THE VALKYRIE'S TRIUMPH

HALF-BLOOD RISING BOOK 3

LUCY ROY

The Valkyrie's Triumph

Half-Blood Rising Book Three

Copyright © 2024 Lucy Roy, all rights reserved

ISBN 978-1-955556-14-9 (paperback)

ISBN 978-1-955556-13-2 (hardcover)

ISBN 978-1-955556-11-8 (e-book)

Map art: John R. Sackett

Cover art: Inessa Sage

Edited by: Jenifer Knox

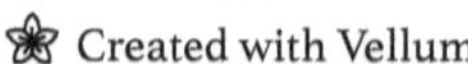 Created with Vellum

To those who patiently waited

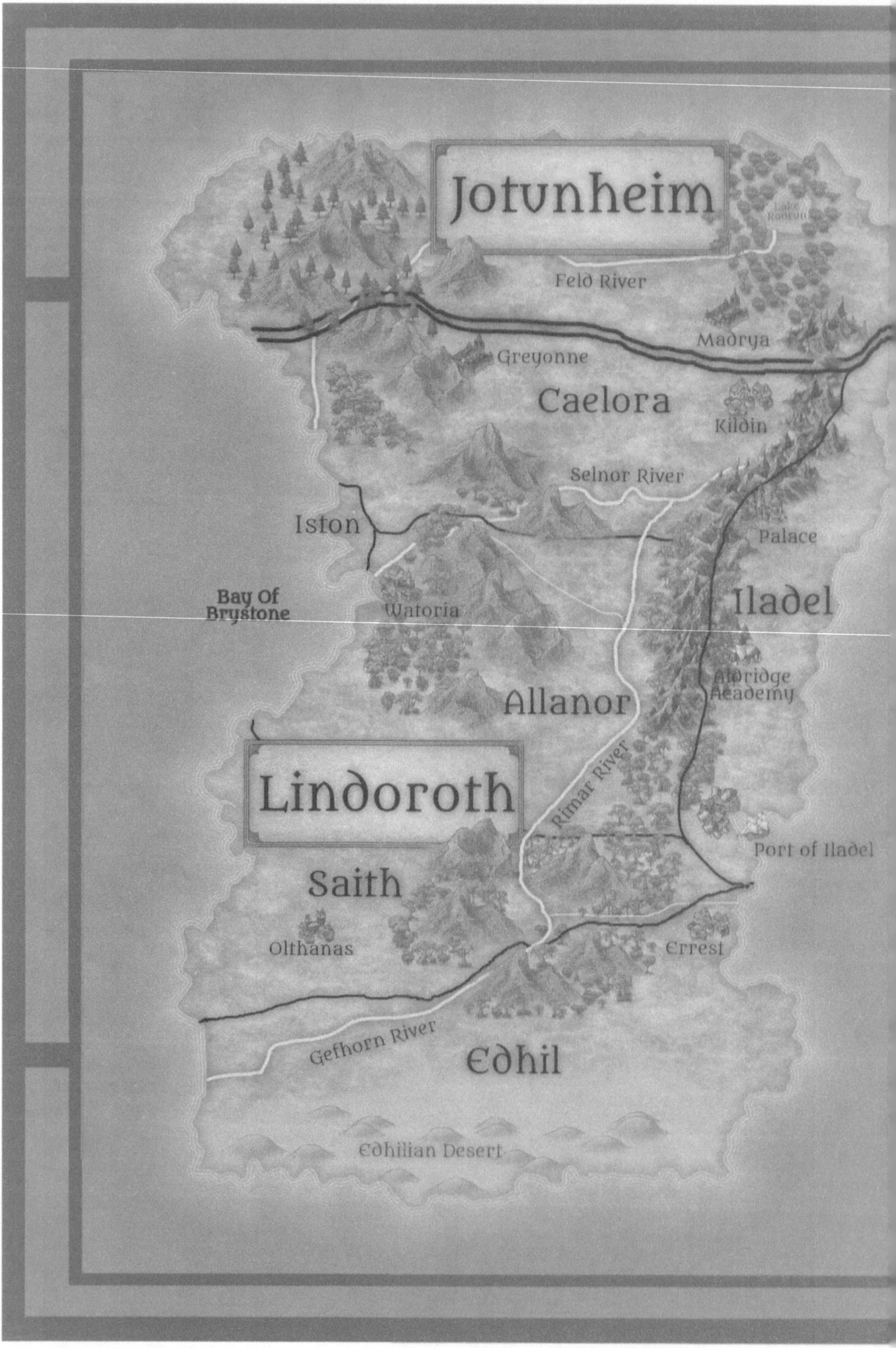

Jotunheim
Feld River
Madrya
Greyonne
Caelora
Kildin
Selnor River
Iston
Palace
Bay Of Brystone
Watoria
Iladel
Aldridge Academy
Allanor
Lindoroth
Rimar River
Saith
Port of Iladel
Olthanas
Errest
Gefhorn River
Edhil
Edhilian Desert
Lake Rootun

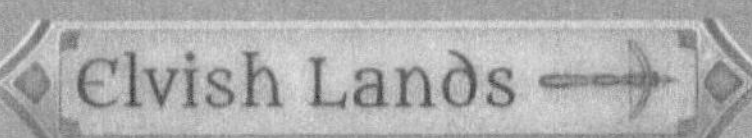

Elvish Lands

Dystone
Teid
Caldel
Port of
Caldel
Aren
Vindarria
Leford

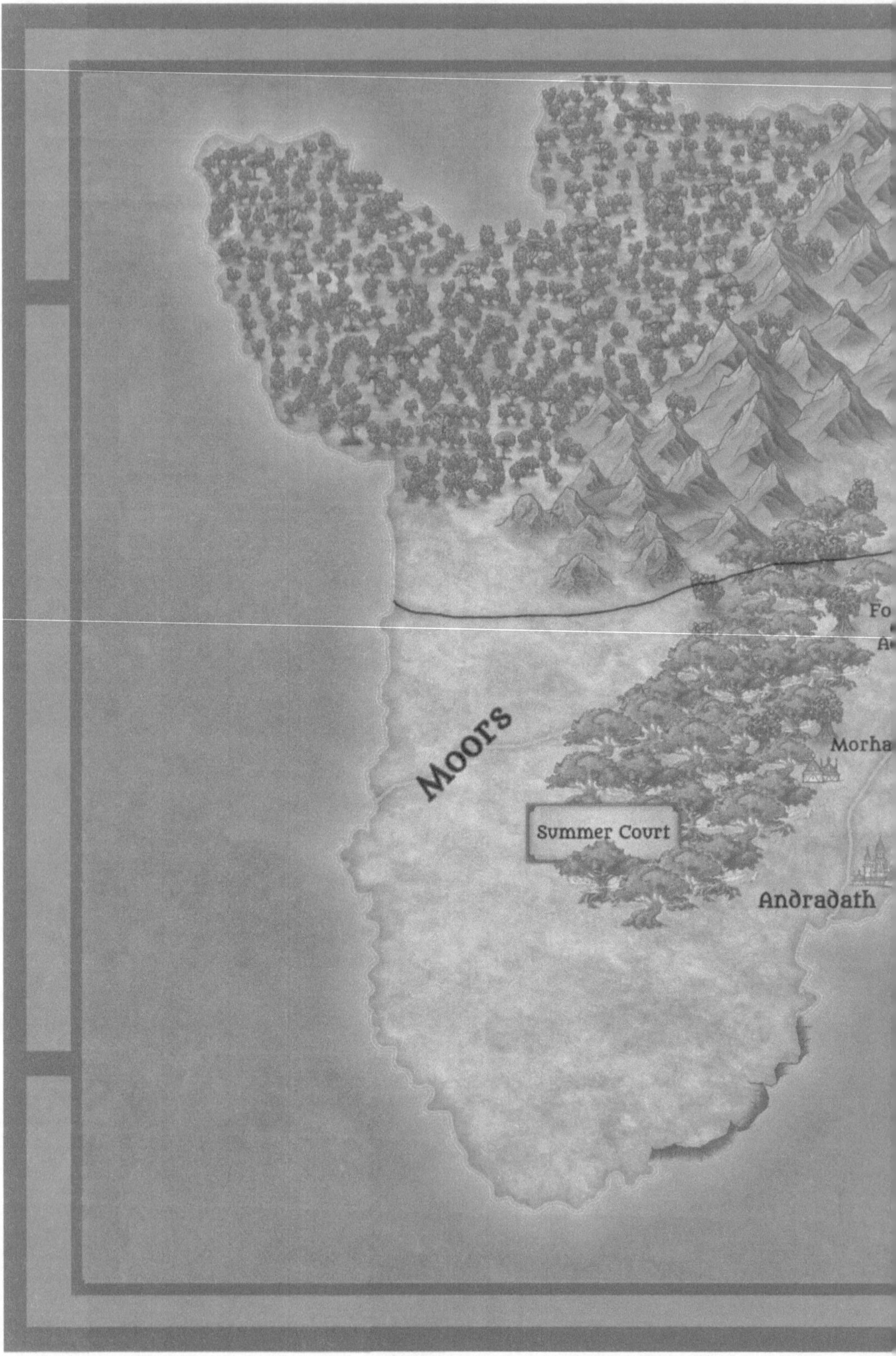

Moors
Summer Court
Morha
Andradath
Fo
A

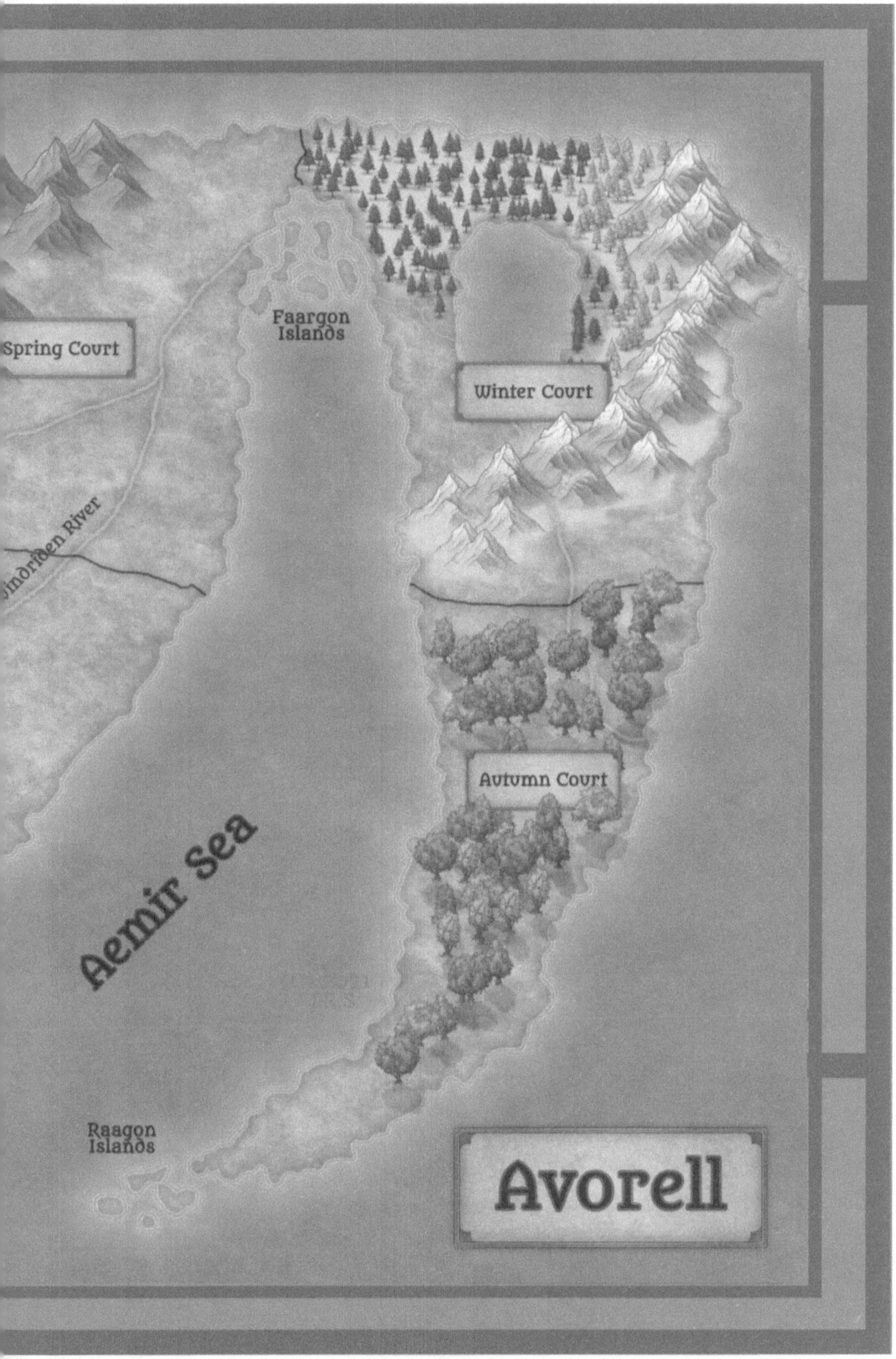

Spring Court
Faargon Islands
Winter Court
Windriden River
Autumn Court
Aemir Sea
Raagon Islands
Avorell

PRONUNCIATION GUIDE

Freya – Fray-uh
Aerelius – Air-el-yus
Grevillea – Gruh-vil-ya
Lazarus - Laz-uh-rus
Collin – Col-lin
Byrric – Bir-ric
Salazar – Sal-uh-zar
Ordona – Or-doh-na
Myria – Meer-ya
Dystone – Dis-tone
Jotunheim – Yot-un-hime
Lindoroth – Lin-duh-roth
Haegin - Hay-gin
Naedan - Nay-din
Nalaea - Nuh-lay-uh
Ruehnar - Roo-nar
Ratatoskr - Ra-ta-tos-ker

1

FREYA

When the queen of Lindoroth was a girl, she hoarded secrets. Discovering a secret was akin to finding a bit of treasure she could keep in a box under her bed, far from her father's prying eyes.

This was something she and the crown prince both shared, so much so, one summer, they held a competition to see who could collect the most secrets.

There had been no shortage of gossip and tidbits from the occupants at the palace that summer. From royal guests consorting with courtesans, to which squires would make the most promising knights. It had been one of the most exciting visits in Freya's memory.

In the end, the prince had won. The revelation that his chambers once belonged to a king's paramour had beat Freya's handful of collected secrets. To eleven-year-olds, that kind of news was scandalous, salacious, something they wouldn't bat an eye at now at nearly twenty.

As she grew, Freya Harridan continued to gather secrets, surrounding herself with them until they became a part of her. The result was that trust never came easily. It had to be earned. Even

Aerelius hadn't been an exception, not until she had deemed him worth keeping in Freya's eyes.

The hidden truths of childhood didn't hold a candle to the revelations she and her husband, now the king, had faced since taking their thrones. Secrets that held more weight, that tested her loyalty, her intelligence, her trust in those closest to her.

And now she was second guessing everything she'd heard.

The most recent revelation was one she took more personally than the rest. Andreus Florian, royal spymaster, deliverer of justice, was elvish royalty. And no one, not even her father, had thought to inform the king and queen. Perhaps it wasn't something Freya needed to be concerned about. Indeed, it likely wasn't. But this brief moment was causing her to question her closest advisors, which was something her overburdened mind was struggling to take on.

Today, as she stood at the gates of Iston, home of the Valkyrie, surrounded by the people she trusted most, she wondered just how much more she could take.

"I think we should bring this inside," Byrric stated, eyeing his daughter warily. She could only imagine how she must've looked to him in that moment.

Anger, annoyance, frustration, and the knowledge that Florian's identity simply shouldn't *matter* warred inside her. Between that and the news that a new human army was preparing to flood her lands made her full to bursting with the need to fly.

"Yes, these are topics better discussed in private," Vara Balthana added. Freya's grandmother had opened her home in the city, to the soldiers and people that Freya and Aerelius now carried with them.

Despite the truth in her grandmother's words, Freya needed a breath before discussing how to handle the humans who'd just crossed into Lindorothian waters–or the topic of Florian's elvish heritage.

"I need a few moments to myself," Freya murmured to Aer. "Get Toskr settled. I'll be there soon." She unclipped the pouch from her belt that held the injured squirrel shifter and handed it to her husband. Brief concern flashed in his eyes, but he took the pouch with a short nod, clipping it gently to the empty sword belt at his waist. She quirked a brow at her father. "I want to see the city from above, get the lay of the land. I'll meet you there." Then, not waiting for a response, she turned and spread her wings, taking to the skies for passage to her grandmother's home.

Thankfully, Aer didn't try to stop her. He knew when she needed to take a moment to breathe, and he especially knew when she needed to take that moment in private.

She needed to fly, needed to see the city below, see that it was safe, just as Watoria was now. Her city had fallen to the Jotnar and humans, but she, Aerelius, and three armies had taken it, wresting it from her enemy's hands and giving it back to her people.

A moment later, she heard the heavy flap of wings behind her. She knew better than to think Byrric would let her fly off on her own, but when he didn't rush to keep up, she realized he was giving her the few moments of solitude she needed.

As they soared wordlessly over the city, Freya shoved all thoughts of war aside and took in the home of her ancestors. The last time she had visited, she'd been in her early teens. It had been only a year or two after her mother's death, and not long before her father decided she would stay in Watoria for good–at least until it was time to return to the capital to marry her prince.

The sprawling lands below made Freya's breath catch. The land had been built for the Valkyrie eons ago, crafted with wings in mind: Training fields, courtyards, and rooftop gardens were all tucked into a rocky valley in the snow-crusted Northwest Mountains.

Freya shifted her sharp eyes toward the north, past the remaining stretch of Allanorian countryside to the Caeloran border. Another two days' journey beyond that sat Jotunheim.

A flare of anger lanced through her at the thought of the enemy lands so close to her own. Now wasn't the time for anger, though. Right now, she needed to draw in the cold air and settle her nerves. So, as was her habit, she soared, taking solace in the fact that, thus far, war had yet to spoil this place.

"It's beautiful," she said to her father once he was in the air beside her. The snapping wind nearly drowned out her words, but he smiled.

"I should've brought you here more often." He gestured toward Vara's estate. "This is your ancestors' home. You should be more familiar with it."

"Perhaps you should've sent me here instead of Watoria," she told him, sending him a smirk. Without another word, she tucked her wings to her sides and plummeted in a wordless challenge, making a straight line for Vara's gated home.

She touched down moments before Byrric, but she had the sneaking suspicion her father had given her this win. When he landed with a soft thump beside her, she turned and looked at the main house.

The Balthana family was old and well-established, so Vara's home was one of the more posh ones in Iston—posh by Valkyrie standards, anyway. There was no ostentatious décor or rising turrets. Instead, the Balthana estate was a sprawling one-story masterpiece of stone, glass, and wrought iron, one that had stood at the center of Iston for centuries. Gardens bursting with winter-blooming and cold-hardy flora dotted the rooftops. She could picture herself there in summertime, basking in the sun, surrounded by verdant, lush foliage.

Today, however, the clouds obscured the sun, and the chill in the air that promised frost made being indoors much more favorable.

"It's going to snow soon," Byrric murmured, as if reading Freya's mind. "Travel east will be difficult if we wait too long."

"Agreed." Turning to him, she asked, "Why didn't you tell us? You had to know we wouldn't have taken issue with Florian being elvish royalty, but why keep it from us?"

"Florian's heritage is his to disclose. You know that as well as anyone." He placed his hands on her shoulders, then waited until her gray eyes met his before continuing. "There will be far more confidential information to come to light now that you're queen, Freya. What's important is that you understand *timing*. When this is all over, Ordona and I will sit down with you and Aerelius and discuss everything we should've the moment you were coronated. Until then, please trust that we are solely focused on getting that bastard that's on your throne out of this kingdom."

Her eyes closed as his words sunk in. Hadn't she spent years hiding who she was? Hiding under glamours and secrets, sharing information only when necessary? Hadn't she tried to *continue* that once she'd gotten to Aldridge?

"I—" Her shoulders slumped in a very un-queenly movement. "Ugh. I'm just tired of having things sprung on me." She rubbed a hand across her forehead. "I'm so, *so* goddamned tired."

"I know it's frustrating," Byrric said. "But none of this has gone how we expected. You need to trust that not everything is a catastrophe."

"You're right," she finally said. "I know you're right. It's just that King Ruehnar and Queen Nalaea were absolutely wretched while Aerelius and I were in Avorell. It's going to take a moment for me to wrap my head around Florian being the king's brother."

He smiled softly, then cupped her chin in his hand and met her eyes. "I can promise there will be no more surprises, at least from my end. If not because you're my queen, then because you're my daughter. Now, let's get inside. They'll be waiting for us."

The rest of their group had just arrived when she and Byrric stepped up to the portico, her two guards, Rissen and Cecilia, shoving open the heavy double doors that led into the foyer. Freya watched as Lea, Lazarus, Collin, and Myria hurried off to find their remaining family members who were recovering in the guest quarters.

Byrric led Freya into Vara's sitting room, her standard place for welcoming guests. Aer hung back and held out his hand, wordlessly inviting Freya to walk with him. Freya squared her shoulders, then gave him a small smile and slid her hand into his. Together, they went into the sitting room, where their guards, Florian, and Ettrian were waiting.

Feeling a bit steadier now that she'd spread her wings and spoken with her father, she looked at Andreus Florian, their most trusted advisor.

"Explain," Aer demanded. "And I don't mean explain why you

lied, Lord Florian. I understand that, to some extent. Your heritage is yours to disclose, of course, but Freya and I need to know how deep your connection with the elves goes in order to make the best decisions going forward."

"I've always trusted you and your judgment," Freya added. "But I'm sure you can understand why my husband and I need more than you've given us."

Ettrian snickered.

Aer shot him a sharp look. "Something funny, Your Highness?"

Ettrian shrugged, then leaned back against the wall, one black-booted foot propped behind him, his golden eyes dancing. "There's always something funny with you lot. But since you asked, I'm simply wondering why this matters to you. Personally, I'd be more concerned with the fifteen thousand human soldiers who just docked in your harbors." Infuriatingly, he examined his nails, rubbing them against the pale blue velvet of his jacket. "Perhaps on that we differ."

Freya felt her cheeks flush with annoyance. Aer, seeming to see her anger rise, put a hand on her back.

"My queen and I need to be able to trust the people around us," Aer said, looking first at Byrric, then at Florian. "As I'm sure you can understand, the news of your true identity brings with it a number of questions." His eyes shifted to Ettrian. "The topic of the human incursion can wait a few more minutes."

Freya sighed. Ettrian was right; they needed to get on with reclaiming their land. But if Florian was elvish royalty, his connections went much further than a simple friendship with Lord Silmar, their guide in Avorell.

"If I may?" Vara asked.

Freya shifted her eyes to the aged woman before her. Vara was somewhere in the vicinity of seven hundred years old, yet her short chestnut hair had barely begun turning gray.

"Yes, Grandmother?"

Vara retracted her wide white wings and folded her arms, gray eyes stern on each of them, her stare brooking no argument. "Perhaps you should let Andreus tell you his story before unleashing that anger of yours."

"We're not *angry*, Grandmother," Freya said wearily. "Just tired of being the last to know. Especially considering he was hesitant to reach out to the elves when we first discussed it." As the royal spymaster, he'd kept things from them before. Secrets Freya knew, at least in hindsight, were necessary. But when she looked at her father, she sighed. "I know there's a lot about the monarchy we simply haven't had time to learn. We just need to know there are no other major secrets lurking about."

"My hesitation was not because I didn't want their help," Florian explained. He held his tall, wiry frame stock-still, showing no signs of chagrin, remorse, or humility. Not that Freya necessarily expected him to, knowing the spymaster as she did, but on the same token, his apathetic expression nearly set her hackles rising. "It was because I knew what they would ask of you in return."

"The Wild Hunt," Aer said.

"We do enjoy our games," Ettrian murmured.

Freya rolled her eyes, then looked at Florian in question. "You didn't think I could win?"

Florian shook his head, his dark expression never leaving his king and queen. "Oh, I had no doubt you would. But welcoming the elves back into our world could cause more problems, which I didn't want you to have to deal with so early in your reign."

Aer looked at Ettrian. "Such as?"

Ettrian lifted his brows. "Let's be honest, Your Majesty. What do you think your citizens will do once they know their dreams can be realized with a simple elvish bargain?"

Outraged, Freya took a step toward the prince, stopping when Aer grabbed her arm.

Florian held up a hand and sent Ettrian a warning look. "I ensured that eventuality was written out of the bargain we made with King Ruehnar and Queen Nalaea." Then, to Freya and Aer he asked, "Why do you think we spent the better part of a day writing that agreement?"

"And how do you think your people will like it if they find out you refuse to let them make elvish bargains?" Ettrian quipped before either could answer. "I'd be quite upset if I were them."

Gritting her teeth, Freya let out a breath. "Lea was right about you, Prince Ettrian."

"That I'm a 'stupid elvish bastard'?" He grinned, his sharp incisors flashing against his lips. "Yes, I'm quite aware. Although, to be fair, my parents and brothers were the ones who made those bargains."

"When we wrote the bargains, we included limits on elvish involvement in Lindoroth." Florian shot a look at Ettrian. "Limits that allow *only* military bargains and can only be made by the king and queen."

Ettrian shrugged. "There are always loopholes."

Aer rubbed a hand against his forehead and sighed. "Prince Ettrian, if you could refrain from attempting to make trouble, we would greatly appreciate it."

"Ah, of course." Ettrian gestured a long, pale hand toward the spymaster. "Carry on."

"I'll be brief." Florian met each of their eyes in turn. "My father was Devdan Tordove, the former king of Avorell and Ruehnar's father. Approximately eight hundred years ago, we had a falling out because I refused to marry the female he and my stepmother chose for me. Instead, I took on mercenary work." Each word was clipped, intentional, and devoid of emotion. "It's how I became so skilled with toxins and eliminating threats."

"You mean killing people?" Freya asked drily.

He nodded curtly, with no hint of shame. "As the second of four sons and only half-elf, I didn't see the need, nor did I have any desire, to adhere to their wishes. When it became clear my father wouldn't stand for my disobedience, I chose to leave my homeland. My father found me when I attempted to leave, punished me, then exiled me to the Forest of Ages. It's where I first encountered Ratatoskr, although I already knew him by reputation."

A chill ran down Freya's spine at the memory of her time in the living forest of Avorell.

"King Salazar's grandfather, Avinald, had heard of me," Florian continued. "When word got to him that I'd had a falling out with my parents, he sent for me, taking care to avoid raising my parents' suspicions."

"He snuck you out of Avorell undetected?" Aer asked sharply. "How?"

"Relations with Avorell were much better back then, at least for the Linds. Avorell had closed its shores to humans after their war, but the Linds still had trade access. I left on a ship with his emissary after said emissary had a visit with my father."

"Your great-grandfather took him in," Vara said to Aer. "Took him out of that gods-forsaken place and brought him here."

"Ruehnar knew, of course," Florian continued. "We were close growing up, and he never cared for the way our father handled certain aspects of our upbringing."

"It should go without saying that Lord Florian's placement in Lindoroth needed to be kept quiet to avoid the ire of King Devdan," Byrric told them.

"And more recently, because your people likely would not have been thrilled at the idea of an elf in the royal court," Ettrian added with a smirk. "Our reclusive nature has garnered us an...unsavory reputation, as you know."

"Half elf," Florian corrected. "Devdan was my father, but my birth mother was human, a visitor from Dystone whose name I was never told. She died in childbirth, as is common for elf-human pairings. Queen Mariona was presented to my father by her parents two years later. She was kind enough and raised me as her own, even though she didn't wholly agree with allowing a half-elf to be in line for the throne. Nor did she care for rebellious children, so she stood by my father when he tried to force the betrothal and when he ultimately decided to disown me."

"We planned to tell you," a soft voice said from the door. "When the time was right."

Aer's hand jerked in Freya's, and her heart stuttered at the sight of Ordona Harridan standing framed in the arched doorway.

"Mother," Aer rasped, his voice filled with a broken relief that Freya had seen so rarely these past weeks. Dropping Freya's hand, he rushed toward Ordona, sweeping her off her feet in a huge hug.

And just like that, Florian's identity didn't seem quite so important.

Freya's eyes stung as she watched Aer greet the Queen Mother. Aer hadn't seen her in more than a month, not since she'd fled the besieged palace after watching her husband die.

Ordona gripped her son tightly, the sight so moving Freya had to look away. Something told her if she started crying right then, she might not be able to stop. Now was not the time for that—she needed to be strong for her people, for her husband, and for the rest of the travelers they'd brought with them to Iston.

After a moment, Aer set Ordona down and took a step back. "Are you alright?" he asked.

"Yes, I'm fine. Lady Balthana has been taking good care of me." Despite the circumstances, she still looked just as regal as the day they'd left the palace. Someone, likely a palace pixie, had ensured she still looked like royalty, even in hiding. Her dark hair was pulled back into a low chignon, with soft curls drifting gently along her cheeks. She wore a soft pink dress that belied her dire circumstances. Instead, it cast a beautiful contrast against her golden skin.

She caught sight of Freya, and her eyes watered. "Freya, dear."

No longer able to hold back her tears, Freya rushed forward to accept Ordona's embrace, squeezing her eyes shut as she buried her face in the former queen's silk-covered shoulder. Even in exile, Ordona carried the regal air only a queen could possess.

"Your Majesty," Freya breathed. "It's so good to see you."

Ordona pulled back and knuckled a tear away from her eye. "Yes, well, I'm just glad we're all under one roof now." She looked around the room, her gaze narrowing briefly on Ettrian before moving on. "I know we have much to discuss, but I'd like some time with my son and daughter-in-law, please."

Vara nodded. "Of course." She shot a look at Byrric. "Come on, son. We have our own matters to discuss."

With one last look at Freya, Byrric left the room, all the rest following behind.

2

FREYA

Once the room was clear, Ordona faced Aer and Freya, her expression hard.

"Sit. Tell me everything." She shook her head when Aer tried to speak. "I'm safe, Aerelius. Sir Ervic brought me here straight from the palace before leaving to meet Byrric in Olthanas. I am *safe*. We can discuss all of that later."

Aer looked like he wanted to argue, but before Freya could agree with Ordona, he took a seat on one of the sofas. Adjusting her silken skirts, Ordona sat across from them on a settee. Although she knew it was silly, Freya couldn't help but feel wildly underdressed, her wool and leather clothing a far cry from Ordona's finery.

"Now, I know you spent the last few weeks in Watoria," Ordona said once they were settled. "The city is in good hands?"

"It is," Aer confirmed. "The marshals and reinforcements we left behind have it under control and are handling the prisoners. Prince Tavian is seeing to it that everything's sorted, and he'll be here tomorrow with Prince Fenian and their knights."

"Good, good." Ordona let out a long, soft breath, seeming to exhale a month's worth of fear in one go.

"Have you gotten word on the wedding guests who managed to

escape?" Freya asked. "Tyna reported only a few dozen in the dungeons."

Ordona's face slipped into a frown. "I don't know how many were able to flee, but Prince Ettrian seems to think most managed to get out, although far too many were killed."

And dumped in a pit behind the palace, Freya thought grimly. Lea had filled them in on Willem and Lessia's dumping ground, a pit of bodies that were no more than carrion for crows at this point.

"Now, tell me about Avorell," Ordona said, forcing a smile.

As concisely as they could, Aer and Freya briefed Ordona on their trip to the elvish lands. Freya wanted to gloss over the Wild Hunt, but Ordona insisted on hearing every detail about the Hunt, their travels, and what they thought of the elvish monarchs. Fear and concern filled her features as Freya gave her the details of her time in the Forest of Ages, replaced with relief and pride when she heard how Freya had beaten her final attackers.

"I'm curious." Ordona's eyes narrowed. "How were you able to make so many bargains with Ruehnar and Nalea without suffering loopholes?"

"It was Florian, actually," Freya admitted, although the telling gleam in Ordona's eyes indicated she already knew that. "Without his help..."

"We wouldn't have made it out of there alive," Aer finished. "I'm certain of that."

"He's a good person." Ordona's expression turned solemn. "He's never once led us astray. You know that, Aerelius."

With a sigh, her son nodded. "Yes, Mother. I know. It doesn't change the fact that he had ample opportunity to tell us how he managed to get us a meeting with Ruehnar and Nalea so quickly. We just assumed—" He scrubbed a hand over his face, his haggard appearance turning more so. "I don't know what we assumed."

"Does it matter?" Ordona asked. "In the grand scheme of things, does it truly matter? You've already said his heritage is of no importance to you. Don't let your offense cloud your judgment here."

"We won't," Freya replied, although she couldn't guarantee that.

Ordona's patronizing look told her she knew as much. "I'd still like to hear more of his story, though."

"You will in time, but it's his to tell. Just know that Salazar and I were both in agreement that Florian's identity be kept a secret to avoid anything getting back to his father and stepmother. Once they passed on, we never saw a need to change the status quo." Ordona smiled at Freya and leaned forward to place a hand on her cheek. "Let's set that aside for now. I was shocked when I heard they made you run the Hunt, but your success is certainly no surprise." Her lips drew into a smirk. "And I hear you brought a stowaway home with you."

Despite all he'd done to help them, Freya couldn't help her frustrated huff when Ordona mentioned Ratatoskr, who'd been whisked away by Rini and Tyna the moment they'd arrived at Vara's home. The gossiping squirrel shifter who'd aided her on her hunt was currently recovering from a stab wound he'd taken during the battle at Watoria, during which he'd barely left her side.

"Yes, Toskr is a bit much, but I can't deny his usefulness in battle." *Or his loyalty*, although she kept that thought to herself, not quite ready to believe it just yet.

"It doesn't surprise me in the least that you managed to pull that rascal to your side," Ordona said, shaking her head in amusement. "From what I've heard of him, I'd say you've made a friend for life."

"Yes, it would seem that way," Freya murmured. "Do you know him?"

"Only by reputation. Florian told me stories of him when I was younger, before Salazar and I married. Warned me of him, rather." She held up a finger and put on a stern expression. "'Never go into the forest, Lady Waisfir. Ratatoskr will trap you there with his beguiling ways.'"

Aer let out a quiet snort. "That sounds about right."

A soft smile played on Ordona's lips. "Well, you're certainly gathering an interesting collection of allies. Now, let's go find the others and discuss what comes next, shall we?"

The three of them made their way through Vara's estate toward the dining room, where Byrric and Florian were helping her flip the table top to reveal a full-relief map of Lindoroth. Prince Ettrian leaned casually against the window sill, surveying their progress but not bothering to lift a hand.

Freya had seen Vara's map of Lindoroth once as a child, but its significance and detail were far more breathtaking when viewing them as an adult, especially considering the context. The paper maps they'd used in Watoria had been invaluable, but nothing could replicate the dips, curves, and jagged edges of the map Freya's ancestors had carved centuries ago—from the depth of Watoria's ravine to the rising peaks of the Aldridge mountains, ending at the red expanse of the Edhilian desert.

Most importantly, it allowed them to view the eastern shores of Lindoroth, where nearly fifteen thousand human soldiers were preparing to invade.

"What's our plan?" Aer asked as they walked in.

"Ideally, we try to prevent the humans and Jotnar from slaughtering all of your people," Ettrian replied.

As far as elvish princes went, Ettrian was by far the most irritating of the three, even if he did seem slightly less homicidal than his brothers. She had only spent two days with him, but his blasé outlook on every aspect of their situation rankled her.

Freya shot him a dry look before addressing her father. "Anything more valuable to add, Commander?"

Byrric ran a hand over his stubbled jaw and exhaled slowly, letting his arm drop to his side. "Unfortunately, no. I've sent Zane, Naedan, and Amara to monitor activity between here and the eastern shores, but it will be a few days before they return. Lord Silmar is assessing the situation in the capital and will return as soon as he has more actionable information. Until we know more, I'm afraid Prince Ettrian is correct. We need to figure out how to keep the humans at bay."

"The best we can do is regroup, and rest here," Florian said. "We cannot stop the humans coming ashore, but we can do everything in our power to ensure we're at full strength when we push them back."

He inclined his head toward Ettrian. "The other princes will be here tomorrow. I'd like to send a few knights directly to the eastern ports to scope out the area, confirm how many humans have landed, but the information Zane and the others return with will help with the journey across the kingdom."

Logical, Freya thought, but not altogether helpful at present. "We need—"

"For the moment, you all need to eat and rest." Vara silenced her granddaughter with a sharp look. "There's nothing to be done today, unfortunate as that might be. I already have the kitchen preparing lunch. There'll be plenty of food and space for everyone."

"I'm not hungry, Grandmother." As if on cue, Freya's hollow stomach let out a soft grumble. She'd barely eaten anything since before the battle, nearly two days prior, her stress removing her appetite entirely.

"You were saying?" Ettrian gave her a look that made Freya want to smack him.

Freya scowled at him, but in the same moment, exhaustion hit, nearly overwhelming her. Aer sensed it immediately. He wrapped an arm around her shoulders and kissed her temple, his support disguised as a soft show of affection.

Wearily, she eyed everyone in the room and the similar signs of exhaustion on their faces. She knew better than to refute her grand-mother's suggestions, seeing as they were correct, but she also knew the only way to get everyone to agree would be to set the example herself.

"Taking time to eat and rest won't make a dire situation any more so," she told them. "Everyone should take a few hours to reenergize so we can hit the ground running tomorrow."

"We'll regroup later," Aer added, dismissing everyone.

Florian and Byrric hung back until the room had cleared of all but them and their king and queen.

"Your Majesties," Florian began. "I want to begin by apologizing, again, for the delay in revealing my true identity. I assure you, the goal was not to deceive you."

"We understand," Aer told him, continuing to frown down at the map, arms crossed. When he looked at Florian, his eyes were filled with exhaustion. "Going forward, though, we expect full transparency."

"It has nothing to do with you being an elf," Freya said reassuringly, hoping to walk back any insult she may have insinuated. "But we must have all the information to make better decisions going forward."

"Agreed," he said with a sharp nod. "While I rarely make errors in judgement, I can acknowledge this misstep on my part. For that, I'm sorry."

With a flurry of pixie dust, Rini, Freya's pixie attendant, appeared above the map. The small silver female had been at Freya's side since they had left the palace, fussing over her at every opportunity. Freya was happy to see her friend's stress wearing off now that she was back with Tyna, her twin. They'd never been apart more than a few hours, as far as Freya knew, so she imagined this separation was like losing an arm for a period of time.

"This way, Your Majesties," she said with a smile, her eyes bright. "Lady Balthana had me prepare your chambers. I've drawn a bath." She looked at Aer through narrowed eyes. "If it suits His Majesty, we'll allow our queen to bathe first and I'll have lunch delivered to the room."

Freya shook her head at the pixie's continued doting. "It's fine, Rini. Aer can go first. I need to—"

"No, you don't." Aer took her arm and tugged her toward the hall that led to the guest quarters. "You've barely slept for two days and haven't bathed in as many."

"Are you suggesting I smell?"

His answering smirk held only a shadow of his typical mirth.

Rini clicked her tongue and flitted down the hall, following them. "Ignore him, Your Majesty. You smell lovely as always."

Amused, Freya continued down the hall, her hand still tucked in Aer's. "No need to lie, Rini."

The pixie tossed an exasperated look over her shoulder but didn't respond.

The guest chambers Vara had assigned Freya and Aer were large but hardly ornate or exquisite. Instead, the massive room held a comforting air. Especially the wide, dark-framed monstrosity of a bed dressed in fresh linens and a thick quilt Freya wanted to instantly sink into. Yet despite Rini's denial, she knew she needed to bathe before wrapping the cloud-like bedding around her body. She'd been off the battlefield for nearly a day, but the grime of battle—blood, dirt, and dark Jotnar magic—seemed to have permeated her bones.

"Your food will be here shortly," Rini told her. "His Majesty can eat while you bathe."

Wearily, Freya nodded. "Alright. I'll be out soon. Who will be attending to the prisoners who were in the dungeons?"

"Most of the other pixies fled here when Willem and Lessia invaded," Rini replied. "They're taking care of the others as we speak."

Freya let out a quiet breath and nodded. "Good. That's good."

"Where are the rest?" Aer asked.

"They've scattered about to the other cities." With a small smile, she touched Freya's arm. "Come, Your Majesty. The bath is ready for you."

The moment Freya stepped inside the bathing room and smelled the soft scent of Rini's rose-infused water, she knew she would not, in fact, be out soon, and would much prefer Rini deliver her lunch directly.

Stripping down, she let herself sink into the soft water, tinged with Rini's magic to ease the aches and stress she'd collected over the last week. Between the Wild Hunt and her first stint on a battlefield, she felt as though her body had been put through the wringer three times over.

Freya had never been in war before. She knew how to fight and, more importantly, how to win; at least in small doses. Yet facing off with her peers in Aldridge's combat yard, or the draugs in Watoria's streets, had done little to prepare her for the repeated blows her enemies had dealt when fighting to save her city. She'd come out with only minor injuries, but the mental toll the fight for Watoria had taken on her—was still taking on her—was heavier than the physical pain.

The sounds of battle, of arrows hitting flesh and armor, bones crunching, the burning stench of a magic and blood-soaked field were images and sensations she wouldn't forget any time soon. Plummeting into throngs of human and Jotnar knights, slicing them down in droves...

Yes, she'd been very, very lucky to come out of it all with her body and mind intact.

Her allies hadn't suffered huge losses, but many were injured badly enough that they might not recover to fight another day in this war. Toskr, who'd dutifully ridden into the fray on her shoulder, was recovering from a stab wound that might put him out of commission for weeks if Haegin and Florian couldn't heal him with their magics and potions. Knowing Toskr, he wouldn't allow such a travesty, despite his initial reticence to fight, and Florian was too stubborn to fail at what he considered a basic healing.

Try as she might, Freya could only focus on injured warriors for a few moments before Rini's soothing magic permeated her thoughts, making it hard for her to concentrate on more than the warm water that sluiced over her skin as she sank deeper into the tub. She knew there was no way she'd come to any conclusions or revelations just yet. Not until she was fed and rested.

So, she let herself slip deeper into the tall bath, allowing the water to cover her chest and shoulders and letting her vibrant hair spread across the surface.

Then she slept.

3

———

LEA

Once she'd arrived at Vara Balthana's home, Lea barely spared anyone else a thought as she and the others rushed off to find their families. Lea and Perida suffered several painful weeks with minimal interaction, not counting their brief conversations in the dungeons. Lea knew her mother was as eager to catch up on recent events as Lea was.

Most importantly, Lea hated that her mother had watched as her only daughter spewed lies about Orrin and was married off to a Jotnar lord. She needed Perida to know it had all been an act Lea had put on for Willem and Lessia's benefit.

Her skin crawled at the memory of being in such a debasing position. She knew without question she'd die before letting herself end up there again.

An act. Perida had to have known that it had *all* been an act, that the lies Lea had told about Orin Calliwell being a horrid person were just that.

Her mother had to know.

The halls were crowded as Lea made a beeline toward the western end of the estate that housed the guest chambers. Pixies flitted about, carrying bedding, medicines, and food. It was a wonder

Vara wasn't losing her mind with the influx of people in her home, considering she spent so much of her time here enjoying her solitude.

The door to Perida's room opened on Lea's first knock. Before Lea could speak, Perida's shoulders slumped as relief filled her features, and she pulled her daughter into a crushing embrace. Perida held her for a few moments, her face buried in her daughter's hair. At that moment, Lea knew her mother had done just as good a job as she had acting her part in the palace.

"Thank god," Perida breathed, pulling Lea inside, hastily wiping away tears.

"Mother—" Lea stepped back, then opened her mouth to spill her apologies, not quite ready to trust the relief creeping into her heart.

"Darling, before you say anything, I know what you were doing at the palace all along." Perida gripped Lea's biceps and met her eyes. "I hoped I was able to hide that knowledge well, but I worry I managed to hide it *too* well."

Lea was already shaking her head before her mother finished speaking. "Mother, you have nothing to apologize for. I worked very hard to make it seem I'd turned on our family, knowing full well you might believe my ruse. I'd hoped you'd see through it, but I've spent weeks preparing for the opposite."

"Oh, Lea... of course I saw through it!" Perida cupped Lea's cheek and smiled softly, her eyes sparking with dread. "My only concern now is—"

"Jonas and I are not married, nor are we mated." Lea rested her hands on her mother's shoulders, gaunt after weeks of malnutrition. Her soft black hair and honey gold skin still carried a dullness left from her time in the dungeon, although the spark that had always lived in her dark eyes had returned in full. "It was all part of the ruse. Ettrian never performed the mating bond and has no authority to perform Lindorothian marriages."

Small furrows formed between Perida's brows, telling Lea that her mother wasn't quite convinced of the elf prince's allegiance. Lea had contemplated bringing Ettrian in to explain, but found it unlikely Perida would believe him. Not yet, at least.

"I know you might not trust Jonas or Ettrian," Lea said. "I don't fault you for that. But... well, we can discuss that later. Right now, we need to focus on getting back to Errest. Prince Ettrian can help us get home to ensure the city remains in our hands."

Perida shook her head. "How can you trust any of them? After everything Jonas allowed to happen to you—"

"Jonas didn't allow anything to happen to me that I hadn't agreed to." Frustration creeped into Lea's tone, but she forced it down. "We carefully orchestrated everything with guidance from Byrric, Freya, and Aer. My attendant, Tyna, ensured everything appeared as real as possible." She curled her fingers around her mothers hands and gave her a beseeching look. "I know some things might've looked terrible, but I assure you, Jonas never touched me improperly or in a way that I didn't approve of." She thought back to their one and only kiss in the hall after their fake marriage ceremony. "Or wasn't out of desperation."

Perida raised her chin a fraction of an inch. "And the elvish prince?"

"Ettrian was there as a spy for the elvish throne." Then, with a frown, Lea shook her head. "No, 'spy' doesn't seem quite the right word. Scout, perhaps. After Freya and Aer left for Avorell, Ettrian arrived at the palace. I assure you, you have nothing to worry about with him. The elves hate the Jotnar nearly as much as we do." A fact that still surprised Lea. "And Freya and Aer have a signed bargain with their king and queen."

Ettrian had given Lea an abbreviated version of the elves' relationship with Jotunheim and how they believed the Jotnar had taken the gift of elvish magic and used it for evil and greed, doing nothing to help the rest of the world. Although the elves were a capricious people, even they seemed to have their limits. Lea hadn't interacted with the elvish monarchs yet, but Ettrian's disdain for the Jotnar had been clear in his tone, his words, and his golden eyes.

Perida still looked doubtful, but she huffed out a breath, then nodded. "As you were in close contact with them all, I'll trust your judgment. If the commander and the king and queen gave their approval, this whole charade must be far bigger than I thought."

For the first time in weeks, Lea's heart flooded with relief. She and her mother needed to secure their home and ensure the enemy knights the Linds were currently holding at bay were pushed back fully. It would take far longer if Lea had to spend excessive time convincing her mother they finally had allies.

"We need to get back to Errest," Lea repeated. "Commander Balthana will help ensure we're well supported, and Prince Ettrian can transport us inside the capital gates. But we must go quickly."

Tyna appeared beside them. Her soft glow shone brighter now than Lea had seen in weeks. "My ladies," the pixie said with a nod. "As much as I'd like to encourage rest, I understand you must be eager to return home."

"A bath and some food are all we have time for," Lea replied. Knowing Byrric, he and the others were already plotting their next steps. "Tyna, will you please see to lunch? I'd like to go find Prince Ettrian."

"Of course, my lady," Tyna replied, pearlescent wings fluttering madly behind her.

"Thank you." Lea gestured to Perida, waving a hand toward the bathroom. "Mother, I'll be back shortly." She softened her tone as she touched the soft sleeve of her mother's wool dress, so unlike the gown she'd been forced to wear every day since the wedding.

When Lea had last seen the ball gown Perida wore to the wedding, its ice blue silk had been stained brown with her father's dried blood. If she knew her mother at all, the dress had likely ended up in a fireplace somewhere, any hint of its beauty destroyed.

Another reason for Lea to see to it Willem met the same fate as his former ally.

Exhaustion tugged at Perida's eyes, lancing through Lea like a blade. Regardless of what Perida knew of their ploy, Lea couldn't imagine the strain it must've put on her mother's psyche.

Whatever shone on Lea's face must've betrayed her thoughts,

because Perida's eyes softened with sympathy. She wrapped her arms around Lea, exhaling a long, shaking breath.

"Oh, Lea," she murmured. It took all of Lea's strength not to let her emotions flow freely, but now wasn't the time.

"It will be alright, Mother." She took a step back. "Trust me."

With a quick kiss to her mother's cheek, Lea hurried from the room, weaving through guests and halls in search of the youngest Tordove prince. She found Ettrian on the portico, his glinting gold eyes watching the road that led to Vara's home. The tenuous nature of their relationship and the fact that he was a bit terrifying had led Lea to avoid seeking him out on most occasions. Unfortunately, if she wanted to return to her home quickly, she would need him to assist her.

"Your Highness?" Lea said, coming to a stop in the doorway behind him.

"Hmm?" Ettrian's gaze shifted slowly to her. "Ah, Lady Calliwell. How are you faring now that you're so far from your tormentors?" His elvish accent added a rolling lilt to his words that Lea might've considered soothing during normal conversation. As it was, despite the lovely softness his language added to hers, she couldn't focus on anything more than simply getting home.

"Just lovely." She took a small step forward. "When can we leave?"

"Tomorrow." Ettrian quirked a brow, challenging the retort he saw on her lips. "Perhaps the day after."

Wisps of annoyance pricked at her patience. "My mother and I want to leave today."

"As my brothers have yet to arrive, that would be unwise, considering we need their knights to accompany us."

Lea ground her teeth, seeking an alternative option, but coming up empty. "And when will they be here?"

"Soon."

"*When* is soon?" She was so close. *So* close to being home, back with her people.

"You know, Lady Calliwell, for someone who needs my help so desperately, you might consider being a bit less demanding." Eyes flashing, Ettrian faced the road once more. "I'd expect you to be more grateful, considering."

"Considering what?"

He slid her a sly look, one corner of his mouth sliding up. "Considering there's an entire continent between you and your home, and you need *me* to get you there."

Stupid elvish bastard, Lea thought, although she couldn't refute his claim *or* the chill that skittered down her spine. The only way to get to Errest in a timely manner was through the Between, and the only way to access the Between was with an elf. *This* elf, apparently, as his brothers, soldiers, Florian, and the rest of the monarchy were currently absent or otherwise assigned.

"Fine." If she wanted his help, she'd need to play this game his way. With a frown, Lea followed his gaze back to the road. "What are you doing, anyway?"

"Watching," he murmured, his brows drawing together. "Listening. There is much going on in your lands, as I'm sure you know. It feels...prickly."

"Prickly?"

"Yes, my lady. Prickly. Among our other skills, we elves have strong spirit magic." His eyes continued to drift over the landscape. "Your peoples' suffering is like a scythe. A dull one, at that."

Lea's tongue turned to cotton in her mouth as she took in his words. She had no doubt her people were suffering. But here in Iston, at the furthest reaches of Lindoroth, she'd never expect anyone, including an elf, to be so affected by a continent's worth of pain.

But then again, what did she really know of the elves? Perhaps they were the cold, calculating creatures she'd assumed on meeting Ettrian. On the other hand, maybe she hadn't given him enough of a chance to shake the mask he wore whenever they were around other people. Which seemed to be nearly always.

"Can you...turn it off?" A stupid question, maybe, but still worth asking to her mind. She couldn't imagine holding onto that feeling indefinitely.

"Of course," Ettrian replied. "If I couldn't, I would've gone insane long ago. It simply helps to get a feel for the state of the world, especially when I've been summoned here to *help* said world."

"And what does this prickly feeling tell you about the state of my world?"

"That your people suffer, but they still have hope." Impatience flicked across his face when he looked down at her and noticed her doubtful expression. "I cannot *lie,* Lady Calliwell, and I believe my statement was quite clear."

Cheeks aflame, Lea nodded. "Yes, of course." She hesitated for a moment. "Is your spirit magic what allows you to do your mind-speak?" It was something that had been bothering her since he spoke to her mentally in the throne room. To the best of her knowledge, no one in her own lands had the ability to speak mind to mind.

"It is," he confirmed. "Why do you ask?"

She shrugged. "Just curious, I suppose." She raked a hand through her dark curls, wincing when her fingers caught almost instantly in the tangles.

Ettrian smirked, running his eyes across her face and hair. "Perhaps you should go bathe before a bird attempts to nest in your hair."

Indignation flared. "You—"

"Yes, yes, all the bad names you can think of." A smile played at his lips as he jerked his chin toward the house. "Go. Bathe, have some tea, and eat something. If not because you smell, then because you *should.*"

"I don't *smell,*" Lea snapped. Out of everything, she knew that to be true.

"Indeed, but you look as though you might pass out any moment." With a frown, he gave her body an appraising look, but then his eyes softened with something akin to concern. "When was the last time you had a good night's sleep, my lady?"

Lea lips parted, the argument on the tip of her tongue. *Not everything needs to be an argument with him,* she told herself. And besides, was he really wrong? She thought she had slept well enough every night in the palace, but upon recollection, Jonas' presence beside her and the lack of weaponry in her bedside table had prevented any *true* sleep. And later, once they had arrived at Watoria, everyone had been so focused on recovering from battle and preparing for Iston there'd been no time for proper rest or bathing.

As though her body realized that, a wave of exhaustion hit, causing her to wrap her fingers around the iron railing in front of her.

"You've never been in war, my lady, or even war adjacent. You should rest while you can." Ettrian looked around, taking in the gray Allanorian skies and sprawling expanse of Iston, which straddled the two northern territories. "Especially in a place so peaceful."

"And if our enemies decide to attack Iston?"

"They won't."

"You can read minds now?"

"Now and again." He sent her a smirk. "But my assumption is based on logic. The Istonians have powerful defensive magic protecting their borders, thanks to your queen's ancestors. Your enemies may know where Iston sits, but they do not have the tools to break through Cantor magic."

"Cina Enrieth placed protective spells here?" Freya's mother had been dead for nearly seven years, but if there was one thing Lea had learned in her time as Freya's friend, it was that her family's magic was strong and enduring.

Ettrian shook his head. "Her coven, but that was centuries before she came to be."

Lea frowned, casting her eyes outward, as if she might see wisps of magic floating about. "How do you know this?"

"All magic tells a story, my lady. Lady Enrieth's mother, Selinda, who was a Cantor by birth, had magic with a long story to tell." He waved a pale hand toward the area around the estate. "The Cantor Coven's magic is old and particularly dense. Nearly impenetrable and quite long-lasting."

"Can elves break through the magic?"

He gave her the same sly look he'd shown her moments ago. "Of course. Now, go get some rest. *Proper* rest."

She wanted to argue, but the desire to return home warred with the sudden need for rest and a hot meal. With a nod, Lea rubbed a hand across her brow, knowing he was right and hating it all the same. "Yes, I suppose you're right. I'll go tell my mother we're not leaving just yet." Perida wouldn't be happy, of course. Everyone needed rest, *adequate* rest, but her mother and the other prisoners more so than she. They were malnourished, weak, and in some cases, injured. In her rush to leave, Lea hadn't considered her mother might not be physically or mentally up to the task.

She hadn't even considered whether she *herself* was up to the task, whether Tyna would be willing to leave her sister so soon, and whether any of them were mentally prepared for what they'd find when they reached home.

Gods above, she hadn't even asked the pixie how she was doing now that she and Rini were reunited.

Some friend you are.

With a faint smile goodbye, she turned and walked back into the house, aiming directly for her chambers. With the uproar caused after Isadora killed Frederick Edrin, sleep had been impossible for everyone. Lea had no doubts Freya, Aer, and her other friends were realizing they were just as exhausted as she was.

Lea's temper flared at the thought of the false human queen who'd spent so long with her own monarchs. She'd spent weeks thinking Dania Edrin, Jonas's sister, was disguised as the human queen in exile with Freya and Aerelius. Instead, the true Isadora had murdered Dania and carried out a different type of ruse.

She hated Isadora for it all, but most of all, her heart ached for Jonas at the loss of his sister, knowing he wouldn't be able to properly grieve until this battle was over. She knew what it was like to have to hide your grief, and it wasn't a fate she'd wish on anyone.

But Jonas was a kingdom away. There was nothing Lea could do to help him, not from Iston. She could only hope Willem hadn't told him of Dania's death or Isadora's duplicitousness. Ignorance would be best in Jonas' situation. Lea was certain of that.

When she turned down the hall toward her room, she smiled at the sight of Iska, the guard who'd been with her since childhood, standing sentry at her door. He'd traveled to Watoria with the other palace guards and they'd been happily reunited when she had arrived with Ettrian. Having him back at her side was a little shred of normalcy that gave her an added layer of relief.

"My Lady," Iska said, his warm smile like a balm. "Your mother decided to rest and has asked me to pass along the message that you should do the same."

"Yes, I'd hoped she would." She smiled at the male who'd become her shadow since birth. "I hope you'll get some rest, too?"

The hulking wolf shifter gave a stiff nod. "I will. I assured your mother I would wait until you returned before I retire."

Lea let out an exasperated huff. "That was unnecessary, Iska, but thank you." She stepped aside and gestured down the hall toward the wing where staff were being housed. "Now, go relax for a while. It's been a long few weeks."

He gave her another soft smile. "That it has, Lady Calliwell. Sleep well."

4

FREYA

The windows were dim, and the fire in the hearth was a quiet smolder when Freya's eyes slid open later that day. Not yet full dark but near enough to sundown to know she'd never sleep that night if she didn't get up and move soon.

After dozing in the bath, she'd awoken long enough to wolf down the bread, cheese, and roast chicken Rini had delivered before sinking into the cloud of blankets on the bed.

Still groggy, she turned her head and saw Aer asleep next to her, his face a peaceful mask that made her loathe to wake him. The downy pillows cushioning her head combined with the warm duvet were nearly enticing enough to convince her to stay put, but she'd only end up restless, and restlessness would wake her husband. Sleep had never been hard for him to find, at least until they were forced to sleep on the frigid forest floor or in musty caves. He'd achieved some respite at her grandparents' estate, but the threat of direct attack had always been imminent there. Here, safe in Iston with warm beds, hot food, and a swarm of battle-ready Valkyrie performing aerial patrols, they could all finally rest.

After placing a soft kiss on his brow, she slid off the high mattress, wincing when her bare feet touched the cold stone floor. She frowned at the dying embers in the hearth, surprised Rini hadn't kept them going throughout the day.

Then again, Rini had just been reunited with her sister. It was impossible to miss the glow that had returned once she was back in the company of her own kind, so Freya was more than willing to give her time to regroup with not only Tyna, but the rest of the pixies who'd made it to Vara's.

Sliding her feet into a pair of lambswool slippers, Freya wrapped herself in a robe and slipped from the room.

Muted voices floated through the halls from the dining and sitting rooms. Byrric's gentle baritone rumbled above the rest in the dining room, so she assumed some type of strategy meeting was taking place. The voices coming from the sitting room, however, were female, likely the ladies Calliwell and Cailen and Queen Ordona catching up on recent weeks.

At first, she turned to join them. Then she remembered she was only wearing sleep clothes and slippers, so instead, she opted for tea and a quiet snack in the kitchen.

When she reached the lower level, she was instantly enveloped in the fragrant air of the kitchens. A cook stood at the stove gently stirring a pot, while three palace pixies kneaded dough on a long wooden table. Although she'd eaten just a few hours earlier, her stomach still rumbled at the scent of baking bread and bubbling stew.

Vara and Ana sat at the opposite end of the table, each with a steaming bowl in front of them. She wasn't sure if she was happy to see them or annoyed she wouldn't get the quiet meal she'd been after.

When Ana saw Freya enter, she smiled and motioned for her to join them. "Can't sleep?"

Freya smiled sheepishly. "I won't sleep a wink tonight if I stay in bed any longer. Aer could sleep for days if I let him."

One of the pixies fluttered away from the dough and gave Freya a small curtsy.

"Can I get you something to eat, Your Majesty?"

Freya eyed the stew simmering on the stove. "Has everyone else had dinner?"

The cook, an older Valkyrie who reminded her of Maghda, the long-time palace cook, glanced over her shoulder. "Oh, we won't do a sit-down dinner this evening, Your Majesty. With everyone needing their rest, Lady Balthana opted to allow you all to eat when you were ready."

"I'll take some stew, then," Freya replied with a smile as she joined them at the table. "Thank you. You two looked quite serious when I came in," she commented, picking up a piece of bread as the cook set a steaming bowl of stew in front of her. "Dare I ask?"

"Plotting and planning," Vara said with a tired smile. "That's all."

Ana rolled her eyes. "Mother," she muttered. "She's your queen."

Vara shot her daughter a silencing look, then looked back at Freya. "We were discussing who we might reach out to for allegiances." She gestured toward Ana. "Ana and I were discussing the merits of reaching out to the Jotnar rebels. As I've yet to bring it up with your father, I thought she and I could work out any kinks in the plan now, to avoid lengthy arguments and 'what-ifs' when we bring it to the table."

Freya gnawed at the corner of her lip. "We haven't talked much about them, but I would think they'd be more inclined to focus their attention northward, no? They *are* rebels after all. A regime change is the perfect time to launch an attack."

"Possibly," Ana allowed. "Then again, Daniel Veldin has been holding Madrya in Lessia's absence. The rebels might not see it as quite the opportunity we do." She shrugged. "We have a distant cousin up there. It might be worth reaching out."

"Do you really think they'd help us?" Freya asked. The cousin Ana spoke of, Vali, had lived in the northern parts of Caelora for centuries, was Istonian by birth, and had taken up with the Jotnar rebels when he met his Jotnar wife decades before Freya was born, helping to spearhead the rebel movement against Lessia Edrin. She'd never actually met him, only heard her father talk about him in passing. She assumed they crossed paths when Byrric visited the

Lindorothian soldiers that guarded the border, but with the hostilities that so often arose between her knights and the rebels, she couldn't imagine the interactions had always been cordial.

"I'm honestly not sure." Vara leaned back in her seat and drummed her fingers on the table. "It's been some time since I interacted with Vali, or any of them, so it's difficult to say."

"Even if he wanted to help, the rest might not see the same benefit," Freya said. "And he's, what, a third cousin? Fourth? I'm not sure my father would go for it." The Jotnar rebels were bent on ousting Lessia Edrin from the throne, so Willem turning on her had likely put him in their favor. On the other hand, Willem was just another ruler who would come in and dictate their lives. The Linds had no desire for Jotnar lands, and Freya was sure the rebels knew that.

On the other hand, a Jotnar rebel had also killed her mother, so it was a struggle to see them in a favorable light, despite how helpful they might be or what family might still be in the area.

Vara laughed. "Your father tends to forget I was a warrior before birthing him. Believe it or not, I know a thing or two about courting allies."

Freya nodded. "Fair enough." She was too tired to consider further discussion about battle right then. Recalling that her aunt had mentioned Vara's recent travels, Freya opted for a topic shift. "So, Grandmother, where have you traveled recently? Ana said you were away when she first returned."

Vara nodded. "Yes, I spent some time in the Raagon islands. I needed a bit of respite from the cold."

Freya started. "You were in Avorell? Recently?"

Vara nodded slowly. "It seems we just missed each other, although the Raagons don't really allow for a quick stopover in Andradath."

"True," Freya murmured. The small cluster of islands was in the eastern region of Avorell, clear on the other side of the continent at the southern tip of the Autumn Court. "I suppose Avorell isn't as closed to outsiders as I once thought."

"Only some," Vara said with a small smile. "I've traveled there a few times over the centuries. Before that I was in Stoestia."

Freya had no experience with the small island kingdom off the southern shores of Dystone, although she'd heard her father mention its inhabitants on occasion. Peaceful, from what she remembered, and they kept to themselves nearly as much as the elves, having little to offer in the way of trade, with most of their commerce being due to visitors seeking a retreat from the colder parts of the world.

"Now that you're building relations with the Tordoves, you should consider a proper tour of the kingdom," Ana suggested, drawing Freya's mind to the present. "I've never been, but if they're to be Lindorothian allies, it would be good to see how they live."

"Yes," Freya agreed. "Aer and I discussed going back, once this is all over. Whenever that might be." Anger, sprinkled with sadness, roiled in her gut as she realized she might never get to enjoy the post-wedding travels she and her husband had been so eager for. Frowning, she looked to her grandmother. "How in the world have you been able to travel so far?"

Vara's lips quirked. "Retirement has been kind to me, and you're not the only one with friends who can travel the Between."

Shaking her head, Freya tore off a piece of bread and used it to sop up some of her stew. "Is Avorell where you met Lord Silmar?"

Vara nodded slowly as she sipped her tea, its steam rising gently toward the plaster ceiling. "A few centuries back, Artin and I crossed paths in Tevielle. We struck up a friendship of sorts. I met Andreus through him. The Tordoves, too."

"So, you've been friendly with the most reclusive people in the world and I never knew?" Freya glanced at her aunt, who shrugged, before shifting her gaze back to her grandmother.

Vara sighed and Ana smirked. "Avorell's borders are closed for trade and politics, not travel," Vara explained. "I visited the elvish lands as a guest and longtime friend of an emissary, nothing more."

"It's a beautiful land," Freya commented. She couldn't help feeling envious of Vara, who'd retired from life as a warrior and now spent her days freely traveling wherever she pleased.

"You should return some day," Ana said. "An allegiance with the elves would be highly beneficial to Lindoroth."

Freya let out a sigh through her nose. "True, but I'd like to acquire a few foreign friends without political motivations. Not every relationship needs to be transactional."

Ana's eyes filled with sympathy. "While that's a nice sentiment, life as a monarch means everything is either political or transactional." It looked like she was about to say more, but her eyes drifted toward the door as someone stepped into the room.

"There you are."

Smiling at the sound of Aer's voice, Freya turned her head and saw her husband, his hair mussed from sleep. "I couldn't sleep anymore." She patted the bench next to her. "Come eat."

Rubbing his eyes, Aer sat down beside her and picked up a piece of bread. "I don't know how I'm hungry already."

"You've been asleep for six hours," Vara informed him.

Lines formed between his brows. "Six *hours?*"

Ana gave him an amused look. "Most kings would be more on their guard, considering."

He sent her a withering look.

Freya bit her lip, fighting a smile. "Most would also run a comb through their hair before gracing their subjects," she added before Aer could respond. "We were just talking about Grandmother's travels. She's spent quite a bit of time with the elves."

Aer leaned back in his chair, his bread momentarily forgotten, and gave Vara a curious look. "Is that so?"

"Here and there," Vara replied. "It helps to know your neighbors, even the ones we don't share a border with."

"Indeed." Aer let the legs of his chair drop to the floor and took a bite of bread. "So, what next?"

"Byrric will want to have a full strategy meeting tomorrow," Ana said. "Ruehnar will be here the day after, so we need to be able to hit the ground running." Lips pressed, she eyed Freya with consternation. "You're still wary of the elves."

"Yes and no," Freya replied carefully. "They made good on their word, but the ways they tried to avoid following through…"

"Were troubling," Aer finished. "But understandable, considering."

"You can't blame them for doing all they can to keep their people safe," Vara said. "I would hope you'd do the same."

Freya nodded slowly. "It's just difficult knowing I'll always have to be on my guard, monitoring every word, every intonation."

The ghost of a smile tilted Vara's lips. "Elves or not, you should always be on your guard. Your parents taught you better."

"I know, Grandmother." Freya leaned against Aer and took his hand. "If our parents had been less interested in politics, we'd likely be in more of a mess than we are now. Knowing that doesn't make it any easier to handle."

Aer wrapped his fingers around hers under the table and squeezed. "But we will. Any suggestions on how to approach them now that we have better information to work with would be much appreciated. Lord Florian gave us more than we could've asked for, but you have the objectivity of someone without blood ties."

Vara nodded. "Yes, my experiences with the Tordove family are much different than Andreus', certainly."

She paused when the cook stepped in and replaced the empty bread basket with a new one overflowing with warm, flaky rolls.

"My first visit was when I was about a century old," Vara went on, her eyes twinkling, "long before Byrric came along. I met your grandfather on one of my trips.

He was Valkyrie through and through," she said at Freya's confused look, "but he'd left Iston when I was a girl, so I'd never met him here. We just happened to be on the same ship traveling to Avorell. Once we saw how well we got on, we traveled everywhere that would have us."

"Where did you stay when you visited Avorell?" Aer asked.

"Where didn't she stay, you mean," Ana muttered, but the words carried amusement.

"I stayed in each of the courts at least twice," Vara replied. "The capital was always too busy for my taste, but I did a few shorter trips there."

Freya frowned. "Where did you meet the Tordoves, then?"

"In Andradath, but I spent time with Nalaea in the Winter Court when she was visiting her family. I met Ruehnar through her on one of my visits. I did some day trips to the capital to sup with them both, but I typically stayed elsewhere to experience more of the land."

They sat in silence for a moment before Aer spoke.

"So, how would you suggest we approach Ruehnar when he arrives?"

"Just as you did in Avorell. With respect and gratitude coupled with the desire to form a lasting relationship. You've proven your strengths as king and queen. Forming that friendship shouldn't be hard."

Logic, Freya thought. Pure logic. Yet as she considered her first meetings with the elvish king and queen, she struggled to see how she could apply Vara's advice now that she and Aer had already made their first impressions. Yes, she wanted a relationship with the elves for a multitude of reasons that would benefit Lindoroth. But reeling in her anxious desire to save her kingdom, a desire that had nearly ruined their chances in Avorell when her gut told her to flee, seemed a major feat.

As she idly poked at the dregs of her stew with her spoon, she shut out the voices of the others and wondered how different things would be now that Ruehnar had seen her skills in action. The Wild Hunt had surely changed the elves' perspective of her as a queen and, in turn, Aer as a king. He hadn't fought her battles for her and she'd won the Hunt, fair and square. The feelings of insult and disgust she'd felt when she first met the monarchs, that they saw her as a trophy queen for Aer, something pretty and eye-catching to set upon a throne, lingered but were dwindling.

Whether they'd dwindled enough to put her at ease with the elves was yet to be seen.

5

FREYA

Freya's father was up at dawn the next morning, sending Rini and the other pixies to wake her, Aer, and anyone else who would have a strong hand in crafting plans for reclaiming their kingdom. They couldn't linger in Iston forever, certainly not with a power switch in play in Iladel, but the idea of leaving so soon was already exhausting her.

When Byrric summoned them all to the dining room, Freya wasn't surprised to see he had already begun shifting the markers around on the map, the furrow between his brows showing how hard his military mind was working. Florian stood at his side, arms folded as he murmured his own thoughts to Byrric.

Tavian and Fenian, the two eldest elf princes, stood opposite Florian, eyeing Byrric's movements. Both had arrived from Watoria not long after sunrise, having spent the last few days securing the city with the marshals and ensuring Commander Alstad had sufficient support when they left. They'd also brought Reginald and Rosie Ristner with them. Between elvish magic and Lindorothian healing remedies, Reginald would be up and about in another day or two, if Florian's assessment was correct. Everyone was at a loss as to how to handle the princess, but as Freya looked around the room and took in the map before them, she knew Rosie was the last thing she needed to worry about at the moment.

Over the next few minutes, more guests shuffled in. Some, like Alyndra Cailen, the Maddixes, the Brytons, and Perida Calliwell, looked far too exhausted to do anything but listen or, ideally, rest. Ettrian leaned against the wall behind them.

Once everyone was settled, Byrric stood at the head of the table, his back rigid, wings tucked tightly between his shoulders. Florian's dark eyes swept the room, seeming to scrutinize everyone in attendance. And, Freya realized, he likely was. That was his job, after all. Take in every detail, ensure his monarchs were making the best decisions with the information he gathered.

Yes, they were lucky to have him.

"We're facing issues on multiple fronts," Byrric began. "We'll start with numbers." Gesturing toward the map, Florian slid a handful of markers toward the side. "We've lost approximately fifteen thousand Lindorothian knights and marshals across our five armies. Of the remainder, I've sent squadrons from the Royal Army to each of the capitals to hold or secure them alongside each realms' knights. We're still waiting for final numbers from Olthanas, but all told, we've destroyed roughly four thousand enemy knights, although, as we all know, there are more of them than there are of us. Avorell has offered three thousand knights, the bulk of which will arrive tomorrow with King Ruehnar." He gave a nod to the princes. "That's more than we'd originally planned, for which we're grateful. Combined with our own forces, we'll have approximately twenty-five thousand knights." Pursing his lips, Byrric rubbed a hand over his stubbled jaw. "We don't have precise numbers, of course, but if Prince Ettrian's assessment is correct, we're looking at roughly twenty thousand men landing on our shores today, putting the humans and Jotnar at roughly thirty-five thousand."

"My numbers are accurate, Commander," Ettrian stated. "Assuming Willem was being truthful, you have a great host heading your way."

"How can you be certain of this?" Perida challenged.

Ettrian sent her a bland look. "I asked Willem where I should direct my own knights. He said, and I quote, 'I have twenty thousand men arriving on the eastern shore of Caelora. Send your forces there.'"

Freya bit down on her lip to keep from laughing at the narrow-eyed look on Perida's face when she had no argument for Ettrian's response.

"Zane and the others should be back within the next few days to confirm," Ana told Perida.

Perida gave a sharp nod of approval.

Byrric's eyes flicked toward Lea, who stood at Ettrian's side. "Lady Calliwell, do you have anything to add regarding Willem or Lessia?"

Lea blew out a short breath. "I can confirm most of what Prince Ettrian stated. There were two Jotnar hosts heading toward Kildin and Watoria, although Lessia never informed Willem of the one set for Kildin, so I'm assuming it was intended to wipe out the human knights there. Willem stated the northern army was 'handled,' though, so one of his scouts must've caught wind of the attack on Kildin, which certainly would've taken out most of Willem's forces there. From what I could gather," she looked up at Ettrian, "and Prince Ettrian, feel free to contradict me, but neither Willem nor Lessia knew the elves were assisting you in Watoria."

"Willem surely knows now," Aer said. "Reykr Traust fled Watoria before the battle was over. I can't imagine he went anywhere other than Iladel."

Byrric nodded slowly. "Yes, I agree. Our scouts are looking for signs of him, but since he's stayed hidden for decades, I don't expect we'll find him easily, at least not until he returns to Iladel."

"Willem will need to regroup now that he knows the elves are involved," Florian said. "It's also worth noting that Jonas has not been crowned emperor of Jotunheim. That may cause a bit of a hiccup for Willem, which, in addition to the news of our new allies, could give us a few days' respite."

"Or he could just have Jonas killed and deal with the issue of

Jotnar succession later," Aer countered. "If at all. He may simply try to take Jotunheim for himself."

"Unlikely," Tavian replied. "Willem will be focused on getting a handle on the Jotnar army. If he thinks Jonas is on his side or he can ensure Jotnar knights' loyalty, he'll guarantee him his crown simply to avoid that 'hiccup.'"

"This is all well and good, but we're forgetting that the Jotnar army might not be amenable to Jonas as their commander," Fenian added. "A regime change in the midst of war is problematic at best. It could work in our favor, of course, or it could make this war far more difficult to win."

"Willem may try to put Traust at the helm of the Jotnar army, considering Lessia put him in charge of advising Frederick Veldin in Watoria," Byrric replied. "He's already trusted among the Jotnar. Willem would be a fool not to consider it, and Jonas would be a fool to argue it."

Freya eyed her father curiously. "Why?"

"Lessia trusted Traust to lead a siege in Watoria," Byrric explained. "The knights will trust him, a male with centuries of experience, over Jonas, a thirty-year-old male who's done little more than travel his entire life."

"Or Jonas could have Traust executed," Fenian said with an exaggerated sigh. "Or he could betray you lot entirely and stand shoulder-to-shoulder with that cretin, with a grin on his face. So many *'ors'* with you lot." His metallic eyes turned to Lea. "As someone who was...close with Lord Edrin, do you believe he'll remain faithful to your cause?"

"Yes."

Fenian's lips twitched with amusement, and Freya arched a brow, surprised at Lea's certainty. "Lea—"

Lea held up a hand to cut her off. "Apologies, Your Majesty, but yes, I think Jonas will remain steadfast. However," she pushed forward, ignoring Freya's attempt to interrupt, "considering we can't easily contact him, we shouldn't rely on him for support just yet."

It wasn't hard for Freya to understand why Lea felt Jonas would remain loyal. By his own account, he'd hated Lessia and wanted to take her throne. Even so, considering he'd planned to take her throne, it was safe to assume, at least in her mind, that his loyalty was tenuous at best. If Lea was open to the idea of him only being moderately useful, it would make pressing forward all the easier.

"I don't think there will come a point when we *can* fully rely on him," Freya replied gently. "But Lea, even if he is still on our side, there's no telling what Willem might be doing to him right this moment. It's entirely possible Jonas is imprisoned or worse."

"Agreed," Byrric replied. "And as you are now here, there's no way to guarantee a consistent flow of information."

"If it's all the same to everyone else, I think we should send a scout who can return more quickly than our own," Aer said, eyeing the elvish princes. "With one of the royal guards, ideally. Both mine and Freya's are prepared to accompany one of your knights," he added, jerking his chin toward their four guards who stood sentry against the wall.

Seeming to sense Aer's wariness, Tavian nodded. "Agreed. We will arrange it immediately."

"Once our father arrives, I'll escort the Ladies Calliwell to Errest," Ettrian said, a dark brow lifting as he looked down at Lea. "I think we can all agree it's best to wait until we have knights to join us before leaving, so we'll leave tomorrow."

Based on Lea's scowl, Freya could only assume her friend had already been pressing the elf prince to leave immediately. Recalling her own insistence at patrolling Watoria, Freya knew all too well what Lea must have been feeling. She made a mental note to have a one-on-one with her later.

"I want to go to my city," Lazarus said, drawing Freya's attention from Lea and Ettrian. The Cailens, alongside Collin's family, had stood quietly as strategies and plans were passed around, but there was no doubting what Lazarus and Alyndra Cailen wanted to do.

"Laz..." Aer murmured.

"Please, Aerelius," Alyndra murmured, her words tinged with pain. "We need to be with our people."

"I know you want to go to Kildin as soon as possible." Byrric's tone was gentle. "However, it would not be wise to dedicate that much of our time and movement to a city that's a seven day march from here and another four to Iladel. Our priority should be the palace and retaking the capitol. We will retake Kildin," he assured them, "but we need our monarchs' thrones back first."

Freya exhaled, knowing he was right and hating it all the same.

"Then how do we ensure my people's safety?" Alyndra asked. "There must be something we can do, more knights we can send."

"I'd like to know the same," Lazarus asked. "My people are–"

"Dying," Tavian said. "Yes, we're aware."

The callous tone the prince took chilled Freya's bones and had her back up as offense for Lazarus and his mother sparked inside her.

Tavian gestured toward the map, at Iladel sitting on the eastern shore, which was wide open to naval attacks. "So are the people in the capital. What makes your citizens so much more important?"

Fury roiled in Laz's eyes. "Nothing. I only meant–"

"You only meant that we should devote our soldiers to securing a city that can be rebuilt instead of the city that holds your monarchs' thrones."

"Thrones are—"

"Thrones are symbols of hope and stability," Fenian snapped. "If those seats are being warmed by a human thief and the heir to the Jotnar throne, your people will lose hope. More than they already have, if such a thing is possible."

Alyndra rested a hand on her son's arm, silencing Laz's retort. "Prince Tavian, you must understand our need–not desire–to retake Kildin. It's a crucial intersection between Jotunheim and the rest of Lindoroth."

"An intersection that is currently in ruin," Tavian countered, his tone only mildly calmer than his brother's. "Sending a full squadron of knights there while a usurper is in your palace would be akin to–what is it your kind say? Plugging a dam with your finger?"

Alyndra took a deep breath. "Caelora's capital has the largest trading center in the entire kingdom. Most of that trade is with Jotunheim, so we can't afford to lose it permanently."

"It also has *people*." Lazarus met her eyes. "People we cannot lose permanently." The pain in his voice was a blade that sliced through Freya's heart, and it took everything in her not to try and comfort him.

Byrric, Freya, and Aer all watched in silence at the volley between the elves and Cailens. Although her instinct was to defend Lazarus, Freya knew this was one of those times that it would be best to listen instead of speak. This wasn't a decision her heart could make.

"I think a compromise might be best at this juncture," Florian suggested, a small frown turning his lips. "The roads to Kildin from the sea and Jotunheim are far too perilous to risk sending a large battalion, and it's likely the humans will attempt to form a base there. If the elves can carry a small group of knights to the outskirts of Kildin, we might be able to offer some aid without limiting our movements to Iladel, get as many people out of the city and into the outlying villages as possible."

"How many could you afford to send?" Byrric asked Tavian.

Tavian's obsidian eyes flashed when he met Byrric's gaze. "I can commit one hundred. Two hundred at most."

"One hundred!" Laz sputtered. Again, Lady Cailen gripped his arm, but he shook her off and took a menacing step toward the prince. "That's hardly any!"

Prince Fenian, let out an exaggerated sigh, then snapped his fingers. Instantly, Lazarus' mouth fell shut, his ability to speak gone.

Moments later, he was engulfed in flame.

6

FREYA

Alyndra Cailen screamed and stumbled back, Byrric catching her as she nearly fell to the floor. Completely ignoring the flames, Collin leapt forward, then crashed hard into an impenetrable shield of magic when Prince Fenian held up his free hand. The same force seemed to hold back everyone else in the room. Including, to Freya's dismay, each of the guards who stood behind them.

"Stop!" Freya exclaimed, her wings flaring as she pressed with all her might against Fenian's magic. It shifted and swayed, writhing like a serpent under her weight, but she couldn't break through it.

Flames licked at Lazarus' immobilized form. Aer took two steps toward his cousin before slamming into the same invisible force that held Freya and Collin in place.

The room was still as a statuary, the only sound the quiet rustle of flames. Freya's heart thundered as she watched Collin fight against his invisible bonds, trying and failing to reach his partner. Her thoughts whirled and her magic pressed against Fenian's, clawing and scratching to be free. Just as she finally felt the slightest give, he let his hands fall.

Freya's hip sang with pain as she stumbled into the table, then she watched in shock as the flames around Laz died out and he stood there, unmarred and furious. Her and Aer's guards, now free from their bonds, rushed forward, shoving Lazarus out of the way and grabbing Fenian, locking his arms behind him.

"Have you lost your mind?" Aer roared, lunging toward the prince. Freya jutted out a wing just as Ordona latched onto his arm, stopping him before he could go further, while Byrric gave the command for the guards to halt.

The prince chuckled but didn't bother pushing against Rodrick and Perinald. "Quite the contrary," he replied calmly. "Lord Cailen seems to think our numbers are insignificant. I believe I just demonstrated how much that is not the case."

The expression on Prince Tavian's face was mildly disapproving, although the same couldn't be said for Ettrian, who appeared on the verge of laughter. Or Byrric, Freya noticed. His gaze, while exasperated, was also speculative. Ordona's gaze seemed to mirror his.

"You've made your point, Your Highness," Florian said. "Enough with the theatrics."

"Your Majesty?" Perinald, one of Aer's guards, asked. "What shall I do with His Highness?"

Jaw set, Aer gave a sharp nod. "Let him go. As Lord Florian said, he's made his point."

"And what *point* might that be?" Laz shouted, shaking off Collin's hand on his arm and taking a step toward Fenian. "You could've killed me!"

"And yet here you are." Fenian shrugged out of Perinald's hold, then brushed his fingernails on his doublet and sighed. "With half a thought, I've slaughtered your leader, incapacitated all of your guards, and bewitched you all with my magic without breaking a sweat. At least, that's what I could've easily done were I not beholden to a bargain made by my parents." He bared his teeth in a cruel grin. "What do you think one hundred of us can do against a bunch of pitiful humans?"

Exhaling a shaking breath, Freya stifled her anger and frustration and met Laz's gaze evenly. "Despite the prince's methods, his point still stands. And...I think you should prepare yourself for a city that may not be fully salvageable." There was no way to soften the blow her words delivered. Despite how true they were, they were also harsh.

"That doesn't mean it isn't," Byrric cut in when Laz's outraged look grew. "It simply means we need to prepare for the worst. We may be too late to save many of the people, but that doesn't mean we cannot retake the city. And Prince Tavian is correct," he added with a disapproving look toward the prince. "At least in regards to the power of his army."

"The elves could—"

"We need to focus on getting your knights to Errest and Iladel," Fenian cut in. "We will not waste more of our own on a fool's mission, and that is my final answer."

"A fool's mission?" Alyndra Cailen stepped forward. "Tell me, Prince Fenian, would you call wanting to save your home a 'fool's mission'?"

"If it was crawling with enemy soldiers? Yes, I would. I would look at the situation as objectively as possible, which you are categorically failing to do." The prince cocked his head, eyeing Lazarus curiously. "Your city is overrun. There is no retaking it quickly, quietly, or safely. I understand its political and economical importance, but that simply does not change the facts. There is no room here for idealistic and naïve thinking."

"Then send our own knights!" Laz exclaimed.

"Lazarus, we need to get to Iladel," Aer said firmly. "It's not what you want to hear, but it's what needs to be done. A kingdom without monarchs is no kingdom at all."

"If we take too many of our soldiers away from the capital, we risk losing the kingdom–not just the governor's seat," Freya added. "The knights we send will be able to help get your people to safety, but that's the most we can focus on right now."

Colin placed a hand on Lazarus' back when he looked like he was about to argue. "Will we be permitted to go with the knights to Kildin? I know my family will go to Watoria." He looked to his parents, aunt, and cousin, who had to return to Watoria to take his father's seat, before looking back at Byrric. "But I am needed in Kildin."

A muscle feathered in Byrric's jaw. "I cannot tell you what to do, my lords. If it were up to me, the Cailens would remain here until we get their city in hand. The wards that protect Iston are the best way to ensure Caelora has a governing family remaining when this war is over. That said," he pressed when Alyndra opened her mouth to protest, "having you both present will also go a long way in boosting your citizens' morale, even if you can only rule from the outlying villages for now." His gaze shifted to Freya and Aer. "What do my monarchs have to say?"

Freya's instinctual response was to keep everyone in their party together. They were stronger together, a fact that had been proven time and time again. Separate, they would splinter like a wooden sword. Together, they were a mace, hard and enduring.

But that was her heart speaking. Not the mind her father had taught to think like a leader.

"I know you two are my king and queen now and I have to do your bidding," Laz said quietly, his voice carefully restrained. "But we're also family. Please, I'm begging you to look at this from my position as your blood, not your subject."

"I agree with Byrric that your presence in Kildin will do more to help your people than if you remain here," Aer replied, exchanging a look with Freya.

"We'll support you if that's what you wish to do," Freya added with a smile.

"Now that that's settled, let's go over positioning and movements," Byrric said, huffing out a sigh and raking his fingers through his hair. Quickly and succinctly, he began shifting markers around, outlining Lind and enemy placements. The first of Lessia's armies had been taken out by the Linds at Watoria, eliminating roughly seven hundred Jotnar and human soldiers. The army she'd sent toward Kildin—one that was, according to Willem Ristner, 'handled'—had been destroyed by the humans two days prior, based on what information Ettrian had been able to obtain from Willem, although more scouting was necessary to confirm. Olthanas and Watoria, the capitals of Saith and Allanor, were considered safe for any Linds fleeing their homes. Errest, the capital of Lea's home realm of Edhil, was at a stalemate, with roughly one thousand enemy knights camped outside the city. The people there had enough notice to set up defenses before the enemy arrived, but no one had gone in or out for weeks. The city itself was safe, although the same couldn't be said for the outlying villages. Many had been pillaged.

For the next half hour, Freya listened as Byrric, Aer, and Florian gave instructions on which families would go where, who would maintain governor seats, and how many knights would travel with each. Ultimately, the sons of Governors Bryton and Maddix would return to Saith and Allanor, respectively, to hold their fathers' seats, each with a squadron of knights. Lazarus, his mother, and Collin, along with Collin's parents, would remain together and travel to Kildin with a total of four hundred knights, both elf and Lind. Lazarus would hold his father's seat, as Rischa Cailen's successor had been slaughtered at the wedding.

"I know leadership isn't what you wanted," Aer said quietly to Laz when the other families began to disperse, leaving only a handful remaining in the room. "But a complete change of leadership will only make things more difficult. Your people know you. It's important to step into the role for their sake."

Jaw tight, Laz took a deep breath, then gave them a smile that looked anything but genuine. "Then I suppose I shouldn't disappoint them."

7

———

LEA

Although Lea already knew she and her mother would leave the next day, hearing Byrric give the official order for everyone to disperse allowed something solid to settle in her chest that replaced the hollowness that had been there for weeks.

Home.

She was going home. And, from what the commander said, it was still in one piece. The last stronghold. She couldn't help but smile as he'd said that, knowing the strength of her people, her knights, and Errest's city walls did what they were supposed to do: keep their enemies out and their citizens safe.

Before they all went their separate ways, though, she needed to sit down and lay out all of the goings-on at the palace to Freya and Aer. Too much had happened for her to write it down or leave it to chance that Tyna could relay everything, and with so much said in that morning's meeting, she wanted a private audience to ensure everything was conveyed properly.

So, after they'd had lunch, they, along with Florian and Byrric, set their sights on the main courtyard, a space designed for broad wings but perfect for privacy. Collin and Lazarus would want to hear her story, she knew, but for the moment, her focus was on telling the people in charge everything she could before she left.

Fortunately, the day was unseasonably warm, making it easy to carry on their business outdoors without catching a chill.

"Where would you like me to begin?" she asked once they'd settled. She, Freya, and Aer sat on the grass, Byrric on a stone bench beside them. Florian stood stock-still, arms folded across his black leather jacket. "I've given you all the most important bits," she added, "but I'm sure you want to know more."

"At the beginning," Aer said, swapping a glance with Byrric, who nodded. "We heard a lot second-hand from Tyna, of course, but she wasn't always there or with you."

With a nod, Lea took a deep breath. "Right. The beginning." *When I was dragged before Lessia and Willem like a prize worth winning.* "Well, for starters, Jonas carried out his oath as best he could." She gave Aer what she hoped was a reassuring smile. "I know you were concerned he'd find some loophole, but as you can see, I'm perfectly safe."

"What was Jonas' reasoning for leaving you in the dungeons for so long?" Freya demanded.

"I'm guessing Lessia and Willem weren't willing to trust you, correct?" Byrric asked Lea.

"Precisely. Jonas and Tyna also needed to seal up any spy holes or other means of entry to our room." Lea grimaced. "I don't blame Lessia or Willem, of course. I wouldn't have trusted me either." She looked at Freya and Aer. "I was angry with Jonas at first...I still am, I suppose, just for other reasons. But forcing the issue with Willem and Lessia would've gone counter to the character he was trying to portray. Willem wanted to let his men fight over me as spoils of war, and Jonas felt it was...imprudent not to rock the boat, so to speak, so he let Lessia take her time deciding how to handle me. The dungeons, at that point anyway, were the best way to avoid any... unsavory interactions, because Lessia wouldn't allow it." Her stomach still roiled at the thought of being handed off to Willem or one of his men. She didn't bother mentioning Lessia's inquisitions and occasional backhands across the face. "I don't know how much of Willem's intentions Jonas knew, but I think Jonas realized that if he put up too much of a fight, Willem's interest in me would grow. We needed to prevent that for a number of reasons."

"Of course," Freya murmured, squeezing her friend's hand. "But your mother..."

"Understood far more than she let on." Lea exhaled slowly. "I know that now. It doesn't change the fact that seeing her in the dungeon, wasting away as she was, is something I hope to never witness again." The hardest part, the part Lea kept to herself, had been the lies she'd been forced to spin about her father, his treatment, and the type of man he was. Orin Calliwell had been dead for a month, yet she could only hope he could forgive her in death for all the terrible things she'd said. Unforgivable things.

It took nearly an hour for her to lay out everything that had happened to her over the past month, of her time in the palace, and how she'd managed to gather information, secreting away bits of knowledge she'd hoped would prove useful in the coming days. She spoke of how she'd had to use her magic to ward off Willem, then hide her magic to ensure everyone thought Jonas was dosing her food with widow venom. Through gritted teeth, she told them of how she'd had to force down her own character to appear docile and submissive to Jonas and contrite toward Lessia and Willem while also being assertive in her 'views.'

Her final days in the palace were the hardest to discuss. Those were the days she had spent living in fear that Freya and Aer were dead, not to mention questioning whether Willem would follow through on his threats to execute her mother. Days she had to decide whether or not it was worthwhile to trust an elf prince with her life, and, as it was, her body. Despite Ettrian, thankfully, *not* mating her to Jonas, she'd spent those days believing she was married to him. She'd had to pretend to be enamored of Jonas, in whom her trust waxed and waned. Yet when Lea began to see hints of the man Jonas was in his homeland, hints his own blood provided about his reputation and past lovers, she suspected she'd been foolhardy and naive to trust his intentions and her own gut.

"But he made a blood bond," Freya said as Lea outlined her concerns. "He couldn't have hurt you."

"No, but his absence gave frequent opportunities for others to," Byrric said, frowning slightly. "Jonas left you alone often?"

"He did," Lea confirmed. "He claimed it was to ensure Lessia and Willem saw him as obedient. It also gave me plenty of time to befriend Rosie and explore the tunnels, though I'm not sure if that was intended or was simply a happy perk." She considered the situation for a moment. "But if I'm being honest, I don't think Jonas was intentionally putting me in harm's way. He just seemed...naïve?"

"A naïve would-be emperor is the last thing we need in this war," Florian said.

"Combined with Willem and it's just a recipe for disaster," Aer agreed.

Byrric, ever the soldier, wore a perplexed expression as he watched her, the wheels in his head surely turning over everything Lea had just divulged. As usual, Florian's dark eyes showed no hint of what he was thinking, but Lea knew him well enough to know he was examining each tiny detail in that elvish mind of his.

She still hadn't talked to Freya or Aer about Florian's identity, but she didn't much have it in her to care. He'd been good to her family and friends, had more than shown his loyalty to the Harridan family, and she simply couldn't muster the strength to worry about anything else.

"For the moment, we have to assume the worst," Byrric finally said. "I'm inclined to trust Lord Edrin, but as he is now on the other side of the continent with no form of communication here, we can't bank on his support."

"Agreed," Aer replied. "Especially now that he has a crown to contend for."

"As Lessia's heir, does Jonas truly need to contend for anything?" Freya asked with a frown. "It's his by rights."

"Nothing indicates Daniel Veldin would betray his sister's wishes, despite currently acting as steward" Florian said. "Although, it's entirely possible he's—"

"Hungry for power and willing to kill his own kin to take it?" Freya muttered in disgust. "Just like the rest of them?"

Including Jonas, Lea thought.

"Precisely." Byrric glanced up at the sky, where three Valkyrie were circling nearby, keeping watch over the city. He looked back at Freya and Aer. "It's time to question Isadora. I didn't want to bring it up during planning, but she'll be able to give us the most information regarding Willem and, ideally, Daniel's plans."

"Agreed." Aer raked a hand through his dark hair. "I don't see that being easy. I think it's best to let Florian lead the inquisition."

"Get Ettrian to help," Lea said, frowning. "Something tells me he'll be able to get quite a bit out of her."

"Something tells *me* he'll enjoy that a bit too much," Freya replied, then looked back toward the house. "But yes, I think he or one of his brothers could be effective."

"Andreus, any thoughts on which prince would be most useful?" Byrric asked.

Florian thought for a moment. "Fenian. He's more deliberate in his actions than his brothers and is best at extracting information through fear over pain."

Aer nodded his agreement. "We'll make a plan tonight and question her in the morning. I'd prefer to speak with Reginald and the princess first."

Lea nodded absently, suddenly feeling a bit overwhelmed. She'd had no shortage of visitors the past few weeks, but for once, she wasn't on her guard and didn't need to watch every word she said. Yet while she should've felt relief, all she felt was anxious, itchy, as though the other shoe was about to drop.

"I think I'm going to take a walk," Lea announced. The scent of earth and air had become too tempting for her. She needed to move away from the walls that surrounded them and give her magic a bit of a workout. "If that's alright with you."

A small furrow flickered across Aer's brow, concern that quickly vanished. "Of course. I'm sure finally having some time to yourself is relieving."

She flashed him a grateful smile. "It is." Even though Jonas had left her alone often, those times were spent looking over her shoulder. "And I'm sure Iska will want to join me."

However, if she hurried, she'd be able to slip away without her guard looking over her shoulder. A bit of time where there was no one overseeing her, where she wasn't putting on a show for someone, was precisely what she needed. Willem, Jonas, Rosie... they were no longer her concern. Well, Rosie might be, but that remained to be seen. She'd have to speak to the girl sooner or later. Just not now.

After saying goodbye to the others, Lea left the courtyard and made her way through the house to the main entrance, pausing only long enough to pick up a fur cloak from her room. She knew little of Vara and even less of Iston, but the urge to walk the village streets *alone* beckoned her past the gates. Prior to her sudden arrival in Watoria, she hadn't seen anyone or anything outside the palace walls since the day she'd left Aldridge, mere weeks but what felt like years. As an earth user, her magic had been woefully deprived since the wedding, her occasional visits to the palace garden doing far too little to prevent her magic from feeling stagnant.

With a grin, she stepped through the portico, her steps quickening in the afternoon sun.

8

———

LEA

As Lea strolled down the drive, she contemplated checking if there was a horse available for her to ride into town. Even as the thought crossed her mind, her feet drew her further down the gravel path, past the carriage house and stables, beyond the hedgerow that bordered Vara's estate, all the way to the road.

Finally, *finally,* she was free of the metaphorical leashes and chains that had tethered her to the palace. Willem wasn't there to leer, Rosie wasn't there to preen, and Jonas wasn't there to give her all the reasons she should stay inside. Today, she could go back to openly loving her father and hating the people she'd spent every moment with for the past month.

And *finally,* she could wear a damn pair of pants without risking Lessia's disapproval. The fur-lined wool leggings, fitted tunic, and boots tipped with Caelorian steel Vara had given her were a welcome respite after being forced to wear rib-crushing dresses and dainty shoes that did nothing to keep her feet warm. For once, she could move freely without hefting layers of tulle and silk about.

With each step, she felt a bit more freedom. Each step carried her away from the confinement of the house and reminded her that she was no longer being watched. Her magic was no longer in danger of being bound or suppressed.

Her conscience flickered with guilt at the talking-to Iska was likely getting for letting her slip out, but the moment she scented the winter air flush with pine and the promise of frost, that feeling of guilt vanished.

Grinning, she ran the last few steps toward the tree-lined road that led to Iston's main village. Vines, thick and green, wrapped around the ancient Allanorian pines. Winter wisteria, only present in the colder northern regions, dripped from the branches in wine-colored clumps and cast a sweet smell all around. The lovely flower was one Lea had only seen once during a winter visit to the palace, but it had quickly become her favorite. Iladel was rarely frigid, but there were times it was cold enough for the blood-red flower to bloom, even if just for a day. Never in Errest, though.

Here in Iston, it was everywhere. The trees were drenched in rich burgundy, coating them so heavily it nearly obscured the stiff green needles.

She stopped in the middle of the forested road, closed her eyes, and inhaled. The air was chillier here in the shade, but she reveled in the sweet scent of life tickling her nostrils and filling her lungs. Pine and cedar, livestock from the nearby farms, smoke from the village.

She was finally free.

Opening her eyes, Lea held out her hand, silently calling on the earth to respond. A moment later, velvet petals brushed the back of her hand and danced along her fingers. She looked up and saw several thin branches curling toward her, their flowers swaying with the movement.

Gently, she brushed the soft blooms, being careful not to damage them. Winter flowers were a beautiful thing; hardy, but often delicate as a snowflake. Despite the frigid air and shorter days, they persisted, lack of sunlight be damned, but the twarmth of a closed hand could easily wilt them.

"I've just saved your guard from a flogging, you know."

Startled, Lea jolted from the flower, the whip-like branch snapping to her side as she spun and faced Ettrian Tordove, who stood smirking a few feet behind her. "What are you talking about?" Her heart thundered in her chest, but she refused to let him see how much he'd startled her.

Ettrian shrugged, his eyes landing on the flower, then slowly traveling up the vine toward its host tree. "You slipped your guard. I assume you want him to keep his post, so I asked the king and queen to send me along as your escort before your mother found out."

Lea narrowed her eyes. "Why would you do that?"

"He seems like a good male, and your mother worries." He jerked his chin toward the flower beside her. "You're a bit like them, you know."

"What's that supposed to mean?"

He took a step closer, holding up a hand in defense when the branch twitched toward him. "Care to call off your friend?"

Pressing her lips together, Lea sent the foliage back to its rightful place, then folded her arms across her chest and looked at the prince. "I was enjoying my walk, so be quick."

He gestured toward the trees. "The flowers. They're persistent, a bit plucky, if you will. Not unlike you."

"If it's all the same to you–"

"It's not." Ettrian looked past her toward town, then, ignoring her question, asked, "So, where are you off to?"

"I'm going for a walk."

He glanced over his shoulder toward the house. "I wouldn't mind a bit of exercise, myself."

Lea exhaled. "Fine." Jaw clenched, she turned and started down the road. She wasn't necessarily opposed to the prince's company, although she typically could only handle him in small doses. It would be easy enough to keep conversation to a minimum and still enjoy her walk in peace, though.

Ignoring her snark, the prince fell into step beside her, his feet nearly silent as they moved across the gravel. The lack of sound made Lea's own steps seem thundering.

"So, how is your newfound freedom treating you?"

"It's...different," she said carefully. "Not having someone over-seeing me at all times." A quiet huff slipped past her lips. "Until now, that is." When she looked up at his handsome face, he flashed her a smile, his fangs glinting in the sunlight.

"Your family are quite concerned about you," he admitted. "What kind of prince would I be if I just let you wander off on your own?"

"A good one," she muttered. "I wanted to see the village. I haven't been able to go outside or be normal in weeks. Iston may not be home, but it's far better than being stuck in that damned palace, having no one to spend time with or talk to but people who are either spying or suspicious." She flicked him a pointed glance. "Although it seems I've yet to escape that."

"Well, I am neither spying nor suspicious, so you don't have to worry about that."

To his credit, Ettrian remained silent as they meandered down the road that wended through the forest toward the village. Since most of Iston's residents traveled by wing, Lea hadn't seen a carriage or horse on the entire mile-long trip into town.

When they arrived in the semi-crowded streets, Lea couldn't help but smile. As with Iladel, Iston had an air of camaraderie, where everyone seemed content to sell their wares, enjoy a bite at an eating establishment, or take in the midday sun. Taverns held the typical raucous patrons, while other residents bustled about. The only sign that they lived in a kingdom at war was the increased presence of armed Lindorothian knights in the streets and Valkyrie patrols in the skies. There had only been a few over Lady Balthana's home. Here, dozens crisscrossed the sky over the city, around the outskirts.

Most of the Valkyrie who wandered through the market had their wings retracted. Still, it was impossible to miss the differences between the powerful females and the witches and shifters who made up the rest of Iston's residents. Their strength was evident in the set of their shoulders, the confident way they navigated the crowds, and in the way their clothing did little to hide strong arms and thighs. Based on the sidelong looks Lea often caught, it seemed Vara had alerted the residents, or at least the other Valkyrie, to the elves' presence, because despite what she might've expected, they eyed Ettrian curiously but without fear.

"It's odd," she mused as they strolled around the edge of the central plaza, where traveling merchants peddled wares from all across the kingdom. "They don't seem concerned by your presence."

"Why should they?" His eyes skimmed the passersby. "I am not here to cause them harm, nor have my kind ever had issues with theirs. If anything, they should be happy I'm here." He gave her a slow smile, his fangs once again glinting in the sun. "My appearance is likely a bit disconcerting to some, I'll admit."

She narrowed her eyes. "Why do you always do that? Show your fangs?" she added when he gave her a questioning look.

"Does it bother you?"

"No, but I think most would find it off-putting if *I* went around baring my teeth like an animal."

"Do you not see me as an animal?"

She arched a brow and tried not to smirk. "Of course not. I don't mind if animals follow me around."

"To be fair, I'm not *following* you so much as *accompanying* you. There's a difference."

"Hardly."

Ignoring her, Ettrian jerked his chin toward an inn across the square. "Do you fancy something to eat?"

"A bit, actually," she admitted. Lunch had been good, but she'd been so focused on what she had to tell Freya and Aer that she'd barely eaten. The inn looked to be bursting with patrons, but the thought of dining in a restaurant, even one that probably smelled of ale and sweat, instantly appealed to her.

They made their way inside, the bar matron hardly sparing them a glance as Ettrian ordered food and a pint of ale for them both. Although Lea's original assumption had been accurate—the tavern in fact *did* smell like ale and sweat—she couldn't help but revel in the controlled chaos around her. Travelers and residents filled the space, drinking horns of ale as they shoveled back roasted meat, bowls of stew, and bread. The cacophony was one Lea welcomed wholeheartedly, as it was a thing she hadn't been able to take part in since the wedding.

Wisps of conversation reached her ears as Ettrian led her to a table near the back. Talk of war, the wedding, rumors about Freya and Aer, concern for those in other parts of the kingdom.

She recalled Ettrian's words from the previous day, about how he could feel her people's suffering from the furthermost points in the kingdom. It was hard to imagine so much suffering going on while they were surrounded by the many people here drinking, feasting, and socializing.

"If they're like this during war, I wonder what they'll be like when we win," Lea murmured.

"Your Valkyrie are built for war," Ettrian replied. "I can only imagine all of the people who live in Iston share a similar way of life."

"Maybe." The tone of the room was enough to make Lea smile, just a little. "So how does my world feel today, Your Highness?" she asked as they settled in their seats.

Ettrian drew in a slow breath through his nose, then exhaled. "It's much the same. Your people suffer, but there is an underpinning of hope." His golden eyes met hers. "It's fading, though."

She didn't have to ask to know he meant their hope was fading, not their suffering.

"I want to help them," she said softly.

"In due time, Lady Calliwell," he assured her, leaning back to allow the bar maid to set their drinks down. He narrowed his eyes. "Have you spoken to the princess yet?"

Lea tapped the side of her thumb on the table, letting her eyes roam over the room and take in the people. She had such mixed feelings on Rosie Ristner. On the one hand, the princess was tiresome to an extreme, with her constant questions, uninformed opinions, and observations of Lea's kind. On the other hand, she was a naïve girl who'd lived a sheltered life. Lea couldn't help but feel a bit sorry for her.

"No." She took a small sip of her ale, wincing at its bitter taste. "Although, I'm assuming I'll need to soon."

The prince's shrewd eyes watched her carefully. "What do you plan to say?"

Lea shrugged. "What is there *to* say? 'How are you feeling after watching your brother murder his ally and wife, realizing I was lying to you all along, and being kidnapped?' That's hardly an easy conversation to have, even if Willem *is* a monster."

His lips twitched. "Perhaps she'll appreciate your honesty?"

Lea sputtered as ale caught in her throat. "You must be joking. We *kidnapped her*, Ettrian. Maybe not intentionally, but that's what we did. In her mind, Prince Reginald is a traitor, I'm a liar, and you're, well, also a liar, I suppose." *Among other things.* "She won't be interested in anything we have to say."

The prince rested his forearms on the table, leaning in so only Lea could hear him. "Then perhaps we need to *make* her interested, Lady Calliwell. As of right now, Rosie Ristner is your people's best chance at unraveling her brother's plans. Giving up—"

"No one is *giving up*," Lea snapped. "Quite the opposite, actually. I'm acknowledging the futility—"

"Presumed futility. Rosie might be more amenable than you think."

Frowning, Lea thought back over Rosie's return to consciousness at the Enrieth estate. The princess had been terrified when she awoke to strange surroundings and Lord Florian and Byrric hovering above her. Freya and Aer had been adamant she be made comfortable, of course, but the lack of prison cell clearly did little to ease the princess's mind in an estate filled with her brother's enemies.

"Your king and queen will want to question her," Ettrian said. "She'll feel more comfortable with you present."

Lea arched brow. "You suddenly care about a human's comfort?"

"I couldn't care less about her comfort, Lady Calliwell, only the quality of information she provides and the fact that her brother undoubtedly has his men out searching for her. If you start out by tormenting the girl, she won't give you a damn thing."

"Says the prince who was ready to torture Isadora for information." The excited look Ettrian wore when he had offered to lead Isadora's questioning in Watoria had been eerie enough to set Lea's teeth on edge, although she'd never admit it to him outright.

"Isadora has set herself up for a proper interrogation and she knows it. She'll be lucky if she escapes this with just a few screws in her thumbs. Rosie, I think we can agree, is naive, perhaps a bit dim, and will likely spill more information than we know what to do with if treated properly." He sent her a deadpan look. "In other words, I won't be bringing out the thumbscrews for Princess Ristner just yet. I cannot say the same for Isadora, though."

"Do you truly think Willem has sent his men out to find Rosie?"

"Of course. He and two dozen knights watched her vanish with us. If he wants to maintain any semblance of humanity toward his kind, he'll have no choice but to send out a search party." He sipped his ale. "My brother and I have already discussed this with Byrric. Some of his knights will come west, but I would not be surprised if he sent a sizeable squadron straight to Errest as well."

"Which is all the more reason we need to leave for Errest as soon as possible!" Lea rubbed a hand across her forehead. "Ettrian, if Willem sends his men after Rosie, which I agree he probably will, I cannot let my people face that alone."

"No one said they will. They're human. It will take them more than a week to reach Errest, and that's assuming they left just after we did. By the time they reach your city, they won't be long for this world."

With a small sigh, Lea leaned back in her seat to allow a server to set bowls of steaming stew in front of them. She barely registered its presence as she rolled her mind over the past few days' events.

"I wonder how much worse off we'd be if Freya and Aerelius hadn't realized Isadora had taken Dania's place," she murmured, almost to herself. Fear for Freya and Aer had nearly consumed her back at the palace, even more so once she realized Dania Edrin was lying dead in a mass grave in the surrounding woods.

"Quite a bit, I'd wager." Ettrian spooned up a mouthful of stew. "Fortunately, your king and queen are quite perceptive." He gestured toward her bowl with his spoon. "Eat."

With a nod, Lea picked up her spoon.

9

FREYA

Before Ettrian helped Lea and the Linds escape from the palace dungeons, he'd informed Vara they'd likely be bringing a prisoner or two back with them from Watoria. That same day, Freya's grandmother had smiths in her cellar erecting iron bars. Now, the old cellar housed wine, dry goods, old junk, and three cells built to hold two prisoners apiece.

Today, there was only one occupant, as the rest of the prisoners of war were in Watoria awaiting execution.

Despite the depth of Isadora's subterfuge, Freya wanted to let her stew down here for a few days before questioning her. However, since time was of the essence, she knew her father's desire to extract information immediately was well-founded. So, once their meeting with Lea was finished, she and Aer made their way to Isadora's cell.

Against Freya's better judgement, they'd brought Fenian Tordove along to question Isadora. Ettrian had been her first choice, but Aer had sent him after Lea, so she settled instead on the prince who had unnerved her the most in Avorell. But there had been true terror in Isadora's eyes when Ettrian had suggested executing her, so there was no doubt in Freya's mind his eldest brother would be effective at extracting information, seeing as he'd been borderline giddy to see

Freya run the Hunt. His methods might have been outside Freya's normal comfort realm, but she wouldn't allow herself to stress over it too much.

"I must say, I'm surprised you invited me along," Fenian mused as they descended the old stone stairs to the cellar. He slid a look at Freya. "I assumed you thought I would be far too quick to jump straight to torture."

"We need information quickly," Aer replied. "Based on Lord Florian and our commander's information, you are quite skilled in that area."

"Indeed," Fenian replied. "Where are Andreus and Byrric, anyway?"

"Florian is with Tavian, planning our trip north." Freya turned down the hallway where the holding cells were located, aiming for the one nearest the end. "My father is waiting for us in Isadora's cell."

"And what information, precisely, are you hoping to get from her?"

"Willem Ristner used her for information and she him," Aer answered. "We want to know what they discussed, what she told him about us, and what he's told her about the goings-on in the palace."

Fenian shot them a dubious look. "Do you truly think he told her anything worthwhile?"

"Unlikely," Freya acknowledged. "But not questioning her would be foolish."

They stopped in front of Isadora's cell, where they found Byrric standing over her. The human sat on her cot, her chained arms folded, a haughty expression turning down her pretty features. Somehow, the magic that glamoured her seemed to have faded slightly, revealing the woman beneath who could pass for Dania Edrin at first blush. The shiny golden hair she'd always been so careful to style like Dania's had gone limp, its sheen dimmed to a honey gold, and her red lips and pink cheeks had lost their color, replaced by a dull pallor wholly unbefitting a queen.

The delicate gowns she always favored were gone. Now, the only garb Vara permitted her was drab brown pants and a beige tunic. No strings, no buttons, no ties. In other words, nothing she could use as a weapon or to harm herself. Freya couldn't help but smirk at the sudden downturn Isadora's circumstances had taken.

Isadora watched her captors wordlessly, her expression shifting from annoyed to expectant, then fearful when she watched Fenian enter the room and cock a hip against the cell door, although she schooled her expression beautifully. If Freya didn't know better, she would've thought the woman to be simply stubborn or stupid. As it was, Isadora was certainly both of those things, but wisely, she was also afraid.

Isadora tilted her chin, choosing stubbornness. "Well? Have you come to execute me finally?"

"Soon enough," Aer replied, coming to a stop beside Byrric. "Fortunately for you, we're opting for diplomacy first."

Isadora's attempt at nonchalance flickered once more, giving a glimpse of the fear that lurked beneath her mask.

"You would like that, wouldn't you?" Fenian asked. "To be a martyr for your people? The sacrificial lamb sent by Willem to ensure our attention was diverted away from him?"

"That didn't work out too well for either of you, though, did it?" Freya asked quietly.

"I'm sure it worked out perfectly well for Willem," Isadora shot back. "Even if you have the elves on your side, he still has more men than you."

"Perhaps," Aer conceded. "Although, with Jonas at the head of Jotunheim's army, it's difficult to say for sure who has the upper hand, isn't it?"

Freya watched Isadora carefully to see how she reacted to that bit of news. To her credit, Isadora's face only paled slightly at the king's revelation.

Aer leaned back against the wall opposite Fenian and let his mask of arrogant nonchalance slip into place. "Haven't you heard? Lessia is dead. Effina, too. Poisoned by Willem. I'm surprised you don't know."

"As Jonas is Lessia's heir, he is the new emperor of Jotunheim,"

Freya added with a smirk. "Pending coronation, of course. Though, I doubt he'll let a pesky thing like that delay him taking power."

"Pending–" Isadora jerked forward. "What are you talking about? Lessia's brother–"

"Daniel is a steward and nothing more," Byrric said calmly. "He may hold Madrya today, but it is not his by blood, law, or rights."

Isadora's body relaxed against her chains. "You think the Jotnar will simply accept Jonas as their leader?" She barked out a laugh and shook her head. "And you fools think I'm the stupid one."

"After Lessia colluded with a man who would see their entire race wiped from the map?" Aer lifted his brows.

"And what of Jonas' collusion?" Isadora met each monarch's eyes.

Aer let out a low laugh, and Freya shook her head.

"What collusion?" Aer shrugged. "I've seen no evidence of that."

"Nor have I," Freya agreed. "Father?"

"Not a thing."

Isadora's lips parted in surprise. "But he–"

"Save your breath," Freya said with a sigh. "We don't know Jonas' intentions any more than you do, which is the *only* reason you're still breathing."

Isadora's lips curled into a sneer. "I suppose you'll never know for sure, will you? He was Lessia's nephew, after all. According to you, he helped Willem murder her." When neither responded, Isadora let out an exaggerated sigh. "Why are you really here?"

"We just wanted to talk," Aer replied as Freya took her place beside him. "Find out a bit more about your whereabouts and actions before you switched places with Dania Edrin."

"I'm more curious about the witch who gave you elvish powers." Fenian stepped away from the wall and eyed her curiously. "That's a crime against Avorell, as I'm sure you've guessed. We don't hand out our magic lightly, and those who violate those laws are punished quite thoroughly." His lips tilted into a sinister grin. "As are any who conspired with them."

Freya glanced at him, then bit her lip when she saw the tiny flame flickering softly on his fingertip. Instinct had her wanting to tell him to stop being theatrical, but logic told her to allow him his games.

The human spy studied them, seeming to weigh the prince's words carefully, her eyes coming to rest on the flame he held. "Why do you need to know what I've been doing? You already know what Dania was up to and you know how I ended up in here. What more do you want?"

Fenian continued to toy with his fire, lighting each finger and blowing out the tiny flames one at a time. "You were spying, yes. We're all aware. You were fed false information, but not everything you told Willem was fabricated, correct?" He looked to Byrric for confirmation. "I'd like to know what else you told him and, more importantly, what *he* told *you*."

Isadora pressed her lips into a colorless line, her eyes reflecting the light of Fenian's flames as he set them dancing in the air toward her. "Warnings, mostly. He warned me that the Jotnar were coming down from the north, that Lessia had undoubtedly double-crossed him, although I could've told him that."

Freya took a few steps toward Isadora. "What I would like to know is, why didn't you reveal yourself sooner? Why stay in Jotunheim when you could've returned home? Surely your family would have wanted to know that someone had been put in your place. *Surely* your family would have wanted to know that their daughter was actually a prisoner in Jotunheim and not preparing to become queen of Dystone."

Isadora jolted forward, her arms straining against her chains as she hissed, "My family was willing to sell me off to fuel their political ambitions. Everyone who met Willem knew he was a cretin since birth, but did anyone care? Of course not. They didn't care that he regularly beat Reginald, or that the parents of girls before me had refused a betrothal because they saw he was a violent little monster."

"And yet you allied yourself with him," Aer replied. "Why?"

"Because in the end, he was the only one that gave a damn about me." She ignored Fenian's derisive snort. "Alive, I could give him information. About you all, about Lessia, about Jotunheim. And he knew if he wanted that information from me, he would have to keep me happy." The corners of her bow-shaped mouth curved upward. "Your Majesties, did you know I got to know Daniel Veldin when I lived in Jotunheim?"

"Oh?" Byrric eyed her curiously. "And what did you learn about him in your time there?"

"Yes, Isadora," Fenian crooned, "what did you, a worthless human—of what, twelve when Lessia took you?-- learn about the man who is centuries your senior and likely looked at you much the way I am right now? Did he truly bring you into his inner circle? For that matter, did Lessia do more than simply house you in the slums of Madrya, or did she at least offer you the comfort of a palace cellar hearth?"

Isadora blinked at his cruel words, and Freya could only imagine how each landed, a solid slap on Isadora's confidence.

Freya pursed her lips, contemplating which direction to go. "Alright. What did you learn from Daniel Veldin that you feel is so crucial? Does he plan to challenge Jonas for the throne?"

Something flickered in Isadora's eyes, as if she hadn't considered that possibility. Possibly fake, but Freya tucked it away.

"What did you hope to gain?" Aer asked.

Isadora opened her mouth to speak, then snapped it shut when her eyes fell on Fenian again. The prince was running a fire-sheathed hand over the blade of his dagger, turning the gleaming metal a dark red.

With a small smirk, Fenian looked at Freya, then paused his movements and took a few steps toward Isadora. "Commander, I have been meaning to ask you something."

With a sigh typically reserved for his daughter, Byrric looked at the prince. "What's that, Your Highness?"

"Forgive my ignorance, but how long does it take a human to heal from, say, a knife wound?" He tapped his finger on the edge of his searing blade, the metal glowing hotter with each tap as he lifted his brows at Isadora. "Give or take?"

Under normal circumstances, Freya might've rolled her eyes at the prince's feigned ignorance. As it was, she found herself tamping down her own discomfort at his seeming nonchalance.

"That would depend on the severity of the wound," Byrric replied. Freya had to give her father credit for keeping a straight face. "A stab wound would take longer, of course, but with Lind healing methods, perhaps a few days."

The prince licked a finger, then touched it to his dagger, smiling softly at the quiet sizzle. "And if one were to cauterize the wound?" He smiled indulgently at Isadora. "I'm quite useless when it comes to human anatomy."

Isadora paled, her eyes darting to Freya, then Aer. Something settled in her gaze that told Freya she'd realized just how dire her circumstances had become.

"Aer looked down at Isadora. "Well? What did you plan to gain?"

Swallowing hard, Isadora dragged her gaze away from Fenian and focused on the others. "Truthfully? I don't know. I thought I might want to be made queen, but on the same token, I don't know that royalty is the right path for me. Why would I want to be a queen? So I could sit pretty in an ivory tower, brought out to bear children, and look lovely for guests?" She clicked her tongue and sent Freya a condescending look. "Like you will be someday, I'm sure. You'll provide your king with pretty winged babies with pretty pink hair, sit on a throne when citizens come to call, and lose every part of yourself. No, I wanted my freedom. From Lessia, from Willem, from my parents, from *all* of you. I want to be free to roam the world."

A twinge of sadness twisted Freya's stomach at the wistful look on Isadora's face. As duplicitous as she'd been, Isadora had been a pawn her entire life. First for her family, then Lessia, and now, Willem. No one had ever consulted her about what she wanted, only what she could do for them. Now, she was once again a prisoner, only this time being used for information.

"Oh come, Lady...Brisbane, is it? That is your family's name?" Fenian frowned, sheathing his flames with a flick of his wrist. "It's no matter. As I was saying, it's unlikely you'll be welcomed anywhere in this world. It won't just be Lindoroth's doors that will be closed to you. Avorell and the western continents will shun you, too, once my family tells their tale. The world will be closed to you and your ilk, and you're a fool if you believe otherwise."

Although he spoke to Isadora, Fenian's words had the hairs on the back of Freya's neck on edge, her own dread mirroring what she saw on Isadora's face. Despite the Avorellians' long absence, there was no question they still held sway. Once again, Freya was struck by how very, very fortunate she was that she'd been willing, and perhaps stupid, enough to run the Wild Hunt.

It also made her wonder how the world would see her and Aer if they lost this war.

Don't even think that way.

With a deep breath, she shoved the thought aside.

"What's your point?" Isadora's previous bravado toward the prince continued to lessen with each word, each motion.

Fenian tapped the blade on the palm of his hand, the scorching metal sizzling but not leaving a mark on his pale skin. "Now, back to the matter of your elvish powers. Kossandra, gave them to you, correct?" He waited until Isadora gave a sharp nod before continuing. "As I said earlier, that's a crime against my kingdom." Letting his hands drop to his side, he strode toward her, then leaned down so they were eye-level. "Anyone who colludes with a criminal from my kingdom will earn an equal punishment, so think carefully before you speak."

Isadora's throat bobbed, her eyes wide as saucers as she looked down at his blade, the glow from the metal reflecting harshly against her skin. "I only met the witch recently," she rasped, leaning away from the prince. "Lessia knew her, but Willem offered her asylum in Dystone." Sweat beaded on her temples, and her words began to spill faster as Fenian brought the dagger closer to her skin. "She would give me the power to walk the Between so I could spy in exchange for safe passage to his land."

Fenian cocked his head, studying Isadora. "And how did this witch come to know our dear Willem?"

Freya watched carefully as Isadora swallowed hard and pressed her lips in a thin line. There was no answer to any question that would guarantee her safety—Isadora had to know that. Even now, though, Freya could see the wheels spinning as Isadora attempted to come up with the best answer.

"I don't know," she finally said. "She's old, though. Very old. Older than I thought your kind could be."

Fenian stood upright, then nodded, a pensive look on his face. "Yes, she's quite ancient."

"You know her?" Aer asked.

"Oh yes. This isn't the first time Kossandra has caused trouble between the elves and the humans." His lip curled in disgust. "I can assure you; any help she has provided is strictly for her own gain. Safe passage to Dystone would only be part of her plan."

"You don't know that!" Isadora exclaimed, then shrunk back at Fenian's cruel smile.

Byrric ignored her and looked at Fenian instead. "How do you know this?"

Fenian gave him a curious look. "Because I know the people of my kingdom, especially those who've been an inconvenience from afar for a large part of our history. She's a monstrous creature who always has ulterior motives. If she wants to maintain asylum in Dystone, it is not because she enjoys the climate."

"Is there a reason you haven't executed her?" Aer asked.

"Elves don't make it a habit of marching into other kingdoms to deal with one witch, troublesome as she might be. Why risk my own kingdom's safety when the humans can simply burn their own to the ground by allying with her?" Fenian eyed Isadora contemplatively, his curious expression unnerving Freya. "But if she and the creatures who work with her happen to fall into our laps..." Cruelty flashed in his eyes. "I think we've gotten all we can out of Isadora for now." The prince looked at Freya and Aer. "I can return later if you'd like?"

Aer nodded his agreement. "Commander, your thoughts?"

Byrric flicked a glance at Fenian, then Isadora, whose face had taken on a ghostly pallor, before giving Aer a curt nod. "I think we're done here."

As they left the room, Freya turned Fenian's demeanor and her own circumstances over in her mind. Luck had truly been on her side during her time in Avorell. Yes, she'd had faith in her abilities, but it had been luck that brought Nalaea to her side enough for her to avoid a loophole that could have proven disastrous. Some might have said it was Freya's strength of character, but strength of character was most certainly not enough to have an elf queen vying for Freya's success. Had she failed in her task, it could've been Freya trapped in the palace dungeons facing an inquisition by a bored and seemingly-sadistic elf prince.

"So, Isadora wants freedom," Aer said once they'd shut and locked the cellar door. "How do we use that to our advantage?"

"The short answer is, we don't," Byrric replied. "We certainly can't free her."

Freya wrapped a hand around the back of her neck and groaned. "No, but I'm sure there's something we can offer her to get her to open up more about Willem. She must have more information we can use to get to him."

"Or she's another pawn on an already crowded board," Aer said with a sigh.

Fenian patted his sheathed dagger. "I find pain is often a good motivator in the absence of one's true desires. She's not being entirely forthright about the witch."

"Perhaps, but sometimes patience can be just as effective," Byrric countered. "Let's not be hasty."

"Agreed," Freya said. "If it comes to that...fine. For now, though, I think we can skip torture."

She nearly laughed at the dejected look on the prince's face.

10

LEA

The afternoon sun was sliding beneath the craggy peaks that surrounded Iston by the time Lea and Ettrian returned from their excursion into town. When they entered the sitting room, they found Perida and Ordona talking quietly with one another, their voices hushed.

When Lea walked in, with Ettrian at her side, her mother's eyes narrowed only slightly before smiling at them both. "Where have you been?"

"I needed some air," Lea said with a frown. "What are you two whispering about?"

"Your mother was giving me her version of events at the palace," Ordona explained. "Conditions in the dungeons, how she was treated by Willem and Lessia when they brought her out, who came in and out."

Lea eyed her mother sharply. "Have you explained any of it to Freya and Aerelius?" It was understandable why Perida would want to unload on her sister about her captivity. Doing so had been equally as cathartic for Lea, when she had spoken earlier with her friends. But if Perida had any information worth sharing, it needed to go to Freya and Aer.

"That's where we'll go next," Ordona assured her. "We're just walking through everything now."

Lea looked at her mother. "Did anything happen you didn't tell me about?"

Perida gave Lea a small smile. "No, of course not. I wanted to speak with Ordona about the servants and guards I came across. I don't know everyone who was employed by the crown, but if any pledged loyalty to the Harridans but served Willem or Lessia, their Majesties should be made aware."

"Of course," Lea murmured, thinking of her own interactions with Oliver, the servant who'd often escorted her to the throne room. "That was actually something I was curious about, myself."

Shifting toward Lea, Ordona gave her a curious look. "Who did you see?"

"Not many," Lea hedged.

Ordona exchanged a look with Perida. "How did they seem?" she asked Lea.

"Those I came across, the few who were allowed to care for me, seemed protective...as though they were faking it. But the only time I ever saw their masks slip was toward the end. I don't think they defected, but I could be wrong, of course." Oliver, in particular, had taken little care to hide his disdain the day after Lea and Jonas's sham of a wedding.

Then, as if it pained her to do so, Perida shifted her gaze to Ettrian, who was leaning silently against the door frame. "What is your opinion, Your Highness? Considering you had so much time to...explore?"

"I'm inclined to agree with your daughter," Ettrian said. He either didn't notice or ignored Perida's suspicious tone. "Some of the servants, I can assure you, *have* defected." He inclined his head toward Lea. "Those assigned to Lady Calliwell had not. Assuming Lord Edrin chose them, he did well."

Ordona eyed Ettrian, her expression nothing short of queenly as she asked, "How can you be certain?"

"I had quite a bit of free time, and there were many passages to explore," he replied.

Perida frowned at her daughter. "Who assigned them to you? *Was it Lord Edrin?*"

Lea nodded. "To the best of my knowledge, yes, it was Jonas. I can ask Tyna, though."

On cue, Tyna appeared in a flurry of silver at Lea's side. "You called, My Lady?"

Lea smiled. "Who assigned my servants to attend me at the palace?"

Tyna hesitated, her tiny pointed tooth digging into her silvery lip. "Lord Edrin, at my insistence."

"Your insistence?" Ettrian asked, arching a brow. "So, you chose her servants?"

Indignation flared on the pixie's face. "Yes, Your Highness, *my* insistence. I know you may not like my kind—"

"I used to make sport of pinning your kind to trees as food for forest trolls," he pointed out, causing Tyna's cheeks to pink with anger. "And considering I helped you convince Lady Calliwell to flee... Well, that should tell you how I feel about you."

Tyna drew in a slow breath. "I know you may distrust the *Avorellian* pixies, but I can assure you, my intentions were sound. I spent my days spying on the help to find any who'd not yet turned their backs on the Harridan family." She looked at the other two females. "Oliver and Dina were the two I held the most faith in."

Eyeing Tyna, Lea gave her a small nudge. "Tell her everything, Tyna. The only way we can advise our king and queen is with all the information."

"There's not much to tell, Your Majesty. I didn't see any outright evidence of deceit, but I've known Oliver and Dina longest, so I thought they would be the most trustworthy. Maghda, too. Many of your servants survived, save a few that were in the ballroom. I cannot say for certain who has defected and who remains faithful."

"Fair enough," Ordona said. "Oliver and Dina have been with us the longest, although most of our servants have worked in the palace for a few decades at least."

"The bigger issue is dissension in the Jotnar ranks," Perida said. "From what I saw, which admittedly wasn't much, there's no love lost between the humans and Jotnar. It seemed very clear to me that the Jotnar thought themselves superior."

"But now they're all under the control of one man," Lea replied. "One human, in charge of two armies. Which will hopefully change once Jonas establishes himself a bit more. For now, though, it's anyone's guess."

Perida's eyes darted to Ordona and, to Lea's surprise, Ettrian, before looking back at Lea. "I understand he... treated you well, Daughter, but I don't think anyone is quite ready to trust him as you do."

"He kept me alive," Lea replied. "He didn't assault me or hurt me in any way, and he ensured I was safe at all times."

"Except when Willem attempted to attack you in the garden," Tyna said, then slapped her hand over her mouth, her eyes widening as if shocked she'd spoken against Lea. "Apologies, My Lady," she whispered through her tiny fingers.

"Jonas was away at the time," Lea calmly explained. "And I could hardly refuse the king when he asked me to walk with him."

"What happened in the garden?" Perida demanded.

"Nothing, Mother, because I put a stop to it."

"And what, pray tell, did Lord Edrin do in response to Willem's misbehavior?" Ettrian drawled.

Lea turned narrowed eyes on Ettrian. "Can't you find someone else to interfere with?"

"Answer the question, Grevillea." Perida said.

Lea winced. "Nothing. He did nothing. He didn't need to do anything, because I shut Willem down on my own. But I'll also point out," she said before Ettrian could speak, "that Jonas refused Lessia and Willem's demands to punish me for defending myself."

"At the risk of sounding argumentative–" Ettrian began.

"And yet...," Lea muttered.

"I think it's also fair to point out how often Willem's men followed you in Lord Edrin's absence," he continued, ignoring her argument.

"What would you have had him do?" Lea shot back. "Jonas wasn't *there*, Ettrian. And neither were you, for that matter!"

"Precisely. He should've instructed you—"

"Instructed me?" Lea crossed her arms and gave him a challenging look. "Instructed me to do *what*, exactly?"

"To stay in your quarters with the door locked, considering Willem seemed to have no qualms about defying Lessia's orders to leave you be." The prince held up his hands in defense. "All I am saying, Lady Calliwell, is that Jonas Edrin was not the protector you continue to make him out to be."

"I think Freya and Aerelius would agree," Ordona said calmly.

Lea's shoulders slumped as she took in her mother's and aunt's faces. As much as she didn't want to admit it, and as angry as Ettrian's words made her, Lea wasn't quite sure why she was so insistent Jonas was trustworthy. Yes, he'd done plenty to ensure her safety, but hadn't she spent much of her time in the palace questioning his true nature or looking over her shoulder? Hadn't she only felt safe once she had an elf prince at her side? Even though Jonas had sealed the room from outside eyes, he'd still left her alone more often than she would've liked.

The things Lessia and Effina had revealed about him continued to weigh heavily on her mind, to the point where she wasn't sure she could trust her own judgement at this point. Perhaps she'd come out of that palace more damaged than she realized.

"I know," she said after a moment. "I acknowledge that my judgment might be a bit clouded, seeing as I had no choice but to put my trust in him." She rubbed a hand across her brow. "I'm a bit tired. I think I'll go lie down for a bit."

Perida rose and held out her arms for her daughter. "Of course, sweetheart," she said as Lea accepted her embrace. "Rest as much as you need to."

With a tired smile and muttered farewell, Lea left the room and made her way through the halls to her quarters.

Lea felt as though she'd slept enough the night before to last her the next week, but she needed to be alone for a few moments, spend some time considering her thoughts. Her aunt and mother certainly had logic for feeling as they did about Jonas. After all, he'd done all in his power to keep her safe, but he'd been bloodbound to do so. Lea couldn't help wondering if the reason he left her alone so often was because he wanted someone else to manage what he couldn't.

No, she thought. *Absolutely not. Don't be stupid.*

Sending her off with Ettrian had been wise on Jonas' part, regardless of his allegiances. If he planned to be loyal to Jotunheim, he would need to put her in someone else's care, return her to her family once his oath had been fulfilled. Telling Willem she was disloyal would be akin to harming her himself, so he obviously wouldn't have done that. Now that she was gone, though, he was free to plot and plan however he liked.

Try as she might, Lea couldn't force her continued skepticism from her mind. Even if Jonas hadn't betrayed her, she was forced to question if he was even someone she wanted on her side.

Her mind drifted toward the elves, the newest allies she'd need to adjust to. Ettrian seemed to be trustworthy enough, although most of her logic there was based solely on his inability to lie and her ability to see his many twisted truths for what they were, which was, admittedly, still a bit lacking. He'd gotten her away from the palace, though, and back to her friends and family.

What family she had left, anyway.

And there it was. The reminder of her father's murder, like a sucker punch to the gut. Unable to take any more steps, she leaned against the wall beside a tall cabinet in the hallway near her bedroom, her hand to her abdomen as she struggled to regain her breathing.

A heavy breath had her throat constricting, the air heavy in her lungs.

Not now, not now.

If she stayed where she was, how she was, allowing herself to feel as she did any longer would draw attention to herself she just didn't want. She needed to busy herself, do something productive.

Rest was no longer an option. So, before anyone could see her small breakdown, she huffed out a breath and righted herself. Then she went off in search of someone or something that would occupy her mind.

MOMENTS LATER, Lea found herself outside the door to the room that housed Rosie Ristner. The princess wasn't a prisoner. At least, not in the same sense Lea had been. Still, Lea wasn't quite sure that was how the human princess saw her current accommodations, and Lea didn't trust Ettrian to reassure her that she could move about Vara's property. Perida was out of the question, as she saw all Ristners in the same light—cruel, vile monsters. No amount of explaining would convince her that Prince Reginald and Princess Rosie were different.

Lea pushed open the door to the princess's room, a small bedroom beside Reginald's, half the size of the room Rosie had occupied at the palace.

The youngest Ristner sibling was curled in a ball in the center of the bed. Her pretty red hair spilled around her shoulders, brushed but unstyled. The eager smile she so often wore was absent, replaced by a listlessness that seemed at odds with her typical bubbly personality.

"Rosie?"

The only indication Rosie gave that she heard was a small huff.

Lea sat down gingerly on the edge of the bed, eyeing the untouched tray of breakfast that sat cold on the bedside table. "Have you eaten anything?"

With a sniff, Rosie rolled over. "Why should I? Don't you all plan to execute me at first chance?"

"Rosie, if we planned to do that, it would've been done." She tried to sound gentle, but she still struggled to show much kindness toward the girl who was so eager to see Lindoroth fall under Willem's control. Naïveté could only excuse so much, in her opinion.

Rosie paled, telling Lea her words had struck a chord. "Then what do you plan to do with me?"

"That will be up to my king and queen."

Defiance flashed across Rosie's face, no doubt a reflection of her desire to tell Lea that *Willem* was king. Wisely, she kept whatever words she wanted to say to herself.

"You aren't a prisoner," Lea forced gentleness into her tone. "I saw your fear in the dining room, Rosie. When Ettrian and I realized you were with us in the woods, I made the choice to bring you with us. Not kidnap you, but *bring* you."

A small furrow puckered Rosie's brow. "Why?"

"I wasn't sure what Willem might do to you if he thought you'd attempted to flee intentionally, or if he'd even give you the chance to explain. That and I had no interest in returning, nor did Prince Ettrian. And... I wanted you to have a choice. If you want to go back, one of the elves will deliver you to the forest where we found you."

"I want *nothing* from you," she spat. "And my brother wouldn't hurt me!"

"If he thought you'd betrayed him? Yes, he would. Without a moment's hesitation." Lea gestured toward the door. "Do you think he'd choose blood over vengeance if Reginald showed up on the palace doorstop?"

"Reginald *is* a traitor," Rosie snapped. "A horrid, rotten traitor."

"And for all Willem knows, so are you."

Anger and uncertainty flickered in Rosie's eyes. Her brother had proven to be a cruel, callous man, but he hadn't yet done anything directly to Rosie that would've hurt her. Yet it was clear that Willem's display in the dining room, killing Lessia and Effina so viciously, had shaken Rosie's trust in him.

"I don't believe you." It was there, though, in Rosie's eyes. A seed of doubt; small, to be sure, but present enough that it would most certainly grow stems and thorns if given time to flourish. Lea could only hope those she left behind to care for Rosie would help cultivate that doubt sooner rather than later.

Lea stared at the princess for another moment, unsure whether she should attempt to push. For all she knew, Ettrian was right and Willem had knights out scouring the kingdom for Rosie. The princess knew that just as well as Lea did, so she opted to let the possibility hang in the air rather than try to convince Rosie one way or another.

"I'm leaving tomorrow, but Reginald is right next door," she said. "For now, the king and queen have given orders not to harm you, but we thought being near your brother would ease your mind."

There was silence for a moment, then Rosie replied, "Reginald is a traitor to my family. Now please leave me alone."

You'd want to be left alone, Lea reminded herself. So, she stood, smoothing the blanket to leave no trace of her presence.

"Eat something, Rosie," she whispered. "You'll need your strength in the days to come."

She left the room, closing the door softly behind her. The latch clicked. A breath later, Lea heard the sound of quiet sobbing from the other side.

11

FREYA

Later, after Freya and Aer both had a chance to be still for a bit, they made their way toward the room Vara had set up for Reginald. He'd suffered a stab wound to the thigh when he'd gone out to patrol the woods just past the estate's borders, not fifty yards past the cloak of magic Selinda Enrieth had laid over the property decades before. As a human, Reginald's ability to recover was not nearly great enough to heal him as quickly as an elf or Lind, but Florian's tinctures and medicines had set him on the path to be fully healed within another day, two at most. Which was quite fortunate, because Freya knew they would need him. Or at the very least, the information he could offer.

"Are we sure about this?" Aer murmured as they walked down the hall. "He's a good fighter, but how much do we truly need to involve him?"

Digging her teeth into her lip, Freya considered it. Reginald had proven himself an excellent fighter during their trip to Watoria. Yes, he'd stolen his brother's wife away, but the woman he'd spent the last month with was not, in fact, the woman he professed to love. It wasn't a leap of logic to conclude he might not be as forthright as he claimed to be.

Either that, or he was much more oblivious to those around him than he let on.

With a glance at her husband, Freya tried to understand how Reginald could've been so blind as to miss the switch between Isadora and Dania. Freya knew every inch of her husband's body, both intimate and mundane. The way his muscles flexed beneath his tunic, how his eyes, deep brown ringed with emerald, glinted when he was amused, and the way he snored quietly, almost soothingly, when he finally drifted off to sleep. And his touch. In no world would she be able to mistake another male's touch for his. Even if their appearance was identical, no one could replicate the love that fueled the caresses he reserved just for her.

So how was Reginald Ristner so easily fooled?

"I struggle," she began, "to trust him. Isadora glamoured herself to mirror Dania Edrin, but that was only on the surface. How on earth could he share a bed with her and not know she wasn't the woman he loved?"

"We were all fooled," Aer reminded her. "He might have known Dania better than the rest of us, but with all that's been going on, I can understand why he might've been able to chalk some things up to her stressors and trauma. Even if she knew Willem and Lessia's plans, no one can prepare you for a siege as violent as this. In Reginald's mind, she was thrust into the midst of war, forced to flee her home long before she intended, and had a bounty put on her head by her husband. It's reasonable enough to think those things might've caused her to act out of character."

"Stressors," Freya scoffed. "She left her wretched husband for the man she's been sleeping with for years. Maybe her plan came to fruition a bit early, but that was still her goal nonetheless. Reginald knew that better than anyone. She was finally *free,* Aerelius. Anything outside of pure happiness would've been out of character."

Aer touched a hand to her arm and came to a stop. "Freya, you need to look at this objectively. Yes, you and I might think it's absurd that things happened as they did. Perhaps you would've been thrilled in Dania Edrin's place. But she's lived a pampered life, protected, never having to worry about sleeping accommodations or her next meal. I don't think it's outside the realm of possibility that she also could've been apprehensive, nervous, even, to have finally broken free. Not to mention, he's human. He wouldn't be as quick as you or I to make the leap to magic or spells." He chuckled at her answering huff. "Believe me, I struggle to wrap my head around it myself. The only other possibility is that Reginald is fooling us just as badly as he wants us to think she fooled him."

"Which we won't let him do," Freya replied with a nod. "We need to go into this conversation examining his words from both sides."

Aer nodded slowly. "We already have guards at his and Rosie's doors."

"Yes, and as much as I trust Lea's assessment of Rosie, I'm not prepared to trust someone who was so faithful to Willem only two days ago." She sent another look toward the princess's room. "Especially one who feels she was taken by force."

"I honestly find it hard to believe she truly feels that way," Aer said, frowning softly in the same direction. "By all accounts, she was clinging to Lea, hiding behind her when Willem and his men attacked."

"As though she was seeing him for the first time," Freya murmured. "So we try to turn her to our cause, then."

"Precisely." He brushed a thumb along her jaw. "It might not be easy, but with your charms, I'm sure we can do it."

Freya snorted. "With Lea's charms, you mean. Or *yours.*" That was easier said than done, of course, but it was the only logical approach. They didn't have the time or, in Freya's case, the inclination to keep watch over an unnecessary prisoner. Even if Rosie was fully faithful to Willem, she was no threat to them in Iston. If anything, she'd be a burden, which was something no one wanted to deal with.

They came to a stop outside Reginald's door. Freya knocked lightly, then stepped aside when Aer gently pushed it open.

The human prince lay propped up on a pillow, arms folded across his stomach, his blond hair lank against his jaw. A dark, hollow look haunted his eyes, a sadness Freya couldn't begin to imagine–assuming it was genuine. She wanted to believe it was, partly because she didn't like being made a fool of, but also because she couldn't handle yet another traitor in their midst. They'd caught on to Isadora's scheming quickly, but that wouldn't always be the case. As it was, if Reginald was betraying them, he'd already gained a fair amount of information he could give to his brother despite the care Freya and the others had taken to limit his knowledge.

Byrric, who'd told them he'd accompany them to question Reginald, sat in a chair beside the prince's bed, his fingers steepled in front of his mouth. It was an expression Freya knew well—his thinking face, the one he wore when he was pondering something just as hard as she was at that moment.

Her father stood, sliding the chair back to its place against the wall, then stepped back to stand beside them.

"Your Majesties," he said. "I've just been discussing our plans with the prince."

"An illuminating conversation," Reginald said with a wry smile. His voice was rough, as though he hadn't had enough to drink or had been silent for a long period. "I suppose you've come to question me now that we're settled in?"

"We wanted to check on you," Aer began. "But yes, we'll need to question you."

"We're sure you understand," Freya added, watching for any sign of defiance or hesitance. Instead, all she saw on his face was resignation. "How are you feeling?" *Show kindness,* she thought. *He'll be more likely to give information.*

Reginald patted his bandaged leg. "Lord Florian says I should be walking tomorrow, fully healed within a few more days. I've managed to hobble around here, change my clothes without help. The medicines in your land are truly a work of art."

"We're happy to hear you're doing well." Aer leaned against the tall bedpost, arms crossed. "I'm sure you know why we're here."

"You want to know how I managed to mistake the real Isadora for Dania Edrin, correct." Grimacing, he looked down at his hands, folded in his lap, his nails still lined with the dark remnants of battle. "Sadly, I don't have a good answer for you."

"Dania Edrin posed as Isadora for years," Byrric said. "She was at your side, your lover, for quite some time." He gestured toward Freya and Aer. "It wouldn't take my king or queen more than a moment to notice if the other had been replaced."

Reginald shifted his gaze toward the window, the peaks in the distance. "I would've said the same three days ago."

Aer scrubbed a hand over his face and sighed, his fingers resting on his chin. "We need to know what you've shared with her, what she might've sent back to Willem."

"Bearing in mind, of course, that much of the information she received was falsified," Byrric added.

From the moment Florian had detected the switch in the forest, they'd all done their best to keep crucial information from reaching Isadora, going so far as to fabricate details such as locations and plans to give her something of substance to offer. All meetings, strategy sessions, and plans were made behind closed doors cloaked in magic, with Rini as the only trusted guard. Still, with so many soldiers and marshals on the Enrieth estate, there was no way Freya, Aer, or Byrric could be certain nothing crucial reached her ears.

"To the best of my knowledge, the only information she had is what you gave me or fed her," Reginald said, eyeing them both. "Information you curated quite well."

Freya didn't miss the resentment in his tone.

"Indeed," Aer said with a nod. "Still, we need to know if she overheard anything she shouldn't have."

"Shouldn't you be questioning her, then?"

"We have," Freya replied, noting the fear that simmered in Reginald's eyes. "As someone presumably on our side, we wanted to speak with you, too."

"Presumably?" Shaking his head, Reginald clicked his tongue and turned away. "I thought we were past that, Your Majesties."

It was hard not to feel bad for the prince who'd not only been duped by an imposter, but who'd just found out his true love was lying in a mass grave behind the castle, no more than food for crows and insects. Holding back her sympathy was difficult, but as Freya reminded herself of the stakes, of the damage Isadora could've done if they'd discovered her deceit only one day later, that sympathy felt shriveled and cold.

"What information would she have sent back to Willem that we might not have shared?" Freya asked.

"To rephrase," Byrric added, "What information did *you*, in particular, share with her that might've reached Willem's ears?"

"The only information I had to give was what you offered me," Reginald replied. He looked at them each in turn, his eyes dim with sadness and exhaustion. "She knew how many marshals you had working for you, of course, which gave my brother an idea of how many were slaughtered by the Jotnar in Watoria. To the best of my knowledge, she knew nothing of the elves' presence until Ettrian appeared in your cellar," he told Freya. "That information obviously did her little good, as she is now captive here."

Freya pursed her lips, considering Reginald's words carefully. Reginald was only part of the picture. They hadn't disclosed Isadora's true identity to anyone else in Watoria, so it was possible she could've overheard bits and pieces throughout the house.

"Can you give us an idea of how often she met with Willem?" Byrric asked.

"How am I supposed to know that?" Reginald asked. "I didn't even know she was *meeting* my wretched brother."

"Were there times you couldn't find her right away, or perhaps she took frequent walks?" Aer suggested. "Her meetings likely weren't long."

With a sigh, Reginald leaned his head back against the headboard and closed his eyes. For a moment, Freya thought he might be attempting to dismiss them, but then he opened his eyes.

"She took baths," he said. "Long ones, daily. I assumed it was because she was used to doing so in the palace and hadn't adapted well to nearly two weeks in the wild. It's possible she could've slipped out then, as I wasn't always in the room with her."

"Every day since you arrived?" Freya shot an alarmed look at her father. "How in the world did she have the amount of power necessary to walk the Between every day?"

"It's unlikely she did," Byrric replied. "Prince Reginald, how often were you present in the room with her when she took these baths?"

Reginald shrugged. "More often than not. She didn't care to bathe together, but there were times she wanted company while she did."

"You didn't find it odd your lover didn't want to relax with you in the tub at all?" Aer asked with a smirk. "I find it to be an enjoyable pastime, myself."

Freya shook her head as she fought back a smile. Byrric's jaw clenched, but by the flicker at the corner of his mouth, she could tell he was trying not to laugh.

"Yes, Your Majesty, I found it a bit odd," Reginald snapped. "She also refused me if I attempted to make love to her, if you'd like to get even more personal. But I chalked it all up to the stress of our travels and the siege, the significant and sudden changes in her circumstances. I assumed she wanted time to herself, so I gave that to her."

Annoyance pricked Freya's mind. They were getting nowhere with Reginald, and they all knew it. Reginald didn't have his brother's confidence, desire to be in charge, or suspicious nature. If he did, he would've noticed something was amiss with Isadora quickly. Instead, he'd brushed aside any odd behaviors and refused to acknowledge something more serious might be at work simply because his love for her blinded him to her deceit. They could sit with him all day and it would be unlikely they'd find anything useful.

Byrric sighed and ran a hand through his cinnabar-streaked hair, clearly coming to the same conclusion. "I hope you understand why we struggle with what you're saying. It's true we filtered the information that got back to her, but you were her lover, Your Highness. We need to know what information you provided outside what we allowed you to have."

"Such as what?" the prince demanded. "We spoke of my brother's cruelty, which we're all aware of, our plans for the future—"

"What plans?" Freya asked.

"*Plans,* Your Majesty. To leave Dystone, travel the world, get away from my brother's rule."

"Where did she want to go?" Aer asked.

"Anywhere but Dystone," Reginald said. "We spoke of traveling to the western continent, to Stoestia, perhaps even taking on new identities in your lands, should you allow us to seek asylum. She mentioned once she wouldn't mind returning to Jotunheim if her brother ever took power." A frown flickered across his face as his own words registered. "Does Lord Edrin know yet of his sister's death?"

"We're not sure," Aer said quietly. "It's unlikely, as we've heard nothing to indicate he's turned on Willem, which he surely would if he discovered Willem's role in her death."

"Oh, Willem will be able to convince him he knew nothing of it, I have no doubts." Reginald sighed. "Your Majesties, Commander, I understand your need for information. I wish I could provide more; I truly do. Yes, there were signs I shouldn't have ignored regarding Isadora, but I cannot change that now. I will do all in my power to help you going forward. That's unfortunately the best I can offer. If I think of anything more, you will be the first to know."

Aer continued to eye him speculatively, then he nodded slowly. "Alright. Let's let the prince rest, shall we?"

"Of course," Freya said, forcing back a sigh.

"We'll come back if we have more questions," Byrric said. "Get some rest, Your Highness."

Florian was waiting for them in the hallway when they left Reginald's room, dark eyes narrowed.

"Well?" Aer asked. "Any insight?"

The spymaster shook his head. "Based on what I just overheard, I don't think he's lying about Isadora's behavior, but he's hiding something, I'm certain of it."

"Any thoughts on what that might be?" Freya asked.

"Something to do with his brother or family would be my guess," Byrric said.

"I agree," Florian replied. "Leave him be for now. Keep guards on him, but allow him to move about if he feels up to it. We'll suss out answers soon enough."

"Florian and I will go discuss things with the others and we'll reconvene in the morning to make our exit plans," Byrric added with one last glance at Reginald's door.

They said their goodbyes, then Aer and Freya started the walk back to their room. Freya hadn't seen Vara's home in years, but as she walked the halls, her memories of the house returned. Her visits had been infrequent due to distance and the nature of her parents' jobs and grandmother's lifestyle, but she'd always loved the space. Had she been given the choice, she would've preferred a palace that held the simplicity of her grandparents' estates with the size and breadth of her new home in Iladel.

She smiled to herself as she thought of the palace and her place there. She was certain they would retake it—she had too much confidence in her people to believe her kingdom would fall completely into enemy hands. They might need to rebuild, but that was fine because it would be theirs. Not the humans', not the Jotnar. No, the courtyards, gardens, gleaming marble halls, and towering columns would be *theirs* and theirs alone.

A small voice nagged at the back of her mind. The voices of Lessia Edrin, of Willem Ristner, and of the rest who believed her home was lost to her. They were thunderous and vile, relentless in their desire to beat her down.

But all they did was provide fuel for her determination to save her kingdom. It was that determination she would use to see to it those voices wouldn't win.

12

FREYA

Freya awoke at dawn the day King Ruehnar was set to arrive. Despite how she'd gotten to know Queen Nalaea in Andradath, Freya found herself wide awake and staring at the molded ceiling, worrying over how she'd interact with the king. The dim light from outside made the room feel a bit like a cave at first, but as the sky slowly lightened, Freya found herself studying the dark wood grain patterns on the beams that framed the dips and whorls and sharp angles carved into the plaster. The lightening sky cast a pinkish glow over their room, promising sun and perhaps a break from the cold again.

She imagined waking in Andradath with the sound of the Aemir sea, its turquoise waves rolling softly just beyond her balcony, the air tinged with the briny scent of the ocean. The skies there weren't cloudy like they were in Iston, although she knew that was unlikely the case all the time. Even still, she couldn't help but miss the quiet serenity she would soak in for just a few moments each day.

"You're awake," Aer murmured, rolling onto his stomach to wrap an arm around her, his voice thick with sleep as he nuzzled her neck. "It's too early."

She smiled, rubbing a hand along his bare arm. "My head is too busy these days for good sleep."

He rolled to his back, concern filling his eyes as Freya tucked herself into his side. "Is there anything I can do?"

"No, it's just…" Her thoughts drifted to Lea, who'd been forced to harden during her weeks in the palace, losing the carefree nature that had been so *Lea* just a few months ago. To Lazarus, who'd looked so lost since his father's death. Myria, her anger like a blade, and Collin, steadfast at Laz's side, despite suffering the loss of his uncle. "I worry for them. Our friends and families."

"For Lea, you mean?"

"Not just Lea. All of them."

"She weighs on you most, though." He brushed a lock of hair behind her ear and smiled at her questioning look. "I've seen the way you watch her. My cousin is strong and smart. You don't have to worry about her."

"I don't worry much for her safety, at least not more than I would Laz or Collin. I worry for what this is doing to her heart and mind." With a sigh, she looked out the window beside the bed, focusing on the landscape beyond, the hills giving way to craggy, snow-capped peaks where Iston straddled Allanor and Caelora. "I worry she won't be able to come back from this."

"None of us will fully come back from this," Aer murmured. "I know that's not what you want to hear, but—"

"It's the truth." Freya closed her eyes, then exhaled a long breath. "Still, not terribly helpful."

"Perhaps not, but it's realistic. The important thing is that we have each other for support. All of us." He touched a light kiss to her forehead before tightening his arm around her. "We'll get through this. Try to sleep some more, though. Even just another hour. You need your rest."

Rest was the last thing she'd attain at the moment. They both knew it.

Freya rested her cheek against his shoulder and inhaled the scent that was so singularly Aerelius. Her husband, her oldest friend, and now, her mate. As if on cue, she felt the bond between them grow taught, his heart beating in time with hers. Then, resting her chin on his chest, she met his eyes. "Perhaps you can do something else to settle my nerves?"

Aer leaned back and kissed her forehead. "What, pray tell, would you like me to do, Your Majesty?"

They hadn't enjoyed each other nearly as much as newlyweds should have, more than a month into their marriage. Their days should have been spent making love on a boat on the Selnor, on a beach in Edhil, or in the snow-capped mountains that swept up the eastern coast of Lindoroth through Caelora.

Instead, they were in Iston, taking refuge from their enemies. Meeting with the elvish monarchy to form a plan of attack on Iladel.

She touched a hand to his cheek. "You are quite beautiful, my king. Have I ever told you that?"

"You've mentioned it once or twice." His hand found the small of her back and gently pulled her toward him. Softly, he touched her lips with his, and she reveled in the feelings of love she felt tugging on their bond, where their hearts beat as one, where their love for each other flowed like a river that would never go dry.

"I love you, Freya," he whispered, then kissed her, long and deep, hitching one of her legs up around his hip.

Freya gripped his shoulder, pulling herself against him as his hands roamed over her body. With a soft gasp, her head fell back as soft hands slid her nightgown up her thighs. Each touch was like a balm to her nerves and senses, each caress calming her in a way only he could. She rolled to her back, letting him take her mouth just as he took her body, burying himself inside her as they made love in the pale morning light.

Their world was in shambles, yes, but here in bed, they could take time to be content in each other's arms, to defy the state of the world, and take solace in a space only they could exist in.

～

THE ELF KING arrived silently at the portico just before lunch. Freya wondered if arriving right at meal time was some type of test, but quickly squashed the idea. Despite how tricky the elves could be, Ruehnar wasn't the type to test hospitality in the midst of war. He was more likely to try to walk Freya into a verbal mousetrap just to see how easily he could pull back his knights and renege on his agreement.

A few moments after Freya stepped onto the portico to meet Ruehnar, the elf princes, minus Ettrian, appeared beside her. She wasn't surprised Ettrian was missing. In the little time she'd known the youngest elf prince, it had become clear he'd be content to torment his parents for centuries with his indifference toward his heritage. She still found it hard to believe he had no interest in the crown, and wondered idly if anyone had ever outright asked him his intentions. Being unable to lie, he could theoretically just avoid the question indefinitely, although she assumed his parents would've seen through that instantly.

Shoving thoughts of elvish succession aside, Freya stood tall between her husband and father, doing her best to channel the strength she'd had in the Forest of Ages. Despite welcoming royalty, Freya was garbed in her preferred leather pants and tunic, wings tucked tight to her shoulders with two blades strapped to her hips and another at her thigh—something Byrric had unsurprisingly chastised her for. Yet as Freya took in the thick leathers and solid-soled boots the king wore, she had a feeling no elf would scoff at her choice of attire.

"King Ruehnar." Vara bowed low from Byrric's left side. "Welcome."

"Vara," Ruehnar said, leaning in to give her a hug. "It's lovely to see you again."

"It's been too long," Vara said as she returned the hug briefly before stepping back.

"Your Majesty, thank you for coming," Aer said. "This is the Commander of our Royal Army, Byrric Balthana."

"An honor to meet you. Your aid will be invaluable, Your Majesty," Byrric said with a small bow. "We cannot thank you enough."

Ruehnar's eyes flicked from Byrric to his sons, then to Freya and Aer, his expression smooth. "It's no matter. Lindoroth has promised to return the favor in kind."

"A promise we plan to follow through on," Freya assured him. "Please, come inside."

Vara led their group through the house and to the dining room, where Florian, Ettrian, and Ordona stood waiting by the table in the center of the room. The massive map on the table's top displayed more markers than Freya had seen the previous night, telling her that her father and Florian must've been up late planning.

Freya allowed Aer to make introductions, as the Tordoves hadn't formally met Ordona in person, only via messenger. From what Florian and Aer had told her, Ordona and Salazar had attempted to reach out to the elves to discuss opening lines of trade but had been denied several times.

"Ah, the Queen Mother," Ruehnar said, his voice tinged with a dash of sympathy. "A role you took on far too soon." He held out a hand to clasp Ordona's and gave a small nod. "It's lovely to meet you, Your Majesty."

"Likewise, King Ruehnar," Ordona replied, squeezing the proffered hand. "It's a meeting long past due."

"Too true, Your Majesty. And Andreus!" Ruehnar greeted Florian, his gentle tone shifting as he turned to his half-brother. "Two visits in as many weeks. We should make it a habit."

Florian smiled indulgently. "So long as it does not involve my kingdom going to war, I'll be glad of that."

"Now, let's hear about the state of your kingdom," Ruehnar said, gesturing toward the map. "I have two thousand knights at the ready awaiting my orders. They're preparing camp as we speak."

"We've retaken Watoria, the capital of Allanor," Freya told him. "Thanks in large part to the knights you provided. The capital of Saith is in Lind hands, and Iston remains untouched, putting most of the western portion of the kingdom in our hands."

"For now," Byrric said, stepping toward the map. He picked up a long, thin plotter's rake and rested it on his shoulder. "We'll send most of our forces to the east and south. Errest, the capital of Edhil, holds firm, but it needs reinforcements on the outside to remove the threat at their walls. We'll send forces to western Edhil, as well, to cover the mines, but the enemy simply didn't have enough time to get that far south or west." He tapped the capital with the rake. "Iladel is, of course, a priority, so we'll divert several thousand there, a mix of both Lind and Avorellian."

"And the north?" Ruehnar asked, frowning at the rocky expanse of Caelora.

"Our capital in Caelora has been overrun," Aer said. "We don't think it's wise to devote a large portion of our knights there, but we do plan to send a strong squadron to help get the people out and to assist those who've already fled." He flicked a glance at Freya before continuing. "We can rebuild the city later. For now, we'll focus on the people."

Ruehnar nodded his agreement, then looked at his sons. "Fenian, Tavian, what are your thoughts?"

The princes began recapping the discussion from the previous day, outlining the plans they'd all laid out and the timelines devoted to each attack. The humans spilling into the northeast from the sea were the biggest concern, although their lack of magic helped level the playing field a bit. Freya didn't want to think what they'd face if it was fifteen thousand more Jotnar flooding their shores.

As the conversation was essentially repeating what she already knew, Freya listened absently while examining the markers Byrric had arranged on the map. Two large squadrons, each a mix of elves and Linds with the majority being the latter, were set to move toward Iladel and Errest. Errest was the last stronghold, but Iladel was the most important target.

The squadron headed to Kildin was far smaller, only a few hundred in total, mostly Lind, with the one hundred elves Tavian had promised. Freya's heart ached at the thought of leaving a city in ruin, but the logical and analytic mind she'd inherited from her parents constantly reminded her that it was indeed a waste of manpower to send thousands toward a fallen city.

There was no denying that Lindoroth was in dire straits, not with the spread of wooden and metal markers strewn across the map. The vast expanse of her kingdom was dotted with soldiers, both enemy and her own. But could they truly stand against the forces bearing down on them? Against the tens of thousands of knights that were no doubt pillaging the coastal villages and the capital cities at that very moment?

Her eyes drifted to the north, beyond Caelora and toward Jotunheim's border, where the rebels had formed their camps to the west, clear across the empire from Madrya. She'd never seen Utgard up close, but from what she knew, the rebels took pride in maintaining their homes and protecting them from outsiders.

Freya thought back to the conversations she'd had with Queen Nalaea about friendship and allegiances. Vara enjoyed a friendship with the Tordoves that had nothing to do with foreign relations, something Freya envied a great deal. She saw much of herself in the elf queen, or her future self, at least. Nalaea's strength, fortitude, and no-nonsense demeanor were all things Freya hoped to nurture in herself as she fell into her role as queen. Yet she couldn't help but want to share a friendship with Nalaea as well.

Sadly, Freya realized, her days of making friends without intent were likely far behind her.

13

———

LEA

When Lea heard news that King Ruehnar was arriving, she wasn't sure whether she should be present or not. On the one hand, he was a foreign ruler and she was the daughter of one of Lindoroth's governors. On the other hand, the elves had more or less held her captive through Ettrian in Iladel while Freya ran the Wild Hunt, making her wary of being anywhere near him.

Fortunately, her mother made the decision for her.

"The commander and king and queen will meet King Ruehnar," Perida told her over lunch. "There are too many of us here to have a welcoming party, so we'll have to introduce ourselves this evening at dinner." If Lea wasn't mistaken, Perida's voice carried a tone of disdain, as if she were mildly insulted she wasn't asked to be present when the king arrived.

"It's probably for the best." Lea took a slow, careful sip of her tea. "No one should be wasting time introducing nobility when our kingdom is at war." Then, sensing her mother's offense, she added, "Try not to take this personally, Mother. We don't have time to fuss with what you think should happen. Freya, Aer, and the commander will make the best decisions for us. And don't forget your sister is with them. Aunt Ordona has more experience with these things than any of us."

Perida stared down at her own tea, her lips pursed. "I suppose you're right." With a quiet sigh, she picked her napkin up from her lap and set it beside her tray on the table. That sigh carried with it all the weight Lea felt in her own heart. She could feel her mother's sadness, despair, anger, and hopelessness all in that single breath. Sitting here watching her mother struggle because she wasn't yet home to help her people was becoming far more painful than Lea liked to admit. Meeting Ruehnar, going through the motions of welcoming him, was at least something she could *do*.

With a soft smile, Lea reached across the table and took Perida's hand. "It will be alright, Mother. We'll be home soon."

Perida didn't meet her daughter's eyes as she turned her hand and clasped it around Lea's. "I know, sweetheart." She knuckled away a tear from her cheek, then forced a smile. "Why don't you go find Prince Ettrian and see about our plans for tomorrow? I think I'll take a nap."

Understanding she was being dismissed, Lea stood and set her own napkin down. "Of course. Call for Tyna if you need anything." She gave her mother a quick kiss on the head, resting her cheek against the dark curls for a moment before leaving to find the prince.

Lea found Ettrian in the courtyard, sitting on a bench, his arms resting on the fountain behind him, face tilted toward the sun. His onyx hair shimmered with the subtlest shades of red in the sunlight, a stark contrast against his ice-pale skin.

"Hello, little witch," he murmured, turning his glinting gold eyes on her before looking back to the sky. "To what do I owe the pleasure of your company?"

She tugged her fur cloak tighter around her shoulders, then sat beside him. The cold stone beneath her seeped through her leather pants, but it was better than being cooped up inside.

"Perhaps I just want some fresh air," she said airily. "It's a lovely day."

"Hmm."

Eyes narrowed, she took in his expression. Relaxed, but there was a tightness around his eyes. "What's wrong?"

Ettrian slid her a look. "My father has arrived with his knights. He's in the dining room with your monarchs and the commander."

Trepidation fluttered in Lea's stomach as she imagined what Ruehnar might be like. Ettrian was an outlier in his family, one who cared little for royal fanfare and was content to flit about the world, ignoring his princely duties. Ruehnar, if the prince was to be believed, was quite the opposite. Cold and calculating like Tavian and Fenian in his thought processes, with the main difference being the jovial mask that Freya had told her about. Although, considering she'd spent very little time with Ettrian, she supposed he could be just as bad.

Lea gave the prince a curious look. "Shouldn't you be with him?"

"Believe me, I have very little I care to offer to their discussion and even less he cares to hear." A touch of derisiveness colored his tone. "I much prefer the company of no one."

Cheeks flushing at the implied dismissal, Lea made to stand. "I'll leave you to no one, then."

"Not so fast." A warm hand gripped her forearm, holding her in place on the bench as Ettrian sat up and finally looked at her. "I was actually just about to come find you. My father will want to meet the person he was holding hostage from across the world." He sat upright, then smirked down at her. "If you don't go now, I can promise, he'll call for you soon enough. Best to get it out of the way sooner rather than later."

She scowled at him and shook off his hold, knowing her stare was hardly effective. "Well, perhaps I'm not too interested in meeting him." Her cheeks burned again when amusement filled his gaze. "And I'm sure he's too busy with my own monarchs to bother with me."

"You say that as though you have a choice." He chuckled, then stood and held out a hand. "Come, I'll act as your bodyguard."

"I don't *need* a bodyguard," she muttered, tilting her chin stubbornly as she glanced at Iska, who was hovering just inside the court-yard entrance. "No offense, Iska."

He flashed her a quick smile.

"And you take too little care in how you speak to Avorellian royal-ty." Ettrian leaned down and took her hand, tugged her to her feet, gripping her hand more tightly as he added, "Just be thankful you'll have me at your side when you meet him."

As if I care, Lea thought. Still, she knew better than to argue. If nothing else, Ettrian's family was the reason she'd avoided marriage and mateship with Jonas. He was also the reason her mother was no longer rotting in the palace dungeons, so she couldn't let annoyance at his bossiness and demeanor allow her to forget those things, even if they had been self-serving and a requirement of the bargain his parents made.

"You have my parents to thank for your safety," Ettrian continued, as if reading her mind. *He probably is,* she thought. "And that of your friends and family. Try not to look so ungrateful."

"I'm not ungrateful," she said, although she knew scoffing at his words would indicate the opposite. "Quite the contrary, actually." Ruehnar and Nalaea had sent him to keep an eye on her in the palace, although if Freya had failed the Hunt, there was no telling where they'd be now. She didn't doubt that Ettrian would've thrown her in the dungeon just as easily as he'd released the others.

Or perhaps he'd take her away just as he'd done, only instead of whisking her off to Iston, he'd have taken her to some other corner of the world that wasn't currently under siege, just to irritate his parents. For a brief moment, the thought of being far from home, far from political machinations and the masks she was always forced to wear these days almost seemed...peaceful. She wondered what it might be like to sit on a balcony as her king and queen had done, taking supper and drinking wine as the sun set over the sea. Freya's account of Andradath's beauty likely paled in comparison to the real thing, but it was hard not to wish to escape to a place that wasn't plagued with war and rot.

Shame flooded her, but before it could take root, Ettrian placed his hands on her shoulders. She met his eyes and was surprised to find pity there. Before she could speak, he turned her toward the entryway. "Come, Lady Calliwell."

Against her better judgement, she let the prince lead her back through the house while butterflies rioted in her stomach, nervousness that shoved away the waves of shame that still crested in her mind. She gave Iska a nod when they walked inside to let him know she was fine, but the look of concern on his face told her he could tell how on edge she was.

As they neared the dining room, she was thankful for Ettrian's proximity, knowing, or at least, hoping, it was unlikely he'd let his father do anything to her. But as she pictured the fangs that rested just behind his parted lips, she thought perhaps some of Rosie Ristner's denial had rubbed off on her.

"You look as though you're headed for an execution," the prince murmured against her ear when they approached the dining room. He placed a hand on the small of her back and nudged her to the door. "Smile, and for the gods' sakes, stop looking so scared. It makes you appear weak."

Her sudden desire to punch him had her steps faltering, but when his hand clenched on her back, she forced her lips to curve upward, then stepped just out of the prince's reach, refusing to let his father think for one moment there was an ounce of weakness or fear in her.

A small sigh of relief threatened to slip out when she saw that Byrric, Freya, and Aer were in the room, too. But they weren't what drew her attention.

King Ruehnar's presence commanded the room, even as he stood silently beside his other two sons. Dark hair draped over his shoulders, his eyes a shimmering bronze a few shades darker than the gold that swirled in Ettrian's. Tan skin hinted at his Summer Court heritage, and the ghost of a smile rested on his full lips, as if he found his circumstances amusing. Sharp eyes that likely missed nothing skimmed over her, taking in the small distance between Lea and Ettrian, lingering on her face in a bemused expression, as though he couldn't quite understand her presence or why she was standing so close to his son.

Fenian and Tavian stood behind Ruehnar. Fenian, a near-copy of Ettrian, was frowning down at the map, while Tavian stood facing the door, hip propped against the table as his black eyes took in Lea and Ettrian's every movement.

The mere sight of them all, their proximity, turned Lea's insides to ice.

If Tavian's feline smile was any indication, the elf prince knew exactly how Lea felt.

Fortunately, Ettrian spoke before she could think too long on the king and other princes' demeanors.

"Father." He gave a cursory bow. "Nice to see you've finally arrived."

Lea sent him a side-long look that he ignored.

"Ah, Lady Calliwell," Byrric said, sending Lea a reassuring smile. "There you are."

"We were just about to send for you," Freya added, her voice devoid of the easy tone she always had when she spoke with friends.

The formal tone surprised Lea, but she quickly recovered herself and dipped into a curtsy. "Your Majesty."

"Lady Calliwell, this is King Ruehnar of Avorell," Aer said. "Your Majesty, this is my cousin–"

"The lovely Lea I've heard so much about," Ruehnar said, smiling in a way that seemed intended to put Lea at ease. "It is so nice to see you have made it here in one piece."

Forcing her mild panic aside, Lea's training kicked in, reminding her to smile demurely. "Thank you, Your Majesty, for all you've done for my people."

"Your queen completed her task," Ruehnar said simply. "We always follow through on our promises."

"That's because you have no *choice*, Father," Ettrian drawled. Lea had to fight the urge to step further away from him, as he was now standing so close their arms nearly touched.

"We had the choice not to make a bargain," Ruehnar pointed out.

"Considering *you* never made such a bargain, I suppose she should be thanking *you* for not leaving her to rot with the humans."

"He has a point, Brother," Tavian said, his eyes dancing with amusement.

Ettrian's jaw clenched, and Lea bit her lip to keep from smiling at his discomfort. She'd yet to see the elf prince cowed by anyone, but a verbal slap by his father was borderline amusing.

"Clearly he knew Mother and Father would've hung him by his toenails had he harmed her after they had just made a bargain with the King and Queen," Fenian replied, glancing over at Ettrian. "Isn't that correct?"

Ettrian shrugged. "Why make an ugly war uglier?"

"We were just about to spread lunch," Aer cut in, looking at Ruehnar. "Would you care to eat?"

"Not yet," the king replied. "I think we are done here for now. I'd prefer to rest a bit, check in with my knights."

Lea sent Ettrian a confused look, curious as to why he'd waited so long to come greet his father.

Byrric gave a sharp nod, "Of course. We'll convene later to discuss tomorrow's travels."

Ruehnar looked at Lea and dipped his chin in farewell. "It was lovely to meet you, Lady Calliwell."

"You as well, Your Majesty," Lea replied.

With one last look toward Lea, Ruehnar vanished.

"I'll need to go check in with our own knights," Byrric told them. "Now that the elves are here, I'd like to get moving as quickly as possible."

"Of course," Aer said. "Do what you need to do."

With a nod goodbye, Byrric left the room.

Once Byrric was gone, Lea felt her insides loosen and she let out a small breath.

Ettrian chuckled. "Relax, Lady Calliwell. He won't bite."

"Try not to let your fear of him show," Aer told Lea. "The elves helped us in more ways than you can imagine."

"You in particular," Tavian added, his gaze flicking up and down

Lea's body in a way that made her feel uncomfortably exposed. "Do your best not to let him think that you are ungrateful."

"I have immense gratitude for everything your family has done for us," Lea replied. "For *me*. Please don't take this the wrong way, Your Highnesses, but your king looks like he would eat me alive if given half a chance."

"Our father is protective of us all, but he's a fair king." Fenian picked up one of the map markers and began tossing it in the air. "But be thankful my mother chose to stay in Avorell. Contrary to what my brother may tell you, she might, in fact, bite if given provocation." He dropped the marker back to the table, then clapped Tavian on the shoulder and lifted his brows at Ettrian. "Father might not care for lunch, but I'm famished."

"Likewise," Tavian replied. "Ettrian?"

"Food sounds delightful." With a quick nod at Lea, Freya, and Aer, Ettrian followed his brothers from the room.

"You did wonderfully, little witch."

Lea jumped at the sudden intrusion in her mind, but relaxed when she realized it was Ettrian's voice and not one of his brothers.

"Thank you."

Lea found her gaze drawn to the three brothers as they passed through the arched entryway. Similar enough in appearance that there was no question they were brothers, but different enough to tell one from the other. The most significant similarity was the power that radiated from them. She'd seen it with Ettrian, power that dripped from the tips of his fingers and flowed around him like water, as though he could barely maintain a hold on it. Seeing it in triplicate and all in one place was...something she couldn't quite explain. Terrifying, certainly. Intimidating, although she'd never admit it aloud.

"That's..." At a loss for words, Lea looked desperately at her cousin.

A smile ghosted across Aer's lips. "You'll get used to them."

"I'd rather not," she murmured, although, even as she spoke the words, she found herself denying them in her mind. The kind of power the princes held and that of their parents was something she was near desperate to see in action.

"Ettrian seems to have taken an interest in you," Freya commented, her sharp eyes lingering where the princes had exited the room. "You might want to decide how to handle that."

"There's nothing to handle," Lea replied.

"Just keep it in mind, because it might matter to his father." Freya's lips formed a thin line. "Who knows if that interest is fondness or mere entertainment?"

Lea followed the direction of Freya's eyes, cursing herself for wondering the same thing. Ettrian had seemed...curious about her since arriving in Lindoroth, but a bored elvish prince was not necessarily something she wanted to invite into her life. Not now, probably not ever.

Lea curved her lips into a smile and gave Freya a small nod. "Then I suppose I should watch my step."

Freya smiled sympathetically. "I wouldn't worry. We want to form a solid relationship with the Tordoves, but hopefully we can wrap this war up quickly. Then we can work on getting back to normal and you won't have to worry about curious elf princes any more."

Once again, Lea's traitorous mind took hold, this time asking her if the prince's presence at her side each day was truly something she *wanted* to end.

No.

She forced the thoughts away, then smiled at her king and queen. "Weren't we talking about lunch?"

Seeming to understand, Freya looped her arm through Lea's. "Let's go."

14

LEA

Vara Balthana's house was teeming with energy the morning of their fourth day in Iston, the day Ettrian would take Lea and her mother home and Freya and Aer would set out for Iladel.

Lea awoke fraught with a mix of nerves, excitement, and fear. General Theodore Lindesson, who Byrric had left to hold Errest, was strong, experienced, and, most importantly, an Edhilian, born and bred. But he was no Orin Calliwell. He might do a wonderful job maintaining the city in the absence of an elected official, but he would never stand up to the legacy of Lea's father. No one would.

Just like that, her nerves evaporated, replaced instead with anticipation.

For the past several days, her thoughts had been plagued with what ruin her capital city might be in. She'd heard reports of Kildin's status and knew Olthanas had been dealt its fair share of blows. And of course, she'd seen the state of Watoria firsthand.

Byrric's reports from Errest were favorable, as were those from the western regions of Edhil, which were fare less populated. Their scouts were supposed to return from the east today, however, which had Lea quickening her steps. She wanted to know what was going on in the north before returning home.

She'd just finished packing her belongings, meager as they were, when Tyna appeared.

"My lady, Prince Ettrian has sent two of his knights to gather your and your mother's belongings. We'll be leaving for your home shortly."

"Thank you, Tyna." Lea was surprised to see the same sadness that had dimmed Tyna's features in the palace had made a return. Her glittering eyes had lost a bit of their spark and her overall posture was listless. "Are you alright?"

Tyna averted her eyes and brushed away a tear. "Yes, my lady."

"Don't lie to me, Tyna."

"Oh, we're all separating again!" Tyna wailed, wringing her hands. "I thought now that we've regrouped, we could stay together, that I—"

"Could stay with your sister?" Lea gave her a small smile. "Tyna, please don't feel obligated to come to Errest with me. Your help in the palace was invaluable, but you shouldn't be away from Rini for so long."

"Nonsense!" Tyna's eyes widened with shock. "I am *your* attendant, Lady Calliwell. Attendants do not *leave* their charges!"

Perplexed, Lea stared at the tiny pixie. Technically, she could order her away, but that would be akin to firing the poor thing, and the last thing Lea wanted was to cause even more distress. "Alright, fine. But I'm telling you *now,* if you miss Rini and want to return to her, I won't hold you back."

Tyna sniffed, then nodded. "Alright, my lady. I appreciate that. But now it's time to go."

Lea buttoned the satchel Vara had given her to transport her belongings to Errest. "Have you spoken with my mother?"

"Yes, she's already in the dining room. They're starting the final meeting in a few minutes."

"Alright. We should go, then." Lea gave herself one last look in the mirror, then, satisfied with her appearance, gestured for Tyna to lead the way. After arriving in Iston, Lea had all but abandoned the gowns she'd worn in Iladel, fully embracing the sturdier leather and wool garb Vara had provided, although she'd be abandoning wool in favor of muslin soon enough. Considering the circumstances, she felt being able to move freely, whether it be to walk, run, or fight, was a necessity.

The dining room was filled to bursting, the energy Lea felt emanating through the house from her chambers intensifying as the day's plans were laid out. Byrric, Florian, Ruehnar, and Aer stood at the table poring over the map, while Freya talked with Fenian, Laz, and Collin nearby. As far as Lea knew, Lazarus and Collin, along with their parents, were staying in Iston for one more night. The Brytons and Maddixes were discussing their own plans with Tavian, who would be returning them to their homes in Olthanas and Watoria through the Between before leaving for Kildin with Lazarus the following day.

Sadness filled Lea as she took them all in. Once again, she and her friends would all be separated. Only this time, more so. Now they'd be spread to all corners of the kingdom with plans to break apart even further once they'd formulated a plan for Kildin.

"Ah, Lady Calliwell." Ettrian broke apart from the cluster of elvish knights he'd been conversing with and walked over toward her. "It's nearly time to go. Have you taken care of everything?"

Lea let out a slow breath, then nodded. "Yes, I have. When will we leave?"

"Shortly. Have you said your goodbyes?"

Lea glanced over at her friends, then at her mother, who was speaking furtively with Ordona. "Not yet."

They stood beside each other in silence for the next few moments, watching as everyone she'd shared a house with the last several days planned to leave. There was an underlying tone of anticipation and even excitement, as far as the elves were concerned. Lea supposed the excitement she felt in the room was due to the self-assuredness, either earned or fabricated, that any soldier might need going into war. After all, if one went into war assuming they were too weak to survive, they'd be more likely to fail. But if one went into war knowing they might die but trusting their skills nonetheless...well, Lea supposed that soldier was far more likely to succeed.

A few minutes later, Freya, Lazarus, and Collin walked toward them, their expressions grim.

Time for goodbyes, then, Lea thought.

Ettrian touched her elbow, causing her to start. "If you'll excuse me, I'd like to go speak to my father." He inclined his head toward her friends. "And I think you have business to attend to."

She gave him a brief smile of thanks, then held out her hands to Laz when she approached.

Collin took her hands and squeezed, giving Ettrian a nod as he walked off. "So, are you excited?"

"To separate again?" Lea's brows furrowed as Laz draped an arm around her shoulder. "No, not particularly." With a sigh, she wrapped her arms around his waist and leaned against his chest. "Perhaps one of these days we'll be able to have one of our old gatherings in the palace. A proper welcome to our new queen."

Laz chuckled and kissed the top of her head. "Yes, once we rebuild this kingdom of ours, many parties will be in order."

"Did I hear someone say party?"

Lea straightened, then smiled when she saw Myria walking toward them. Her long blonde hair was tied back in a tight braid, but despite the utilitarian hairstyle, she still bore a slim-fitting pale pink gown that perfectly suited the pretty lady of Saith. In no world, war torn kingdom or no, would Myria Bryton be caught wearing anything less than a proper lady's attire when returning to her home. Considering she, her mother, and brother all housed lions beneath their skin, Lea supposed dressing for potential battle meant something much different for them than it did her.

"Yes," Collin said, "apparently we're planning celebrations already."

"I was planning a month ago," Freya said with a shrug as she and Aer joined them. "This will end in our favor." She looked at each of them in turn. "I want you all to know that."

Aer slipped an arm around Freya's waist. "I second that. On both counts."

Myria rolled her eyes in feigned annoyance. "If you all insist on having a victory party, at least let me have a hand in planning it."

Freya's eyes widened and gave a look of shock. "Lady Bryton, we would never dream of doing otherwise."

This time it was Myria's turn for a wry smile. "I'd like to apologize to you again, Your Majesty, for the way I treated you when you first arrived in Iladel."

Lea snorted, unable to hold back her amusement, but she bit her tongue when she saw Freya's gracious smile.

"I appreciate that, Myria, even if you did refer to me as a smelly pigeon."

"And you proved me wrong quite neatly," Myria replied, then winced at some memory before adding, "And painfully, I might add."

Lazarus rubbed his hands together. "Alright, so we'll see each other at the palace soon, then, yeah?"

"We will." Aer gave a sharp nod. "Count on it."

There was a moment of tense silence as Lea, and likely the rest of them, thought about each of the stars that would need to align in order for them to celebrate the way they wanted. Lea couldn't even begin to imagine where they would start to rebuild a kingdom, considering how long that might take. By now, the eastern shores were likely overrun with humans and Jotnar pillaging and burning whatever they found no use for. She wouldn't be surprised if they were fighting their own battle amongst themselves and worsening Lindoroth's state further. Although, if that were the case, it might give the remaining people a reprieve, a chance to flee the cities while the enemies were focused on one another instead of their bounty.

Freya cleared her throat. "All right, then. So this is goodbye for now."

Collin glanced over his shoulder at his aunt and cousins, then exhaled a quiet breath. "Yes. Goodbye for now."

Then, as though they were simply parting ways at the end of a term at school, they hugged, gave kisses on the cheeks, and smiled their goodbyes with teary eyes.

Finally, they all separated to their own corners.

Lea knew they would see each other again. There was no question of that in her mind. She would see to it, no matter the cost. The only uncertainty that remained was about the circumstances surrounding their next meeting. Not even the most powerful seer could reassure her they would come out of this alive and free.

Left alone once more, Lea scanned the room, watching as her mother conferred with Byrric, Ordona, and Florian. The spark in Perida's eyes had gone sharp as she took in Byrric's instructions, words of caution, and whatever else he felt the need to tell her before the journey home.

Ettrian reappeared at her side. "Are you ready?"

Slowly, Lea exhaled a breath. "If by 'ready' you mean mildly terrified of what I'm about to walk into, then yes, I am." She gave him a rueful smile. "I don't think I have much choice, Your Highness."

"Lady Calliwell, was that a *joke*?" Ettrian put a hand over his heart and closed his eyes. "If a heart attack was enough to murder me, I would be dead at your feet."

"Idiot." But she couldn't help the small smile his own joke forced from her lips. Turning somber, she glanced over at her mother. "How will your knights know where to go?"

"Their allegiance ties them to my family," Ettrian explained. "Where I go, they can follow." He smirked, then added, "So long as I let them."

"Ah." It seemed efficient enough, although Lea wasn't entirely sure she wanted to know how the Tordoves ensured allegiance of that kind. Before she could ask, Perida stepped away from her conversation, touching her sister's arm before joining Lea.

"Have you said your farewells?" she asked Lea. When Lea

nodded, she sighed. "Ordona will return with us. She feels useless here, and Aerelius won't have her going with them."

"That's understandable," Lea replied, frowning at her aunt and cousin, who were in a tense discussion with Byrric and Freya. "I'm surprised Aer is going for it, though."

"He knows if his mother comes with us, we'll have the benefit of her earth magic," Perida explained with a wary glance toward her king. "He may not want her in battle, but he wants us all safe. We're better off together." She inclined her head toward a cluster of knights near the door. "We'll be taking her personal guard with us. Ervic escorted Ordona here, so Aerelius trusts him with her continued safety."

"You're probably right." Lea knew Ordona wasn't coming with them solely to offer her magic. Ordona would never leave her sister to recover after being in those dungeons for nearly a month, starved and neglected. As it was, Ordona had barely left her side, spending every moment separated from Aer with Perida. And, of course, having the Queen Mother in Errest would go a long way in boosting morale among the citizens.

"Mother, I was thinking..."

"Don't you dare." Ettrian's voice in her mind nearly made her jump, but she ignored him.

Perida looked at Lea in question. "I see that look, Grevillea. What are you plotting?"

Lea bit her lip, then, ignoring Ettrian's disapproving words, asked, "What do you think about bringing Rosie along?"

Confusion filled Perida's eyes before understanding settled. "You want to bring the princess."

Lea gave a curt nod. She'd been considering it, toying with the idea of bringing Rosie since the night before. Logically, she knew this wasn't the best time to bring it up, but, well, she was allowed a bit of self-doubt now and then when it came to potentially reckless decisions.

"Might I register my disapproval of this plan?" Ettrian asked.

"No," Lea replied flatly, not breaking her mother's stare.

After a moment, Perida let out a suffering sigh. "Willem will come looking for her."

"He'll do that no matter what, as the prince pointed out to me previously," she added, quirking a brow in his direction.

Ettrian's lip curled. "Have you spoken to your king and queen about this?" he asked. Lea nearly smiled at the frustration in his tone. "Seeing as she is technically *not* yours to do with as you please."

"Actually, I have." She glanced over at Aer, who gave her a quick nod. "They agree that having one less mouth to feed here will be beneficial."

"And her brother?"

"Reginald has already spoken to the king and queen about meeting up with them once he's fully healed, which should be in the next day or so. Although, if his sister stays here, he plans to as well."

Perida's lips formed a thin line, then she blew out a breath. "Fine. But she is *your* responsibility. If General Lindesson so much as suspects she's making trouble—"

"We have a dark and gloomy wine cellar to toss her in," Lea finished.

A moment later, Ordona walked over, joined by Aerelius.

"Aunt Perida, I'm guessing by that look on your face Lea has explained what she'd like to do?" Aer asked with an amused smile.

Perida slid a look at Lea, then nodded. "She has. You think this is a good idea?"

Aer shrugged. "No, but it's not a particularly bad one, either. We need Vara focused on coordinating with our points of contact here, not monitoring a human princess." He tilted his head toward Lea. "If nothing else, she trusts Lea slightly more than the rest of us."

"Which says little, considering she does not trust any of us at all," Ettrian muttered.

"And if Willem comes to Errest?"

"You'll be backed by a full squadron of elvish and Lindorothian knights," Aer replied.

"It will be fine, Per," Ordona murmured. "Let the girl come with us."

Lea's mother looked torn between accepting her older sister's guidance and wanting very badly to side with the prince. Finally, Perida let out a resigned sigh. "Like I said, she's *your* responsibility, Lea. She can have the room beside yours."

Lea blew out a breath, flicking a curl away from her forehead. "Whatever you say, Mother."

15

FREYA

Taking to the skies was often the only thing that eased Freya's nerves during times of stress, so after saying her final farewells to Lea, Ordona, and Perida, she excused herself from the dining room and went for a flight. She knew Aer would want company once his mother left, but Freya also knew he'd want a few moments in private to say goodbye.

It didn't come off as surprising that Ordona would want to travel with her sister, or that Aer would support her. The Queen Mother had been idle since fleeing the palace, unable to do anything to help her people. After centuries of having her hands in every aspect of running and protecting her kingdom, Freya could tell Ordona wasn't content to sit on her hands. They all agreed it didn't make sense for her to come east and she had no interest in continuing her stay in Iston. So, Errest was the next logical choice. She'd be safe behind the city walls and able to offer valuable counsel to Perida as she shifted into her new, albeit temporary, role.

It had been hard for Freya to say goodbye to the woman who'd been like a mother to her, but she knew how it felt to want to be useful.

As she launched herself into the sky, Freya looked around the city, eyeing the borders to see if there was any sign of scouts or enemy knights. Several other Valkyrie flew closer to the city's edge, circling and watching just as she was. Iston was safe. Of that, Freya was sure.

Slowly, she drifted over rooftops, roads, and the central plaza, watching as people went about their day as if it were any other. As she flew past the soaring sentries in the sky, craggy, snow-capped peaks rose before her, jutting up from western Caelora. To the south and east, there was nothing but rolling blankets of forest. First pine, then, beyond where her eyes could see, deciduous oak, maple, and beech. And at the western edge of Iston, its waters glittering and blue, sat the Brystone Sea, the saltwater expanse that stretched from Lindoroth to the western continent of Tevielle, another place she'd dreamed of visiting that seemed eons beyond her reach.

She flew for nearly half an hour, taking it all in before she shifted back toward Vara's home, glancing toward the southeast as she did. Lea was likely home by now. The thought brought hope and sorrow. Freya hated being separated from her friends, friends who'd become family during her time at Aldridge, people she'd want as part of her life for as long as she lived. She'd never made the same connections with friends in Watoria as she did with Lea, Lazarus, and Collin. Even Myria, who'd been so hostile to during her first days at Aldridge, had become someone she'd always consider a friend.

As she aimed toward the estate, she couldn't help but wonder what it would've been like if her father actually *had* sent her to Iston as a girl so she could grow up with her northern family. What little family she had, anyway. She wouldn't trade her life in Watoria for anything, but it was hard not to question what she could've learned from the other Valkyrie that now soared in the sky with her.

A few moments later, she touched down on the gravel path that led to the front door. As she climbed the stairs, Aer stepped outside, a slight smile on his face as he watched her approach.

Taking her hand, he kissed her cheek, then rested his temple against hers. For a moment they just stood there, breathing each other in before he spoke. "How was your flight?"

"It was nice." Leaning back, she looked up at him, staring into his warm brown eyes. "Did your mother leave?"

He nodded. "Just before you landed."

"Are you alright?"

Aer sighed, then took her hand and led her back inside. "I am, but I can't help but worry. I don't like being separated from her and Lea again."

Freya hummed her agreement. "I don't think we could ask for three better women to take charge of Errest."

"Agreed." Aer gestured toward the dining room. "Come on. Lord Silmar has returned from the east."

The news had Freya's steps quickening. Ever since the day Zane, Silmar, and their scouts left, she'd been on pins and needles waiting for news. Not knowing what Jonas, Willem, and Ryker Traust were up to had caused her mind to concoct scenarios that made it impossible to sleep some nights. With Lord Silmar back in Iston, they might actually be able to make some headway.

When they arrived in the dining room, her father, Florian, Ana, and Silmar were standing at the head of the table arguing with Ruehnar and Fenian.

"Lovely," Freya muttered. "This can't be good."

"Indeed," Aer said with a sigh. Then, raising his voice slightly, he said, "Lord Silmar! It's wonderful to have you back. Hopefully you have good news?"

With irritation clear on his face, Silmar looked at Aer and Freya, giving each a nod of acknowledgment. "Your Majesties. I was just filling the commander and my king in on my observations from the east. Unfortunately, Reykr Traust has found his way to Iladel in one piece."

"And?" Freya looked to her father, then back at Silmar. "What role is he playing now that he's in the capital?"

"It appears he is now answering to Willem in Lessia's absence," Silmar replied. "Whether that will continue, I do not know. It's safe to assume he will act as an advisor, perhaps assist Lord Edrin with leading Jotunheim's army. Based on what your commander and spymaster have told me about him, I don't see him tolerating answering to a human for long."

"And Lord Edrin?" Aer asked sharply.

"Slipping into his role as leader quite nicely, from what I can see. His knights seem to have accepted him, and Willem shows no sign of suspicion."

"Then what seems to be the problem?" Ana asked.

"There's no evidence Lord Edrin has betrayed you," Silmar said slowly, swapping looks with Florian. "But there is also no evidence to the *contrary*." He sent a look toward Byrric. "If I am to be honest, I would say the evidence of his defection is greater than evidence against it, but of course, there is no way to be certain. In any event, I would proceed with caution when it comes to him."

Heart sinking, Freya nodded. In the absence of absolute proof of his loyalty, they had to treat him as their enemy.

"So, this Reykr Traust fellow made it across the kingdom carrying a grudge against your commander," Ruehnar said, "and Jonas Edrin is leading your enemy's army and may or may not order them to march against you. Do I have that correct?"

"It would seem so," Byrric replied.

"A grudge that is due to you marrying the woman he hoped to take for his own?" Ruehnar shook his head, then gave Freya a smirk. "Your father's romantic history seems to have added quite a complication to this war."

"Funny, I said almost the exact same thing to him not two weeks ago."

Ana snorted a quiet laugh, then schooled her features at her brother's sharp look.

A flicker of appreciation flashed in the king's eyes. "Traust will be more difficult to take down than the human king. Vengeance is a far more powerful motivator than greed, which is all you'll face with Willem."

"He's also only one Valkyrie," Florian replied.

"One Valkyrie who is aiming specifically at your queen and commander. Willem wants your kingdom, which requires slaughtering your armies." Ruehnar shifted his eyes to Freya. "Traust simply wants you dead. That is, it seems, his only goal in this. He has no other, what's the phrase? Dog in this fight?"

"He won't get near her," Aer said. "Near any of us. We're too well-guarded."

Ruehnar's brows shot up. "Then how was he able to attack her previously? Where were your guards then?"

Freya felt her cheeks redden at the stern looks her father, husband, and aunt sent her. "That was due to my...poor judgement when seeking information. It isn't a mistake I'll make twice."

"Let's hope you are right, Queen Freya," Ruehnar said. "Your kingdom depends on you, so you mustn't allow an insatiable curiosity interfere."

"Has there been any word from Zane or the other scouts?" Ana asked Silmar.

"I was able to speak with Lord Ristheld before returning," Silmar replied. "He is still insisting on traveling the kingdom by foot and wing, but I did convince him to allow me to return for him and his companions in three days' time."

"Where?" Florian asked.

"The eastern shore of Caelora, near Midstal, a few miles from the mouth of the Selnor river."

"Were you able to assess how many humans landed?" Aer asked. "Or where they went?"

"Twelve thousand, from my estimate, Your Majesty, but Lord Ristheld will get more detailed information regarding movements, planning, and so forth. I've instructed two of his companions to fly to Madrya to assess the situation there, as well." As if sensing her question, Silmar shifted his gaze to Freya. "Even with my ability to travel the Between, I cannot perch on a fencepost or tent in the midst of an enemy camp like your hawk shifters can."

"And Kildin?" Aer asked. "Were you able to see anything there?"

"Briefly. I was able to travel into the city under an invisibility glamour, but I didn't stay long. From what I can gather, it's significantly worse off than Watoria, likely due to the Jotnar's element of surprise. However, it appears the Jotnar Lessia Edrin placed in charge has been killed." His eyes flicked between them all. "The city is now under human control."

Freya nodded slowly. One less Jotnar in power could be a good thing, seeing as the humans had no magic of their own to wield against the Linds. "How did the people seem?" she asked.

"As is to be expected for a city in Kildin's condition. I couldn't say how many citizens were able to flee, but those who remained are well-hidden, detained, or dead. I've relayed the information to Lord Ristheld so he knows what to expect when he flies through."

Aer let out a heavy breath. "Alright. I suppose that's better than nothing." He looked at Byrric. "If you don't mind finishing without me, I'd like to go update Lazarus."

Once Aer left, Freya turned to Silmar, frowning. "Lord Silmar, how were you able to get such detailed information at the palace if you didn't want to linger so long in Kildin?"

He gave her a small smile. "We elves have varying levels of power. My invisibility glamours only last for an hour, two, at most, but your palace is rife with hidden passageways," he said, casting a glance at Florian. "Lady Calliwell's attendant also offered her assistance in navigating the tunnels."

Freya smiled. "Yes, Rini and Tyna are quite skilled at gathering information discreetly." She still hadn't made a solid decision as to whether Rini would accompany them when they left, although knowing the pixie, Rini likely wouldn't have it any other way.

"Commander, have your Valkyrie find the best route to the east," Ruehnar said, contemplating the map. He drew a finger along the line of the Selnor River. "Perhaps half a days' march north of here. We will send the first round of knights there to establish camp. It will give us enough cover that we will be able to clear any enemy knights we find, but fast access to the waterway if need be."

Byrric gave a sharp nod, then looked to his sister. "Ana?"

"Two of the other Valkyrie and I will fly east," Ana replied. "Between us and the hawks, we'll find you a clear path forward."

Freya drew in a slow breath, then exhaled quietly. "Alright, then. It looks like we have a plan."

If only she could feel as confident as the words she spoke sounded.

16

LEA

Lea had traveled through the Between three times before. Once from the palace dining room to the woods of the Aldridge mountains, again from there to Watoria, and a third time to Iston. Each trip had been cold, nauseating, and more than a bit unnerving. Her fourth was no different, although the feeling was starting to become easier to ignore. Despite her better judgement, she clung tightly to Ettrian's hand, hating that she was showing any sign of weakness but knowing it was better to feel grounded while traveling in such an unconventional way. And, as much as she hated to admit it, his warm grip offered a sense of comfort as well.

Unfortunately for Rosie Ristner, *her* fourth trip proved just as troublesome as the first two, causing her to faint against Ettrian the moment their feet touched the warm wood floor of the governor's mansion. His hands slipped from Lea's as he caught Rosie, leaving Lea to recover her sea legs, as she liked to call them, on her own. Iska caught her elbow and steadied her, waiting a moment to ensure she was steady before letting go.

"Gods above." Ettrian huffed, pushing the princess toward Lea, who caught her deftly. "I suppose you have a space for her in mind?"

With a hiss and a jerk, Rosie stepped back before Lea could help, scowling at their new surroundings as she straightened her dress and smoothed back her hair.

Once Rosie seemed able to stand still on her own, Lea took a moment to survey her surroundings. Ordona merely brushed a stray hair out of her eyes, then put her hands on her hips and greeted the waiting staff with a queenly nod. Perida, as usual, looked perfectly elegant and unruffled, her gaunt frame showing no ill effects despite the harsh trip she'd just taken.

Lea was pleased to find the governor's mansion in Edhil had managed to remain unscathed, although the servants that greeted them appeared a bit worse for wear.

My home is secure, Lea thought as she took in the entryway. Nothing was out of place. The paintings that had hung in the hall were perfectly straight, the white plaster walls uncracked. The windows, open to the warm breeze, showed no destruction. The city seemed quiet, as though an entire army wasn't waiting on the other side of the gates. Although, without walking the estate's walls, she wouldn't know for sure what the extent of the city's damage might be.

Tyna appeared at Lea's shoulder, then smiled at the others, concern etched on her face as she took in Lea's home. "Oh, thank goodness," she said with a sigh, her expression relaxing. "I was so worried."

Nearly all the staff, roughly a dozen Linds, awaited them in the foyer, their faces a mix of relief, sadness, and, as they took in the elf and human companions, apprehension. Brutus, a hulking wolf shifter who'd been running the household during the last twelve governorships, stepped forward to greet them first.

"My ladies," he said, dipping into a bow. "Your Majesty. Welcome home."

"Brutus," Perida said with a nod. "It's lovely to be home, thank you." She looked around at everyone, instantly taking charge. "If someone could help us with our things, we'd like to have an update on the state of our city as soon as possible." She snapped her fingers toward a younger female, a girl named Ora, who was about Rosie's age. "Take the princess to the room beside my daughter's. See that she's comfortable."

Ora nodded but eyed Rosie suspiciously. "And shall I have the windows spelled, Lady Calliwell?"

"Yes, please do," Perida replied, flicking a glance up and down the human girl. "We won't have her leaping to her death without permission just yet."

Rosie blanched, but Lea hoped the not-so-subtle threat would keep her in place for the time being.

"I'll be up once you get settled," Lea said gently. "Ora will bring you whatever you need." She glanced at Iska. "Iska, if you wouldn't mind keeping an eye on the princess until I'm able to come up?"

He gave her a short nod. "Whatever you need, Lady Calliwell."

Rosie huffed and folded her arms. "I don't *need*—"

"If you are going to say you don't need anything from the Ladies Calliwell," Ettrian drawled, "I would thoroughly rethink that. Food, water, all of those annoying little human things that you creatures require to exist...I'd be more grateful if I were you."

Lea nearly cut him off, but based on the flicker of fear on Rosie's face, Lea thought it might help the princess to be a bit scared. When she glanced at her mother, Perida's expression told her she felt the same.

"How else might we be of assistance, Lady Calliwell?" Brutus asked as two other staff began picking up the meager belongings Lea, Perida, Ordona, and Ettrian had brought with them.

"I'd like to speak with General Lindesson first," Perida replied.

"Of course. He's coming along now."

As he spoke, a tall, slender Lind warlock came toward them, walking briskly down the hall. "My ladies," he said, a bit out of breath. "Your Majesty," he added when he saw Ordona. "I'm General Lindesson."

"Ah, yes," Perida said with a nod. "You've been keeping my city under control?"

He nodded. "Yes. I was just wrapping up a strategy session with the knights. Whenever you're ready, we can go over everything that's happened in your absence." His eyes lifted to the elves behind the ladies of Errest and the Queen Mother. "And, of course, we need to determine how best to spread out our newly acquired allies."

"Not to worry," Ettrian said. "I've already sent my knights out to assess the area. They're concealed with invisibility glamours," he added at Lindesson's look of objection. "I want to hear from my own knights what we're facing so we can secure things by nightfall."

"Fair enough, although I can assure you, the city is secure," Lindesson said, his expression still carrying a hint of suspicion. "If you'll accompany me to the drawing room?"

"Drawing room?" Perida asked sharply. "My husband's office—"

"I thought it best to wait until your arrival before using his space, My Lady," the General said. "It seemed inappropriate, considering the circumstances, to do otherwise, and the drawing room is bigger."

"It will have more space, Perida," Ordona murmured, touching her sister's arm.

Perida gave Ordona a sharp nod, then turned to face the prince. "Your Highness? If you wouldn't mind joining us, I'd like you to fill General Lindesson in on the information you've gathered."

"Of course, Lady Calliwell." Then, lowering his voice, he touched a hand to Lea's back. "I'll come find you later."

For a moment, Lea considered going to her room, calling for tea and sending Tyna to check in with Freya. But as she watched her mother walk down the hall discussing battle strategy with the elf prince and General Lindesson, she was overcome with an urge to be a part of that. She'd spent so much time sitting idly by that the thought of doing nothing for another moment made her want to crawl out of her skin.

Tyna, always more perceptive than she let on, gave Lea's shoulder a small nudge. "Go, My Lady," she whispered.

So, without giving herself time to second guess her choice, Lea hurried to catch up, falling into step beside Ettrian.

"Mother? I'd like to join you, if that's alright," she said, cutting off whatever Ordona had been saying.

Indecision warred in Perida's expression, and it took everything within Lea not to argue her case, but Perida finally gave her daughter a sharp nod. "Of course." She looked at Lindesson. "My daughter should fill you in on her time at the palace, anyway."

Lindesson gave Lea an understanding smile. "Yes, of course. Come, I'll bring you all up to speed on everything."

The group made its way toward the drawing room down the hall, the space Lea's parents had always taken guests at the start of any party or gathering. It was an old wood-paneled room with towering windows draped in gauzy white curtains that were tied back with gold braided ropes. Everything about it, from the heavy ancient wood furniture to the paintings and sculptures scattered artfully throughout the room, highlighted bits and pieces of the heritage Perida and Orin had brought into their union.

It was the portrait of her parents on their wedding day that drew Lea's eye, though. The gilt-framed painting that hung above the fireplace was so lifelike Lea often felt as though Perida and Orin's eyes followed her throughout the room. Today, though, a heavy curtain, typically used to protect it from sunlight and dust when the room wasn't in use, hung over the piece. Lea couldn't think of the last time it had been concealed in such a way, but she could only assume it was the work of their servants, who would mourn her father nearly as much as she would.

Perida's back stiffened as they entered the room, and Lea was sure only she heard her mother's quiet intake of breath when she saw the covered painting. She recovered herself quickly, but it was Ordona who turned to Brutus.

"Uncover the painting, Brutus." Ordona gripped Perida's hand as her eyes drifted back toward the covered piece. "Let us all see the constant reminder of what these people have done to us."

"Of course, Your Majesty," Brutus murmured, hurrying across the room. With a single tug on the golden cord, the curtain fell from the painting, revealing the jovial face of Orin Calliwell, grinning broadly from his place beside Perida.

Lea took her mother's other hand and squeezed, thankful when she felt Perida return the gesture. "Aunt Ordona is right, Mother. We should always see his face."

General Lindesson led them toward a broad table covered with maps and other documents, pens and inkwells, and piles of wood and iron map markers. When they got closer, Lea realized it wasn't one large table, but the four smaller tables that had been spread throughout the room previously.

"How much information have you received from Commander Balthana?" Ordona asked as they came to a stop beside the table.

"His last update came four days ago," Lindesson replied. He gestured toward the map while they all spread around the table. "As you can see, that information didn't include numbers for the elvish army."

"The bulk of our knights will stay with my father," Ettrian said. "But my brother Fenian, who controls our armies, sent a healthy squadron with us."

"Excellent," Lindesson replied. "As I said, the city is secure, but having your type of magic will help ensure it stays that way. Now, let's go over the rest."

Lea listened as they went over much of what she'd already heard in Iston regarding positioning, numbers, and movements. It was hard to keep a focus on what they were all saying when it sounded so repetitive, but she did her best. Lindesson's report of Errest's conditions was more interesting, although unsurprising.

While Errest was nowhere near the state of ruin she'd seen in Watoria, the General reported quite a bit of damage. Before The Linds had been able to push the humans and Jotnar back, the enemy had managed to pillage and burn several villages a few miles outside the city walls, but many had been able to flee into the city. Fortunately, the city itself had remained untouched aside from a bit of damage to the wall and gates.

"For now, we'd like to allow as many as possible to relocate inside the city walls as possible," Lindesson said. He shifted his gaze to Perida. "If you agree, Lady Calliwell?"

Perida nodded slowly. "Yes, I think that's best. Send some of your men to find inns with space. Be sure the owners know we'll compensate them for use of their rooms."

"Of course," Lindesson replied. He sighed, then glanced up at the painting of Orin and Perida before looking to Perida. "On a final note, we need to discuss the issue of leadership. For now, Commander Balthana and I think it's best if I remain at the helm until this siege is over, but you will have the authority to override decisions if you feel it's necessary," Lindesson explained. "However, if you have an objection to that, we can certainly have a longer conversation."

Lea nearly objected, but Perida was already nodding. "Yes, Byrric and I spoke about that last night. Joint leadership is best right now, considering the circumstances. As you hold the military experience, I will certainly accept that guidance. We'll hold an election once this all blows over."

"I agree," Ordona added, meeting Lindesson's eyes calmly. "Lady Calliwell will sit at your side, General, and I will sit at hers." The warning in her words was clear.

"This should go swimmingly."

Lea's jaw clenched at the sound of Ettrian's voice in her head. No matter how many times he used his ability to speak in her mind, she didn't think it was something she'd get used to easily.

So, she smacked his chest with the back of her hand but couldn't help the small smile on her lips. If she knew her mother and Ordona, General Lindesson would have his work cut out for him.

17

LEA

It was long past midday when Perida finally dismissed everyone from the drawing room, leaving Lea with little to do. There was no question in her mind that she wanted to be as much a part of getting Errest back on its feet as possible, but for the moment, there was little to be done as Lindesson, her mother, and Ettrian organized who would go where and when. Tyna likely already had the servants sorting through the belongings Ettrian had managed to sneak away from the palace, which is how she found herself wandering the halls of her home that afternoon.

She ignored the knights that hurried about preparing for battle and the servants heading in one direction or another, but with each footstep, she found herself drifting through the echoes of her father's presence. No matter where she went, hints of him remained. The emerald green curtains he'd chosen in the northern hallway, the vases dotted with Edhilian gems he'd ordered servants to always have filled with peonies for Perida, the stone archway that led to the small courtyard garden he'd given to Lea and her mother to cultivate...

Everywhere she went, he was there.

Suddenly, the walls felt as though they were closing in around her. The house was old and solid as a fortress.

She needed to be out.

Before she knew where her feet were taking her, Lea found herself rushing toward a short bridge on the third floor that led directly to the battlements that ringed her home. Errest's proximity to Iladel's borders and ports led the first governor to craft his home of solid stone, surrounded by tall battlements, with a clear view of the surrounding landscape from every corner of the wall. Now, those safety measures were the only bit of freedom she could manage.

She rushed past servants and knights, letting the fresh air and thrums of magic emanating from the earth draw her upward until she reached the southern wall. Everyone seemed to have a place to go, but she didn't care. She needed to be *out.*

By the time she reached the wall that allowed a direct view of the southern desert, her lungs felt ready to burst. Hot desert air blew from the north, bringing with it the scent of sand, wisps of power that were so utterly *home,* and just a touch of elvish magic from their new allies.

Hands braced on the crenellated wall, Lea closed her eyes and inhaled deeply, feeling the magic of her city, her people, and the land she so desperately wanted to save.

After a few moments, her breathing steadied and she opened her eyes. She realized with a start that the sun was sliding toward the western edge of the world. Still, the dimming light did nothing to block the view before her. Rolling hills of red sand and scraggly brush extended for miles beyond the walls of her city, giving way to barren desert as far as the eye could see. Beyond the horizon lie the red canyons that opened seemingly out of nowhere, carved eons ago by a river that had long since dried up in the burning heat. The Southern Ocean, where the Brystonian and Elysonian Seas met, was another hundred miles past the canyons, a salt water oasis that fed freshwater tributaries on land that anyone traveling the desert would never reach.

A true deathtrap that began not ten miles beyond Errest's city walls.

If only the humans had attempted to come in through the south.

Tears threatened her eyes as Lea contemplated how different their fates would be had the humans made such a grave mistake. One small piece of false information is all it would've taken...

But of course, it was far too late for that. They were here at her home, camped along the northern edge of her city, the knights too smart to risk getting pushed into the desert from the south.

When she felt the first tear drip onto her cheek, she forced her eyes away from the desert's beauty. It wouldn't help anyone to wish for the past to change, so all she could do was help her mother figure out how to protect their future.

She stepped back from the wall and walked away, letting her fingers trail along the warm stone as she considered what she would do now that she was home. Help her people recover, of course. But she needed to see the city, see that it hadn't been bombarded like Watoria. First, though, she needed to see what they were up against. She hadn't gotten a view of the human and Jotnar encampments yet. Some small part of her wanted nothing to do with that knowledge. But if she wanted to have any part in ending this war, hiding from the bad parts would make that impossible.

As she neared the western wall, something in the air, a prickly feeling that was unmistakably elvish, had her picking up her pace. The moment she turned the corner, the distant sound of metal-on-metal reached her ears, and magic, elvish magic, at that, sizzled along her skin. She had felt it each time Ettrian used his power near her, but this was heavier, a wave that coated her body, thickening with each step. Her first instinct was that they were being attacked, that they'd been too late and more enemy knights had arrived. Alarm coursed through her and she moved faster, running full sprint until she hit the northern battlement, crashing into the limestone and sending her hip bones singing with the impact. Alarm turned to shock as she slowly processed what was in front of her.

Far below on the grounds before the city gates, nearly a mile from where she stood, the elves had joined forces with the Linds and were battling the enemy knights. She struggled to reconcile the planning meeting they'd just had with Lindesson with the battle before her.

There was no way General Lindesson would've sent the elves out so soon to start a battle, certainly not without speaking with the Errestian army general. When Ettrian sent his knights out, she thought it was for reconnaissance only, to get up to speed on things.

Instead, she heard the thrum of distant shouts and men, undoubtedly human, fleeing north as magic pulsed in the air around her. She realized with a start that Ettrian, fool that he was, had likely ordered his knights to attack while they were meeting in the drawing room.

"Idiot," she muttered, and her nails dug into the stone. The gods only knew what he had said to ensure the Lindorothian knights this was at the behest of Lindesson, but there, in front of her, were more than two thousand knights pushing back the human and Jotnar armies that had been camped at Errest's gates for weeks.

Slowly, the shock began to fade, replaced with a feeling of grim satisfaction. General Lindesson and Perida would likely be furious with the prince, but as she watched the rapid destruction in the distance, it was clear Ettrian had opted to ask forgiveness rather than permission. A small part of her respected him for that.

"Lady Calliwell?"

She jumped at the sound of Iska's voice. He stood beside her, his chest heaving with exertion.

"Yes?"

"I must ask that you go back inside for safety reasons. Your mother insists."

With a frown, Lea looked back at the battling knights, wishing she could stay and witness her enemies' destruction. She knew Iska would alert her mother if she didn't comply, though, so she sighed and nodded. "Of course." Then, as he led her quickly toward the small bridge that would take them back inside, she asked, "How long will it take? To dispatch the enemy here?"

Iska's disapproving expression told her discussing warfare with her was the last thing he wanted to do, but he relented. "Only a few hours more, considering the reinforcements you brought. The elves will make the work much quicker."

"And the people of the city?" Those closest to the walls had to know what was happening on the other side. "Are they safe?"

"Yes, my lady. They've been ordered to stay in their homes until our marshals alert them it's safe to come out."

"Good." She nodded, looking down at the city streets that stretched outward from her home were empty, the shops and taverns all shuttered. "That's good."

Iska stepped to the side when they reached the bridge, then gestured for her to walk forward. "Please, my lady, you shouldn't see this."

She sent one last look past the city gates, watching for a moment as more dust kicked up, obscuring then clearing her view. With one last sigh, she smiled at Iska. "Lead the way."

Silently, she followed him to the main entry hall, far from any entrance to the battlements, where she found her mother waiting. The windows along the hall were shuttered, the only light the flickering sconces along the walls.

"Lea!" Perida exclaimed, pulling her daughter into a hug. "Where have you been?"

"On the wall, Mother," Lea replied. "Why didn't you tell me—"

"Oh, that fool prince you brought home with you launched an attack while we were in our meeting. He put a blasted *silencing* spell on the door so we wouldn't hear the knights calling!" Perida's eyes flashed. "General Lindesson is furious and he's ordered us to stay here." She looked at Lea's guard. "Iska, have the knights inside finished sealing the doors?"

"Yes, my lady. The door to the northern wall was the last one, and I've posted knights along the wall and at any entry points."

"Good. Come," Perida said, hurrying Lea down the hall. "We shouldn't have anything to worry about here, but I'd rather be in the center of the house."

Quietly, Lea followed her mother to the drawing room, one of the safest rooms in the house thanks to its central location and six-inch-thick wooden shutters that locked with Caelorian steel bolts.

"How long will this take?" she asked. She wasn't the least bit surprised Ettrian had pulled such a stunt. In the short time she'd known him, Lea had sensed patience was not one of the prince's strong suits. Nor was communication, it seemed.

Perida shoved open the doors to the drawing room, where Ordona was sitting on a chaise talking with Tyna. Rosie sat in a huff on a chair in the corner, the furthest spot from anyone in the room, wearing a haughty expression. "General Lindesson said the elves took the enemy by surprise," Perida explained. "Unfortunately, they also took our *own* knights by surprise," she added, her voice full of derision, "but they found their footing quickly. Hopefully by nightfall they'll no longer be an issue."

"Well, that's something," Lea murmured. "If that idiot ends up being the cause of our city's destruction—"

"Oh, no need to worry about that, my lady," Tyna said cheerily, fluttering up from the chaise beside her. "I've checked in with His Highness and things are going quite well on the battlefield. Nearly half our enemy are defeated and many have fled."

Lea stared at the pixie in alarm. "You've spoken to the prince? In the midst of battle?"

Ordona laughed. "The pixies are a valuable source of information, Lea. You know this."

Tyna nodded emphatically. "Yes, yes, my job is to attend to your every need, Lady Calliwell. That includes keeping you informed of all that's happening around you."

Lea rubbed her forehead. "While I appreciate your help, Tyna, I'd feel much better if I knew you were safe. Popping in to check with an elvish prince while he's fighting our enemies goes quite counter to that."

"If only you'd seen him!" A small flush crept across Tyna's cheeks as she fluttered closer. "I watched from the air as he took down *three* men with one swing of his sword."

"Tyna!" Perida chastised.

Lea smirked at Tyna, then gave her shoulder a small poke. "Stay inside from now on, alright?"

Tyna let out a small huff, then said glumly, "Yes, my lady."

With a huff, Lea dropped down on a leather wingback beside her aunt, then looked at her mother questioningly. "What do we do now?"

Perida took a seat on a matching chair across from Lea, ankles crossed, hands in her lap. "For now, we wait."

Lea closed her eyes in defeat. She'd thought her days of waiting and standing by were over. Now, thanks to that stupid elvish prince, she felt like she was right back where she started.

18

FREY

A gray sky blanketed the world when Freya awoke the next morning. Even through the closed window, she could feel the promise of snow. It was the last thing they needed during their travels, but she comforted herself with the fact that traveling through the Between would keep their time outside to a minimum.

Her instinct was to burrow deeper under the warm quilts her grandmother had provided, but logic had her swinging her legs over the edge of the tall, plush mattress. The moment her feet touched the frigid wood floor, she nearly recoiled, wanting nothing more than to dive under the covers once more.

"Don't even think about it," Aer murmured from beside her. "We told Byrric we'd be up at dawn."

With a slow nod, Freya slid from the bed, pulling a pair of slippers from the wardrobe beside the window. "At least Grandmother acknowledges how cold her home is." She began pulling clothes from the wardrobe, donning fleece-lined leathers and a wool tunic, and had just finished lacing up her boots when Rini appeared to attend to her hair. As was her habit, she twisted the long pink and brown locks into a braided coronet that had been her favorite style recently. Freya appreciated the practicality of the style far more than the pretty twists and curls Rini had been so partial to previously.

"The commander is in the dining room waiting for you both," Rini said as she secured the last bit of Freya's hair with a pin. "He's been pacing for the past hour."

"Unsurprising." Freya patted her hair, admiring Rini's work. "It's been some time since he's been in battle, and with new allies in the mix..."

"Yes, I'm sure it's difficult." Rini sniffed. "The elves are a curious bunch."

Freya met Aer's eyes in the mirror as he finished buttoning his leather doublet, then looked to Rini. "Are you still angry about what the princes have said about their feelings for the pixies in Avorell?" She frowned when Rini gnawed her lip in response. "Rini, you know we would never allow them to lay a finger on you or any of the other Lindorothian pixies."

Rini flitted forward, adjusting the combs in her glittering hair in the mirror. "I know, Your Majesty. And I don't blame their distrust, not entirely." She turned in the air to face them. "My sisters in Avorell...well, you saw them when you were there. Their magic diverged from ours long ago...it went dark somehow." She took a deep breath. "So, Tyna and I have decided that we will do all in our power to ensure the elves see that *we* are nothing like the creatures they are used to."

Freya smiled. "If anyone can do it, it's you two."

Rini blushed, then went back to tending to her own hair.

Freya gave herself one last once-over in the mirror beside Rini, then exhaled and faced her attendant.

"Rini, I want you to go to Errest, help Tyna get Lea and the princess settled," she instructed. Before Rini could object, she held up a finger. "I will call for you when I need you, but Rosie Ristner needs a kind hand, and Lea has too much to handle right now. You and Tyna are the only ones I would trust with her."

Rini deflated a bit, her mouth turning down in a frown. "I suppose I can't quite blame you for that, Your Majesty," she muttered.

With a scowl, she folded her arms and averted her eyes. "As you wish."

Aer chuckled. "Try not to worry, Rini. You'll have your hands full; I promise."

Rini wrinkled her tiny nose. "Full with that bratty human princess. What fun."

Freya grinned. "She's far from home and more scared than she lets on. She may be tiresome, but we need to treat her kindly. And you'll be with Tyna. I'll see you soon, okay?" She opened her arms, and Rini sniffled, then flew toward her, wrapping her spindly arms around Freya's neck.

"Oh, please be safe, Your Majesty." Her words were thick with tears. "I'll be just a shout away."

Tears burned Freya's throat, so she gave the pixie a small squeeze, then disentangled herself from the embrace. "Travel safe, Rini."

Rini took a deep breath, straightened her back, then nodded. "You, as well. I'll come the moment you call."

Then, she vanished, leaving Freya feeling a bit less whole.

WHEN SHE AND Aer arrived in the dining room, Byrric and Florian were finalizing plans for their trip through the Between, determining where they should land. Her father gave her a nod of acknowledgment when she walked in, then went back to poring over a map with Florian.

She was surprised to find Reginald beside Fenian, a pack at his feet, his shortsword on his hip.

"Your Highness," she greeted him. "You look well."

Reginald smiled in greeting. "Commander Balthana came to me this morning. Lord Florian has checked me over, and as I'm fully healed, we've decided I will accompany you on your journey."

"That's good to hear," Aer said, although Freya could've sworn she saw apprehension tightening his eyes.

"I was just explaining to Prince Reginald that we'll travel through the Between to the eastern edge of the mountains, just north of the Selnor," Fenian told them, leaning back against the table and eyeing Byrric and Florian. "They've been arguing about how far into the forest we should land for the last twenty minutes."

Freya smirked. "It's always entertaining to see the commander a bit ruffled."

Wordlessly, Byrric shot her a disparaging look.

"Considering I am one of those who will be carrying you lot, you'd think my opinion might hold more weight," Fenian continued. "Our scouts have found a favorable area to camp for a few days, long enough to transport our knights and allow mine to rest, and send aerial patrols further east."

Freya frowned as she considered their method of travel. Going through the Between made the most sense, of course. They could be at the valley in an instant, allowing them to avoid potential battles or skirmishes along the way. Since the western portion of the kingdom was largely in Lind hands, their best option was to get to the central regions immediately.

But at the same time, there were dozens of villages and towns between there and Iston that were probably still filled with people. People who could be hurt, captive, or worse. After seeing how many Linds had been pulled from their homes and carted off by enemy knights between Iladel and Watoria, Freya knew the villages had probably been pillaged, leaving the people with little in the way of supplies.

"I see your face, Your Majesty," Fenian crooned, pulling Freya from her thoughts.

She tried to conceal her small sigh. "As one might, when they're standing before me."

"If I could hazard a guess, I would say you want to travel the long way to allow you and your companions time to check on the villages along the way." At her questioning look, he shrugged. "I've committed the Lindorothian map to memory. There are twenty-six villages between here and there, if you were to travel a direct route. If I have learned anything about you and your king in recent days, it's that you'd want to help as many people as possible."

"And that's a bad thing?" Aer asked, lifting his brows at the prince's answering smirk.

"I just want to be sure we're helping as many people as we can," Freya explained to Fenian.

"What, precisely, do you expect to be able to do in these villages?" Fenian gave her a look that dared her to challenge his logic. "We certainly won't be lugging supplies to dole out, no weapons to offer or food to provide. So, what good will your presence do? And do not speak to me about hope, Your Majesty. You know as well as I, that will do nothing to help your people."

Freya opened her mouth to speak about letting the Linds see their monarchs in the open and *not* hiding behind an army. But the words died on her lips as *his* registered. With a sigh, she looked at Aer, seeing the same resignation on his face.

"He's not wrong, Your Majesty," Reginald said quietly. "Unfortunate as it is, the prince is correct."

"We'll accomplish our goals more quickly if we stay the course," Aer said quietly.

"We also don't want any Jotnar or humans in the area to see us coming," Byrric added, finally stepping away from Florian. "Willem currently has scouts scouring the kingdom for you both. Presumably Traust does, as well. We need to keep you as concealed as possible."

"And I think it goes without saying that having three monarchs, two princes, and your army's commander traveling about in the open is a wretched idea," Fenian added. "As a *huntress*, I'm sure you would agree."

Freya bristled at his tone. "The difference is no one will be looking for us that far north. They might be watching Iston, but if we travel from here through the Between to the nearest village—"

"Freya." Byrric's tone was somber, and when she looked at him, his expression brooked no argument.

It took all her strength not to let her shoulders slump, but she refused such a display of weakness. Even a defeat as minor as this weighed heavily, adding to the heap of guilt she carried that had been growing for the past month. She wasn't sure how much more she could bear.

Aer turned toward her, taking her chin between his thumb and forefinger. When she met his brown eyes, she softened, the anger and frustration melting away at his gaze.

"We'll help our people best by winning this war quickly," he promised.

"You can't save everyone, Your Majesty," Fenian quipped. "Best to learn that now."

Aer's jaw clenched as Freya felt her own irritation flare. This time, though, she chose not to rise to his bait.

"Do we have everything we need?" she asked her father as Florian strode from the room.

He nodded. "Florian is settling a few things with my mother, first."

"Alright." She cinched her pack on her back, then adjusted the pouch she'd secured to her waist. "I have one more companion to get."

She only grinned at her father's suffering sigh. "Of course you do," he muttered.

A SHORT WHILE LATER, Freya and Toskr, now fully healed and on two legs, met the rest of their party back in the dining room, where Vara and Ana were waiting to see them off. It was clear Fenian wasn't happy about their additional companion, but Freya had come to bond with Toskr after they'd flown into battle together. More importantly, his ability to shift into a small animal would make reconnaissance much easier.

Presumably Fenian acknowledged the same thing, so all he said was, "My father sends his regards. For now, we all agree it is best for him to stay with our encampment and minimize the number of knights traveling in one cluster. Once we have secured the area, he will join us with the rest of his knights, and yours."

"Of course," Aer replied.

Freya turned to her aunt and gave her a sad smile. "It feels like we're constantly leaving one another."

"I'll see you in a few days." Ana inclined her head toward Byrric. "Hopefully, once we meet up, we'll have a better idea of which direction to head. I'm not as convinced as some of you that Kildin is fully lost."

Freya appreciated her aunt's optimism, even if she didn't share it. She kept that to herself, though, and squeezed Ana's hands. "Let's hope you're right."

Ana took her in a tight embrace. "I'm very much looking forward to settling with you in the capital once this is all over."

Pulling back, Freya grinned. "And here I thought you were going to live out the rest of your days with our kind. Does this mean you'll be my palace physician?"

"Of course." Ana shrugged. "It's not nearly as lovely here as I thought. Too cold and there aren't many males to choose from up here."

Shaking her head, Freya laughed. "Then let's get you to Iladel, where the suitors will be lining up to meet you."

Ana gave her a rueful smile and patted her cheek. "Be careful, Freya," she said, her tone turning grave. "The Between will make this a quick trip, but the gods only know what might be waiting for you on the other side." Her eyes shifted to Aer, who stood just beside Freya. "Keep one another safe, you hear me?"

"Always," Aer replied.

After giving her final goodbyes to Lazarus and Collin, who'd be leaving for the outskirts of Kildin the following day, and her grandmother, who instructed her to "get this damn war handled," Freya turned to Fenian. "Are we ready?"

The prince gave a sharp nod. "We are."

Wordlessly, Fenian took her and Aer's hands and transported them away.

Although she knew what to expect when they traveled the Between, Freya was still startled by the swirling, cold gray that surrounded her when Fenian transported them all to the Caelorian Forest. She didn't feel the same nausea she'd felt after her first trip to Avorell, but it was still a bit unsettling to go from standing in the warmth of her grandmother's home to the frigid pine forest of central Caelora.

They landed roughly a mile from the western edge of the valley, allowing themselves plenty of time and space to assess their surroundings, and to allow Toskr and Florian to see if there were any scouts in the area that might not be immediately visible.

"It's quite cold," Toskr commented, rubbing his hands up and down his leather-clad arms. "Is it always so cold up here?"

"We could send you back to your forest," Fenian muttered.

Toskr winced, but kept his mouth shut.

A moment later, Freya heard the quiet *hoot* of a mourning dove. Then, a tall, dark-featured elf materialized in front of them. Beside him stood a Lindorothian knight she recognized as Commander Birchard, a lion shifter and the recently-promoted commander of the Caeloran army, who'd received his post when the previous commander was killed during the siege of Kildin.

"Lethyra, what news do you have?" Ruehnar asked the elf.

"We have prepared camp in the valley," Lethyra replied. "Patrols have been monitoring the perimeter regularly and we have detected no disturbances as of yet."

"If you're ready, we can go over which places between here and Iladel we might want to use for arrival points," Birchard added, addressing Byrric.

"How long do we anticipate remaining here?" Aer asked.

The two knights exchanged a look. "Ideally, no more than a day," Lethrya replied. "Two at most."

"There have been some differing opinions of which areas are the best places to transport our knights," Birchard added.

"Of course," Aer said with a sigh. "Lead the way."

19

LEA

Lea and the rest waited in the drawing room until nearly midnight before Lindesson finally came to them and reported the enemy defeated. Even Rosie, sullen and angry as she was that her brother's army had been defeated, had seemed relieved when they finally were told they could go to their rooms and get some sleep. Fortunately, Rini had arrived that morning, so Lea hoped, between Rini and Tyna, they'd be able to help Rosie get into a better place.

A small part of Lea hoped such close proximity to war would show Rosie what an evil man her brother was. Another part of her knew that Rosie was undoubtedly biding her time until Willem sent his men in to rescue her. Lea didn't have the heart to tell Rosie that was unlikely to happen, and even if it did, it was even less likely to be successful.

As thrilled as she was that the human and Jotnar encampments outside Errest were no longer a threat, Lea slept fitfully, putting her in a sour mood the next morning.

Prince Ettrian, on the other hand, was positively joyful when he appeared for breakfast, conveniently just after Perida and Ordona had left to meet with Lindesson.

"Why so glum?" he asked as he dropped into a chair across from Lea. "Have you not looked outside?"

Lea's hand tightened around her fork as she held his gaze. Perida had spoken to Ettrian sometime in the night after he and General Lindesson had wrapped up the battle outside Errest, so Lea knew things had fared well for her city. The humans and Jotnar were either dead, captive, or fleeing to the north. The captives were held in stockades, while the dead enemy knights had been piled in the desert nearly two miles beyond the southern walls of Errest and were currently burning. She'd seen the column of smoke rising in the distance past her window when she rose at dawn but hadn't had the stomach to actually look for the source.

"We lost one hundred and sixty-two knights," Lea replied. Her mother had informed her of the loss at breakfast, and while it wasn't a large number, it still stung.

"Well, it might've been far more had we waited for those creatures to attack us," Ettrian said, stuffing a bit of egg into his mouth.

"You put your knights under *invisibility glamours* the moment we returned, Ettrian! No one but us knew they were there!"

"Yes, *Lea*, and those invisibility glamours allowed us to overhear the plans your enemies were developing." He took a sip of tea. "They were terrible, of course, but the element of surprise was crucial at ensuring those plans did not come to fruition."

"You could've at least warned my knights! For the gods' sakes, this is supposed to be a partnership!"

"The knights outside became aware of our plans quite quickly. There was no time to fuss with strategizing with everyone *inside* when your enemies were right in front of us, all but asking to be slaughtered." He popped a piece of bacon into his mouth. "Damned fools, the lot of them. I might have a word with their general if I hadn't already beheaded him."

It took all her willpower not to growl. She was caught between being furious he'd only been in her city for minutes before using his power to deceive her people, and grateful that he'd managed to be so wildly successful. This entire incident was a stark and necessary reminder that she couldn't always take him at his word. He'd agreed to help keep her city safe, but clearly their definition of such differed wildly. She couldn't assume his methods would align with hers *or* Lindesson's. She also couldn't assume that his methods were wrong just because they were different.

That flicker of respect she'd felt when she watched the battle he waged returned.

"You can't do that again," she said quietly. "We all need to be on the same page, or else someone will get hurt."

"Isn't that the point?" The corner of his mouth twitched upward. "For many, *many* people to get hurt?"

She clenched her teeth and took a steadying breath. "Someone *we don't want to get hurt* could get hurt. Is that clearer?"

"Fine, fine. I will inform any and all interested parties if I concoct such a deviously effective scheme again." He held up a finger and leaned forward, resting his elbows on the table. "I will not, however, apologize for tilting the battlefield to our benefit."

"Possibly. Not definitely."

Refusing to be cowed, Ettrian gave her a cajoling smile. "I'd say the hundreds of dead enemy knights currently burning in your desert would disagree." He grinned at her answering scowl, then jerked his chin toward her plate. "Eat, then give me a tour of your lovely home."

"Shouldn't you be heading back out to the battlefield to help the knights sort through everything?"

"Already done. I've assigned my own knights to work with yours to round up the stragglers. " His eyes flicked to the window above her head, then he met her eyes and smiled. "What more would you have me do?"

"Oh, I don't know. Perhaps strategize?"

He waved a hand dismissively. "I'm not really one for strategy, Lady Calliwell, as I'm sure you've gathered. I'm far better at delegating, and my brother has trained his knights to be good at what they do. His generals and yours are more than capable of collaboration."

Disbelief had her mouth falling open. "Are you truly going to spearhead a battle that ended in the deaths of more than one thousand enemy soldiers and then ask to spend the day meandering through my home?"

The first flicker of impatience shone in his golden eyes. "What, precisely, would you like me to do? I've assigned interrogators who will report to Lindesson. There are guards at the stockades, knights gathering escapees, and a rotation of knights to ensure the fires continue until all bodies are ash. As a general in the Royal Army, Lindesson has my blessing to direct my knights as he sees fit, with the understanding that if any believe he is *not* working in your city's best interest, they will report to me."

"Paperwork?" She was grasping at straws and she knew it.

He snapped his fingers and a sheaf of papers appeared in his hand, then he dropped them on the table between them. "This is a full report of all that transpired yesterday, including casualties and resources used, sent in triplicate to General Lindesson to share with Byrric and my father." He leaned back in his chair and gave her an expectant look. "My job is not to be a bureaucrat, Lady Calliwell. I was sent here to solve a problem. You may disagree with my methods but you cannot deny their effectiveness."

Jaw tight, Lea held his gaze, not quite knowing why she was so hell bent on proving him wrong. If there was one thing she'd learned about the elf prince it was that he was not one to be trapped by logic, because, while hasty, he didn't make illogical decisions.

With a sigh, she looked toward the window and imagined what the smoking heap of bodies to the south looked like after ten hours of burning. Closing her eyes against the image, she shook her head, then met his gaze. "This is hardly the time for a leisurely tour, Ettrian."

"Lea." He waited until she looked at him before continuing, and she struggled to ignore the feeling in her chest at the way he said her name. "If not because I'm bored, then because you are clearly in desperate need of a distraction."

"I don't need a distraction."

"Your hands were tied in the palace and you have no tasks to complete here," he pointed out. "Until your mother finds something that allows you to be productive, you need a distraction."

She gave him a wry smile. "And a bored elvish prince who starts battles for fun is a good distraction? If anything, you're likely a bad influence."

"Oh, I am without question a horrid influence," he agreed. "Truly, you should spend as little time with me as possible. Nothing good could ever come of it."

Something loosened in her, and she found herself fighting back a smile.

"Fine." She dabbed her mouth with her napkin and set it beside her plate. "What would you like to see first?"

His lips tilted into a full grin. "Perhaps your—"

"My personal chambers are not part of a friendly tour, Your Highness," she said drily.

"I was merely going to suggest a tour of your gardens," he said smoothly. "But now that you mention—"

"I mentioned nothing of the sort." She pushed back her chair and stood. "Now, if you'd like a tour of my home, we should get started. I'm meeting my mother and Aunt Ordona for lunch, neither of whom are very happy with you at the moment."

"Well, we wouldn't want to upset them further now, would we?" He stood, then gestured toward the door. "Lead the way."

Despite her annoyance with the prince, Lea was grateful to have his company while she waited to catch up with her mother and aunt. Ettrian was rash and foolish, but she couldn't deny that he'd turned things around for Errest quite quickly. Far more quickly than her own knights, although she'd never admit that out loud.

Lea led Ettrian toward the entrance to the courtyard that was currently in full bloom. She wasn't at a point where she wanted to bring him to the living spaces yet, and the garden would take up a fair chunk of their morning while she waited for lunch to come around.

"Gardens always seem like a safe starting point, don't they?" Ettrian mused as she pushed through the garden door in the east hall.

"They are," Lea agreed, waiting until he'd stepped over the threshold before shutting the wrought iron gate. "My father built this one for me and my mother."

"Because of your earth magic?" he asked as his eyes traveled over the garden.

Lea nodded. "She and I are the only ones permitted in here." She followed his gaze, wondering what he saw as he looked over one of the best gifts her father had ever given her. It was a large square split into four beds with narrow gravel paths leading between them toward a bigger circular bed at the center. Raised beds were attached to the walls of the courtyard, and a narrow path encircled the space. Hers was nowhere near the size of the one at the palace, nor as extravagant, but her father had taken great care to give her and her mother everything they needed to build the garden they wanted. Unfortunately, in their long absence, much of it had become overgrown. "That's why it looks a bit unkempt," she admitted, suddenly realizing it must look like a bed of weeds compared to the ones in Avorell.

But he surprised her by saying, "It looks well-loved." He slid a look her way. "Can you show me your favorite?"

"Oh." She cleared her throat. "Um, the jewel fruit trees," she said and pointed a finger toward the center bed. "Just over here."

They walked toward the small path that led to the circular bed, where half a dozen short trees, their branches heavy with glittering red and yellow fruit, formed a ring around the perimeter.

"They look like they need some help," Ettrian commented.

Lea smirked. "Why do you think I've brought you here?" She nearly laughed outright when his mouth fell open in shock. "You have to make up for throwing my city into a frenzy yesterday. Delivering the governor's jewel fruit to the market will help with that."

"You expect me to harvest fruit?" He looked as though the mere idea was unfathomable. "I've never—"

"Done any manual labor in your life?"

"Quite funny, but no. I was going to say I've never helped tend a garden before, but I suppose there can be a first time for everything." With a sigh, he unbuttoned the wrists of his sleeves and rolled them up, revealing the smooth skin of his muscular forearms. "Alright, then. Tell me what to do."

Lea shoved her own sleeves up, then picked up a basket off a nearby bench and walked toward the nearest tree. "It's quite complicated, you see." She reached up and gently twisted one of the ripe yellow fruits from a low branch and dropped it in her basket, then tossed him a smirk. "The trick is in the twist."

Ettrian pursed his lips. "Is that sarcasm, Lady Calliwell?"

"I wouldn't dream of it, Your Highness." She picked up another basket and pushed it against his chest. "Now pick."

20

LEA

Lea and Ettrian spent nearly an hour harvesting fruit. By the time they'd finished, they had three baskets filled to the brim with fresh produce. After depositing them with the kitchen staff, who would select some to preserve or use in recipes while setting the rest aside for the market, they were still left with nearly two hours before Lea was set to meet Perida and Ordona for lunch.

"Where to next?" Ettrian asked as they left the kitchen. "I feel quite energized."

Lea couldn't help but smile as she looked up at him, his dark hair falling across his forehead in a very un-princely way. "Yes, spending time in the garden often does that to me, too. Someday soon, my mother and I will go set the whole thing to rights. Come on, I'll show you my favorite spot in the house."

She led him through the halls and up the stairs that led to the wall around her home. It was a long walk, as the kitchens were clear on the other side of the house from where they were going, and on the ground floor, so they ended up passing through almost the entire building.

She paused when they reached the hall that would take them past both her room and the room Rosie Ristner was staying in. She didn't hear the princess's voice, but she could hear Rini and Tyna chattering away inside, clearly trying to get the princess to do something other than mope.

"I feel as though I should do something for her," Lea murmured. "Now that Rini is here, she and Tyna have been occupying Rosie, but I feel as if we should take her with us or something."

"She will jump off the roof the moment she has the opportunity," Ettrian replied.

"No, I don't think she will. She's too idealistic, too quick to assume her brother will send help for her."

"If he does, it will only be for appearances."

"Of course, but she's not prepared to accept that." With one last look toward Rosie's closed door, Lea continued down the hall.

When they passed the hall that led to her father's study, her stomach flip-flopped and she had to force herself to face forward and not look down the short hall to the door that still remained closed.

Not one to miss a thing, Ettrian nudged her arm. "What's down there, Lady Calliwell?"

"My father's study." She straightened her shoulders. "Come on, the stairs are just this way."

Something in her tone must've conveyed the message that her father's study wouldn't be a part of their tour, because Ettrian shifted the conversation without a single question.

"Where did you stand yesterday when you watched me vanquish your enemies?" he asked teasingly when they started climbing the stairs to the next floor.

Lea blew out a quiet breath and laughed, thankful he hadn't pushed. "That's actually where we're headed. Well, sort of," she amended. "You'll see."

"So you *did* watch me, then?" He smirked when she sent him a disparaging look. "Your words, not mine."

"No, I didn't watch *you*, Your Highness. Once our guards realized where I was, they insisted I come inside."

"Pity," he quipped. "You would've enjoyed it."

"Contrary to what you may think of me, viewing beheadings isn't exactly my favorite pastime."

"Then I'd say you haven't seen the right ones."

She slid him a look as they approached the door that would lead them out. "Has anyone ever told you you're a bit disconcerting?"

"Yes, but somehow I do not think that's a problem for you."

She ignored him and pushed open the door to the small bridge that would take them from the house to its battlements. She instantly detected the scent of smoke. It wasn't strong, thankfully, since they were upwind and on the opposite side of the city from where the dead were being burned, but it was enough to have her reconsidering their destination.

"Ah, the scent of burning flesh." Ettrian inhaled deeply as Lea shut the door. "I was *so* hoping we could get a bit more fresh air today."

"It's not my fault your elf senses are so strong." As they stepped onto the battlements, she turned left, aiming away from the smoke in the west that drifted south across the desert. When they reached the southeast corner, she stepped up to the wall, then gestured for him to join her in looking out through the wide crenelation.

"This is my favorite place when I'm home." She pointed to where the ocean met the eastern coast of Edhil nearly ten miles to the south. "Because of that."

Ettrian rested his hand atop the merlon beside them as he followed her gaze toward the place where the dense brush outside the city gave way to scorching sand. "It's quite beautiful," he said, his eyes drifting over the landscape. "I saw a bit of it from the ground, but the view from above is another beast entirely."

"It is," Lea murmured. "I like looking past the forest here and seeing the shift in the landscape. And at night, the view of the sky is unlike anything." She leaned against the wall, pressing her hands to the warm stone. "The desert has always been a... protector of sorts in my mind. Comforting in a way." She felt her cheeks warm, suddenly feeling a bit exposed. It was rare she brought company up here, mainly because it was rare she had visitors in her home for anyone other than her parents. Most of her time with friends or her cousins had been in Iladel, and none of her friends locally were the type to appreciate such a sight. Yet somehow it didn't surprise her that Ettrian did.

"I find it amusing how you speak of a thing that would kill an ill-prepared traveler in a single day as if it's something to cuddle."

She shrugged, appreciating his humor. "It's where my mother used to take me to practice my earth magic." She pointed toward an area a bit further inland. "There, right where the hills give way and the brush disappears."

"Your mother made you walk all that way just to practice your magic?" The prince let out an appreciative huff. "She and mine would get along quite well, I imagine."

"Based on what my queen has told me, I don't doubt it." Lea gave him a wry smile. "My grandmother did the same for my mother and Aunt Ordona when they were girls. It's a rite of passage, so to speak. There are no distractions, it's peaceful, and—"

"Hot?"

This time, her smile was more rueful. "Very hot, and therefore very motivating. Is there any place like this in your kingdom?"

Ettrian stared out at the dwindling forest and desert beyond. "The Summer Court has deserts, of course. None quite so vast, though. Or so deadly."

For some reason, that surprised Lea. "It's where your father's family originated, right?"

"It is. Most of my lineage is Summer. My mother is the first queen from any other court Avorell has had since Gregory and Helena married."

Lea didn't bother to hide her incredulity. "Why? That seems like something that would cause your people to be...upset." Probably not the best word choice, but it was all she could come up with.

The prince shrugged. "The elf females who run the Wild Hunt come from all over Avorell. Summer tends to have the strongest contenders, thanks in large part to carefully arranged marriages." He nodded toward the desert, then glanced her way and smiled in a way that softened something inside her. "But also due to...rigorous training in their youth. My mother proved Winter can be just as ferocious."

Again, Lea looked out at the place where her mother had helped her hone her magic to a fine point. "Yes, I suppose that makes sense." It still boggled her mind that the elves chosen as potential queens were forced to run the Wild Hunt to win the king's hand. She'd also never aimed to be queen or hungered for power in any way, though, so she supposed she couldn't understand the logic that went into such a brutal contest.

With a deep breath, she pushed away from the wall. "Come, I'd like to see what's happening out front before I go meet with my mother."

Turning away from the wall, they began their journey toward the entrance of her home.

"You know what I find amusing, Lady Calliwell?"

"No, but I'm certain you're about to tell me."

"I saw your expression when I mentioned our queens running the Hunt. You think my people are a vicious lot, correct?"

Seeing no sense in denying it, Lea nodded. "At times, yes."

"Yet here you are, leading me toward the place where you witnessed a battle yesterday, hoping to see more." He lifted his brows. "That takes a bit of a 'vicious' heart, wouldn't you say?"

Although her instinct told her to refute his claim, she forced herself to examine his words critically. She'd never considered herself one to enjoy violence or seeing revenge exacted on those who'd wronged her. But Ettrian was right—she wanted to see where her enemies had been slain the day before, to ensure they were, in fact, destroyed. And as they walked toward the western wall, she couldn't deny that her eyes itched to drift to her left where the plume of smoke was growing larger.

No, her heart hadn't grown vicious. But she couldn't deny that it was filled with a desire for vengeance. And that, she knew, could be the most destructive emotion of all.

21

FREYA

Freya, Aer, and the others spent nearly two days in the valley planning their path east. Each time a scout returned, they reported more humans on the Selnor, more Jotnar traversing the land, and fewer paths forward. Fortunately, the elves and Linds had combined their magic to set concealment charms around the valley, offering enough cover to conceal the camp without fully draining anyone's magic.

Ruehnar and his knights arrived once they'd settled into camp, nearly doubling the number of knights in their party. Freya marveled at the sight of them, with their gleaming armor, slim helmets, and bows that looked light as feathers. The armor looked far too thin to be effective against any type of assault, so she could only assume it was some magic of elvish craftsmanship that made it sturdy enough for battle.

On their second day in the valley, Silmar set out to retrieve Zane, Naedan, and Amara, promising to return as soon as possible. Despite their desire to continue monitoring northeastern Lindoroth and Madrya, Byrric and Ruehnar were insistent that the hawk shifters rejoin them for the remainder of the trip, allowing them to join Freya and Aer's guards in leading the rest of the shifters. Since it seemed the best path forward would be smaller jumps through the Between, they wanted as many shifters as possible to hide in plain sight, clearing the way for their massive party to arrive.

Impatience made it difficult for Freya to focus on everything they'd have to do before reaching the capital. A year ago, she might have insisted on taking the fight directly to Willem, ending him before he could launch any type of counterattack. Now, she saw how foolhardy that plan would be. His knights had flooded the eastern part of her kingdom and were quickly heading west, killing and pillaging unchecked–if her scouts' reports were accurate. They needed to be eliminated just as much as Willem, if not more so.

The only benefit to his men taking time to pillage the villages and smaller cities was that it slowed their progress into the kingdom. When she said as much to Byrric and Reginald, she was surprised when they both agreed.

"Greed makes fools of men," Byrric said, slurping up a bite of soup Florian had prepared when they stopped for the night. They hadn't been fortunate enough to find a cave to sleep in, but with a glamoured encampment of knights with them, they were well-protected sitting around a campfire in the middle of a field of tents.

"It will most certainly be their downfall," Reginald added.

"Let's hope so," Freya murmured as she tore off a chunk of hard bread and stared into the fire. "They have far less to lose than we do."

"They have their lives," Reginald countered.

"How much do they really care about their lives if they risk them in foreign lands for no reason other than the greed of their master?" She frowned. "What could he have promised them that would make this all worthwhile?"

"They're knights, Freya." Byrric leaned back against a large rock. "They follow orders."

"We humans have been told many lies about your people," Reginald told her. "The Jotnar, too. That you're monsters or barbarians with wicked magic that you'd use to kill us without a thought. If those were the types of stories you'd been raised on, you might not feel so badly about stealing from the lands you were invading."

Freya looked over at Aer, who was sitting with Florian and Ruehnar around a nearby fire. She and Aer had opted to divide their time between Reginald and the elves as much as possible. Unfortunately, that meant spending less time together, and on a trip such as this one, she desperately wished to spend as much time with her husband as possible. Any moment could be their last. She'd come to grips with that long before they'd set out on this journey, back when she had fought her way out of the forest in Avorell. It didn't change the fact that she wanted to spend as many moments as possible together, and not on the lookout for possible deceptions from the people who claimed to be allied with them.

There was nothing she wouldn't do to return her kingdom to its rightful state. But then again, wouldn't anyone say that before being faced with the improbable? If she'd taken off the blinders she'd been wearing to focus on getting her throne back, would she be so quick to run the Wild Hunt or ally with the elves? She'd been so focused on winning this war that she hadn't taken the time to consider what would happen if they didn't.

All of her thoughts sent her down a spiraling hole of what-ifs and worst-case scenarios that had been plaguing her lately. The idea of Lazarus and Collin, already established with Alyndra and several hundred knights in a small camp outside of Kildin, terrified her, knowing how quickly that tiny piece of Lindoroth could be decimated. The elves and Lindorothian knights would do their best to ensure that didn't happen, but even the most powerful of creatures couldn't stand in the face of overwhelming numbers.

And then there was Lea. Freya had never worried so much about a friend as she did Lea, despite how strong she'd proven herself to be. The regular updates Tyna had given were hopeful, but sporadic, so it was difficult to say whether her friend was truly alright.

Freya still struggled to trust Ettrian, despite the number of times he'd proven he was capable and willing to protect Lea's life. Lea seemed to trust him, though, which said something. She just wasn't sure what.

Abruptly, she set her canteen down and stood, cutting off whatever Byrric and Reginald were discussing. "I need to go for a walk," she muttered.

"Bring Rissen and Cecilia," Byrric called after her.

Right on cue, her two guards appeared at her side, both in their brown-black wolf forms. It took all her strength not to snap at them, tell them to stay behind and give her some desperately needed space.

It was their job to protect her, though. Just as it was her job to protect her kingdom.

And after the fiasco with Traust in Watoria, she'd sworn to the others that she would try to be less impulsive.

Aer reached up and took her hand briefly as she walked past, giving her a smile of understanding and a small nod of acknowledgement that he'd leave her be. Her heart squeezed at the knowledge that he knew her so well, although part of her wanted to reassure him that she would never push him away if he wanted to join her.

So, instead of thinking it, she said, "Care to take a walk, Highness?"

He smiled softly. "Of course." He excused himself from the others, then stood and brushed off his pants. "I wouldn't mind stretching my legs."

Rissen nudged her hand, a silent warning to stay close. Freya smiled at the way Cecilia bumped his hand out of the way, her own way of telling him to leave them be.

"We won't go far," Freya promised.

Aer slid his gloved hand into Freya's and they started down the path that cut between the small campfires, tents, and steaming kettles of the encampment. The knights had spread their tents and bedrolls throughout the valley and surrounding woods, scattered about in small clusters that formed an arc around the area, but all within twenty paces of one another.

"So, what's going on?" Aer asked once they'd put some distance between themselves and the rest of their party.

Freya tightened her cloak around her shoulders and exhaled, watching as her warm breath frosted the air in front of her. The frigid night promised snow, something she'd normally be excited for, but considering the circumstances, she could only pray to the gods that bad weather held off a few more days. At the very least, until they made it to the capital.

"I'm tired. Of walking, traveling, sitting, guessing." She looked at him in question. "Do you ever feel that way?"

Aer nodded, his boots passing quietly over the frozen forest floor. "Only always. Each morning, I want to ask Fenian to transport us directly to Iladel so we can end things with Willem right now. But it's not the best path. Not yet, at least."

Aer stopped, then turned to face her, taking her chilly hands in his. She wished she'd remembered to put on gloves. "But Freya, we *will* come out victorious. This war will end with Willem's head on a pike. I assure you of that."

With a small sigh, Freya leaned forward and rested her head against her husband's solid chest.

"How can you be so sure?" she whispered. "And why can't I have your confidence in us?"

Strong hands ran a path down her spine, pulling her close. "I believe we will come out victorious because I believe in *us*." Aer wrapped both arms around her and rested his chin on her head. "No matter where we are, we'll be together. That's enough for me."

With narrowed eyes, she pulled back and scowled at him. "We'll be *here*, Aerelius. In our kingdom, right where we belong, with Willem Ristner rotting in a pit somewhere."

Aer chuckled. "Well, if you said it, it must be true," he said as he led her further into the forest. When Freya glanced over her shoulder toward the camp, she saw just how well it had been hidden from sight, only visible if she focused her mind on its existence. Human eyes would simply look straight through it.

"Where are we going?" she asked. It was colder than she thought, and now that they were far from the warm fire in their tent, she was beginning to regret being so hasty in her need for solitude.

Aer shrugged. "Away. Rissen and Cecilia are close, and they'll call us back if we've gone too far."

They walked in silence toward an opening in the trees, where the ground dropped off into a gully. In the wet season, it would likely run with water, feeding the Selnor a few hundred yards beyond, clearly visible now in the absence of tree cover. Now, though, all she could see were fallen trees bridging the gap from one side to another and dead leaves and pine needles coating the bottom, so white with frost she could practically feel them crunching beneath her feet.

"Care to warm us a seat?" Aer asked, gesturing toward a wide, flat boulder that took up nearly half the width of the gully. They were on the outermost edge of camp, with knights patrolling the area. With the knights under glamours, Freya could pretend for a few moments that they were alone.

Smiling, Freya released his hand and pressed her hands to the boulder's surface. She closed her eyes, allowing her fire magic to heat the surface.

Once she was done, they sat down on the rock, legs pressed together, Freya's head on Aer's shoulder. On any other day, she might find it romantic. A moonlit stroll, sitting quietly in a grassy field, watching as the stars twinkled above.

"So, tell me, Freya Harridan," Aer began, "what will you do once this war is over?"

With a smile, she linked her arm through his. "When we win? First, I'd like to take our honeymoon. I'd say we're due that much."

"Ah." He nodded. "Yes, months of traveling around the kingdom, visiting governors and nobles, simpering for our subjects."

She punched him lightly on the thigh, then sighed wistfully and rested her head back on his shoulder. "I was thinking more along the lines of making love on a ship as we sailed down the Selnor or on a beach in Edhil, but if you'd rather simper, I suppose that's fine."

"Hmm." Aer brushed his lips across her brow. "Your plan sounds much better than mine, if we're being honest. Perhaps—"

With a start, Freya sat up, her sharp eyes trained on the tree line across the field. Aer stiffened beside her, then slowly stood, pulling her up by the arm. At the same moment, Rissen and Cecilia shifted to two legs and two elvish knights materialized in front of them.

"Are those lights on the river?" Cecilia whispered.

"Yes," Rissen replied. "Your Majesties, we need to go back to the camp now for orders."

The two elves drew their bows, the quiet whisper of wood on string barely audible in the dark. Without shifting focus, one turned his head slightly to the side. "Get the king and queen back to camp, now!"

It took everything in her not to ignore the knight's order, break into flight, and set the whole ship ablaze.

"Don't even think about it," Aer murmured, tightening his grip on her arm. "Let's go."

"But—"

"Let's go, Freya," Aer repeated, his tone brooking no argument. "Now."

Without waiting for her response, he tugged her away, Rissen and Cecilia flanking them.

"Do you think they know we're here?" Freya asked as they rushed toward the woods that would lead back to camp. "Or just coincidence?"

"Coincidence or not, they'll have confirmation shortly," Cecilia said grimly. "Our knights are on the move."

Suddenly, Fenian appeared beside them. "They've caught wind of us." As if on cue, an arrow flew past her ear, missing her by inches, when Rissen pushed her and Aer out of the way. Another flew, and Aer's magic lashed out, catching it and breaking it in two.

Without a word, Fenian gestured for Rissen and Cecilia to join hands with Freya and Aer, then he transported them all back to their tent.

22

FREYA

A moment later, they were standing in the middle of camp, in front of Byrric, Florian, and Ruehnar. Ruehnar was barking orders to the knights camped closest, switching between Elvish and Lindish, while Byrric and Florian were instructing everyone else on where to go and what to do.

"How do they know we're here?" Aer asked.

Ruehnar's face was grim as he paused to address them. "A tracker would be my guess. Even the best spells have weak spots; we all know this. They must have found one."

The hard line of Fenian's mouth twisted into a sneer. "Fortunately, we expected as much. The valley is surrounded by knights on all sides. The humans will not get far."

"I scented the change in the air when they rounded the curve just upriver," Florian said. "Two ships, but we won't know how many men until our scouts return."

Freya exhaled a sigh of relief. "Thank you, Lord Florian."

"We have more than enough knights to handle them," Ruehnar assured. "I do not think we should reveal our full arsenal just yet, however."

"I agree," Aer said. "All they would need is one man to flee upriver, and every human coming this way will know how many we have within two days."

Freya slowly started cracking the knuckles of each finger with her thumb, a nervous habit she'd picked up in recent weeks. Her body was coiled tight as a spring as her mind roved over the possibilities of where the next moments could lead them.

Another attack. They'd managed just over a week without a fight, without any losses. All she could hope now was that the enemy's numbers were low enough that they could be handled quickly.

An elvish knight loped toward them, coming to a stop beside Fenian. "What are your orders, Your Highness?"

Fenian sucked his cheek between his teeth, his eyes narrowing briefly toward the river before looking at Byrric. "We should split our knights off. Keep the bulk here and hidden, of course."

"Agreed," Byrric said.

With a nod, the knight ran off toward the others, shouting orders as he went. Fenian frowned, his eyes going distant. "Where is that damned--"

Rini popped into the air beside them. Her iridescent wings fluttered madly, glittering despite the dark night and studiously ignoring Freya's stare. "The humans are spreading out on the shore," she said before Freya could question why she was there without being called for. "Approximately fifty are heading toward the village down river near the foot of the mountain. In total there are approximately seven hundred human knights."

Freya's heart lifted a bit at that. The humans were vastly outnumbered.

Aer's eyes shot in the direction of the nearby village, only a few miles away. "And the second ship? The one that hadn't landed?"

"They were preparing to lay anchor just a few moments ago."

"Take out the ship that hasn't docked yet," Byrric told Fenian, then tilted his head toward Florian. "Save any supplies you find useful, but don't go out of your way to salvage." He looked at

Ruehnar, and when he nodded, Byrric added, "King Ruehnar and I will handle those who've docked."

Aer looked back toward the river, then to their spymaster. "Lord Florian, we'll leave the village raiders to you."

There was a small scuffling sound at Freya's feet, but before she could pull her magic forward, Toskr shifted into his elf form. "Where may I be of assistance, Commander?"

"You'll stay here with the king and queen," Byrric said. "Remain with their guards."

Freya opened her mouth to protest, her disappointment mirroring Toskr's, but her father cut her off. "Not this time, Freya. Now more than ever, keeping you both safe is crucial to this mission. Our monarchs need to be in one piece when we arrive at Iladel, and we have more than enough knights to handle this."

She looked at her husband in the hopes of finding support, but all she found was a grim determination mixed with resignation. Before she could protest further, Florian appeared at Byrric's side.

"The Valkyrie are waiting on the other side of camp," Florian told them. "They are going to help me on land. Their Majesties' guards will stay here, along with aerial support."

"Time to go!" Fenian shouted as his own soldiers began leaving camp. He added a few additional commands in Elvish, then the entire lot of them vanished.

It took all of Freya's strength not to insist they find some way for her to be put to use. There was no sense wasting time when there would be plenty of opportunities for her to fight later.

With a sigh, she looked at her father. "Be safe. All of you."

Once they were gone, Freya was too keyed up to sit still, and based on Aer's pacing, he felt the same. Toskr dropped down on the ground and leaned up against one of the tent poles, while Rodrick, Perinald, Rissen, and Cecilia stood watch in their wolf forms, all but ensuring she would never get past even if she were foolish enough to try.

"I hate feeling useless," she murmured to no one in particular, watching as her guards paced on quiet feet.

Aer paused his own pacing to take her hands. "You're anything but useless, Valkyrie, but this isn't like Watoria. We'd be more of a hindrance here than anything."

"He is correct, Your Majesty," Toskr said. "With my people and yours combined, it will not take long to defeat those invaders. This is not a war on two fronts spread wide across your lands as it was at your home city. Humans on a ship are child's play for my kind."

There was no valid argument against either of their points, but it didn't lessen Freya's frustration at all. Annoyed, she watched as their guards paced in front of the command tent. When movement drew her eyes upward, she saw two Valkyrie circling high above, their black leather garb nearly obscuring them in the night sky.

She didn't know whether she should be insulted that none of them seemed to trust her or thankful they all clearly knew her so well.

"I think I prefer the warmth inside," Toskr said, heaving himself to his feet and flinging open the tent flap.

"That's probably for the best," Aer murmured. He stood and pulled Freya to her feet. "Better to stay warm while we can."

When they got inside the tent, Freya sat down on a pile of blankets, reaching her hands toward the smoldering brazier in the center to absorb some warmth. Toskr laid down on the ground, tugging a blanket around himself as if falling back asleep in the midst of battle was a simple task.

Freya eyed him as he lay there, his face a peaceful mask despite all he'd been through, not only the past few weeks, but the last few millennia. His time in the Forest of Ages had jaded him, no doubt, but it still surprised her that he could close his eyes and rest at a time like this.

Aer nudged her with his elbow. "What's on your mind, Valkyrie?"

She jerked her chin toward Toskr, whose eyes had drifted shut, and smirked. "I'm just trying to figure out how one can sleep while a battle is raging just beyond our camp."

A smile twitched Toskr's lips, and his black eyes opened and met hers. "Thousands of beings have been killed in my presence, Queen

Freya. Slaughter has become little more than background noise to me."

Freya didn't quite know how to respond to that, so she clamped her lips together and kept her thoughts to herself.

"How is your side?" Aer asked, his expression a bit horrified as he shifted topics. "Is it healed fully?"

"It is," Toskr replied. He pulled back the blanket and lifted the edge of his tunic to expose the thin white line that was the only remnant of his stab wound from the battle the previous week. "Lord Florian is a gifted healer."

"Would it have healed on its own easily?" Freya asked.

"In time," Toskr replied, letting the hem of his shirt fall back into place and tightening the blanket once more. "When there is a lot of blood loss, injuries tend to heal more slowly."

Freya arched a brow. "In other words, had you told someone you were injured sooner, you might've healed more quickly?"

A sly smile curved his lips. "Of course, Your Majesty. But how else would I have received such wonderful treatment from the caretakers at Lady Balthana's home?"

Aer huffed out a laugh and Freya rolled her eyes. "You're absolutely incorrigible," she said, but she couldn't help but smile.

The three of them fell silent, Aer lightly stroking her knuckles with his thumb as Toskr curled tighter into his makeshift bed.

Freya had just decided to follow his lead and get more comfortable when the shouts and screams of battle reached her ears. Aer stiffened beside her, his hand tightening around hers. Low growls rumbled from the wolves' throats outside, their heavy footsteps halting.

Freya met Aer's eyes; her fear mirrored there.

They're close.

But even as the thought formed, the sounds of fighting ebbed, drifting further into the distance.

The minutes ticked by slowly as they waited for news, the sounds dying slowly as the battle ebbed. Freya wanted to leave and investigate things herself, and by the way Aer kept tapping his left foot, she could tell he wanted to as well. But each time she considered the thought, she'd be plagued by her father's disapproving voice in her head.

"I know what you're thinking, Freya," Aer murmured, his eyes steady on the tent opening. "Your father will be back soon enough. Be patient."

"I am patient," Freya muttered, then smacked Aer with the back of her hand when he snickered. She was about to chastise him when Rini appeared in the air beside them, causing them both to jolt forward. Toskr sat up in his makeshift bed.

"What's happened?" Freya demanded.

"I just wanted to give you an update, Your Majesties," Rini said. The tiny pixie was out of breath, her wings fluttering madly. "The elves have destroyed the ship that was still coming in. All of the men aboard are dead and the ship is in pieces."

"Thank goodness," Freya murmured.

"And the other ship?" Aer asked.

"Unfortunately, many of the humans scattered when they disembarked. They saw what was happening on the other ship and fled before attempting to fight. The commander and King Ruehnar are rounding up stragglers now, but it appears we have caught most of them. Lord Florian and the others were able to head off the men going toward the village."

"Have we lost anyone?" Freya asked. The elves would likely minimize their losses, but that couldn't keep her from hoping the Linds and their allies would come out of these smaller battles unscathed.

"Several are injured, but they should be able to heal quickly," Rini said. "We've been quite fortunate."

Too fortunate, Freya thought, but she kept her negative thoughts to herself. "Have we taken any captives?"

"A few," Rini said with a nod.

"Good," Aer said. "I'd like to question some of the captives."

"Of course, Your Majesty. I'll let the commander know."

Once Rini was gone, Freya frowned at Aer. "Why do you want to question them?"

His brow was furrowed in thought. "We still haven't heard much about Reykr Traust. I doubt these knights have seen what he's up to in the capital, but it's worth asking." He shook his head and peered toward the darkened forest. "It's making me uneasy."

"You and me, both, my love," Freya said with a sigh.

"I'd just like to know if we should expect him to pop out from behind a tree somewhere between here and home."

"Wouldn't that be nice?" Freya murmured. Aside from getting her kingdom back, the thing she wanted most was to put down Reykr Traust. She couldn't let a man who was so quick to spit on her mother's memory get away with it. Especially not one who professed to hold any amount of love toward Cina Enrieth.

A heavy quiet suddenly settled over the tent, one so viscous it had Freya holding a hand up to silence whatever Aer had been about to say. For a brief moment, she thought the fighting was done, but the feeling in her gut told her the opposite.

Slowly, she stood, snapping her fingers at Aer to pull him up with her.

Toskr went still, his head tilted as he cocked an ear toward the tent flaps. "Nothing good ever comes from that much silence," he whispered.

"No, it certainly doesn't," Freya replied as she let her magic flicker at her fingertips.

"Dare I ask if we could simply stay here?" Toskr asked.

Freya sent him a withering look. "You may stay if you like, Toskr, but we're going out there."

"We can't stay," Aer agreed. Freya felt his spirit magic humming, two blue ropes of power twining around his forearms and fingers.

The shouting suddenly resumed, only nearer now and accompanied by the snarl and snap of wolves' jaws. Several *thuds* sounded from outside the tent, the sound of Valkyrie landing around them.

"Toskr, are you coming?" Freya asked. When she looked at the elf, she saw indecision warring with agreement in his eyes, his desire to save his skin mingling with the promise he'd made to her.

"As king and queen, you both should stay put," he hedged.

"Toskr…"

"We won't be able to see anyone sneaking up on us," Aer said. "We're going out there to help our knights. Do what you wish, Toskr." Not waiting for either of them to respond, he moved toward the door, letting his magic unfurl as he moved. He'd gone half a step before Freya joined him. A moment later, Toskr had shifted to his squirrel form and scurried up to her shoulder.

23

FREYA

What Freya saw when Aer threw open the tent flap had her stopping in her tracks. Ruehnar and Fenian were leading Lindorothian knights, wolves, and elves against dozens of Jotnar knights. Jaws snapped and grunts of pain sounded, screams of anguish as blade met blade and teeth met flesh. Preparing for the worst, Freya summoned a handful of daggers using her air and fire magic.

There wasn't a human in sight.

In the center of it all, Reykr Traust and her father were fighting each other.

"Freya—" Aer said.

She ignored him and stalked forward, Toskr's tiny nails digging into the dip in her shoulder with each movement. Aer was at her back, his magic flaring to either side as he charged after her, whipping toward any enemy knights that came at them. Two wolves ran toward her, Rissen and Cecilia, likely to push her back, but she'd have none of it.

A Jotnar charged toward her, but she tossed a dagger at him, lodging it in his throat. Just as he fell, Traust caught her eye over

Byrric's shoulder. With a laugh, he ducked Byrric's sword as it swung toward him, throwing up his own sword to parry the blow.

"There she is!" he shouted as he shoved Byrric back. "The disgraced queen and her orphaned king." He grunted as Byrric shoved a boot in his gut, sending Traust stumbling to the ground. He flared his broad, black wings and stabilized himself quickly enough to catch Byrric off guard with a blow to the jaw.

Freya threw her daggers out, slicing at knights that came toward them. She felt the sizzle of spirit magic as Aer reinforced her own power, ensuring all the knights she hit stayed down. Rissen and Cecilia hadn't bothered trying to hold her back, focusing instead on keeping the enemy away from their king and queen.

When she was within a few yards of Traust and her father, she began flinging her magic blades at the monster fighting Byrric. He deflected them all easily, but they drew his attention enough that Byrric was able to launch his own attack.

"Weak, just like your father!" Traust roared, blocking a punch from Byrric. "Come fight me with your fists, little girl!"

Toskr squeezed her shoulder twice, then leapt, shifting mid jump to take on two Jotnar that were approaching from Aer's blind spot.

"Get back to the tent, Freya!" Byrric roared. He threw another punch at Traust, but the distraction allowed Traust to clip him with the pummel of his sword.

"Oh, let the child come and fight," Traust taunted, stepping just out of range of her father's sword. "It'll make it that much easier to end her life."

"I wouldn't count on it," Freya snapped, continuing to chuck daggers at him, one after another, drawing on her deep well of magic.

Somehow Traust still managed to fight off both her magic and Byrric's brute force. Knights continued to charge, but her focus was solely on the man trying to kill her father.

"Freya watch out!" Aer shouted just as Rissen grabbed her by the hem of her jacket and tugged. She ducked, narrowly missing the swing of a Jotnar sword. Aer caught it with a rope of his magic and yanked the knight forward, catching the weapon and using the male's own blade to impale him.

Keep going, she told herself. The closer she got, the harder it became to fight through the knights attacking them from all sides. She could see her father tiring, but she knew he wouldn't give up, not until Traust was dead.

Just as she reached them, Traust kicked out a leg, tripping Byrric and sending him to the ground. But instead of aiming his blade at Byrric, Traust turned toward her, his massive sword poised to strike. She raised her two short blades to meet his, but it was too big, too broad for her to hold him off for more than a few moments.

Aer's spirit magic unfurled once again, twining around Traust's blade and stopping his momentum. Byrric rose from the ground, immediately ducking out of reach of Traust's other arm. Traust yanked at his sword, gaining an inch, then another. Suddenly, he dropped the weapon and roared, slapping a hand to his neck as he whirled in fury to the squirrel that was now scurrying off into the darkness. Silver dust exploded all around him as Rini appeared, her pixie dust temporarily blinding him.

Byrric took the precious seconds Toskr and Rini had given them and kicked Traust's sword away. Freya threw four more daggers at Traust's back, and this time, they hit their mark, lodging in his wings.

With a roar of fury, he rounded on her. It took everything in her to hold his vicious gaze and not stumble back at the enormity of him.

Then, he was airborne, leaving his sword and his knights behind.

"Godsdamned coward!" Freya shouted as he became no more than a flash of dark against the full moon.

"Freya, Aerelius, go!" Byrric shouted, picking his own sword up from the dirt and wiping his bloodied nose with the back of his hand. "Get away from here!"

She ignored her father and looked at Aer. "You go left, I go right?"

He gave her a sharp nod. "I love you."

"I love you, too."

She ran to help the others, glancing back only long enough to see him dive into the fight with the rest of their people. It took most of her energy not to look at the ground, see which of her own were dead. She saw at least one pair of wings, but she ignored the twisting in her heart as she pushed forward, letting her magic unfurl around her as they took out the rest of the enemy knights.

BY THE TIME DAWN CAME, the Linds and elves had lost a combined fifty-two knights, including one Valkyrie. The humans had been handled within a few hours, including those who'd been heading toward the village upriver. Fortunately, they hadn't been hard to take down, so those who'd been sent to deal with them were able to return to camp and help with the rest of the Jotnar knights that Traust had left behind. It was clear the humans had been sent as a distraction by Traust to clear a path for him and his knights to attack Freya and Aer.

"I suppose we should thank him, really," Freya said to her father as the sun rose over their camp. Aer was off with Ruehnar and Fenian, so she'd taken a few minutes to talk with her father in private. "Traust hand-delivered us seven hundred human men to eliminate from Willem's army. I'd call that a partial win, at least." Her eyes scanned the camp, covered with bodies, both of her own people and her enemies. "What do we do with the dead?" In Watoria, they'd been burned, the fires tended to for days.

"Burn them," Byrric replied. "Once we clear our camp, we'll pile them there," he gestured toward the center of the valley, "and light a fire. We'll leave a few knights behind to keep it going until they're ash. If nothing else, it might cause those looking for us to come here while we head east."

Freya nodded, then rolled her neck, letting out a few cracks. It had been hard to ignore the grunts and groans of the injured and dying the last few hours, but it had finally gone quiet in the valley. Healing magic was flowing into the Linds and elves who'd been hurt, and the few humans they'd captured for questioning were tied to a tree awaiting transport to their next destination.

A shadow passed overhead, but before her fear of Traust's return could register, a large vulture landed atop one of the bodies nearby, quickly joined by a second. She glanced up and saw several more beginning to circle overhead. Soon, the valley would be full of carrion birds looking to eat their fill.

Stomach roiling, Freya turned away and went off in search of her husband. Hopefully he could give her something to keep her mind off the pile of corpses they were about to leave behind.

24

LEA

Rini received word of the attack on Freya and Aer's camp not long after dinner. She barely said goodbye to Tyna before fleeing to be with Freya, refusing to be anywhere but by her side during battle. Although the numbers she'd give Lea—two human ships against more than two thousand Lind and elf soldiers—were nearly concrete proof of a human defeat, Lea was still on pins and needles all night, unable to sleep until Rini finally returned during breakfast to tell them all was well. When Rini gave Lea, her mother, and Ordona the news, Lea nearly wept with relief.

"All is well for now," she said as she hovered over the end of the dining table. "They'll be moving on today."

"Thank you, Rini," Perida said. "Will you be staying with us?"

"No, Lady Calliwell." Rini glanced at Tyna, floating beside her. "As much as I would like to stay with my sister, my place right now is with my queen."

"I thought she wanted you to stay here?" Lea asked with a frown.

"I am hopeful Her Majesty will allow me to remain with her," Rini said. "If she refuses me, I'll return here."

"Her Majesty gave you *orders*," Tyna ground out, silver eyes simmering. "Very specific *orders*."

"And *I* think Her Majesty's desire to keep me safe with be a hindrance–"

Tyna gasped. "Are you questioning Her M–"

"Alright, enough," Ordona said, holding up her hands as Lea covered her face with her own to conceal her amusement. "Tyna, no one is questioning the queen's orders. But Rini, as the queen's attendant, refusing to obey orders could lead to your dismissal. Is that something you're willing to risk?"

Rini pursed her lips and rolled her shoulders back. "Yes, Your Majesty. I am willing to risk that if it means my queen will be safe. I was not by her side in Avorell and that is something I will always regret. If she chooses this to be the reason to dismiss me, so be it."

"We all know that won't happen," Lea said.

"Be that as it may," Perida said, "it's best to be aware of the risks. Rini, you're welcome to return here at any time, whether you are in the queen's employ or not."

Rini blanched a bit at that, but she forced a smile. "Let's hope Her Majesty is in a forgiving mood." She darted forward and grabbed Tyna in a tight hug. "I will see you all soon!" Then, she vanished.

The rest of the day was a blur of updates from the elvish and Lind soldiers outside the city. Planning for reopening areas that had suffered in some way or another since the war began became the main focus. Many shopkeepers and business owners had taken hits when the city gates were blocked, making them unable to acquire the necessary resources to run their businesses for several weeks. Some, such as the grocer, had been able to use earth magic to keep some things from spoiling, but not all had been so lucky, and those who were didn't have a bottomless well of magic.

With her mother occupied with Ordona and Lieutenant Lindesson, Lea had little to do within her own home. Everything had settled back into business as usual once they had returned, and she quickly found she didn't have much to contribute to the planning meetings that were taking place.

So, the following morning, she met with her mother after breakfast to discuss her role more explicitly. After a bit of back and forth,

Perida agreed that Lea should start making rounds in the city to check in with the citizens in the market district. Even if there was nothing she could do for them immediately, her presence as a member of the governing family would at least show them she had every intention of helping get things back to normal.

"Be careful," Perida said sternly as they wrapped up their conversation in the drawing room. "And bring Tyna with you. And Iska."

"Of course," Lea said with a nod. "I don't think they'd allow me to do otherwise," she added.

"Yes, I suppose you're right." Perida pursed her lips and sighed. "I want you to know, Lea, that I'm not keeping you inside because I don't think you can handle any of the work we're doing. I just want you to be safe."

"I know, Mother," Lea replied softly. "But being kept safe nearly drove me to tears in the palace. Regardless of why Jonas kept me sequestered so much, I can't handle that solitude and inaction anymore."

Perida's expression softened. "I know, darling. For now, though, please just stick to the market. We need to reassure our citizens that we will bounce back from this, and that we'll be at their side in the meantime."

"That's my goal." Lea stood from the chair in front of her mother's desk. "I'll check in when I return?"

Perida nodded, then rose to see her to the door.

Lea opted against taking a carriage, instead choosing to walk from her home to the central square. It wasn't particularly close, but it would give her a chance to stretch her legs. The influx of elves and Linds had allowed them to seal the city more effectively from invaders, giving her added confidence that she could take a walk in peace instead of fear.

It also gave Tyna the opportunity to burn a bit of her own energy. Despite how much she'd been flitting back and forth between Lea, Rini, and the other pixies that remained in Lindoroth, Lea knew her attendant had been feeling just as confined as she had. Iska, not so much, but even his steps seemed lighter as they moved into the city.

"How do you plan to help them?" Tyna asked as they moved leisurely along the cobblestone street. "If we still can't get out of the city?"

Lea glanced at Tyna. "Mainly, helping them figure out what to do with any surpluses, arranging accommodations, that type of thing. But if nothing else, I hope seeing that my mother and I are back in the city and taking steps to improve our city's circumstances will help."

Tyna did a slow dip, then fluttered her wings and did a graceful spin in the air. "Oh, your presence has already done wonders in that respect," she said with a sigh as she tilted her shining face toward the sun. "I've been monitoring things throughout the city, checking in here and there, and I can tell you without question that things are already looking up."

Lea smiled faintly. "Well, I hope that's truly the case. It could take weeks to safely reopen the city gates. I can't imagine what the past month has been like for them."

"Everyone is struggling, my lady, but your citizens know what you've been through. I can assure you, word of your time in the palace has spread. Everyone knows how much you helped the king and queen, and as far as I can tell, any who've spoken ill of your intentions have been silenced swiftly."

As her smile grew, Lea was suddenly more grateful for Tyna's presence than she had been in some time. "You *have* been spying, haven't you?"

Pink tinged Tyna's cheeks as she ducked her head. "It's part of my job, Lady Calliwell. I know more than most would probably prefer, but I do it to keep those I care about safe."

"And you do it wonderfully," Lea replied with a grin. "Now, since you're so knowledgeable, where to, first?"

Tyna tapped her chin as she floated along in the air. "Grocers who offer mainly dry goods are doing well enough, so I would suggest starting with the produce peddler. He has a surplus of fruits and vegetables due to citizens being unable to enter the city to buy their food, so he's at a loss as to what to do. He's been using his earth magic, but it's beginning to wear thin."

"Perfect. I'd like to speak with some residents, maybe other shop-keepers to see if they might be willing to donate canning supplies to help with storage for the time being." Relief filled Lea's heart as a solid problem and solution materialized in front of her.

"Of course, Lady Calliwell."

"Thank you, Tyna," Lea said after a moment.

Tyna sent her a curious look. "For what?"

"Everything." Lea smiled. "You've kept me sane these last few weeks, and now here you are, advising me on how to help my people. You're a wonderful friend."

"Oh, but I'm your attendant, Lady Calliwell!" Tyna put a hand to her chest, her eyes wide. "This—"

"Is what friends do, Tyna." Lea softened her tone and smiled. "Your job as my attendant is to do my hair and makeup, find the right outfit for each occasion, give me advice on personal matters. It is not to help me rebuild my city and spy on my enemies. And yet, here you are, doing just that."

Tyna blinked her wide, silvery eyes several times. Finally, she gave a hard sniff, wiped her nose with the back of her hand, then nodded.

"Thank you, Lady Calliwell. You are...a wonderful friend as well. I'm fortunate to have the honor of your company."

Lea beamed. "Likewise."

Tyna gnawed at her lip, her tiny fang threatening to draw blood. "My Lady there's one more thing..."

Lea looked at her friend curiously. "What is it?"

Tyna began wringing her hands. "Oh, perhaps it's improper—"

"Out with it, Tyna."

"I think you should try to spend more time with the princess," she said in a rush. "She may push you away, but she is just so terribly lonely. Rini and I tried to keep her company, but she wasn't receptive at all. And now, with Rini back with the queen...perhaps you can encourage her to come to breakfast with you? Or lunch? Tea?"

Lea pursed her lips but kept her eyes forward as they continued down the street. "Have you been spying on Princess Rosie, as well, Tyna?"

"Yes, of course," she replied, as if it were the most obvious thing in the world. "You all seem to think the poor thing will chuck herself off a balcony the moment she gets a chance." Her shoulders slumped a bit as she drifted in the air beside Lea. "She cries so much."

"I don't know what to do for her, Tyna," Lea muttered. "She declined my last three offers to join me for a meal and refuses to acknowledge that Willem is vile, despite what she witnessed in the dining room. I've tried talking to her, but for the gods' sakes, we did take her from the forest. We couldn't exactly leave her there unconscious for as long as it would've taken her to wake up from traveling the Between, and going back into the palace simply wasn't an option."

Tyna deflated even further.

"I'll try to talk with her again," Lea said softly. "But I can't promise you the outcome you'd like." She gave her a small nudge. "You could befriend her, if you'd like."

"I've tried," Tyna responded morosely. "She threw her slipper at me, so I tossed some pixie dust in her eyes. It truly was not my best moment, Lady Calliwell."

Lea couldn't help but smile at that.

LATER THAT AFTERNOON, General Lindesson called a meeting with Lea, Perida, Ordona, and Ettrian. When he found her just as she and Tyna returned from their walk, Lea shot a confused look at her attendant. She hadn't been outright invited to any type of planning meetings since the day they arrived, which she assumed would be the norm going forward.

"What's this about?" Perida demanded once Lindesson had shut the drawing room doors behind them. "Has something happened?"

"I've spoken to my scouts. It seems Jonas Edrin has left Iladel with a small squadron and is headed this way." Lindesson looked at Lea. "I think you should prepare for the fact that he might be coming here in an attempt to take you, and probably the princess, back to Iladel."

Lea's brows flew up, unsure she'd heard him correctly. "Excuse me? Why on earth—"

"It would be...poor form for him not to come after his wife and for Willem to leave his sister to fend for herself," Lindesson replied. "To be fair, I think any attempt Jonas makes will simply be to appear loyal to Willem in front of his knights." His eyes flicked to Perida's. "Assuming he's remained loyal to us, that is."

"Jonas has plausible deniability when it comes to Willem, as I'm the one who took you and Rosie from the dining room," Ettrian told Lea. "He was left behind, therefore Willem has little grounds to believe he colluded with me."

"But he let me go!" Lea protested. "This wasn't a matter of him being left behind, and we both know Willem knows it."

"One of two things is happening here," Ettrian told her, his tone going firm. "Willem either knows Jonas is a turncoat and is using this mission as a way to get Jonas out of his hair. Or he believes I stole you and the princess away and is sending Jonas to bring you both home 'safely.'"

Tyna put a small hand on Lea's shoulder. "You must know how this looks, my lady."

"Do you truly think this is a concern? Him taking Lea?" Perida frowned at Lindesson, then her sister. "Ordona?"

Ordona's lips were a thin line as she appraised Lindesson and Ettrian. "Even if Jonas is still loyal to us, he would need to come to save face with Willem, regardless of his plans for when he arrives." She turned sad eyes on her sister. "So yes, Perida, I do think this is a legitimate concern. Even if we destroy this squadron, Willem will just send another. I don't think he would be as focused on Errest if Lea and the princess weren't here."

"Make no mistake, Lady Calliwell, we will be able to easily handle the group being led by Jonas," Lindesson assured her. "It's a small squadron, so eliminating them won't be an issue even if you want to spare Jonas." He nodded toward Ettrian. "His Highness and I have also sent out scouts in case Willem sends additional knights behind Lord Edrin, which is the larger concern."

"Can't you just destroy them all like you did the ones who were here when we arrived?" Lea asked, directing her question at Ettrian. "Make Willem believe Jonas has been captured?" The thought of handing Rosie back to her brother, a man who would undoubtedly punish her for the show of fear she displayed when he killed Effina and Lessia was nauseating.

"That is the plan, but unfortunately the element of surprise has left us," he replied. "The knights we killed when we arrived were taken completely off guard. Few had weapons at the ready, none were expecting our type of magic. Willem must know we're here by now. Any humans or Jotnar who come south will expect us and plan accordingly."

"Rest assured, the elves and Linds will keep them at bay," Lindesson said. "But we need to decide how to handle Jonas...politically when he arrives."

"This is ridiculous," Lea snapped. "Willem didn't go after Isadora when she fled with Reginald. Even though he knew Dania was impersonating Isadora, he would've needed to pretend to care if he wanted to appear the loving king and husband."

"Willem led his men and his people to believe she'd been kidnapped and murdered by your king and queen in collusion with Reginald," Ettrian countered. "He only spoke of her betrayal in closed meetings with people who were fully aware of the circumstances. As Isadora was well-loved, that type of fuel will undoubtedly add to his support in Dystone, as will news of the princess's supposed kidnapping."

Lea crossed her arms and arched a brow. "And how, exactly, did he spin his immediate marriage to Effina?"

Ettrian shrugged. "All kingdoms need a queen. Willem, gracious as he is, opted to set his grief aside and give his subjects a new queen to help ease them more smoothly through...turbulent times."

Tyna cleared her throat. "The last time I checked in at the palace, I heard Willem had sent out notices that Lessia had betrayed them all by poisoning Effina, giving Willem no choice but to kill Lessia," she said. "The knights who'd assisted him in the dining room when he poisoned Lessia and Effina have been...silenced to avoid having any witnesses who could dispute his version of events."

"Gods above," Lea muttered. She'd heard absolutely nothing from Jonas regarding Willem's portrayal of Isadora's disappearance to his own people; she assumed everyone knew Isadora had run off with Reginald. Thinking back, it made more sense for Willem to pretend he'd been betrayed by his brother, not his wife. It also didn't come as a huge surprise that he'd found a way to make himself out to be a martyr in the midst of invading another kingdom.

Ettrian sighed. "All of that said, Willem has done more than enough to attempt to save face considering the circumstances. Jonas will need to follow his lead, which means he will need to at least pretend he plans to rescue you from a traitorous elf."

"I'm sorry, but do we really think anyone in that palace actually believes I was taken against my will?" Lea looked at them each incredulously. "Willem made it clear he didn't buy my story about my 'wretched' family. I can't believe he's the only one who saw through it."

"Many believed your story, my lady," Tyna replied. "Not staff, so much," she added with a quick glance at Ordona, "but the humans and Jotnar there believe Prince Ettrian kidnapped you and the princess. I haven't spoken to him, but I would imagine Jonas feels he can't say otherwise, not while he's in the capital."

"Lea, you must understand that Jonas is stuck between a rock and a hard place," Ordona said. "Lord Edrin needs assistance to ensure he maintains control of Jotunheim. If he thinks he can guarantee Willem's aid by returning you to Iladel, well, that's something you should prepare yourself for."

"Then we'll guarantee our allegiance in helping him settle in Madrya," Lea said. "Right?"

"That's our plan, yes," Lindesson replied. "However, with the king and queen fighting their own battles, we need to be a bit more creative with our numbers. For now, we will wait until Jonas reaches us. When he does, we will reassess our stance on how to aid him."

Lea found herself looking to Ettrian as she considered her response. "If he comes here, do you think he'll truly try to bring me back to Iladel?"

"I think Jonas is not so much of a fool that he thinks that would be possible." His molten eyes bore into hers. "And if he does try, I will be happy to send him back to that bastard of a king, minus an appendage or two."

For whatever reason, his words brought more comfort to her than she liked. The thought of Jonas being so duplicitous...it just wasn't something she was prepared to accept. But knowing Ettrian would follow through on his threat made that possibility a bit easier to swallow.

She held his gaze for a moment, then gave a small nod, hoping he could see the gratitude in her eyes.

25

LEA

After their meeting regarding Jonas, Perida and Ordona went off with Lindesson to have a brief strategy meeting, while Ettrian went to check in with his knights, and Tyna flitted off to check in with her sister. Lea, having no place with any of them, found herself alone for the rest of the day.

She'd hoped to dine with her mother, but when no one had returned by sundown, she opted to take dinner in her room. She was already verging on feeling lonely. So much so she found herself walking toward Rosie's room in the hopes of enticing the girl to join her for dinner. Even if they ate in silence, at least Lea would have company and Rosie would have a break from the stale air of her room.

When Lea reached Rosie's room, she hesitated, her knuckles hovering a breath away from the door for a moment before she gently rapped on the wood.

Rosie's answering huff was loud enough to be heard through the door, so Lea took that as an invitation to enter and pushed open the door.

She found the princess sitting in an overstuffed chair by the window, knees drawn to her chest, head cocked against the chair's tall back. Her eyes seemed to focus lifelessly on the scenery outside the window. When she didn't protest any further at Lea's entrance, Lea stepped into the room and waited silently for Rosie to look at her.

After a moment, Rosie dragged her gaze from the window to meet Lea's stare. It nearly broke Lea's heart to see the sadness and anguish there, the anger that had been so present just a few days earlier, gone.

"What do you want?" Rosie asked.

Lea folded her arms and leaned against the wall beside the door. "You need to leave this room."

"Why? So you can try to convince me to come around to your way of seeing things?" Rosie sniffed. "No thank you."

Lea shook her head. "I'm not trying to convince you of anything, and we can send you within a few hours' walk to the palace the moment you say the word. But you know that already."

The princess scowled. "Knowing how those wretched elves work, whoever you send me with will likely take me to the middle of that desert—" she jerked her chin toward the window "—and leave me there to starve," she said scornfully. "So again, I say, no thank you."

Lea gave the girl a curious look. "You know, for someone who claims to want to go home, you're certainly doing very little to get yourself there."

"Like trust you to transport me with that elf you whored yourself out to?"

Lea snorted. "That elf is bound to adhere to the bargain his family made with the true king and queen of Lindoroth. If he's ordered to take you back to Iladel, he will."

"Why bother?" Rosie asked airily. "My brother will come for me soon enough."

Lea was dangerously close to aborting her mission of kindness. "Ah, yes, when he sends his army here to slaughter even more of my people."

"Perhaps if you hadn't kidnapped me, you wouldn't have to worry about your people."

"Oh?" It was taking all of her willpower not to scream at the princess. "Then tell me, Rosie. What did the people of Lindoroth do to deserve a mass slaughter at my king and queen's wedding? What did the people of Errest do to deserve the incursion that caused this city to seal itself off from the rest of Edhil? We hadn't kidnapped a princess then, had we?"

"My brother tried to keep Lessia's knights under control!" Rosie cried. "None of that was his plan. He wanted a peaceful takeover."

"Do you know nothing of history, Rosie? Did you truly believe he and Lessia could come to a royal wedding and ask nicely to take over the godsdamned kingdom? Gods above, were you ever allowed to leave your home, or did Willem ensure you stayed stuck in your room with nothing but fairy tales to read?"

"My brother loves me," Rosie snapped.

Lea knew she should let it go, but the anger of the past month had been simmering beneath her skin, itching to be let loose.

She took a step closer to Rosie. "Are you truly so delusional as to believe the man who poisoned his ally and wife, the man who attempted to take me as his wife while he continued to lead the slaughter of my people, actually gives a shit about your well-being?" She clenched her fists, ignoring the stricken look on Rosie's face. "The man you saw in that throne room, Rosie, the man who threatened to throw you in the dungeon for showing fear, is the same man who threatened to hang my father's corpse at my city gates to get my people to bend to his will. He's the same man who allowed my mother to rot in a dungeon covered in her husband's blood for *weeks*." She eyed the princess with dangerous calm. "You profess to love your betrothed. How would you feel if someone slit his throat and forced you to soak in his blood for a month?"

Rosie recoiled as if she'd been slapped, and Lea had a feeling she might've taken it too far.

"I'm sorry if my words were harsh," she said quietly. "But that's who your brother is, Rosie. The sooner you come to grips with that reality, the better." She smoothed her hands over her dress and collected herself before looking at the princess again. Her face was completely devoid of color. "I'm going down to dinner now. You can call for food or come down and join me."

Rosie's lower lip began to quiver.

"I understand that may not be what you want right now," Lea continued. "But I'm going to leave this door open. It was already unlocked, which I'm sure you knew, but in case there was any doubt, now there's no question. With a few exceptions, the house is open to you."

With that, Lea turned and stalked from the room, now more than content to dine on her own.

AFTER DINNER, Lea made her way to her mother's library in the drawing room, hoping a good story might distract her from that disastrous conversation with Rosie. Yet when she curled up in a chair to read, her mind kept drifting toward war, deceit, and betrayal, making it impossible to focus on the romance novel she'd plucked from the lowest shelf.

Later, as she tossed and turned in bed, trying and failing to focus on the gentle breeze blowing outside her windows. The clock in the center of town struck midnight, its heavy gongs echoing mournfully through the city. Lea found herself counting each one, listening as the last rang out, its sound fading into nothingness.

With a huff, she kicked back her bedding, suddenly feeling too confined beneath the layers of fabric. She sat up, letting her bare feet rest on the wood floor. The old wood was smooth with age, warm to the touch, and instantly put her senses at ease.

It was late enough that she was unlikely to run into anyone in the halls, but she still grabbed a satin robe from a hook on her wardrobe door and shrugged it on over her nightdress.

As she'd expected, the house was silent, the halls empty. Most of the sconces were extinguished, but the rest offered enough light to navigate the halls in the dark without stumbling. On a normal night, the silence mixed with the low light would've calmed her. Her home had always felt safest at night, when she could hear the silence from outside and know that all was right within her city.

Tonight, she saw knights standing guard outside as she passed the windows. She could make out the faint glow of firelight from the encampment through the windows in her hall, elves and Linds who'd taken the place of the humans and Jotnar that once surrounded her city.

Willem's face flashed unbidden through her mind, and she was instantly seized with hatred so powerful it turned her vision red.

Pushing thoughts of Willem aside, she continued through the halls, stopping only when she realized her bare feet had led her to the uppermost floor. At the end, the door to her father's office was shut tight. She knew it had been opened in her absence, as Byrric would've needed to ensure Lieutenant Lindesson had everything he needed to run the city. But Orin Calliwell hadn't darkened its doorway in over a month, nor would he ever again.

She took a few steps closer, then closed her eyes and exhaled a quiet breath before closing the distance. Steeling herself, she lifted the latch and pushed open the door.

His scent hit her first. She'd barely taken in the dark wood and leather that surrounded her when the smell of amber and smoke, a scent so unique to her father, flooded her nostrils. This was the closest she'd been to him since Freya and Aer's wedding night. The closest she would ever be again.

The space was just as he'd left it. The rough-hewn desk made of Edhilian driftwood and studded on the front with two large emeralds —her realm's prized export—sat silent in the middle of the room. Moonlight from the window behind it cast shadows on the inkwells, notebooks, and other accouterments that adorned its surface. Everything was in order and waiting for the governor's return.

Quietly, Lea leaned against the wall beside the door, unable to move further into the room and unsure if she even wanted to. As she let her eyes drift about the room, taking in the sheafs of paper on his desk, the book that lay beside his blotter, the chalice that sat where his right hand would've rested, she felt her heartbeat and breaths quicken.

The papers on his desk would go unsigned. The ink in the well was likely dry by now. The jug of wine that sat on the shelf behind his chair would have grown sour in his absence. The flowers one of the maids had arranged so artfully on the side table had long since wilted, the pretty pink petals nothing more than a muted brown.

As everything that had happened over the past month crashed into her, surrounded her, flooded her with emotions she'd kept buried so, so deep, Lea felt like those flowers. Wilted. A shell of who she was. A little girl playing at being an adult. One small touch, a gentle breeze, would cause her to shatter.

Never again would she spend afternoons at her father's side learning all she could about how to run a city. There would be no more afternoons together, no more parties, no trips to the sea. No weddings.

No funeral.

Her father had been dead a month, and there had been no funeral. And the days she should've spent mourning him with her mother had been spent spinning lies about him, instead.

Guilt crashed into her, twisting in her gut.

"What would they say about him?"

Lea jumped, her hand flying to her face to wipe the tears that tracked down her cheeks, then spun to face the door. Ettrian stood in the doorway, not quite inside, an unsettling picture of uncertainty.

"I'm sorry?"

He gestured toward the desk. "Your father. What would they say about him?"

Lea felt that lost little girl inside of her stir. "What are you—"

"I'm trying to ask about your father," he replied, his eyes gentle. "Your mother took control of this city quickly. I can only assume that had much to do with the respect your people held for Orin."

Lea exhaled, then looked back at the desk, frowning slightly as she tried to settle her racing heart. "They would say he was kind. Friendly. Jolly, even." A smile ghosted across her lips. "He was larger than life in every way." She brushed away another tear. "They would say he was a great leader, and the world is a lesser place without him."

The elf prince took a step toward her. "I would have liked to have met him."

But you never will.

That thought slapped Lea harder than any blow she'd taken from Lessia in the dungeon. Harder than every realization that had battered into her since stepping into this room. Her throat began to tighten, so she turned away from the prince, not wanting him to see her weakening composure.

But as she looked around the room, taking in the space that held so memories of her father, her composure fled. A tremor shook her knees as sudden sobs, harder than she'd ever felt, built in her chest. Her hand flailed out when she fell against the wall, her fingers curving around the wood trim on the door as ragged breaths tore from her throat.

Arms tightened around her waist, catching her just as her legs gave out, and she pressed her face to Ettrian's chest, clinging to him as all her grief crashed into her. The ache in her chest intensified with each wretched gasp of air, with the river of tears that sluiced down her cheeks, dampening her nightdress and his shirt.

I'm going to pass out, she tried to say as dots blurred her vision. But she couldn't; words were impossible to form. Instead, she acquiesced to the prince, allowing herself to show this weakness she'd been holding in for weeks.

For once, Ettrian didn't speak. He simply rested his chin on top of her head and held her as her tears spilled across the sleeve of his shirt, darkening the pale fabric. His cool hand brushed the hair from her face, tugging the strands away that were sticking to her skin.

After a few moments, Ettrian put his lips to her ear. "Come, let me show you something." His voice was so gentle, so out of character, it nearly sent her into hysterics again.

She eyed him with confusion, but allowed him to take her hand and pull her to her feet.

"What type of magic did he wield?" he asked.

Lea sniffed, blinking back tears. "He was a shifter. Bear."

He nodded, then led her to Orin's desk.

"Pick something up," he whispered. "Anything."

After a brief hesitation, she picked up her father's letter opener, a thin blade with a wood handle inlaid with gold, then looked at Ettrian in question.

The prince wrapped his hand around hers, keeping their gazes steady, then tightened his grip. After a moment, shimmering bronze magic flickered from where their hands were wrapped around the blade's handle, seeping into the air. In the next instant, her father's magic wrapped around her. The brief crackle of magic letting off a scent so singular to the shifter that it was unmistakable–it was the smell that filled the air when he shifted into his ursine form.

Her grief continued to try to suffocate her, but his magic slowly began to fill her with life.

"How..." She followed the glittering magic as it fluttered around the room and wrapped around their hands. "How are you able to do this?"

But even as she asked, she didn't care one bit how an elf prince was able to pull the dregs of her father's magic from a simple letter opener. All that mattered was that he could.

He brushed a thumb over her knuckle and smiled softly. "Our magic permeates everything we touch. For someone as old and powerful as your father, his presence will linger for years to come."

A fresh wave of grief, this time muddled with relief, flooded her heart.

"Thank you," she rasped, staring in wonder at the magic that continued to dance around the room. "Thank you, Ettrian."

Her legs trembled, so the prince pulled her in close, keeping one hand on the letter opener and embracing her with the other. As he pressed a cheek to her head, she allowed herself to cry.

26

FREYA

Despite their plans to stay for another day, Byrric and the others all agreed their location had been compromised and they needed to leave the valley as soon as possible. That, and with so many bodies to dispose of, no one was particularly inclined to remain where they were.

As the knights broke down camp, and Byrric, and the others ordered everyone about, Freya and Fenian sat by a fire eating their breakfast near a tree where two humans Ruehnar had plucked from the melee were tied up. They'd opted to hold off on questioning them until they reached their next destination, and when Freya pointed out it had taken Rosie Ristner nearly a day to awake from her first trip through the Between, Fenian merely waved a hand dismissively.

"Rosie is weak," he told her. "But my brother could have woken her if necessary."

"How?"

"Uncomfortably." He slid her a look, then took a sip of tea. "You will not have any trouble questioning them. You have my word."

She held his stare for a moment, then nodded. "Thank you."

"This Traust fellow…," Fenian said after a few moments of silence.

"He's a coward," Freya said. She set her own cup down and looked at the prince. "This is the second time he's flown off instead of seeing a fight through to the end, despite hating my father and me so much he wants to see us dead."

"Then he should be simple to kill," Fenian replied. "And yet here we are."

"It seems his desire for self-preservation outweighs his desire to kill me," Freya muttered. "Hopefully we can use that against him." She frowned, then watched as the prince's narrowed gaze followed Reginald Ristner as he crossed the camp with two of Byrric's knights. "Or against Willem, seeing as Willem seems to trust him to run missions like this one."

He pulled his gaze from the human prince and nodded. "Yes, well, the more I learn about Willem Ristner, the more I think he may have fallen from his mother's womb head-first onto a stone floor."

Freya snorted. "You and me both, Your Highness." She smiled when she saw Florian heading toward them. "Any word on our travels, Lord Florian?"

Since none of them seemed terribly concerned with how the humans handled their trip, Freya opted to let those with more experience than her handle the arrangements. While the bulk of their companions worked to clean up the immediate area, Ruehnar went with two of his knights, along with Florian and two of Byrric's knights, to set up shields that would obscure the arrival of an entire army at their next landing spot.

"Yes, Your Majesty," Florian replied, taking a seat beside Fenian. "We found a good location. A valley a half day's walk from the southern edge of the river." He took a hunk of bread from the metal plate in front of Fenian. "It should be secure within the next few hours."

She exhaled a breath. "Thank you, Florian." She looked around at the mess that still remained. "I'd like to be away from this place as quickly as possible."

"In due time, Your Majesty," Fenian said. "My knights are quite thorough, so you must be patient."

Easy for you to say, she thought.

It was another two hours before Byrric finally announced it was time to leave. They made their leap from the river to the valley in central Allanor that afternoon, then spent the next hour setting up camp. Once the command tent was up, Freya and Aer met with Byrric and the others to discuss what information they needed to extract from the prisoners they'd taken.

After significantly more conversation than Freya felt was necessary, they all agreed that the most important thing was to find out how Traust found them despite all the magical safeguards they had put in place.

"He was able to see through my invisibility glamour in Watoria," Freya said. "It stands to reason that at least some of the knights he's leading, would also have similar capabilities."

"While that's true, it didn't seem like he was able to see through the elves' magic in Watoria," Aer pointed out.

"He should not have been able to see through my knights' magic," Ruehnar agreed. "Although, Jotnar magic is essentially a watered-down version of elvish magic, so it is theoretically possible some could feel it, so to speak, and make assumptions based on those feelings."

"Unlikely," Fenian said. "But possible, nonetheless."

"Fair enough," Freya said. "Lord Florian, I think we'll let you take the lead."

"Yes, I think that's for the best," Aer agreed.

Florian dipped his chin in a nod. "Of course, Your Majesties."

Byrric gave a sharp nod to Rodrick and Perinald, who stood waiting by the tent entrance. "Bring the first one in."

The guards left, then reappeared a few moments later, a human dangling between them. The man's head hung low, his entire body slumping heavily. Based on Rodrick's bloody knuckles, it was safe to assume the man had already been beaten quite severely.

"Sit him there," Florian said, gesturing vaguely toward a chair in the center of the tent as he opened his large leather satchel and began pulling out small containers and lining them up on the small table near the chair. "No need to bind him."

Aer's guards dropped the knight into the chair. Freya continued to watch as Florian lined up the poisons he'd chosen for his task. She recognized most from her toxins exam at the end of her semester at Aldridge. Lindberry root extract, ore powder, saithwater, and hemlock were the first few he brought out, but it was the last two, the firebloom serum and the glittering green *eitr*, that had her heart quickening. The former had turned her pen to ash with just a touch during her final exam, and the *eitr* was one of the poisons Willem used to murder Lessia Edrin.

She flicked her eyes back to the human and swallowed back the bile that threatened her stomach.

Florian nodded at the guards. "That will be all for now. Please ensure the next one is ready when we're done here."

Once Rodrick and Perinald left, Florian flicked a hand, and Freya felt the tingle of magic as a silencing spell dropped over the tent.

They stood in silence for a moment, then Florian kicked the human's chair, jolting him awake. He lifted his head, and Freya stifled a gasp as she took in his battered face. Bruises encircled both eyes, dried blood crusted his nostrils, and a gash sliced through one eyebrow, the blood dripping into his eye.

When he took in the people standing around him, his battered face twisted into a sneer.

"Filthy creatures," he muttered, then spat blood on the floor. "What more do you plan to do to me? I already told your animals I know nothing."

Florian nodded slowly, then slid a long, thin blade from the sheath at his hip and touched the point to the human's chin. "We're quite good at rephrasing certain questions." He pressed harder, drawing a wince from their captive. "Now, let's talk about Reykr Traust."

~

THE HUMAN'S screams were permanently etched into Freya's eardrums by the time Florian had completed his interrogation. It took nearly three hours for them all to be satisfied that the first human knew nothing, and by that time, he was so cut to shreds and riddled with burns from firebloom serum that Freya wondered if he'd survive beyond the night. She knew without asking that magical healing would be out of the question.

As much as it pained her, she opted to wait outside for the next interrogation. The last thing she wanted was to appear weak, but those screams...they were pure terror. Florian had played judge and executioner for the Harridan family for centuries, so this type of thing was old hat for him. Freya knew he wouldn't let any of the men off easily, nor would she want him to. But the sounds of the man's flesh sizzling, the hacking cough as he choked on his own tongue from the saithwater Florian dripped on it, stuck in her mind more than all the battlefield screams she'd heard the past two weeks.

She needed a break.

So, when Rodrick and Perinald dragged the second human in for questioning, she excused herself from the tent.

"Do you need me?" Aer asked with a frown.

"Always," she replied with a smile. "But you're needed here. I just..." She sighed, then looked toward the empty chair, now surrounded by a circle of blood and other things she'd rather not think of. For a moment, she contemplated ordering them to give the human a dose of eitr and putting him out of his misery.

He ran a hand down her arm, then kissed her forehead. "Take whatever time you need. I just need to see this through."

She closed her eyes and placed a hand on his chest. "I hate this," she breathed.

"It'll be over soon," he reassured her. "After Avorell...you don't need to be here for this."

She nodded, then gave him a smile she hoped was reassuring before leaving. Since Florian had dropped a silencing spell over the tent, she sat down outside, taking a spot on a fallen log someone had dragged in front of one of the campfires. As she settled on the damp bark, she rested her elbows on her knees, and rubbed her eyes, trying to erase the images that were now seared in her mind.

"Can I ask what causes your aversion to all of this?"

Freya jerked from her thoughts at the sound of Toskr's voice beside her.

"Gods above, make some noise next time," she muttered. When she met his eyes, his face was an open mask of curiosity.

"You killed so many in the forest," he continued, then gestured toward the tent. "Why does this trouble you so much?"

"I was ending their lives," she replied, surprised at how easily the answer came. "I didn't prolong their suffering." She rubbed her hands over her face. "There are some aspects of this—" she waved her hand to indicate the war camp, the battle, everything else "—that I don't think I'll ever get used to."

Toskr made a small sound in the back of his throat and sat down beside her. "Interesting."

"Why is that interesting?"

"I truly thought one so adept at slaughter would have the stomach for a standard interrogation."

Freya grimaced at what she supposed was some type of compliment. "Sorry to disappoint you."

"Oh it's no disappointment, Queen Freya," Toskr assured her. "Only surprise and perhaps a bit of concern."

She frowned. "Concern?"

"This war is far from over," he pointed out. "Would you not agree that learning to oversee something like this would be more helpful in your case?"

"How would I do that, Toskr?" Freya asked. "How, in the limited time we have here, would I be able to learn to watch a man have flesh peeled from bone without flinching?"

He shrugged, then flicked a piece of bark from his fingers and sent it sailing toward the fire. "You are, of course, allowed to leave the dirty work to your spymaster. But I've always been of the mind that if a ruler cannot handle watching a bit of torture carried out under their orders, are they truly ready to rule?"

She stared at him, unblinking, as his words sunk in. He was baiting her, there was no question.

But at the same time...was he wrong?

No one could prepare her for what they were currently dealing with, and it was unfair of Toskr to presume someone had. She'd been nearly a year away from taking her crown when it was figuratively forced onto her head. Of course she hadn't been prepared to rule yet.

Again, her irritation with her father reared its head. Perhaps he could've helped her prepare for situations like this, like Aer clearly had been. Perhaps if she'd lived in the capital, grew up and trained with the royal family, she wouldn't be sitting on a log outside a tent as a man sent to slaughter her entire people was interrogated.

It might be unfair, but in that moment, as she sat by the fire, annoyance at everyone who'd had a hand in the decision to keep her away flared.

"Me sitting out here has nothing to do with my ability to be queen," she finally said. "And it's unfair of you to imply such a thing."

He shrugged. "Then go back in there and face your enemy. It does not matter if he dies at Lord Florian's hand tonight or by one of your pretty daggers tomorrow. Ultimately, his blood will be on your hands, and those of your husband. You must own that responsibility, Queen Freya."

She slid him a look. "I'm beginning to like Prince Fenian's plan to turn you into a footstool for the Queen."

"Decorative cushion, Your Majesty, not footstool." He nudged her with his elbow. "And I do not believe you mean that."

She shook her head and sighed. "Of course I don't, Toskr."

Before he could reply, the tent flap opened and Byrric stepped out. Freya and Toskr both leapt to their feet.

"He's talking."

Freya nodded and brushed off her pants. "Alright." She looked at Toskr. "Thank you, Toskr."

He gave a quick bow. "Of course, Your Majesty. Best of luck in there."

Then he switched to his squirrel form and ran off into the dark.

27

FREYA

The tent smelled of fresh blood and excrement, immediately causing Freya to want to turn around and leave. The human knight slumped in the chair, all manner of bodily fluids encircling the space around him.

"How did it go?" she asked Aer, who stood by the entrance beside Ruehnar.

"Better than the first," he replied. "Once Florian is done, we'll go over it all."

"Good. That's good."

Ruehnar glanced over at her. "He seems to know quite a bit more than the last one." His shrewd gaze turned back to the human. "Or he is far less stupid."

"I would go with the latter, personally," Aer said.

The human sneered in response, but a kick to his chair from Byrric had him shrinking back.

"Our friend was able to share a bit more about Reykr Traust than his companion," Florian said, placing a cork in one of his bottles. "Including how they were able to find us on the river last night, isn't that right?"

The human huffed out a breath. "Yes, that is correct."

"How?" Freya demanded.

The human's brown eyes flicked up and down her form, disgust twisting his mouth as he took in her wings. "Traust sent us upriver with some of his kind who had strong abilities to sense magic. He said wherever you had been before, you'd used magic to shield, so he assumed you'd do the same."

"How do you know this?" Aer asked.

"I overheard him talking to some of his knights the night before he sent us out," he wheezed. "We were to reinforce the Jotnar who were on our boats seeking weak points in your shields. Those spots would allow us to break through."

"There were no weak points," Ruehnar snapped.

The man coughed, then spit a mouthful of blood on the floor before continuing. "Not physically weak. The one who was on my ship could find a spot of magic that was more pronounced than the rest. Once we knew the shield was there, it was easier to see through." He slumped back in his chair and looked around at all of them. "It wasn't perfect and we couldn't get the full picture until the elves attacked us." He smirked at Ruehnar. "So thank you for that."

"Where is Traust now?" Byrric asked.

"How should I know? The only time I saw him was when he sent us to find you all. I had no idea he planned to join us and I have no idea where he fled to."

"Where were you when he gave the orders?" Freya asked.

"We had reached the river junction in the east, the one at the base of a mountain pass. He was there waiting for us, so I assume somewhere in that vicinity is where he returned." He rubbed a filthy hand over his face. "I obviously came here expecting to die, so I don't care what you do to me."

"Alright, so you know nothing of Traust," Freya said, nodding. "What about your king? What are Willem's plans?"

He shrugged. "King Willem wants your land, pure and simple. One of his generals was with Traust when we reached the river junction. That's who we took orders from—orders to destroy any Lind we come across, especially if that person is traveling with the king and queen."

Unsurprising. "And you have no idea what Traust's plans are? What Willem has ordered him to do?"

"As far as I can tell, Traust will continue following the river in search of you both. Whether those were my king's orders, I can't say."

Then we need to get away from the river, Freya thought.

"And the humans who arrived in Lindoroth most recently?" Byrric asked. "Where are they now?"

"I don't know. We came from the North and met at the river junction, but I don't know what their orders were once we left."

"So your companions have been here since the siege, then?" Florian asked.

He nodded.

"Who will be accompanying Traust as he travels the river?" Aer asked.

"He has many scouts that he'll be sending out to search for you in the surrounding areas. All Jotnar, I presume. I don't know what my army's orders were, but if Traust is focused on the rivers—"

"He'll be sending more human ships." Byrric nodded.

"You and your kind will be vastly outnumbered, Commander." The human jerked his chin toward Freya and Aer. "I would suggest getting your king and queen as far from the river as possible." His lip curled into a sneer. "Or as far from this land as possible. Save it from the blight you've brought upon it."

Florian flicked his obsidian eyes toward Freya and Aer. Aer gave a sharp nod, then Florian stepped forward wordlessly and sliced through the human's neck, leaving him to choke on his own blood.

"So where do we go from here?" Freya asked once Rodrick and Perinald had dragged the human's body out of the tent. "It seems Traust is looking for us, specifically, not simply slaughtering our forces."

"Willem likely wants to witness our executions himself," Aer replied. "Make a show of it in the capital."

Byrric nodded in agreement. "Yes, I'm guessing Traust has been given orders to bring you there alive." He sighed. "Whether he'll adhere to those orders is unlikely, based on his most recent attack."

"Our options now are to hunt him down and kill him, or let him continue expending energy to find you," Ruehnar said. "I am of the mind that we let him continue searching and bolster our own defenses to prevent him from locating us."

"Yes, I think that would be best," Florian agreed. "We can adjust our own movements, send out scouts to monitor where Traust goes and find areas further away to transport."

"Unless he's biding his time, he doesn't know where we are currently," Byrric said. "Silmar should be returning any time now. I think we should wait to hear what his thoughts are, now that he's seen a larger stretch of the kingdom than we have."

"Fair enough," Aer replied. With a frown, he looked back toward the chair the human knight had just occupied. "It's late. We should all eat, get some rest."

Rini appeared beside them and put a hand on Freya's shoulder. "Come, Your Majesties. I've made sure your tent is warm."

After saying goodbye to Byrric, Florian, and Ruehnar, who didn't appear to be going to sleep any time soon, Freya and Aer followed Rini toward the tent she'd arranged for them. Freya didn't miss the way Rini very clearly avoided meeting her eyes as they walked, instead fluttering just a few feet in front of them.

So, Freya waited until they got into the tent to finally confront her. "I told you to go to Errest, Rini," she said quietly. "Why are you still here?"

Rini paused in midair in front of the brazier that was warming the space. Then, she turned, her wings fluttering madly as she flew back to Freya.

"Oh, Your Majesty, I couldn't leave you behind! My sister didn't *need* me in Errest, and you were here preparing to fight a battle, and what kind of attendant would I be if I left you alone? And that princess is so *rude!* My place is with you, Your Majesty."

Rini's small hand twitched toward the small bag that held her comb. Before she could attack Freya's hair in a fit of nerves, Freya touched her wrist to stop her.

"I told you to go, Rini. I'm not one to say 'you should have listened because I'm your queen,' but if that's what it will take for me to ensure your safety, I will."

Rini's silver eyes went round as saucers. "I didn't mean to be disobedient!" Tears started rolling down her cheeks. "Please don't send me away! I only meant to help!"

Freya pinched the bridge of her nose and sighed. "Since Prince Fenian seemed aware of your presence, I can only assume he was keeping you informed on what was happening with us?"

Rini nodded. "Yes, I asked him before I left Iston to keep me updated. He said he would. Although it wouldn't surprise me if he only did so because he thought you would get angry enough that you'd let him feed me to the forest trolls." Rini flew forward and latched onto Freya's sleeve. "Please don't allow him to feed me to the trolls!"

Gently, Freya released Rini's fingers from her arm. "You know I would never allow such a thing, nor would I ever dismiss you. It hurts a bit that you'd even consider it. I understand why you're here. I wish you weren't, because I want you safe, but I understand."

Rini blinked back her tears. "So you'll let me stay?"

"Yes, Rini, I'll let you stay."

Rini squealed, then threw her arms around Freya's neck, surprising her with her strength.

"Let's get some sleep, shall we?" Aer ran a hand down Freya's back. "Tomorrow will be another long day and we need all the rest we can get."

"Yes, of course Your Majesty," Rini said with a bow in Aer's direction. "Hopefully tomorrow will bring good news."

Freya patted Rini's arm and smiled. "We can only hope."

28

FREYA

"Your Majesty?"

Freya jolted awake at the sound of Rini's voice. Their tent was still dark, save for the glowing embers still in the brazier.

"What is it?" she asked, shaking Aer to wake him up.

"Lord Silmar has returned," Rini said.

Moments later, Freya and Aer were dressed and hurrying toward the command tent. Byrric, Ruehnar, Fenian, and Florian stood there surrounded by Silmar, Zane, Naedan, Amara, and Ana.

The relief Freya felt when she saw her aunt standing there among the other scouts nearly had her legs collapsing beneath her.

"Freya!" Ana said, rushing forward and enveloping Freya in a tight embrace. "Thank the gods."

Freya held Ana for a moment before pulling back. "Please tell us you have good news."

"We do," Ana confirmed. "I'll let Lord Silmar lay it all out for you, though."

"To start, we found a place to set camp," Silmar began. "A field in Allanor to the west of the Rimar River. We would be able to make our final plans for breaching Iladel from there." His features tightened as he exchanged a look with Ana. "However, it would be remiss of me not to mention that Kildin has nearly emptied of enemy forces."

The tent went silent, and Byrric and Florian exchanged a look. Freya stayed quiet, but Aer tensed beside her.

"Are you suggesting we go to Kildin?" he asked.

Silmar looked at Ruehnar, then Byrric, then finally, Aer and Freya. "I would like you to have all relevant information before making your choice as to where to go from here."

"This could be a good thing," Aer said after a moment. "If all of Kildin is emptying out, those forces are either going to Iladel or Errest. We can attempt to take out a portion on the road to wherever they're going."

"It could just as easily be a trap," Fenian pointed out.

"Unlikely," Zane replied with a shake of his head. "Too many left. When we left, none remained in the city, and very few were in the surrounding area. Most are already too far south to easily return to Kildin to fight. We would fully secure the city before they'd manage to make it back."

"We'll have to go in and look more thoroughly, of course," Ana added. "But the searching we did revealed an empty city and thousands of knights on the march."

The possibility of Kildin being saved set Freya's mind whirring with plans. Yes, Kildin was crucial as a trading crossroads, but it would also be the fourth of five capitals that could be put back under Lindorothian control, fully tipping the scales in their favor.

"Did you speak with Lazarus or Alyndra?" she asked Ana.

Ana nodded. "They're currently safe in a nearby village surrounded by Avorellian and Lindorothian knights. Lord Maddix is with him, but the rest of the Maddixes have gone back to Watoria to help the governor's family get settled in."

"We can send a small squadron," Byrric said. "They can accompany those already traveling with Lord Cailen."

Fenian sighed. "I can spare some knights, but I would like it noted that I strongly oppose this plan and believe we should go *directly* to Iladel."

Before Freya could object, Ruehnar cut in. "I might agree, son, if not for the fact that leaving a capital city open to further marauding could prove to be more catastrophic."

"Don't forget, Your Highness," Florian added, "that Lessia Edrin's brother is currently sitting silently in Madrya only a few days' march from Kildin. If he gets word it's open for the taking, he'd be a fool to not capitalize on that opportunity."

"That considered, we'd have to send far more knights than would be wise to push back a force that large," Ana said. "Elvish magic will go a long way against them, of course, but Jotnar also have magic. A battle like that, control of Kildin could go either way."

"So we get there first," Zane said. "Encircle the city, repair the wall."

Aer nodded. "Earth and air wielders could certainly get the repair underway, but it will take days before any sufficient progress is made toward securing the city."

Freya watched and listened as they all volleyed ideas around the room, struggling on her own to decide which would be the best option. All of her frustrations over leaving Kildin in the lurch flooded back now that they might have a viable path forward. But that path came at the cost of sending fewer troops toward Iladel. They needed to retake Kildin, but decreasing the assault on Iladel simply wouldn't be wise.

Her eyes drifted around the room, watching each person as they argued for one path or another, before landing on Florian. His dark eyes met hers, and he seemed to have already come to the same conclusion she had.

"It's not enough," he said, his voice snapping above the others who were talking in raised voices, trying to be heard. "We can and should secure Kildin, but we also need to swarm Iladel as swiftly as possible. The forces we have are not enough."

"We can't split up now to find more reinforcements," Aer said. "We did that already and it took a week. We don't have that kind of time now."

"No, that's precisely what we need to do." Florian looked at Byrric.

"Your mother and I had a talk before we left Iston. Her ideas were somewhat compelling."

"What ideas were those?" Byrric asked.

"She suggested going to the rebels," Freya murmured with a glance to Aer. "We spoke with her about it, too."

Florian nodded. "And we would be remiss not to consider it now."

"The Jotnar rebels?" Fenian asked. "*That's* who Vara would call in at the eleventh hour?"

"It could be worth considering," Ruehnar said, silencing his son with a look before looking at Byrric. "What is her logic here?"

Byrric sighed and rubbed a hand over his face before cupping it around his chin. "I have a cousin up there. We grew up together in Iston. He left for the rebel camps, what is now Utgard, nearly a century ago when he met his wife, a female from somewhere in Western Jotunheim. He helped found Utgard, and last I heard, he'd become quite the leader among them." He shook his head. "But they're all focused on relieving Jotunheim from the Edrin line."

"How many knights would they have to support us?" Fenian asked. "Would it be enough to make a difference?"

Byrric shrugged. "They aren't exactly knights, not in the strictest sense. They have little in the way of military organization, but by all accounts, they have somewhere in the vicinity of one thousand males and females who protect their lands."

Fenian's brows rose. "That's quite a number, considering our own."

"Quite a number of people with little discipline in the way of battle," Byrric countered.

"It's worth consideration, though," Freya said. "I'm not sure about your conversation with my grandmother, Lord Florian, but she seemed fairly confident they'd be open to a discussion, at the very least."

"What harm could it cause?" Ruehnar asked Byrric. "Take a day or two and travel to their lands, see what they might have to say."

"A day or two of separation can set us back significantly," Aer countered.

"Not if we only send a few," Ruehnar replied. "Send your Queen, your commander, my son." Fenian shot him an incredulous look at that. "You can be there and back within two days, and in the meantime, we can continue making plans for Kildin."

"As I am the one tasked with leading our army, do I not get a say in this?" Fenian asked.

"Do not forget who *put* you in charge of said army," Ruehnar said drily.

"What about scouts?" Naedan asked. "You can't go without aerial support."

"You will accompany us," Freya said. "The Valkyrie and Zane can handle aerial scouting for this group for the time being, right?" She looked at Ana for confirmation.

"Yes, of course," Ana replied.

"Zane, you'll remain here to lead the aerial shifters."

"Of course, Commander."

"I'm not separating from you again," Aer said to Freya. "Not after last time."

"This will be nothing like last time," she reassured him. "We're not in Avorell, I'm not stuck in a forest fighting monsters alone." She nodded toward her father and the others. "Fenian can get us out, and if he can't, my father and I are more than capable of getting away."

Aer's mouth settled into a frown, his brows furrowed in an expression Freya always considered his "thinking" face. She waited patiently as the logic battled it out in his mind. Finally, he puffed out a breath.

"Alright, fine. I'll support it." He pointed a finger at Byrric. "Two days. Two days before I find whatever elf will take me and come find you. We need the help, but we don't have limitless time to convince people of that."

Freya looked past him at Ana. "You won't let him out of your sight while I'm gone?"

Ana's lips quirked in amusement. "Not for a moment."

Silmar rubbed his eyes, the exhaustion of his constant back-and-forth travel over the last week clearly wearing on him. "Well, you cannot go into this without a plan, and a solid one, at that."

"Alright, then," Byrric said with a sigh. "Let's begin."

THEY TALKED for the rest of the day and into the night to develop their plans for traveling to Utgard. Their main concern was keeping their initial arrival peaceful, which would require a lot of fast talking and the ability to maintain a level of calm that would go heavily against how the rebels would be inclined to react. Ultimately they decided Byrric would be their best option at neutralizing the situation when they arrived, with Florian and Fenian prepared to act as negotiators between Freya and Vali.

It was nearly midnight by the time Freya and Aer fell onto their bed.

"Do you think we'll be successful?" she asked as they settled beneath the heavy furs. She found his hand and linked their fingers, letting their hands rest on the cot between them.

"I believe you're capable of anything," he said. "If anyone can convince the people we've been pushing back from our own borders to fight at our sides, it's you."

She smiled, then brought his hand to her lips and kissed his knuckles. "Sometimes I question the amount of faith you have in me."

"And sometimes I feel you forget your own strength," he countered. He shifted forward and slid a hand across her hip, pulling her toward him. "You will, without question, succeed tomorrow."

As he laid one last kiss on her head, she snuggled closer to him and settled under the weight of his arm. "I love you," she murmured, tugging the furs up around them.

"And I love you." He pulled her closer, tucking her head under his chin.

Before she knew it, she'd drifted off into her dreams, where she was allowed to be blissfully unaware of what dangers might wait for her tomorrow.

29

LEA

The morning started off as the previous three. She and her mother awoke, met with advisors, discussed courses of action in regard to rebuilding and pushing back against the invaders, who to send word to in the western mines, and checked in with their people. They'd opted to allow certain citizens to visit them in their home for the day to streamline the process of sorting out any issues that might be ongoing. By early afternoon, Lea had met with her tenth business owner in the drawing room and Perida her twentieth, ensuring people throughout the city had what they needed, coordinating with business owners to set up shelters for those who'd fled the surrounding villages, and, most importantly, to reassure everyone that the Calliwell's had returned to lead the city back to normal. They'd also convened with the marshals more than once to make sure they were spread out evenly across the city, with slightly heavier patrols around the walls and entry points.

Just after lunch and only a few moments after she'd sat down with her mother and aunt for tea, Lea felt a shift in the air. They'd received word from Rini that morning that Freya and Aer had moved their camp and were contemplating some new path forward, so she nearly chalked her feeling of unease up to worry over her cousins.

But a few moments after the odd feeling registered, an Edhilian knight rushed into the drawing room. When she saw Ettrian stroll in behind him, Lea felt that strange tingle down her spine.

"My ladies." The knight halted in front of them, forcing deep breaths so as to be able to speak.

"What is it?" Perida asked, setting down her cup.

The knight looked first at Perida, then at Lea before addressing Perida once more. "Jonas Edrin has arrived and has requested passage for himself and his party to the city gates."

"The knights with him—are they only Jotnar?" Perida asked.

Please be only Jotnar, Lea thought. If Jonas had humans with him, it was a sure bet that the knights were not friendly. At least if they were his own knights, they had a slight chance at a peaceful encounter.

The knight's face turned grim. "No, Lady Calliwell. It appears humans make up the bulk of the knights he brought."

Lea exchanged glances with her mother then shot an exasperated look at Ettrian when he let out a low chuckle. "You find this funny, Your Highness?"

"Oh, I find it most amusing," the prince replied. "Did you truly expect Willem to send Jonas with *only* Jotnar knights? How else would he be able to ensure Jonas returned you and the princess in one piece? If anything, this confirms our suspicions that Willem doesn't trust Jonas, which is a good thing."

Lea gnawed on her lip as her mind ran over the potential outcome of Jonas' arrival. It wasn't surprising that Willem had sent his own men. There was no way he was foolish enough to trust Jonas to follow through with their plans. He also had to know that there was no way Jonas would be successful in Errest, which told her he had no intention of sharing any glory with him.

Perida's expression went stony. "Are you telling me he *is* here to take my daughter?"

Lea wanted to reach out and take her mother's hand, to smooth the look of resignation resting below her mask, but she knew now was not the time.

"We knew this was a possibility," Ordona said. "Let's not lose our heads just yet."

"Might I suggest something?" Lindesson said. His eyes darted between Ordona and Perida, before settling on Lea. "Address him. Those knights, not to mention Willem, believe you are Jonas' wife. Tell them you've made your choice." He inclined his head toward Ettrian. "Our own forces can handle the rest."

Lea considered his words, then looked at Ettrian. "What are your thoughts?"

His eyes roved over her face, then he gave a sharp nod. "I think parading you before him is a risk, but one worth taking." The prince looked at Perida. "He has a small squadron, only enough for a show of force, but not enough to do serious damage, considering you have my knights defending your city and most of his forces are human."

Perida's brow furrowed. "Prince Ettrian, what do you believe Lord Edrin's intentions are with my daughter?"

"His orders from Willem are likely to take her, kicking and screaming, back to Iladel." Ettrian sent another look toward Lea. "Which we, of course, won't allow. It's also unlikely he'll push to follow through. To be honest, it wouldn't surprise me if his goal was to be captured so he has a solid reason not to return to Iladel."

Lea held his gaze for a moment, trying and failing to read whatever was swirling in his golden eyes—eyes that had gone softer in the last few days. "Alright." With a deep breath, she looked at Lindesson. "I'll do it."

"If Lady Calliwell agrees?" Lindesson asked Perida.

Lips set in a thin line, Perida looked at each of the room's occupants before finally nodding her head slowly. "Alright. Do what you must."

Sudden panic rose in Lea's chest as she realized what the outcome of this encounter would likely be. Jonas would either come out of this alive but imprisoned, or burning along with the rest of his men in the desert if he got trapped in the fray. At least the imprisonment was something she would have time to talk her mother out of.

"General Lindesson, what do you plan to do with Jonas and his men?" she asked.

"Take him captive until we can confirm his loyalty. If he's remained loyal to us, he'll be a fount of information, and a willing one, at that."

"We can't put any faith in his knights, though," Ordona said. "They think their goal here is to return you and the princess to Iladel."

"Your aunt is correct," Ettrian said. "Willem will take you from Jonas just as he intended to a month ago. You know it as well as I do. So yes, we will take him into custody, separate him from his knights and see what he has to share."

"Why are you so certain Willem wants my daughter?" Perida asked, sounding far more panicked than she had at the prospect of Jonas taking her.

"One of the reasons my parents sent me to Iladel was to keep Lea safe while your queen completed her task." Ettrian's expression went grim. "The idea to make Lea his wife did not come to Willem until he'd killed Lessia and Effina, but it rooted quickly, within moments, which was when I took her from the palace. Presumably he would still like to see that happen."

A lump formed in Lea's throat as she remembered the proprietary way Willem had looked at her in the moments before Ettrian took her away. "Willem wanted me to convince our people that Lessia had bewitched him and that Freya and Aerelius had abandoned our people," she told her mother. "He thought I would be able to help turn the Linds to his side. I don't believe Jonas is the enemy here."

"Neither do I," Ettrian agreed. "But as Her Majesty said, we all know we cannot place that same faith in his knights, not when they've already gotten a taste for battle."

"No one is going to hurt him," Ordona reassured Lea. She took a deep breath. "As long as he cooperates. At the very least, we need him separated from his knights."

"Fair enough." There was no doubt in Lea's mind that Jonas knew as much. "But I want his knights to hear from my own lips that I have no intention of returning to Iladel."

Ordona nodded. "Yes, I think that's wise."

"Is that safe?" Perida asked.

"A small risk that could yield great benefit," Ettrian said with a shrug. "As long as your daughter stays with me, she will be perfectly safe." He gave Lea a questioning look when she arched a brow at him, then rolled his eyes. "*I* will keep her safe."

Indecision was written all over Perida's face, but after a moment, her furrowed brow relaxed. "Alright. But can we send Iska to monitor Rosie? She'll get wind of this one way or another, but I don't want her doing anything stupid."

"Of course," Lindesson said.

After spending a few more minutes hammering out the details of their plans, Lindesson gave the go-ahead for Ettrian to take Lea to the city wall. She held her breath against the swirling gray Between, then exhaled in a whoosh when they landed at the base of the stairs that led to the top of the ramparts.

"Are we sure about this?" Lea turned to Ettrian as a dozen Lindorothian knights filed up the stairs before them. "This seems as if it could go very, *very* badly." Even as she said it, she heard shouting from the city and the pounding of feet as citizens near the wall fled to the inner parts of Errest.

Just a precaution, she reminded herself. *They're all safe.*

Ettrian waited until the last knight had passed, then turned to face her, his shimmering eyes boring into her own. "Do you trust me?"

"I...yes, I do." She let her eyes fall shut as she pictured the scene that was about to be before her. "But I'm scared," she finally admitted, opening her eyes and looking up at him.

His features softened, but there was a hardness in his eyes that unnerved her. "I promise you, I will keep you safe."

"How?" she whispered. "How can you promise that?"

He touched a finger to her chin and smirked. "Because I am a prince of Avorell and those knights out there are little more than shit on the bottom of my boot." Then, he tilted her face toward his. "And because I'd very much like to ensure you are still here when this war is done."

Her heart thudded in her chest as his eyes darkened. "Why?"

The corner of his mouth curved upward. He laced his fingers through hers, tugging her hand to lead her up the stairs. "Let's go, little witch. Your husband awaits."

30

LEA

The ramparts surrounding Errest were tall and foreboding, made of ancient Edhilian stone mined from deep within the desert. In all her life, Lea had only stood atop them once, but she'd been young and there hadn't been hordes of soldiers blocking her path away from the city. Even still, they'd been terrifying. Now, the towering height and width offered her solace as she looked over the parapet to where Jonas stood with a dozen knights, mostly human, with a few Jotnar. He wore his standard white attire, leather, but no armor, which surprised her. The pale hair he normally wore loose around his shoulders was tied back, highlighting the stern set of his jaw, visible even from fifty feet above him.

She shifted her gaze toward the encampment, where she could see a solid line of elves and Linds blocking the rest of Jonas' companions. There weren't many in comparison to the hordes protecting her city, but the sight of so many enemy knights so near her home was unnerving.

"It's almost insulting," Ettrian murmured. He stood so close Lea could feel the heat of his body against her back. "Two hundred of his knights at his back while you have thousands to stand against him."

"Willem either sent him to die or just wanted him out of his hair,"

Lea whispered back. "Either way, he has one hundred poison-tipped arrows aimed at him," she added, nodding toward the knights that lined the wall. "He poses no threat."

"I've come for my wife!" Jonas shouted, breaking the tense silence. "Lea, it's time to come with me."

Lea stiffened at his words, but relaxed when Ettrian slid a hand up to squeeze her shoulder. There was no way Jonas missed the movement, but the only grumbles rose from the small cluster of knights with him.

"I'm quite content here, thank you!" Lea replied. "You can be on your way now."

One of the human knights snickered, ignoring the sharp look Jonas sent back at him.

"You're my wife, Lea," Jonas replied. "The future Empress of Jotunheim. Did you truly believe we wouldn't come for you?"

"Perhaps if you thought I needed rescuing." Lea looked around at the knights on the wall, then gestured out at the encampment. "As you can see, I'm perfectly safe."

"She has made her choice, Lord Edrin," Ettrian called down. "You have no place here."

"And you do?" Jonas' sneer was so convincing Lea nearly second-guessed her assertion that he was on their side. "Did you come to Lindoroth to steal my wife, *Your Highness?*"

Ettrian chuckled. "Did you not hear, Lord Edrin? I seem to have misplaced my credentials to perform Lindorothian weddings! Consider your marriage annulled."

The whispers amongst the knights grew louder as they exchanged confused looks. One stepped forward, a Jotnar, and whispered something in Jonas' ear. Jonas replied with a sharp shake of his head before returning his attention to Lea.

"Is that the lie he told you, Lea? That our marriage is mere fiction? We spoke vows before witnesses!"

"Vows spoken under duress," Lea shot back. "I would think a person of your stature would prefer a willing wife."

Without warning, a human knight lifted his bow and fired an

arrow straight toward Lea and Ettrian. Before she could register what was happening, Lea called up a branch of morning glory from the wall, grabbing the arrow and snapping it in two just before it would've hit the prince.

Ettrian chuckled. "Thank you, Lady Calliwell. Quite nice to know you care."

"Oh, shut up," she muttered. "It wouldn't have hurt you. I just needed them to see how serious I am." Then, raising her voice she added, "I suggest you put a leash on your knights, Lord Edrin."

The fury on Jonas' face was clear even from her place atop the wall. He spun, jerked the knight forward by the neck of his armor, then shoved him to the ground. Lea couldn't hear what words he hissed toward the knight, but the knight raised his hands in surrender. Jonas stared at him for a second longer, then turned and faced Lea and Ettrian again, missing the look of pure contempt the human sent his way.

"Come talk to me, Lea," he called. "I don't want to resort to violence."

Ettrian snickered, then silenced himself when Lea elbowed him in the stomach. Clearing his throat, Ettrian stepped forward. "You have one more chance to return to Iladel, Lord Edrin, before I give these knights the order to fire."

"Let's allow him in," Lea whispered to Ettrian. "Enough of this."

"Are you sure about that, Lady Calliwell?" Ettrian gestured toward the knights, signaling them to draw their bows. Lea heard the growl of wolves below, shifters who waited at the gates with General Lindesson.

She tensed at the elf's warm breath at her ear, hating herself just a little bit for actually considering his words, before addressing Jonas. "You can come into my city, Lord Edrin," Lea said. "But only you. Your goons can stay out here."

Jonas held her gaze for a moment, then gave a sharp nod.

Stupid, Lea thought. He knew her, of course, but he knew nothing of the people who guarded her and protected her city, especially the elves. She might not wish him harm, but the rest of her people, the elves...the same simply couldn't be said for them.

"Quite the brain trust, that one," Ettrian muttered as Jonas approached the gates.

Lea shook her head. "Let's just see what he has to say. Tyna!"

Tyna appeared beside Lea. "Yes, Lady Calliwell?"

"I'd like you to accompany us to meet Lord Edrin, verify anything you've seen in your visits to the palace. I need to be sure we can trust him."

"Considering he's allowed himself to come inside unaccompanied, I'd say he's either trustworthy or painfully stupid," Tyna replied.

Ettrian clicked his tongue. "My money is on both." For a moment, he stared down at the knights that had stood behind Jonas moments before. "What are your thoughts on letting my knights fire on those cretins?"

Her knee-jerk reaction was to say no, to tell him it was senseless and pointless, that Jonas was here to help. That killing the men who came with him might not keep them in his good favor.

But even if that were true, it didn't change what those men would've allowed to happen to her had she stayed in the palace. They would've followed each of Willem's orders, no matter how cruel, how depraved. And she wouldn't be standing here right now, holding their lives in her hands.

It was a heady feeling, knowing what power she held in that moment. It might send her to the worst places in the afterlife to do it, but she knew she'd do much worse before this war was over.

She hoped she'd do much worse. For her mother, for her father. For her king and queen, aunt and uncle. She could stand on this wall for days and still have names to add to the list of people she planned to avenge. The human king might not stand at her feet, but she would happily dismantle his army, one man at a time, until there was nothing left but a small, pitiful man begging for his life.

So, she tilted her chin and stared down at the soldiers leering up at her, their fingers twitching to fire on both of them. "Only the humans. Keep the Jotnar in custody until we speak with Jonas."

Ettrian's hand wrapped around her arm. "Are you sure?"

"Do it," she whispered, keeping her back straight as she leaned into the prince's solid presence. She could do worse, but she wouldn't stoop to Willem's level of needless violence.

A moment later, arrows flew toward the knights below, a whisper of wood through the air, and the men fell. Before the humans hit the ground, Edhilian knights grabbed the few Jotnar who'd stood at Jonas' side, leaving an entire army between Jonas Edrin and the rest of the soldiers who were there to protect him.

31

FREYA

Freya only managed a few hours of sleep before she awoke just after dawn. Not wanting to wake Aer, she lay quietly in bed listening to the sounds of the encampment; knights talking around fires as they traded watch, the gentle rustle of wind, and the sound of footsteps as people moved about camp formed a soothing background noise that would've lulled her to sleep on any other night. All she could think about, though, was how those sounds would increase in the coming hours, especially once her father and the others gave their new orders.

Her eyes had just started to drift shut when Rini appeared at the tent entrance.

"Your father sent me to get you, Your Majesties," she said quietly. "He wants to be at Utgard by midday."

Aer grumbled a response, but heaved out a sigh and sat up.

Freya smiled as she sat up and swung her legs around the edge of the cot. "Tell him we'll be along shortly."

"Of course," Rini replied with a small bow, keeping her eyes averted. "I'll be back soon to prepare you for the day."

Freya's eyes narrowed when the pixie vanished. "Did she seem off to you?"

"How so?"

"Just...off." She frowned. "Like she's angry."

Aer snorted. "Well I'm assuming it's because you didn't invite her along to Utgard with you." He stood and began tugging on his pants. "Combine that with you sending her away to Errest, and I'd say she's feeling a bit underappreciated."

"I appreciate her!" Freya exclaimed as she stood and exchanged her nightdress for a tunic and pants. "I just worry about her. *For* her. It's all too dangerous for her here. She'd be safe in Errest."

"She's your attendant, Freya." He shrugged into his jacket, then took her hands, causing her to pause and face him. "Her job is to stay with you. Short of relieving her from her duties—"

"I would never!"

"I know that." He slid his hands onto her shoulders. "Deep down, so does she. But the poor thing is anxious enough as it is. She can vanish in the blink of an eye, so just let her be at your side." He kissed her forehead. "Come on. Get your boots on and let's go."

The encampment was bustling when they left the tent, with knights hurrying throughout, presumably adjusting to the shift in orders their commanding officers had doled out.

"I wonder what Byrric told them," Freya murmured as she watched the knights and servants break down their tents, pack up their bedrolls, splash water on embers.

"Knowing your father, the truth." Aer flashed a smile. "In detail."

They found Byrric and the others in his tent, all dressed and ready to move.

"Ah, good, you're here," he said when he saw them. "Let's finalize everything before we head off."

"My scouts have secured the landing place Lord Silmar found," Fenian said. "It will put us in a good position to go north to Kildin or continue east, should circumstances change."

"The plan is to wait for two days at most before attempting Kildin without additional aid," Byrric said. "His Majesty will lead the elves," he said with a nod toward Ruehnar. "Ana, the Valkyrie. King Aerelius and Zane, our knights. Rodrick and Cecilia will remain with Aerelius and join his guard temporarily."

Freya nearly smiled at the twin looks of frustration on her guards' faces. Clearly they opposed the decision, but being the good soldiers they were, they'd never oppose Byrric. At least not openly.

"What about Reginald?" Freya asked. "Whose command will he fall under?"

"Ours," Zane said. "His Majesty and I will keep him with the Lind knights."

"When you go, the most important thing to remember is that the rebels want freedom from Lessia's rule," Florian said. "Now that she's dead, the Linds can help them put a solid leader in place."

"If they pause to hear us out before attacking," Fenian muttered.

Freya turned to Rini, who was hovering silently near the door. "I know you want to come with me, but I need you to stay here." At the pixie's look of frustration, Freya added, "Stay, keep an eye on Reginald, help in whatever way you can. Utgard is just too volatile to risk more of us than necessary, and we need to get in and out as quickly as possible."

Rini huffed out a breath, then gave a sharp nod. "Alright, then. As you wish. The last thing I want is to be in the way."

Freya bit back her sharp response and tried to soften her words. "Rini, this has nothing to do with you. I need you to know that. I always want you by my side, but this time, the fewer of us that go, the better."

Rini's expression relaxed slightly. "I suppose that makes sense, Your Majesty. I will stay with the King and ensure all is well here in your absence."

"Thank you." Freya turned to her father. "When do we leave?"

"Within the next few hours," he replied. "We need to go over exactly how we'll handle Vali and whatever else we'll have to deal with while we're there."

Dread pooled in Freya's stomach at the thought of what 'whatever else' might be, especially considering the various creatures she'd had to fight off of Watoria's streets in years past. But some niggling feeling in the back of her mind told her draugs would be the least of her worries.

DESPITE BYRRIC'S desire to leave by midday, it took several more hours to make final preparations before leaving camp. It was nearly an hour after they'd finished lunch by the time Freya said her good-byes to Aer and took hands with Fenian to travel to the chilly mountain forest of the northern borderlands. As soon as they touched down among the trees, Naedan took flight, shooting from the trees to scan the surrounding area.

The last time Freya had been this far north was not long after her mother died. She'd traveled with Byrric to the border to wait as he investigated the circumstances surrounding Cina's death. At the time, all he came away with was that a prisoner had fled from Jotunheim a few miles from Utgard. Cina had attempted to take him into custody, prepared to bring him south into Caelora, but he'd had a small wooden vial of ore powder in his pocket no one had noticed. He'd tossed the poisonous powder in her eyes, killing her within minutes.

The Jotnar male had wanted freedom, and he believed Cina wanted to prevent that. Freya couldn't blame him, but it didn't alleviate the cold that clenched its fist around her heart as she imagined what her mother must've felt in those final moments.

She was jolted from her thoughts by a tugging at her waist. Exasperated, she unbuttoned the pouch on her hip and let Toskr leap to the ground.

"You know, all you had to do was ask," she told him as he shifted. "I knew you were there the entire time."

He leapt to his feet, then dusted himself off. "I could have asked, Queen Freya, but that would have given you the opportunity to say no. Better to ask forgiveness than permission, I like to say."

"Yes, and how has that worked out for you in the past?" Fenian drawled.

"There is always room for improvement, Your Highness," Toskr replied. "Now, where to first?"

"We aren't far from the edge of the forest," Byrric said. "We'll head that way, meet with Naedan closer to Utgard, then decide the best approach."

Quietly, they started walking, the only sound the crunching of pine needles beneath their feet.

"Do you think Vali will help us?" Freya whispered after they'd been walking for a few minutes. She knew little of her cousin aside from what her father told her, which hadn't been much.

"I don't know." Her father frowned as he scanned the forest around them. "From what I recall of him, he's stubborn, often short-sighted, but intelligent. My mother seems to have a high regard for him, which is the only reason I've agreed to this."

"Did you know him well when you were young?" Fenian asked.

"Not really, no. We share a third-great-grandfather on my mother's side. We always got on well enough, but our relationship was nothing like what Aerelius has with Lazarus or Lea."

She assumed as much, but to hear just how little her father knew of the person they hoped to court as an ally, the person who lived in the same empire that would see hers crumble, unnerved her.

Crack.

All her senses immediately went on alert, but she hardly had time to react to the muffled sound and sudden pull of magic before an arrow, the iron tip swirling with pearlescent magic, flew forward, halting mere inches from her eyes.

Hands up, she swallowed, then checked her periphery, noting her father and Fenian were in a similar predicament. She barely had time to register her surprise that the prince had been so caught off guard, when three Jotnar, each tall and fair-haired, dressed in heavy furs and leather, emerged from the trees, their movements smooth as a blade cutting through water.

A fourth, taller than the rest, walked forward.

"Vali said you might venture our way, Commander." His voice carried the typical accent of northerners, but had a harsher tone, not nearly as smooth as other high-ranking Jotnar Freya had met, although it was clear in his demeanor and the way the other two deferred to him that he was just that.

Still frozen, Freya slid her eyes to her father. "Friend of yours?"

The male's pale eyes shifted to her. "And you've brought a queen, I see." His lips curled when he saw Fenian. "And an elf." He snapped his fingers. "Bind their magic. Take them to Vali. He'll figure out what to do with them." He sent another sharp look at Freya. "And keep those pretty wings out of sight."

THE GATES of Utgard were only half a mile from the tree line, a short trek across a rolling expanse of grass that exposed Freya, her father, Fenian, and the Jotnar who led them toward the gates to anyone who might be watching. Observing the situation now, Freya knew there had been very little chance of them arriving and approaching the gates without being seen, so she could reason that being taken in by guards was actually the most efficient way to get into the village.

Their boots crunched over the frozen grass as they traversed the open space. Several more rebels had slipped from the tree line to join them, effectively caging her party in with no means of escape. Her magic itched beneath her skin; a crawling thing that made her want to tear the layers of flesh away from her body. She'd never had her magic bound before, although the elvish monarchs had threatened with Aer when they were in Avorell. Now, as she felt the prickles of trapped magic beating against her rib cage, she understood why it was such an effective threat.

Her eyes fell to the group around her, but she didn't dare look too closely at any of her escorts as she walked. They weren't here as enemies. They weren't here to attack or pillage or cause harm. Perhaps she was naïve, but she hoped that once her cousin saw them, they would be allowed to enter without armed guards escorting them.

She cast her gaze about, taking in the hamlet's fortress-like construction. It was clear this wasn't a place they had built to look nice or feel like home. Instead, it had been built for survival. The weatherbeaten wood ramparts were easily thirty-feet tall, with a spiked cheval de frise offering additional protection against invaders. Guards paced along the wall, bows at their sides and quivers at their backs, watching the surrounding landscape for any hint of attack.

She looked up, exhaling a breath as Naedan continued to soar high above in his hawk form, drifting away from Utgard and, hopefully, avoiding suspicion.

As they neared the gates, Freya shifted her focus as discreetly as possible to the Jotnar who escorted them. As far as appearance, they were nothing like the nobles of Jotunheim she'd already met. Instead, they were more reminiscent of her own people in Allanor and others in the northern lands. The air of hostility and deceit she often felt around Lessia and her ilk was absent, replaced with a sharp determination that was nearly palpable in each measured look the guards sent her way. Despite the scratches and scuffs that covered their leather, it was obvious highly skilled leatherworkers had crafted their attire. The heavy garb did little to hide the stealthy grace with which they moved, however.

Her only solace was that her father was at the front of their group speaking furtively with the Jotnar who'd put an arrow to their faces minutes earlier and was now leading them to the gates. As he spoke, his motions showed a mixture of aggravation and frustration, but Freya saw no fear or apprehension there.

When they were about thirty yards from the tall wooden gates, one of the Jotnar called ahead. She held her breath as the gates creaked open and a tall fur-and-leather-clad figure strode out.

At first glance, Vali Balthana looked nothing like the other Balthana family members she had met in her time, although that number was admittedly few. Where most of her relatives had hair in varying shades of brown, his leaned more toward dark blond. Two tight braids ran along his temples into the thick, flowing hair that fell past his shoulders. The cocky expression he wore, however, made their shared bloodline undeniable. It was an expression she'd seen on her father's face many times. She couldn't help but smile at just how much she saw her father, her grandfather, and likely every Balthana that had come before, reflected in that one expression.

"Byrric!" He folded his thick arms across his chest, revealing two large blades at his hips. "Give me one good reason I shouldn't send you lot straight to the pillory for crossing into our lands!"

From her position behind him, Freya saw her father tense. "Does blood count for nothing this far north?"

Freya cocked her head, surprised at the commander's lax tone. As she did, Vali's gaze shifted to her, his brows winging up. "And look at your little Freya, all grown up. Where's your crown, girl?"

Freya straightened her shoulders and gave him a wry smile. "It awaits me in Iladel."

With a small smirk, Vali looked back to Byrric and started walking toward him. When the two males faced off, Vali's face broke into a broad grin. "What took you so long, cousin? We've been waiting for weeks."

Freya's shoulders nearly slumped with relief as Byrric accepted a handshake and a one-armed hug from Vali. The males who'd been standing around them shifted, relaxing their stances.

Vali looked back to her before giving them all a sharp nod. "Alright. Let's get inside. It's fucking cold out here."

He shouted a command to the guards atop the wall, and a moment later, the gates opened fully, allowing their group passage into Utgard.

32

FREYA

Freya wasn't sure exactly what she expected to see when she stepped into the rebel stronghold, but the bustling town that faced her wasn't it. A main thoroughfare of hard-packed dirt allowed wagons and horses easy passage, while narrow paths and alleys extended from the walls in all directions, with one broad road that appeared to encircle the entire town. People moved up and down the walkways with purpose, heading one place or another. All wore some variation of the clothing Vali wore—a mix of leather, lambskin, and fur in various states of wear. She didn't see many children, either due to the cold or her group's unannounced arrival, but based on the few she did see, it was clear Utgard was no longer just home to fighters.

As they walked through the village, Freya kept her eyes ahead to avoid looking at the people who'd stopped to stare. The party turned right, at the end of the main thoroughfare, where a narrow road led to a wooden longhouse that was a slightly larger version of those around it. A moment later, the guards ushered them inside Vali's home, where they were instantly hit by the warmth of a large stone fire pit in the center of the room and the scent of roasting meat.

Her mouth watered at the thought of warm stew, but that would have to wait.

Vali took a seat at the head of a long table, then gestured for them to sit. Freya and Byrric took seats to his left, while Fenian sat beside Toskr across from them.

"Where is your friend?" Vali asked as he skimmed his gaze over them. "The hawk who traveled with you?"

"Scouting," Byrric replied. "I'm sure he'll be along soon."

Vali jerked his chin toward his guards. "Go find him. Bring him to me."

With curt nods, the guards ducked through the door and left to find Naedan.

Once they were gone, Vali turned toward them, his eyes settling on Freya and softening a bit. "You look like your mother. I was very sorry to hear she died."

"She didn't die," Freya corrected, ignoring the sharp kick she felt from Byrric. "She was killed."

Vali's gray eyes went cool. "The person who killed her was attempting to flee what he saw as certain death. He had only recently fled Jotunheim. Those of us who'd been here longer knew the Linds were here on good terms. Do not think Cina's death went unmourned or unpunished." He tapped a hand on the table. "But there will be time later to discuss past hurts. For now, let's get you settled in. We have much to discuss, and it will do you all some good to have a proper meal." With a frown, he looked at Toskr. "Although, I must ask...how did you come to keep the company of a criminal from the elvish lands and an elf prince?"

"The elves have offered allegiance," Fenian told him, then sent Freya a look that clearly said, *"You can explain the squirrel."*

"As Prince Fenian said, we've come to an agreement with the elves. Ratatoskr was my guide in Avorell," Freya explained. "And he rode with me into battle to save Watoria."

"I was quite valiant, I assure you," Toskr said.

"Is that so?" Vali sent Byrric an amused look. "I heard of your success in Watoria, and I look forward to hearing the story of how you all managed to get into Avorell and back without losing your lives."

A stout young female appeared, arms laden with food, and began to set a spread in front of them. Vali brushed a hand along her arm and smiled softly. The female, whom Freya assumed was his wife, returned his smile and squeezed his shoulder before retreating. Once she was gone, Vali refocused on them.

"While we eat, tell me your story."

If Freya learned anything in her time with the elves, it was that patience was crucial when it came to courting allies. It appeared the rebels were no exception, so she forced down her annoyance and need for haste. With as bright a smile as she could muster, she nodded.

Fenian leaned forward and picked up a piece of bread. "Thank you, Lord Balthana," he said. "Your hospitality is much appreciated."

Vali snorted. "I'm lord of nothing, Your Highness. Now eat."

They dug in, Freya listening as Byrric laid out the events of the past month, from the attack on their wedding night to their retaking of Watoria. She noticed that he held back some information, including how many people they'd had in their party at Iston and where the others had gone. Byrric also didn't tell Vali the extent of the elves' involvement, leaving out the fact that most of the royal family was currently on Lindorothian soil spreading their strength and resources to all corners of the kingdom. He mentioned nothing of Lea's involvement with Jonas or *Jonas'* involvement in Lessia's murder, instead sticking to the basic facts: Willem had been her ally, turned her own knights against her, and murdered her and her cousin. He left out anything regarding their desire to find out what Daniel Veldin's stance was on Lessia's death or how he felt about her alliance with the humans since their recent coup.

"So, now you want our help to get Kildin and the rest of your kingdom back," Vali said, dipping a hunk of bread into his stew after he'd listened to their account for nearly two hours. "We have our own battles to fight up here, you know. A leader we've despised is finally out of our hair. It's the perfect time to attempt an attack on Madrya. Why should we set that aside to help you?"

"They have triple your numbers," Freya pointed out.

"We're an industrious people," Vali countered.

"Jonas Edrin is Lessia's heir," Byrric said. "Assuming you met him, you'll know he's a far better person than his aunt."

Vali looked at Freya. "Do you believe that, Your Majesty?"

Freya's eyes itched to look toward her father for guidance, but she kept her features schooled. "Having met them both, I believe he will be far better than Lessia, yes."

Vali lifted his brows, then looked at Byrric before addressing Freya. "And what if we believe Daniel Veldin is the leader that would best suit our needs?"

"Jonas has been a strong ally against Lessia," she said. "Daniel, from all accounts, hasn't shown the same tendencies."

"Jonas Edrin sat pretty as Lessia's heir for years, only choosing to rebel against her when it became convenient to do so." Vali sipped from a thick ceramic mug. "A person with those decision making skills isn't one who inspires much confidence."

"One person alone can't fight against an empress," Freya pointed out. "As you well know."

"I do know," he agreed. "However, as you can see, I am not by myself here. We have amassed much support for our fight against the late empress. Jonas, by all accounts, has enjoyed his time in Lessia's employ, traveling as her emissary around the world. So, you'll forgive me and my people if we're wary of supporting his quest for leadership."

"Are you saying you won't help us?" Freya asked.

"I'm saying I don't think I can support Lord Edrin," he replied. "As for you...I can't make that decision just yet."

"Why not?" Fenian demanded.

"I must first convene with my council," Vali replied. "I am not saying no, but I won't make that choice for my people when we are already fighting our own fights here."

Perhaps it was the long-held picture of disorganized chaos she'd envisioned in Utgard, but Freya was surprised to hear Vali had a council. Noticing her surprise, he smiled.

"We're just as civilized as the rest of you," he said smoothly.

"Aren't your people the Linds?" Fenian asked, seemingly stuck on Vali's refusal to give an immediate response.

"I've lived in Jotunheim for more than a century. My wife, my children are all Jotnar born. Blood and kingdom do not always guarantee allegiance, as your friend Jonas will tell you. I saw how Lessia treated the people of Jotunheim, and I felt for them. So, I joined them." His eyes flicked toward the room where his wife had disappeared to, then he thumbed away a speck of food from his cheek and stood. "I'm going to meet with my council now. My wife has made sleeping arrangements for you. As for discussing joint efforts...that will have to wait until morning, as there are many opinions to consider. We won't make this decision lightly."

With a final nod, he left them to finish eating.

Freya smiled her thanks as he walked away, doing her best to ignore the sinking feeling in her heart.

33

LEA

It took nearly fifteen minutes of arguing, but Lea was able to convince her mother and Lindesson to take Jonas to the drawing room instead of the cellar, which was where they wanted to hold him. It was a small victory, but she knew in her heart that Jonas was still on their side. The last thing they needed was for him to turn on them because they already considered him a traitor.

It finally took Ordona pointing out that Jonas would be far more likely to help them if they at least pretended to treat him as an ally.

"We won't detain him in the cellar," Perida said, "but if he so much as looks at my daughter the wrong way—"

"I will remove each of his fingers with a dull knife," Ettrian offered.

Lea elbowed him. "That won't be necessary. Shall we allow him entry now?"

"He'll be of no threat," Lindesson told Perida. "If I get the slightest hint he's being deceitful, we will detain him properly. With all of his appendages," he added, shooting a warning look at Ettrian.

"Very well," Perida said with a sigh.

The moment Perida gave her approval, Lindesson nodded to his knights, who stood with the elves who'd escorted Jonas to the gatehouse of Lea's home.

"Go with them," Ettrian told his knights. "A united front in the same room will help us better gauge his intentions."

The knights gave their salutes and turned to leave the room.

Lindesson remained behind, and once the knights were gone, he faced Perida. "I would like to make him wait a bit."

"Agreed," Ettrian said with a nod.

"Why?" Perida asked.

"I'm inclined to believe your daughter regarding Lord Edrin's intentions here," Lindesson replied. "But it's worth noting how he reacts to not being welcomed with open arms, especially now that he's away from his knights."

"Lea has already made her lack of welcome clear," Perida countered.

"If he has half a brain, he'll know her show was all an act," Ettrian replied.

"He's right, Perida," Ordona murmured. "Jonas Edrin might be foolish at time, but I do not believe he is truly a fool."

Perida scoffed, but Lea couldn't help but agree with her aunt.

"Well, he's already waited nearly half an hour," Lea said. "I'd say that's long enough."

"As you wish," Lindesson said.

They made their way back inside the house, then downstairs to the drawing room, General Lindesson leading the way. There was a complete absence of staff, making it clear someone had given the order for everyone to tuck themselves away until they got things with Jonas sorted.

The nearer they got to Jonas, the quicker Lea's heart beat. Despite the circumstances, she had considered Jonas a friend for several months now. When all was said and done, she hoped that friendship could endure.

A cool hand brushed down her arm, and before she could look at Ettrian, his lips were at her ear.

"Why is your heart beating so quickly, little witch? Are you nervous to see your lover?"

Her teeth ground together in frustration, but she refused to give Ettrian the satisfaction of riling her up.

"I just hoped...ugh." She tugged at one of her curls in annoyance. "I just hoped he would stay in Iladel, that Willem would convince him to let me go the same way he'd let Isadora go."

"Isadora's disappearance was something Willem could use to his advantage," Ettrian murmured. "A human queen kidnapped by evil Linds is just what he needed to garner widespread support from his men."

They reached the drawing room, where Tyna was hovering in the air beside the door waiting for them. General Lindesson stopped at her side and turned to face the rest of them.

"Lady Calliwell, I would like to request that you allow your daughter to go in before us," he said to Perida. "Prince Ettrian and Tyna can go in with her for added support, if you'd like, and Iska and our knights will be in there, of course," he added.

Perida looked like she wanted to argue, so Lea cut off any retort. "That's fine with me." She flicked a look at Ettrian. "Your Highness?"

He gestured for her to move forward. "After you."

Surprisingly, but thankfully, Lindesson hadn't had Jonas restrained in any way. However, the half-dozen knights surrounding him, all elves and magic wielders, were likely more effective at keeping him in one place than any type of bonds.

"Lea!" Jonas rushed forward, relief flooding his face as she entered the room. Two Lind warlocks blocked his path. He paused, his mouth turning down when he saw Ettrian come in behind her.

"Jonas, what are you doing here?" Lea asked, flicking her hand so the knights would step aside, allowing Jonas to relax. "You sent me away so I would be safe, yet here you are with a fully armed squadron, shouting about bringing me back to the capital."

Jonas scrubbed his hands over his face, his eyes a bit wild as he attempted to compose himself. "Obviously Willem sent me on a 'rescue' mission for you and the princess. If it were just a matter of coming after you, I would've convinced him you weren't worth our time. He's expecting me to bring you both back to the capital."

Lea eyed him warily. For someone who normally seemed so confident and put together, Jonas seemed to be hanging by a thread. His typically pristine white leather was filthy from travel, his long hair lank without its usual shine. He was the picture of a male who'd gotten in way over his head.

"You are aware that will not be happening, correct?" Ettrian asked. "You bargained with me to keep Lea safe. I swore to do everything in my power to do that."

Jonas' jaw clenched, his eyes full of distrust at the threat Ettrian's words carried. It annoyed Lea to no end that he would look at Ettrian with such distaste, when he'd put her life in his hands not two weeks earlier.

"Of course I know that," Jonas snapped. "And why are you still here? That wasn't part of our bargain. You should be with the king and queen."

"Yes, about that bargain," Lea cut in before the prince could speak. There was so much she wanted to talk to him about, such as what had been going on in the palace since she left, but her anger seemed hellbent on taking charge. "Why, did you find it necessary to go behind my back and make a deal with not only Ettrian, but Willem, too? Of all the people to make a deal with, Jonas, you chose Willem? We were supposed to be a team!"

"I saw an opportunity to make my empire a better place, so I took it. I didn't have time—"

"To tell me you wanted to send me off with an elvish prince you knew nothing about?" She was horrified to feel tears burning the back of her eyelids.

"I promised Willem to help get rid of Lessia in exchange for your safety," Jonas said slowly, as if he were speaking to a child. "Prince Ettrian swore in blood that he would take you wherever you needed to go to escape Willem *safely*."

Lea folded her arms, her face a mask of dangerous curiosity. "Oh? Did Prince Ettrian promise to bring me safely and directly to Freya and Aerelius? Did he promise to bring all of the prisoners *safely* and *directly* to Vara Balthana's estate? Did he swear to you, in blood, that I would be kept here in Lindoroth with my family, or was that aspect of your bargain so open-ended that he could've brought me 'safely' to Avorell?" She ignored the look of horrified realization he now wore. "Or did you not consider that level of betrayal?"

Jonas' wide eyes turned to Ettrian.

Ettrian chuckled, moving to stand at her side. "She has you by the balls, there, Lord Edrin. And to be fair, she is not wrong. I did consider it. Briefly," he added with a smirk in Lea's direction. "I could've whisked her away to the other side of the world," the prince continued, stepping slowly toward Jonas until they were almost nose to nose. "Kept her safe my own way, in my own lands. One does not need to be home to be safe, Lord Edrin." He flashed a smile, wicked and just wide enough to show his fangs, to remind everyone in the room of the monster that hid beneath his skin. His final words came out in a hiss. "I could have locked her in a tower in Andradath, where she would live out her days without illness or injury, without the threat of harm, her mind filled with so much magic she wouldn't know fantasy from reality. Safety is relative, and you, my lord, should remember that the next time you attempt to make a bargain with an elf prince."

Jonas' face paled, and he took a step back from the prince.

Heavy silence filled the air as the knights watched the two males staring each other down. Loud buzzing filled Lea's head, and her eyes fell shut as she absorbed the gravity of Ettrian's threats. Each time she let herself forget who and what he was, he reminded her before that memory could slip too far away. He could've done all of that, could still do it, if he chose to. All it would take would be one touch and she'd be in Avorell, a captive, so filled with elvish magic she would be deluded into believing her life was a perfect thing.

"You are a fool if you think I would do such a thing."

Her eyes flew open at the sound of Ettrian's voice in her mind, at the reassurance his words instantly brought her.

Ettrian turned away from Jonas, his eyes locking onto hers briefly before he returned to her side.

"Your point is well made, Your Highness," Jonas rasped. "But Lea, I only wanted to help you. I did everything I could to protect you in the palace, I—"

Lea shook her head. "I know you did. It doesn't change the fact that you left me out of the one thing I *should* have been consulted on." She turned her head and looked at Tyna, who hovered by the door, her face solemn. "Tell them they can come in now."

As they waited for the others, Lea eyed Jonas, who still seemed quite shaken. It was a struggle for her to reconcile her desire to defend him just a few minutes ago with the anger and disappointment she felt looking at him now. The blood bond he'd made with Aer required Jonas to protect her, yet his agreement with Ettrian showed just how flawed that agreement had been. Perhaps she'd need to speak with her cousin about fine-tuning his own bargains...

Shame flooded her the moment the thought crossed her mind. The circumstances between Aer's agreement with Jonas and Jonas' with Ettrian were worlds apart. Aer had just watched his father be poisoned to death after his palace had been invaded on his wedding night. He'd had kingship forced on him moments later and was getting ready to part from his mother so they could all flee into hiding, with no knowledge of when they'd see each other again, if ever.

Jonas had simply wanted a crown.

No, the two were nothing alike.

She shook herself from her thoughts when General Lindesson, her mother, and Ordona entered the room. Lindesson seemed to sense a threat in the room immediately, likely due to his shifter senses. He cast a look between Ettrian and Jonas, who now stood several feet apart. Ettrian at Lea's back, Jonas, surrounded by knights, his face still leached of color.

"Lord Edrin," Lindesson said. He gestured toward the knights. "I hope you understand why we're taking precautions here."

Dragging his focus away from the prince, Jonas met the general's stare with a sharp nod. "Yes, of course. I would do the same in your shoes. I'm just glad to see Lea has made it home safe."

"Why are you here, Lord Edrin?" Perida asked. "I hope you don't think you're taking my daughter anywhere with you."

Ordona looked as if she wanted to take her sister's hand, but Lea was glad she chose not to. The last time Jonas saw Perida, she'd been a malnourished, bloody mess. She'd been nothing like the female who stood before him now who radiated strength and glowed with power; all traces of weakness gone.

"No, Lady Calliwell, I had no intention of trying to take your daughter anywhere." He shifted his attention back to Lindesson. "I'm here to help in whatever way I can. That's why I only came with a small squadron."

"All of whom are currently in shackles," Ettrian said. "Aside from the humans, of course. They'll be on the pyre soon enough."

Jonas' mouth dropped open. "I don't care about the humans, but the Jotnar are loyal to me!"

"They won't be harmed," Lea assured him.

"They were loyal to Lessia, too, were they not?" Ordona asked in her most queenly voice. "You'll forgive us for not wanting to take any chances."

Lindesson clasped his hands behind his back and stepped toward Jonas. His gruff face and dark hair were a stark contrast to Jonas' smooth features and white-blond hair, making him appear even more ominous. "So," he began. "Now that we've established you're on your own here, let's discuss Willem Ristner."

Jonas swallowed hard, but to his credit, didn't show any fear.

"I'll tell you everything you want to know."

34

LEA

They spent nearly two hours interrogating Jonas. Lindesson and Ettrian did most of the talking, while Lea, Ordona, and Perida observed silently. There were many times Lea wanted to interject, but her aunt had been firm when they spoke earlier about allowing the leaders of each army to handle the questioning. Part of it bothered Lea, considering she'd been in the palace with Willem, but she also had to acknowledge that Ettrian and Lindesson were far more experienced at this type of thing than she would ever be.

Unfortunately, they came out of his questioning with little more than they'd gone in with. Assuming Jonas was being truthful, which Lea believed he was, all they learned was that Willem had not known the full breadth of the elves' involvement. However, that had been a week ago, when he'd sent Jonas away from Iladel. So, for the time being, Perida had ordered the staff to house Jonas in the guest quarters with four guards on him at all times. Comfortable, but still under lock and key.

"Reykr Traust will have returned to Iladel by now," Lea said as they discussed Jonas' reports. "Willem certainly knows more now than he did when Jonas left, so it's unlikely we'll get anything else out of him that would be useful."

"Yes, Willem will have heard by now where Freya and Aerelius are," Ordona said. "And now that he has Traust at his disposal, it's likely he sent Jonas here to keep him from being underfoot."

Lindesson nodded his agreement. "I think we've gotten all we can from him for now. We'll let him simmer a bit, allow him to get more comfortable." He looked at Lea. "I don't think he expected you to welcome him with such distrust."

It wasn't distrust. More...disbelief. He truly didn't see how horribly wrong this all could've gone. Lea sighed. "I didn't expect to welcome him that way, either. I just wish he knew more." All they'd learned from speaking with Jonas was that he didn't know where Traust was, he didn't know any useful details about Willem's plans now that more human reinforcements were present, and he assumed the Jotnar would follow him into war against the man who was currently their ally.

She folded her arms and turned toward the window, then stared out over the landscape toward the ocean and muttered, "I suppose it shouldn't be surprising."

"Well, we'll keep him where he is for now," Lindesson replied. "If that's acceptable to you, Lady Calliwell?"

Perida seemed to struggle with his question, and Lea had no doubt her mother's instinct was to toss Jonas in the cellar.

"We can trust him enough to keep him in the guest quarters," Lea said. "Treat him as an ally, but with reservations."

"We'll keep him under watch," Lindesson agreed. "But you catch more flies with honey, as they say."

Perida held Lea's gaze for a long moment, her eyes hard, before she looked at Lindesson and nodded. "We'll keep him comfortable for now."

Lea let out a quiet breath of relief, thankful her mother hadn't taken too much convincing. At the end of the day, Jonas had been a friend to her before Freya and Aer's wedding. She hoped that friendship could prove beneficial when they took back their thrones.

∽

THEY LET Jonas stay in his room for the remainder of the day and into the night. The kitchen had sent up the same dinner Lea and the others had shared–roasted chicken with fresh vegetables and wild rice–and he'd been given a room with southern exposure, one of the nicest guest rooms in the house.

Ettrian, being who he was, had suggested the room furthest to the west. Ever the passive-aggressive, Perida had clearly seen the benefit to putting Jonas in the room closest to the smoldering pile of bodies in the desert.

Once sundown came and went, Lea ascended the stairs to the third floor where Jonas' room was. She wanted to ensure he was comfortable, but she also needed to speak with him away from the eyes and ears of her mother, the general, and perhaps most importantly, Ettrian.

It wasn't that she wanted to hide her meeting with him. She just wanted to speak with him in private without heaps of anger and suspicion weighting the room down. Although, with Iska tailing her as he was, she knew that would be virtually impossible.

She had to force her chin high, though, when she stepped past the knights standing on either side of his door and knocked.

"The door must stay open, Lady Calliwell," Iska said from behind her. "Your mother's orders."

She sighed, but gave him a quick smile.

The look of relief on Jonas' face when opened the door told her he'd been hoping she'd come.

"Thank the gods," he muttered as he ushered her inside.

She sent a small smile to the guards, knowing word of her visit would reach everyone in the house soon, then stepped into the room.

"Are you alright?" Jonas asked, taking a seat in an armchair.

"Of course. How are you?" Lea sat down gingerly on the edge of the bed. "They're treating you well?"

He shrugged. "As well as to be expected. The windows are spelled, but otherwise, the conditions for a prisoner could be far worse."

Then, as if realizing what he said, he grimaced. "As you would know, of course."

She nodded slowly. "Thank you for answering all of our questions earlier. And as for the guards–just give my mother a bit of time. You can't really blame her, considering."

Awkward silence stretched between them before he finally asked, "What did you come here for, Lea?" A smile flickered on his lips. "I know it isn't for the pleasure of my company."

She smiled. "Jonas...do you understand why I was—am—so angry with you?"

"Now that I've had time and space to reflect, yes, I do." He leaned forward and rested his forearms on his knees. "But Lea, I swear to you, I felt I was acting in your best interest. I needed to get you out of there and away from Willem. I thought making a deal with him to help kill Lessia would make that possible."

"Anyone who spent five minutes with the man would know he'd double-cross you without a second thought." Her words were harsh, but she didn't care. "The only good that came from this is that the world is now short one sadistic ruler."

"I know. And I hope some day you'll forgive me for putting too much trust in him, when it should've been placed in you."

As he held her stare, she wondered if he'd had the same thoughts she'd had, the wisps of a potential future kicked off by drunken dancing and laughing with friends that had all but vanished the night of the wedding. When his pale eyes dropped from hers, full of sorrow and regret, she knew they'd shared and lost those same fleeting thoughts.

Exhaling a slow breath, she gathered her courage to follow through with her main reason for coming to him. "Jonas...you should know...your sister..." Her words stuck in her throat as tears for a female she'd never known burned her eyelids, pity for the last remaining family Jonas had lost. She'd asked her mother and Lindesson to leave news of Dania Edrin's death out of their line of questioning, both out of respect for the sister Jonas lost but also because, if he hadn't known of her death, it could completely derail their interrogation.

Jonas' throat bobbed, but he kept his eyes trained on the smooth wood floor. "Yes, I assumed as much when I heard the real Isadora had been traveling with your cousin." He shifted in his seat, resting his head against the chair's high back. "I wish I'd known Isadora had been allowed to live as a child. I would've tried to help her."

"Why do you think Lessia let her live?" Lea asked quietly. It was one of the unanswered questions she'd found most perplexing.

"My guess is she didn't know," Jonas said. "She likely handed Isadora off to a healer when she was near death and never followed up to hear of her progress. Lessia made no secret of her disdain for humans, but the palace healer had always had a soft heart. It's a wonder she's been employed as long as she has, to be honest." He smiled softly at some unspoken memory. "She would have done all in her power to save the girl, and it wouldn't surprise me in the least to learn she'd lied about Isadora's death to Lessia."

"She would've helped her start over in Jotunheim?"

"Without a doubt. Isadora would've been just barely old enough to find work of some sort."

"She told Freya and Aer she worked as a seamstress in Madrya," Lea murmured.

"Unfortunately, as a human in Jotunheim, it's unlikely her life was as comfortable as she let on, even with our healer's help." Jonas pressed his fingers to his eyes. "She would've been desperate for escape, so I can't blame her one bit for fleeing with Willem."

They sat in silence for a moment. Lea didn't know what was in Jonas' mind, but all she could think of was that it was doubtful he'd ever get to hold a proper funeral for his sister.

"I'm very sorry for your loss, Jonas," she murmured as she got to her feet. She placed a hand on his shoulder, closing her eyes when he squeezed it, resting his head against her side. His breath came out in a long, shaking gasp so full of grief, Lea's own threatened to rear its head.

"Thank you, Lea," he whispered.

Then she left him to his tears.

35

FREYA

Dusk came and went with no word from Vali or any member of the council he was supposedly meeting with. Naedan arrived stone-faced just after dark, escorted by two of the males who'd brought Freya and the others from the woods. He had little to report other than to provide more information on the layout of Utgard and its defenses. Which, while valuable, wasn't terribly useful considering their current circumstances.

As Freya lay on the straw-filled mattress in a small cabin not far from Vali's home, her mind switched between frustration at their lack of momentum and missing Aer. She hated that they'd separated again, but she knew dividing and conquering was their only option at this point.

It didn't change how much his absence in her bed weighed on her, or how badly she wanted to get back to him as soon as possible.

So, she lay there, listening to the sounds of the others talking—well, all but Toskr, who'd fallen asleep on a cot in the corner of the living area as soon as they'd returned from dinner.

Sometimes she envied the elf's ability to fall asleep in a snap, no matter the circumstances.

Fenian, Naedan, and Byrric stayed up most of the night talking quietly about what they might do if Vali turned them down. The first and most obvious plan was to skip Kildin for now and go straight to Iladel. She hated the idea because they needed Kildin to come back under Lind control. Setting aside its people, whose safety was paramount, its proximity to the river junction, the mountain pass, and its status as a trading crossroads… It was crucial to regain control of it. If the city ended up beyond salvaging, any rebuilding efforts throughout the rest of the kingdom would be infinitely more difficult because any supplies they would bring in from abroad would need to be rerouted to smaller, less central ports.

More than once, she considered giving up on sleep and going out to join the others, but each time, exhaustion tugged at her mind. Eventually, she dozed off, sleeping fitfully for several hours. She wasn't sure how much time had passed when she was woken by a sharp rapping at the front door, but when she glanced out the window, she saw the sky was just beginning to shift toward the purplish hue of dawn.

Within moments, she had her boots and jacket on. Before she rushed out, though, she paused, took a breath, and forced a neutral expression before opening the door and walking into the living area. Her four companions all stood there fully dressed, although Toskr was notably bleary eyed. Vali stood in the door frame, his body backlit by the gray morning sky.

"Little cousin," he said with a nod. "I hope you slept well."

She slid a look at Byrric, then to Vali. "It was quite comfortable, thank you."

"We've reached our decision." He looked at each of them in turn. "If you'll accompany me, we can discuss everything."

She fought the urge to look at her father again and smiled. "Alright. Lead the way."

When the bitter pre-dawn cold hit her skin, Freya tugged her fur-lined jacket tightly around her body and forced herself to think warm thoughts: beaches on the Errestian coast, scenting the Aemir sea in Avorell, lounging on the deck of a ship as it sailed down the Selnor in Summer.

One day, she thought. *One day I'll do it all.*

A sharp gust of wind hit her, whipping her hair around her face in a stinging mess, reminding her that those warm thoughts were just that—dreams of another time that was far in the future.

So, she shoved them down and refocused on the tangible world in front of her.

With a sigh, she pushed a touch of fire magic into her clothes. Warmth filled her fur and leather garb, coated her gloveless hands with soothing heat, and eased its way into her boots, warming the toes that had already begun to go chilly.

As they walked the final yards toward Vali's house, Freya found herself surprised again by how civilized the rebels were. She never considered them animals, of course, but she found it startling they'd managed to build not only a community but an entire village, at that, despite being under constant threat. She'd expected near squalor, with crude shelters that protected them from the elements and little more, all resources directed toward protection and their cause.

Instead, she found...life. People standing in doorways talking to neighbors, the warm scent of food being prepared for the day. It almost reminded her of growing up in Watoria, where the telltale sounds of people starting their day always made her feel at ease.

Considering how established and organized the rebels were, it was hard to understand why Lessia would've left them alone for so long. She could only imagine the former empress simply didn't believe the small clan of Jotnar were strong enough to amass any kind of assault against her. And with Madrya being clear on the other side of the empire, it might seem silly to waste resources when the Linds could take the rebels on sight the moment they entered Lindoroth. Which was undoubtedly what Lessia had been hoping for.

Although, it would seem that wasn't the case. If anything, the Linds had done quite the opposite, helping the rebels establish themselves instead of slaughtering them, which would've been an easy feat considering the lack of Jotnar support. But with Vali to act as a liaison between the Lindorothians and Jotnar, and the Linds' constant presence at the border...yes, it was safe to assume Lessia left them alone to avoid tangling with the Caeloran army, not because she feared the rebels would be successful on their own. Not to mention, if a chunk of the Lind army was focused on rebel activity in the West, that was that many who weren't focused on a potential incursion from the East.

She glanced over at her father as realization hit. "So I'm going to go out on a limb here. Is the reason you and Governor Cailen didn't send a significant amount of reinforcements to the borderlands because you didn't want Lessia looking too closely at the rebels?"

"Partly," he allowed. "She saw them as largely disorganized and viewed our presence as protecting our lands. So, while Lessia would handle any factions that appeared or spread further east, she more or less assumed we would deal with those in the west."

"And those rebels who slipped into Lindoroth?" She lifted her brows. "What of them?"

"More often than not, they were unaware of the relationship we had with the rest of their kind. Vali has become an excellent leader here, but methods of communication between an existing rebel encampment and those who might be making their way here are difficult at best. Many reach the borderlands, see our knights, and assume the worst."

"Like the male who killed Mother," she said quietly.

"Yes." Byrric looked down at her. "I've never lied to you about the circumstances surrounding Cina's death."

She slid her hands in her pockets and let her eyes travel over the village, its people, its place in this world. "I know," she replied after a moment. "I think I just didn't truly understand it until now."

"Most of us admired your mother a great deal," Vali said, falling back to walk beside her. "I told you her death did not go unpunished, but you should also know she was mourned by many."

She gave him a tight smile, but was saved from responding when he shoved open the doors to his home and they were blasted with heat from a roaring fire in his hearth. Retracting her magic, Freya let the warm air heat her skin instead. The window coverings were drawn shut, the only light inside from the fireplace and a few small candles. The open space was filled with the scent of cooking food.

But it was the male at the dining table who had her halting in her tracks. Even seated, legs sprawled out as he leaned back in the chair, it was clear he was quite tall. But it was his face and its unmistakable pale features, his thick black hair, and long, straight nose that had dread pooling in her stomach as recognition hit.

In almost every way that mattered, Daniel Veldin looked nearly identical to his sister.

"Well, this is an interesting turn of events," Fenian whispered in her ear.

36

LEA

As Lea sipped her tea at breakfast the next morning, she found it hard to ignore Prince Ettrian's eyes on her.

It had become a habit of theirs the past few days to take breakfast together just after her mother and aunt left to handle things throughout the day.

She found, to her surprise, she'd started to look forward to their morning ritual, enjoying their verbal spars and his shameless innuendos. They offered a peace, a sense of normalcy she so desperately needed.

Except for this morning, the one after she'd visited Jonas. She could feel the prince's disapproving stare searing through her.

"Something on your mind, Your Highness?" she asked primly as she reached for her third croissant.

"You're too kind for your own good, Lea."

The insult behind his words hit her like a slap.

"Is being kind a crime now?" She reached for the butter dish, but it skirted out of reach, sliding across the table toward Ettrian's place, where it came to a stop beside his plate. Refusing to be deterred, she opted for jam, but it joined the butter beside his tea.

With a scowl, she stared him dead in the eye and took a stubborn bite of her dry croissant. When he smirked, she nearly threw it at his perfect, princely face.

"Kindness is not a crime, but it can make you weak." He picked up his own croissant and began slathering it with butter.

"His sister was murdered," Lea snapped. "He deserved to hear that from the closest thing he has to a friend in this kingdom, regardless of his poor judgment or potential to be a traitor."

The prince scooped up some jam and added a healthy dollop to his roll. "You were quite angry with him yesterday."

"For one reason or another, I've been unhappy with him for weeks. This was the first time I was able to tell him exactly how I felt about my time in the palace."

Ettrian's dark brows inched up. "And all is forgiven now?"

She took another bite of her flaky roll, longing for the butter and jam currently dripping off of Ettrian's. "He knows why I'm angry, he's fully aware of why we're all struggling to trust him, so there's no sense in further beating that dead horse. A bit of compassion toward him and what he's going through isn't hurting anyone."

"So you went to his room after sundown to give him news of his sister's death?" A smile tugged the prince's lips. "Nothing more?"

"Yes. Do you think I went in there to tell him all our secrets? " Lea angled her head and eyed him curiously. "Or do you think I snuck in for a late-night rendezvous with the male I'd thought was my husband?"

Ettrian's smirk widened as he took a sip of his tea. "And how did Lord Edrin take the news of his sister's demise?"

"As well as you'd expect. He already had an idea once he heard the real Isadora had been off with Freya and Aerelius. They were very close."

"Were they, though?" Ettrian watched as Lea took the final bite of her croissant, then slid the butter and jam back across the table. "He only saw her, what, once a year? There would be no reason to visit Dystone more than that, lest he raise suspicions of his true purpose, and any letters certainly would have been intercepted either there or in Jotunheim."

"True," Lea allowed. She was stuffed, but she picked up another croissant and started buttering it, just to spite the prince. "But they shared a childhood bond. That doesn't simply evaporate in one's absence."

"Fair enough." He set his napkin beside his plate. "As it happens, I agree with you. His knights are dead or captured, he knows as well as anyone that Willem will never send in a rescue mission, and you have now confirmed the human rodent has murdered his sister. He'd have to be a dimwitted fool to be loyal to such a creature."

His expression told Lea he felt Jonas was entirely capable of being so dimwitted and foolish.

"And now that the elves are involved, my people are the better allies in Jonas' eyes," she said.

"Precisely. See, you are quite a smart little witch."

She rolled her eyes, but something in the way the nickname rolled off his tongue sounded...different. More personal. As wary as she was to admit it, something had shifted since the night he'd found her in her father's study. They hadn't spoken of her breakdown or the compassion he'd shown her in response, but there hadn't been a moment where she didn't wonder where she'd be if she hadn't been able to experience her father's presence one last time.

What she hadn't settled on was how to tell her mother. Perida had been going nonstop since they'd arrived, barely pausing long enough to sit for meals. Lea knew it was a coping mechanism, but once this was all over, she would show her mother how thoroughly they'd be able to mourn her father.

"Something is troubling you." Ettrian rested an elbow on the table and propped his chin in his fist. "What's wrong?"

She opened her mouth to tell him to mind his own business, but stopped when she realized she had no reason to do so.

"I haven't told my mother what you did for me in my father's study," she said quietly.

"I see. Any particular reason why?"

She shifted her gaze to the open window, the cloudless sky, and breathed in softly, inhaling the warm air. Then with a sigh, she looked back to the prince. "I don't know," she finally said. As she thought it over, she couldn't put her finger on a single reason why she hadn't sought out her mother, told her everything. "Perhaps because I know what it will do to her, knowing she can touch my father's power even though he's gone. It will break her, Ettrian." She lifted her eyes to his. "And we're in the middle of a war."

He ran his eyes over her face, assessing her, then he nodded. "I understand. Do you wish I hadn't shown you?"

"No," she replied instantly. "Not at all. If anything..." Her eyes fell closed as tears threatened. "Gods above, Ettrian, that was the kindest thing anyone has ever done for me."

He raised an eyebrow. "Kinder than saving you from being made Willem Ristner's unwilling bride?"

She gave him a half smile. "Considering saving me was something you had to do? Yes."

"Why don't you trust your mother to feel the same?"

"It's not—I just don't want to add anything to her plate."

"What do you want to do, then?"

She held his shimmering gaze and considered his question. Speaking with her mother now was out of the question. Maybe later tonight, after dinner, when they could have a private conversation. Or tomorrow, when Jonas' arrival was no longer so fresh. Then again, spending so much time with Ettrian had helped her feel at ease ever since the night in her father's study. Perhaps her mother might feel the same.

"Something distracting." Then, seeing his suggestive smirk, she added, "I'd like to get out of the house."

His smirk broadened into a grin that set a few butterflies fluttering in her stomach. "What do you have in mind?"

Her gaze again drifted to the window before she met his eyes. "I want to go outside the walls. The city walls."

She nearly burst out laughing at the look of shock on his face.

"While I'm always one to enjoy skirting the rules, even I have to say I don't think that would be wise," he told her. It was there, though. In his eyes, she could see the speculation, the interest brewing there.

"And yet here you are, figuring out exactly where you would land if we stepped through the Between," she crooned. It was a shot in the dark, but when his jaw hardened, she smiled.

He gestured with his hand. "Let's say I agree to this...Where would you want to go?"

She bit her lip. "I want to see the encampment."

To his credit, Ettrian kept his face and tone neutral this time. "I doubt the elder Lady Calliwell would appreciate that."

"That's what you're worried about? Shouldn't you be more concerned for my safety?"

He shrugged. "We both know you're perfectly safe with me. Your mother, on the other hand, might decide to feed me to the rats if she caught us."

Lea shot him a challenging look. "Are you saying you don't know how to avoid getting caught?"

"I could order my knights to keep quiet, of course, but Lindesson's knights are not under my control. If they think I have put you in danger in any way, they will report back to your mother." His golden eyes turned curious. "Why do you want to go out there?"

She ran a finger along the delicate edge of her saucer. "I know I'm doing more now that I'm home. I've been able to go out into the city, talk with people, meet with citizens here. Maybe it's because I know my friends are out there in the thick of it all, but I just want to see the people who are fighting this battle for me. Right now they're a faceless mass of soldiers, and I don't like it."

"It's more than that." He rested his elbows on the table. "What is it?"

Annoyed that he was once again able to read her so easily, she sighed. "Willem will have sent more troops by now. We'll have a few days at most before this relative peace we've had evaporates." She stared down at her tea cup. "I want to see the city from the outside one last time, and the only way I can do so safely is if..."

"Is if someone can bring you there instantly?" Ettrian snorted.

"Trying to guilt or sweet talk me into something will never work, Lea. I'll gladly take you, but you should be prepared that you might not like what you see."

"I assure you, Your Highness, I'll survive," Lea said drily. "As long as you're prepared for the potential reaming you'll get from my mother when we return. I can handle her, but you..." she clicked her tongue and shook her head. "I'm not sure about you."

The corner of his mouth drew up in a smile. "That, Lady Calliwell, sounds like a challenge."

She gave him a grin in return. "Then let's go."

37

LEA

The Errestian battlefield stretched from just outside the city, where it consisted of constant perimeter patrols, to the dense forest that lay at the horizon leading to the realm of Saith. Ettrian transported them to the edge of the forest, which was dim and, despite the blazing sun above, cool.

"Why are we so far out?" Lea asked as she regained her footing. "Wouldn't the center be the better place to be?"

Ettrian nodded toward a tall elf who was talking with a few other knights. "General Thallan is on his rounds right now, so he agreed to meet us out here."

"I see," she said with a nod. It didn't escape her notice that Ettrian had brought her to a place with no sign of prisoners or interrogation spaces. The only indication outsiders existed here, aside from the elves, was the makeshift corral of horses. She recognized some as a stocky northern breed, most likely the Jotnar, but the rest were a Dystonian breed she'd only seen in the stables at the palace just before the wedding.

"What will become of the horses?" she asked as they waited for the general to join them.

"They'll be sold off and the money will be used to rebuild

Lindoroth," Ettrian replied, watching as the horses calmly chewed grass.

"Why not take them to Andradath as payment for your services here?"

The prince chuckled. "We have our own breed of horses in my lands. They don't do well with outsiders."

"Yes, Freya told me about your horses. She spent a bit of time worried she'd get thrown, if I recall correctly."

"Smart of her, too," Ettrian said. "Our horses are quite particular, even judgmental, when it comes to someone attempting to ride them. My palace's horses even more so." He glanced down at her. "Do you ride often?"

She lifted her brows. "How else would I get from place to place? We can't all flit through the Between like some people."

He smiled. "Fair enough. Do you enjoy it?"

She shrugged. "Sometimes. I usually prefer a carriage, but sometimes it's nice to feel the breeze on my face."

Just then, General Thallan joined them. He was tall, even for an elf, with long, pale hair tied back at his nape and an easy expression on his face. He gave Ettrian a quick bow.

"Your Highness," he greeted. "You've brought a guest?"

"Indeed." Ettrian gestured toward Lea. "This is Lady Lea Calliwell. She wished to pay you and your knights a visit."

The elf gave her a surprised look. "Is the elder Lady Calliwell aware? Or General Lindesson?"

Lea tilted her chin up a fraction. "No, General Thallan, although I'm aware they will likely know before I return home. I wanted to see how you're all faring out here and to thank you personally for assisting Edhil's knights in securing the city."

General Thallan gave her a smooth smile. "Of course, my lady. Your thoughts are much appreciated." He gestured around. "As you can see, we are as comfortable as can be expected being so far from home. Your knights have been welcoming to my own and quite helpful when it comes to navigating the surrounding area."

"I'm glad to hear it," Lea replied. She glanced toward the horses that were penned nearby, then looked back at the general. "What happened to the knights who rode those horses here?"

Thallan exchanged a look with Ettrian before responding. "The holding areas for the prisoners are near the southern edge of camp." He frowned. "We can take you there if you would like, but I would not recommend it."

Lea frowned. "Why is that?"

Thallan's lips settled into a thin line. "The knights here, both elf and Lind, have not been kind to the prisoners, as I am sure you would expect. His Highness has told me of your...tenacity, but those images are not things that should be taking up space in your mind. Not now."

Lea gritted her teeth. "You think I can't handle seeing some injured knights?"

"Not injured, Lady Calliwell," Thallan said. "Mutilated, half-dead, often beyond recognition."

"And before you say more," Ettrian cut in, "I'm quite sure you can handle what you would see there. That doesn't mean you need to, nor would it help in any way."

She chewed the inside of her cheek as she looked back and forth between the two elves. Thallan knew nothing of her, but Ettrian knew her well enough to know how she might feel coming away from the prisoners. However, she couldn't help but feel General Thallan thought her weak.

The image of the pit of dead bodies behind the palace flashed into her mind. Corpses mottled with rot, picked over by animals and insects, crows cawing in the air above as vultures tugged at sinew, completely oblivious to her presence.

"Now imagine if those people were alive."

Her eyes darted toward Ettrian.

"The difference is that I want that fate for the knights held here."

But even as she sent the words to him, she knew he was right. Seeing those prisoners would just confirm what Lindesson had already told her—that the knights were being interrogated and held as prisoners of war, but would be disposed of in the desert once they no longer proved useful.

So, she dropped the subject and smiled at the General. "Alright, then. I would like to meet some of your knights, though, if that's alright. And some of my own."

Thallan looked mildly relieved at her decision. "Of course, Lady Calliwell. Your knights have spoken highly of your father and his before him, so they will all be happy to meet his daughter." He gestured toward the makeshift path that cut between the nearest tents and wound past the paddock. "Right this way."

With a smile, she followed the elf into the camp, the prince close at her side.

38

———

FREYA

Vali's house was silent for all of three seconds before Freya rounded on her cousin.

"What is the meaning of this?" she demanded as Byrric stepped in front of her, his hand on the pommel of his sword. The two guards at Daniel's back mirrored the move in response.

Vali held up his hands and stepped between Byrric and the male seated at the table. "Hear him out, cousin. You might like what you hear."

"I would listen," Toskr whispered to Freya. "What can it hurt?"

She shot him a silencing look. He shrugged in response, then took a small step back.

"Sit," Vali said, gesturing toward the table. "Let's discuss this like civilized people."

A tense moment passed before Freya heard Fenian's voice in her mind.

"The rodent is correct."

"It's fine," Freya glared at him, then murmured, "Let's hear what he has to say."

Byrric stepped forward and pulled out a chair, then stepped aside and gestured for Freya to sit.

Slowly, she settled into a seat and watched as Fenian sat across from them. Finally, Byrric took the seat beside her, motioning for Naedan and Toskr to stand behind her. Toskr was doing his best to hide his interest, but Fenian looked positively joyful at the prospect of an undoubtedly dramatic conversation.

As everyone settled, Freya took a moment to appraise Daniel, taking stock of how physically similar he and Lessia were, right down to the mildly haughty expression on his pale face.

Where they differed, though, was in how he wore his authority. As formidable as Lessia was, she'd had to fight to hold her throne when her husband died, and there were many who would've been content to see her removed and replaced with a male. She'd proven herself worthy, but only barely. In the brief time Freya spent with Lessia, she'd seen how tightly she clung to that power with her words, her stance, her demeanor. As if she needed to reassure the world that she was as fearsome as most believed.

Daniel's power radiated from him in a way that it hadn't from Lessia or from Jonas, the true heir to the throne. He wore it casually, as though it was simply a part of him, not something he needed to convince others of. It was in that moment that Freya knew the male in front of her, who shared no blood with the former emperor and therefore had no legitimate claim to the throne, would be the preferred ruler if the Jotnar people were given a choice between him and Jonas.

His cold eyes barely skimmed over her before settling on Byrric at her side.

Once they were seated, Vali began introductions. "Daniel Veldin, this is Freya Harridan, rightful queen of Lindoroth. Byrric Balthana, their Royal commander, and Prince Fenian Tordove of Avorell." He gestured toward Naedan, who remained by the door acting as sentry. "This is their aerial support."

Daniel sniffed in Toskr's direction and his mouth turned down. "And the rodent?" His voice was a smooth, cold drawl that was thick with a Jotnar accent.

Toskr's eyes narrowed, but Freya spoke before he could comment. "Ratatoskr is an ally," she told Daniel.

"He helped Queen Freya survive the Forest of Ages," Vali added with a smirk. "If you believe the stories."

Freya sent him a sharp look, and was surprised to see him flash her a quick wink in response.

"Lord Veldin and I were just beginning our own discussion about allegiances when you arrived yesterday," Vali explained with a grin at Byrric. "We hadn't yet gotten to the good parts, so your timing truly could not have been better."

"I find it interesting, Your Majesty, that you managed to convince the elves my sister so carefully drew into her corner to fight for your side instead," Daniel commented, drawing Freya's attention to him.

"Perhaps her methods weren't so enticing, after all," Freya suggested with a shrug.

"Or perhaps we had no intention of assisting that wretch to begin with," Fenian told him. At Daniel's hard look, Fenian smiled. "No offense, of course, but we all know your sister was absolutely horrid."

Freya's eyes fell shut. Then she drew a measured breath and offered a placating smile. "What the Prince means, Lord Veldin, is that King Ruehnar and Queen Nalaea had not yet made a determination as to who to offer their allegiance to."

"Mmm." Daniel steepled his fingers in front of his face, touching them lightly to his chin as he appraised her. "And they chose you because you managed to kill a few monsters, correct?"

"I ran the Wild Hunt and won," she replied, refusing to acknowledge his vast oversimplification of the task that had almost killed her several times over.

"Do you think my sister would not have won?"

"I think your sister had no rightful claim to the Lindorothian throne," Freya said. "So, based on the rules of the Hunt, she wouldn't have been given the chance."

Daniel's brows flicked up as he looked at Fenian. "Prince Fenian?"

"Only true queens can run the Hunt, Lord Veldin." Fenian scratched his chin. "Your sister was no such animal."

"She was Empress of Jotunheim," Daniel countered.

"And had she been vying for the throne of her own land, we would've considered her request," Fenian replied. "Now, can we get to the point or are we going to continue to volley insults?"

"Lord Veldin, what is your goal here?" Freya asked. "Why aren't you in Madrya?"

Daniel shifted his hard eyes to Freya, then to Byrric. "Why do you allow her to be so demanding?"

"I—" Freya's words were cut off by her father's chuckle.

"I encourage you to spend a bit more time with my daughter, Lord Veldin, and tell me if you think you'd be able to 'allow' her to do anything. Just because your kind doesn't take kindly to females in charge doesn't mean the same for mine."

"We've had a female sitting on the throne for centuries."

"And how many people did she have to slaughter to ensure that?" Fenian shot back.

"Alright, alright." Vali held up his hands. "Enough of this pissing contest. Daniel, stop being a prick and tell them why you're here."

"We can only assume if you're speaking with us that you have an interest in ruling Jotunheim," Byrric said, then looked at Daniel expectantly. "Is that correct?"

A muscle flickered in Daniel's jaw, then he nodded. "Lessia's nephew is a fine emissary but would make a worse ruler than my sister. He's too impressionable. I couldn't care less about Lindoroth and would be happy to leave you alone to rot for eternity." He leaned forward, resting muscular, leather-sheathed arms on the table. "But we all know the only way to acquire any throne is through intelligence and military savvy. I have both, but with the bulk of Jotunheim's army in Lindoroth answering to a human and Lessia's nephew," he sneered, "I lack the manpower I need to rally Jotunheim's remaining forces."

"Considering our circumstances, we currently lack the manpower to give you," Byrric said. "I'm not entirely sure what you'd expect us to do."

Daniel looked at Freya, then Fenian, then back to Byrric. "Jotunheim's knights will not follow Jonas. Everyone at this table knows that. They *will* follow me, however."

"You seem very certain of that," Freya commented. "Why?"

Daniel sent her another cold look. "I still have three thousand knights in my capital city who are loyal to me. Believe me when I say I have good reason to trust the rest will follow my lead."

"Your sister made her wishes quite clear," Fenian pointed out. "She wanted Jonas to take over in her absence."

"And why do you think she would have done that, Prince Fenian?" Daniel asked. "If she had named someone stronger than her as her successor, she would have been overthrown, likely assassinated, the moment word of that successor got out. By naming someone weaker and less desirable, she knew she was the best option and everyone who served her knew that as well."

"And you think you are the better option?" A note of derision colored Prince Fenian's words, and a small smile twitched his lips. "As Her Majesty said, why?"

"Aside from the support I've already amassed among Lessia's knights? Logic. Jonas has no experience in the military or as a leader. As emissary he is an excellent salesman, but that's about it."

"Not so excellent." Fenian shrugged. "He never managed to get my people to open our shores."

"Lord Veldin, Lessia trusted you enough to leave Madrya in your hands while she overthrew a kingdom." Byrric said, ignoring Fenian's snark. "You must understand why we'd be wary of your words."

A small smile played on Daniel's lips. "My sister wasn't always the best judge of character. Willem Ristner," his lips twisted at the name, "is case in point. She mistook him for weak-willed simply because humans are physically weak." He looked at Freya. "Yet here we are, with a human warming your seat and my sister presumably nailed to the palace gates."

Freya frowned at the image. "You don't seem very upset about your sister's death, Lord Veldin."

"Do not mistake me, Your Majesty. I will mourn my sister greatly." Grief flashed in his eyes. "But her death has given us a common purpose. We all want to see Willem dead, albeit for different reasons. I have no interest in taking over your kingdom, so the sooner we get the humans off your land, the sooner I can get on with settling myself as Jotunheim's new ruler."

Freya took in Daniel's words, weighed them carefully against logic and what she might do in his place.

Everything he said made sense. Jonas was, without question, a weak option for a ruler. Despite the mild friendship she'd built with him during his time in Lindoroth, he'd never come off as assertive in any way. If he had the qualities of a leader, he certainly hadn't demonstrated as much. Even Lessia's death hadn't been by his hand. Instead, he'd gone along with someone else's plan.

"My king and queen will require an agreement in writing that you will not revisit the idea of invading Lindoroth or the lands of our allies once you've settled yourself," Byrric said. "As I'm sure you can understand."

Daniel nodded. "Of course."

"If I may?"

They all looked to Fenian.

"Yes, Your Highness?" Freya asked.

"I think you should insist on an elvish contract," the prince replied, eyeing Daniel shrewdly before looking at Freya. "I don't trust this one, nor should you."

"Agreed," Freya said. "You'll assist in crafting the agreement?"

Fenian nodded slowly. "It will be iron-clad, Your Majesty." He gave Daniel a curious look. "Out of curiosity, what are your plans for Jonas, should you succeed?"

Daniel's shrewd gaze narrowed. "I haven't decided yet. If he chooses not to yield to me, I'll challenge him just as I challenged Lessia when the Emperor died."

Freya cocked her head. "How did you lose when you challenged her?"

"I didn't," Daniel replied. "A fight for the crown wouldn't have benefitted either of us in the long run, especially because, between the two of us, it would've been a long, hard fight. So, before things could get too ugly, she offered me stewardship. I accepted, knowing if she were to be absent for any length of time that required me to act on my duties, it would likely lead to her death. In other words, I would get what I wanted eventually. Biding my time meant less bloodshed, and I needed to keep as many of the Jotnar loyal to me as possible."

"And you don't think a fight between you and Jonas wouldn't be drawn out?" Fenian asked.

Daniel shook his head. "Jonas does not have the same level of support I've amassed over the decades."

Freya eyed Vali. "What's your take on this?"

Her cousin shrugged. "Lessia is out of our hair, and the two options to replace her are far better than we could've asked for. My people will help get the invaders out of your land, but we all agree Daniel will be the better leader. He's also agreed to discuss terms with us, which Jonas has not."

"Nor is he likely to," Daniel added. "He might've hated my sister, but he never made a secret of his thoughts on the rebels."

"Which were what?"

"In his words?" Vali snorted. "He considered us barbaric, traitorous, and selfish. And before you ask, yes, I heard him say as much with my own ears."

"I can assure you all that I will be a much more amenable ally than my sister," Daniel said. "And I'm willing to sign a treaty stating as much. Lessia's rule was unnecessarily cruel, and while I don't disagree with her methods and stance on all topics, I'm capable of being far more diplomatic than she was."

Freya schooled her surprise. "If you felt she was so cruel, why not do more to rein her in?"

"And give her cause to remove me from my post?" He smirked. "That wouldn't have made much sense, now, would it?"

Freya gave a tight smile in response. "No, I suppose not."

Byrric drummed his fingers on the table, then looked at Freya. "Your Majesty?"

"Considering the suddenness of this proposal," Freya slid an irritated look at Vali, "I'll need to confer with Aerelius. As I'm sure you can understand," she added to Daniel.

"Of Course, Your Majesty. Take your time."

39

FREYA

The moment they returned to the guest house, Freya whirled on her father.

"What in all the gods' names was that?" she demanded.

Byrric held up his hands in a placating gesture. "Calm down, Freya. Let's take a moment to discuss things. This could be a good thing."

"Your father is right," Fenian said. "With the proper bargains in place, Daniel Veldin could be a formidable ally."

"Oh, I know that," Freya snapped. "I just don't appreciate being ambushed!"

"None of us do," Fenian said. "But that is, unfortunately, what just happened, so I would encourage you to deal with it."

Freya closed her eyes and exhaled a slow breath through her nose. She knew in her gut that, in the absence of another option, Daniel Veldin was their best chance. But annoyance flooded her as she thought about her cousin's duplicity, regardless of how well-intentioned it was.

"Vali knew damn well what he was doing, throwing Veldin at us like that," she muttered.

"Would it make you feel better if I reassure you the elves will happily annihilate Daniel Veldin and his knights if Daniel turns on us?" Fenian asked.

Despite her annoyance, she smiled at the prince. "That does help, Your Highness."

"Let's have a longer discussion with Veldin and Vali back at camp," Byrric suggested. "Hear them out together."

Even though she knew working with Daniel was their best option, Freya's stomach roiled at the thought of bringing Lessia Edrin's brother, of all people, into the innermost parts of their battle camp.

But they had come to Utgard to recruit those who they'd once seen as enemies...

"Fine," she said with a sigh. "Let's get back to camp."

THEY ARRIVED BACK in Byrric's command tent a few hours later. Freya, Toskr, and Byrric arrived first, while Fenian arrived right behind them with Naedan, Vali, Daniel, and two of Daniel's guards.

There was a brief moment of chaos as everyone present in the tent scrambled to call forward their magic or draw blades. At the sight of the four strangers, Freya and Aer's guards morphed into their wolf forms and poised to launch themselves at the intruders.

Byrric held up his hands just as Ana flared out her wings and the wolves crouched to lunge. "Everyone be calm!"

"What is this?" Aer demanded. His magic hovered in blue wisps around his hands.

Freya mirrored her father's position. "They're here to talk. Let's lower our weapons." She slid a look toward Rissen, then Cecilia. "You can stand down."

The wolves sat back on their haunches, but they maintained their stance protecting their king.

Florian sheathed his dagger with a bit more force than necessary. "You might have warned us first," he told Byrric.

Vali jerked his chin toward Aer. "This your king?" he asked Freya, ignoring Aer's sharp look.

She nodded. "Aerelius Harridan, meet Vali Balthana."

Aer dipped his chin in greeting.

She gestured toward Daniel. "And this is—"

"Daniel Veldin." Florian's sharp eyes assessed the Jotnar steward. "Another one vying for the throne, I presume?"

"Aren't we all?" Daniel said with a nod. "Your reputation precedes you, Lord Florian." He looked at Ruehnar. "As does yours, Your Majesty," he added with a slight bow of his head. Finally, he looked at Aer. "My sister has told me much about you, King Aerelius."

"Interesting, as I've heard nothing about you." Aer's stance relaxed slightly. "It seems there's a bit of a story here. Would you all care to fill us in?"

Vali strode forward and dropped into a chair at the table set up at the back of the tent. "I believe your Queen is running this show."

Toskr looked around at everyone, taking in their angry faces. "I do not believe my presence here is necessary." He gave Freya a brief nod. "Please call if you need anything, Queen Freya." With that, he shifted into his squirrel form and scurried off.

Freya rubbed a hand across her brow. "Alright. Everyone sit so we can run this through just once."

She waited as everyone took seats and the guards took up positions around the tent's walls. Then, as succinctly as possible, she explained their meeting with Daniel and Vali. Here and there, Byrric and Fenian added in their own thoughts, but she did her best to keep things as straightforward as possible.

"So you're offering the bulk of the knights remaining in Madrya to help remove our enemies from Lindorothian land," Aer clarified once they'd all finished speaking. "That's quite an enticing offer, considering our circumstances. Why should we believe you?"

"We want the same things, albeit for different reasons," Daniel said. "I want Willem gone and this war over so I can go about taking control of Jotunheim. That, of course, requires me to pull all of my knights back into my own empire. Both of those things align with your needs."

"What are you offering?" Silmar asked.

"I am offering full military support restoring your kingdom to your rule. In addition, I will provide all information in my possession that I gained from working alongside my sister. Battle plans, her goals in taking your kingdom, information she gathered regarding your lands, as well as all of the intelligence she gathered on the entire Ristner family. That information may or may not be useful, but consider it a show of good faith." Daniel pursed his lips. "In return, I ask for two things. First, I would like your support, both militarily and politically, in taking the Jotnar throne, despite who Lessia named as her heir."

"And the second?" Aer asked.

"Access to Lindoroth's raw materials," Daniel said.

"Out of the question," Florian said before Freya or Aer could answer.

"Why?" Daniel demanded. "We've been importing your goods for centuries. Why not allow us the ability to craft our own using your steel, your lumber, your textiles, your gems, at a lesser cost to my people?"

"And our spellwork?" Freya said drily. "We work spells into most of our materials, Lord Veldin. That's what makes our exports so valuable."

"Spellwork that would be far easier to reverse-engineer from raw materials," Ruehnar added. "Do I have that right?"

"Indeed," Daniel said with a nod. "But I would be willing to sign however many agreements you require to utilize those materials, including replication and reverse engineering clauses that would require us to work with your materials as you send them and not attempt to replicate your spells. We will not modify them in their raw form or once they've been crafted into their final product," he added at Freya's sharp look.

"Or during the creation of said products," Aer added. "No loopholes, Lord Veldin."

Daniel's lips twitched with a look of appreciation. "Of course, Your Majesty. I am not here to play games. In case you haven't noticed, our lands are currently at war. Playing games would be a waste of your time and mine."

"And what do you hope to get out of this, Vali?" Aer asked. "Our intention was to work out terms with you, should you be open to them."

"I want my people left alone. From all of you," he added with a level look at Daniel. "No more fighting at the borderlands, no more threats from the capital. I want it known in both Lindoroth and Jotunheim that we are not the enemy so we can live peacefully."

"You want me to go to war to acquire an empire and give you control over a portion of it?" Daniel looked as though he was about to laugh, but he took a deep breath. "How much?"

"From the Western Mountain Pass to the Brystone Coast."

Daniel actually did laugh at that. "That's a third of the gods-damned empire! For a few thousand people!"

If Freya knew him any better, she would've given him the same kick her father would've dealt her. As it was, she kept her face neutral and watched as the two males spoke.

"Most of that land is mountains," Vali replied calmly. "Home to draugs and huldra. In exchange for keeping them at bay from Jotunheim and Lindoroth, and offering our own swords in this war and any future Jotnar conflict, we want the freedom to settle permanently, form our own system of government, our own trade agreements with other lands."

"Apologies, but I thought we were here to discuss retaking Lindoroth?" Fenian said. "I did not bring my knights here to fight Jotunheim's civil war."

Freya rubbed her fingers over her eyes as Aer's head fell against the back of his chair.

"Lindoroth would not be in a position to aid Jotunheim with anything until after our monarchs are back on their thrones," Florian said to Vali and Daniel. "We cannot set anything in stone until then."

"Lindorothian support in Jotunheim will, of course, be contingent on King Aerelius and Queen Freya retaking control of the kingdom," Daniel replied, then looked at Vali. "We will honor an agreement with your people, Vali, so long as you assist me in my endeavors, and the Linds in theirs."

There were a few tense moments where everyone in the tent sized each other up, considered the proposals before them, and, at least in Freya's case, began forming their own opinions.

"While your terms aren't unreasonable, my King and Queen will need to discuss your proposal," Byrric said after a few moments. "We'll prepare accommodations for you for the night and reconvene in the morning to finalize and sign agreements."

His gaze traveled over everyone in the tent. "You're all dismissed."

MANY HOURS LATER, after discussing Daniel and Vali's terms at length with Byrric and the others, Freya and Aer lay in bed, silent save for the sounds of camp around them.

"I'm struggling to actively work against Jonas," she whispered as she rested her head on Aer's shoulder. "It feels almost traitorous."

Aer kissed the top of her head. "We can't make plans based on assumptions and hope. Yes, we've worked with Jonas so far. But after he went behind our backs, not to mention Lea's, scheming with Willem, I don't know that I trust him not to deceive us again to further his own goals."

"Aren't we doing just that, though?"

Aer nodded. "You could look at it that way," he allowed. "Or you could acknowledge that we're all working with the best information available."

"Lea trusts him," Freya said.

"True, but we have far more to lose than Jonas does. A kingdom, for example."

True as that might be, it was hard to reconcile abandoning the male they'd spent the last several months with in favor of one they'd known for a day and who'd had a direct hand in Lessia's ability to take control of Lindoroth. If Daniel hadn't been willing to hold Madrya in Lessia's absence, Lessia would've had to risk her entire empire in favor of conquest. Greedy as the empress might've been, she'd never struck Freya as a fool until Willem managed to deceive her so thoroughly.

"We no longer have the luxury of Lea hiding in plain sight," Aer continued. "Anything Jonas says now that he's in Errest should be taken with a huge grain of salt."

Freya scratched her head and blew out a breath. "I thought, when he helped Lea escape, that this would be just what we needed to turn the tide in our favor. It seems he's given us more questions and less help."

"What frustrates me," Aer said, "is that I don't truly believe he's a bad guy. But until we can be certain, we have to do what's best for us. Jonas is a smart person. He knew the moment he let Lea go that communication would be cut drastically."

"So that begs the question, do we have Lea tell him what our plans are? I think we owe him something."

"Let's run it by Byrric." Aer frowned. "It could go either way. Supporting Daniel could spur Jonas to prove his loyalty to us, sure, but it could also cause him to try to escape Errest and enlist Willem in helping him take on Daniel."

"And in turn, helping Willem defeat us." Freya pressed a hand to her forehead and sighed. "Gods above, why didn't we make our agreement with him more specific?"

It was something she'd wondered for a while. Their agreement with Jonas, which bound him by blood not to harm any who shared Aer's blood, had been made in haste when they were in the caves fleeing from Lessia and Willem's attack and was intended specifically to protect Lea. Unfortunately, that didn't spare them from his ability to order others to cause harm, making it all but void.

"Freya, this isn't something we can blame ourselves for. We were under duress and didn't expect things to play out as they did. He planned to leave with Lea and opted to change that plan without discussing it with anyone first."

Like a damn fool, Freya thought. "What do you think your father would do in our shoes?"

Aer took a deep breath, then nodded. "I think he would make the best decision based on the information currently in front of him. We have the ability to have a signed, ironclad agreement with Daniel Veldin to ensure the help of a large portion of Jotunheim's army. Even if we knew Jonas' intentions, he holds tenuous control, at best, over the Jotnar knights in Lindoroth."

"So even if he remains true to our cause, accepting Daniel's help is our better option." Resigned, Freya sighed. "Do you think he'll forgive us?"

Aer tightened his arm around her shoulders. "I'm not entirely convinced Jonas wants to rule Jotunheim. And...callous as it may sound, he'll have no recourse should the people and soldiers of Jotunheim choose to stand with Daniel, especially considering the rebels have made their choice."

"You're right. It's just hard to acknowledge that. But if Daniel gives the rebels their land, it could prove how willing he is to change Jotunheim for the better."

"Exactly. Try not to stress too much over this, Valkyrie. Jonas took a big risk when he cut communication with us. He knew that, and if he didn't consider it..." He shrugged. "Then I think that says a lot about his ability to lead."

"I suppose that's fair." If Jonas had even the slightest mind for battle, he would've accounted for the potential for Daniel's involvement in his own planning process. And if he hadn't, well, Aer was right. A good leader should plan for all logical eventualities. Jonas, it seemed, had not.

Freya smiled and drew herself closer to him. "You have valid points now and then, Highness."

"One of the many reasons you love me, I'm sure."

40

LEA

When they returned from the battlefield, Lea found herself ascending the stairs to the uppermost floor, her feet aimed toward the bridge that would take her to the walls surrounding her home. She found herself at the northwest corner, where she leaned against the warm stone wall and stared out over the encampment that now seemed so much larger than it did when she stood among the soldiers just a short while ago.

Perida had, of course, been furious when they returned. She blamed Ettrian for foolishly taking Lea into harm's way, and Lea for asking him to take her in the first place. Lea took the scolding, understanding why her mother was worried, and seeing no sense in trying to convince her otherwise. She was still frustrated at her mother's response to her visiting the soldiers. She could also understand and acknowledge why her mother was so upset. Even though Ettrian hadn't taken Lea to the camp where the prisoners were held or where she might face danger, he still took her outside the city walls. Lea knew if her own child had been in such a position, she probably would've reacted the same way.

But still, she'd felt so confined the last few weeks. Even though she knew she could go out and wander the city more or less as she pleased, knowing she couldn't leave the actual city had been slowly driving her insane.

She inhaled a deep breath of hot air, then let it out on a sigh, doing her best to exhale her frustrations.

As she stood there quietly taking in her surroundings, her mind drifted to Willem. Unsurprisingly, fury rose in her gut as she considered everything he had taken from her, how all of his actions had allowed her heart to become so full of hatred that she nearly didn't recognize herself anymore. She thought back to the days with Freya and Collin and Lazarus and remembered the times they spent together in the garden sipping on pilfered bottles of wine. She thought of the days she and Freya spent wandering Iladel looking for new clothes. All she wanted was to go back to that time, to that same level of happiness and contentment with her friends and family. But even as that desire attempted to replace the fury in her chest, anger supplanted it immediately. Even if Willem was defeated, and Lindoroth was brought back under Lind control, much of the damage the human king had done to her was irreparable.

She turned away from the scene in front of her and slid down to sit with her back against the stone. She hated that Willem continued to make her feel like a prisoner. He continued to make her feel as if all choice had been taken from her, as if she was no longer in control of her own life. She knew it wasn't true, of course, but the fact that his presence and his actions had turned her into someone that she struggled to recognize was infuriating.

She closed her eyes and pictured the northern horizon without the encampment marring its beauty. The grassy hills that gave away to dense foliage in the south. It was a beautiful sight, but she couldn't help but wonder how long it would be before that sight was marred with soldiers coming across the horizon to attack her city. She wondered what those knights had been told about her and her people, what they'd been promised by their king and future ruler.

The more she thought about the threat to her city and to her family and friends lives, the more her head began to hurt, until all of those concerns and fears formed a throbbing pain she didn't think she could outrun. But she needed to. So, she pulled herself to her feet and began walking back toward the direction she'd come in search of a distraction.

She found that distraction in the form of the elf prince, when she nearly crashed into him as she descended the stairs to the main floor of the house.

"Ah, Lady Calliwell," Ettrian said as he gripped her arms to steady her. "Going somewhere?"

She pursed her lips and sighed as she stepped back slightly. "Yes, actually." After a pause, she added, "Would you like to go into the city with me, Your Highness?"

He lifted a dark brow. "Have you forgotten how angry your mother is at the moment? With me, in particular?"

"I'll be in the city, which is perfectly safe," she replied. "If you don't want to join me—"

"Oh, I'm happy to join you," he said with a grin. "I just want to be sure you know what you might return home to."

"I'm well aware, trust me." She looked down at the fitted pants and tunic she'd donned that morning, now coated with a slight dusting of reddish dirt. "I think I'll go change first."

He smirked. "Wise choice, Lady Calliwell."

41

LEA

After Lea changed, she and Ettrian slipped from her home through a side door. Despite her protests, Iska insisted on accompanying them, which she allowed only on the promise that he wouldn't hover. Also because she knew he was furious with her for slipping away earlier, even if he'd never admit it.

"You know that I'm more afraid of your mother than I am of you." Iska said with a smile as he held the door open for them to pass through. "But you also know I can hover without imposing."

"We welcome your company, don't worry," Ettrian said. "Don't let the Lady give you a hard time."

With a scowl, Lea elbowed him, but returned her guard's smile. "Alright, fine. I suppose there are worse shadows to have," she added.

Dusk was beginning to settle over the city as they made their way down the street toward the center of town. Unlike Iston, where everyone seemed to have a purpose, even if that purpose was meandering, Errest seemed to move at a slower pace. Part of that, Lea knew, was due to their current circumstances. It seemed many people weren't going out and wandering the streets as much as they once had. Instead, she saw many darkened windows with curtains drawn tight against any outside observers.

As they moved into the areas of town that housed businesses and other establishments, she felt a bit of hope. Citizens and merchants seemed to have perked up since the reinforcements arrived. People had started to frequent taverns and pubs more than in the weeks prior, more stores were open, and the pixie lights along the street had been relit thanks to the pixies that came out of hiding once Tyna arrived.

"So," Ettrian said, as they approached the main square after walking for several blocks, "as it's getting near dinner time, would you care to show me your favorite restaurant?"

Leah sent him a side-long smile. "Of course, Your Highness. I would never forget to ensure my visiting prince was fed and watered."

"Your prince, hmm?" He smirked down at her. "That sounds... interesting."

She rolled her eyes. "Come, it's just this way.," she said as she led him toward a restaurant at the edge of the square that specialized in Edhilian cuisine.

"This place is nearly three centuries old," she explained as they took their seats at an outside table. Iska, true to his word, sat at his own table twenty paces away. Close enough that he could be protective without being overbearing. "The family is spread across the realm, but the owners have been citizens of Errest for nearly five hundred years."

As they settled into their seats, Lea couldn't help but feel sad as she looked around.

"Why the long face?" Ettrian asked. "Aside from the obvious, of course."

She gestured toward the area around them. "The crowds are so thin, and most of the people present are marshals or knights. The restaurants are barely half full, which is far from typical. It just makes me sad to know that's likely due to the citizens' fear of leaving their homes."

"It's hard to blame them, though, isn't it?" He looked around. "And it certainly seems better than it was."

Lea nodded slowly. "Yes, I know." She looked around again.

A server came over and greeted them. Before Ettrian could speak, Lea rattled off a number of dishes and two drinks apiece. Then, she gestured toward Iska. "And please make sure my guard is seen to, as well."

The server smiled and gave a small nod. "Of course, my lady. And may I say it's wonderful to see you out?"

Lea gave her a gracious smile. "Thank you. That means a lot."

Once the server walked away, Ettrian leaned forward. "Do you not trust your prince to order for himself?"

She winced. "I'm sorry. It's a habit I have when I bring someone to a favorite restaurant. I did it with Freya when she first arrived in Iladel."

"Ah, I see. Does that mean we're friends now?"

Lea felt her cheeks warm at the low tone his voice had taken. "I suppose we're not *not* friends."

"I think I'll consider that a win, then," the prince replied.

The server returned a few moments later with bread and their drinks, both specialities the restaurant was known for, and set them down. Once she'd walked off, Ettrian sat back in his seat and picked up his glass.

"So, why this restaurant and not one of the others?" he asked.

Lea pulled her own drink forward and took a small sip, smiling at the burst of lindberry that disguised the bitter taste of alcohol hidden beneath. "Aside from its history? This was my father's favorite. He'd bring us here weekly, for as long as I can remember."

A soft smile settled on his lips. "I find it quite endearing that you care so much for your people that you cast aside any concerns about being out in public."

She eyed him with surprise. "Are you saying you don't care that much?"

He shrugged. "I care for my people, but I prefer traveling to places where I'm not instantly recognized the moment I set foot outdoors." He wrinkled his nose. "I don't like to be fawned over."

She smirked. "See, now that *does* surprise me. I would expect the opposite."

He leaned across the table and lowered his voice. "I suppose that would depend on who's doing the fawning."

Smiling, she mirrored his position. "What a pity for you I'm not one to lavish unnecessary attention on visiting princes."

"Oh, I'd hardly call it unnecessary." His eyes held hers for a moment before he spoke again. "So, Lea, I just realized something."

"Oh?" Lea picked up her roll and pulled a small piece off. "What's that?"

"I know very little about who you actually are. I know who you pretended to be in the palace and who you're forcing yourself to be now, but I don't feel as though I've actually gotten to know the real you."

"You mean the 'me' who attended my cousin's wedding?" She nodded and took a small bite of bread. "No, I suppose you wouldn't."

He gestured with a pale hand. "So, tell me about yourself, then."

She gave him a deadpan look. "You know that's literally the worst question you can ask a person? Ask something more specific."

He chuckled. "Very well. What do you plan to do once this war is over and you can go back to your semi-normal life?"

Ask something easier, Lea thought.

As if reading her mind, he gave her a challenging smile. With a huff, she forced herself to look past her immediate circumstances and far into the future, once Lindoroth was rebuilt, when no encampments existed outside capitals and she could move about the kingdom freely once again.

"I think I'd like to finish my education," she said after a moment. "Aldridge will resume classes relatively quickly, I'd imagine, and barring another attack, my city will be in good straits. And being back at Aldridge will put me in a good spot to help Freya and Aer in whatever way they need it."

"You think returning to school is the best course?"

Her instinct was to tell him yes, of course she would return to school. But as she turned over the simple question in her mind, she was struck by how out of touch the idea of returning to a classroom felt. It just seemed so...

Small.

"I want to, yes," she finally replied. She set her roll on her dish, then spun the small knot of bread back and forth between her fingers. "I know it seems a bit silly, the idea of going from all of this to sitting back in a classroom listening to professors teach me about the world."

"What would your alternative be?"

She flicked her eyes up to the prince and found him watching her with a careful expression on his face. As if he was concerned he'd upset some balance in their conversation, taken them to a point where she wouldn't want to talk anymore.

"The world is a big place," she finally said. "I think I might prefer to learn more through experience."

One corner of the prince's mouth kicked up. "That's quite a worthy way to learn, I assure you."

"What about you?" Lea asked, desperate to shift the focus away from herself. "What are your plans once you're no longer obligated to be here?"

He shrugged, then took a sip of mint tea. "Continue as I was before, most likely. Spending time anywhere but home, letting my brothers battle it out for the crown, and hoping to the gods I don't live to be as old as some of my relatives."

Lea smiled. "I find it amusing you actually hope to die. And why don't you have any interest in serving your kingdom?"

"I am more than happy to serve my kingdom," Ettrian replied. "But as my family has a history of misery among kings and queens, I'd much prefer to serve those who are miserable from afar, rather than become miserable myself at home."

"That's a painfully grim way to look at things, don't you think?"

Before he could answer, their server returned and set the first course before them. Putting aside talk of serious topics, Lea went to work explaining each course and dish to Ettrian, starting with the flatbread crusted with cheese and meats, and ending with the yellow and red jewel fruit sorbet topped with shimmering pieces of fresh jewel fruit.

"The best part about this one," Lea said as she spooned up a bite of the slowly-melting dessert, "is that you and I helped ensure it was made. Or should I say, my father ensured it."

The prince gave her a surprised look as he dug into his own dessert. "This was made with the fruit from your personal garden?"

She smiled wistfully. "Yes, it was. It has been for years."

Ettrian looked up at the restaurant, then back at Lea. "Relatives of yours?"

Lea shook her head. "No, we don't have any close relations in Errest proper. This is the only place in the city who specialized in jewel fruit desserts at the time we began growing them. My father offered to allocate a portion of what we bring into the city to them, since he'd enjoyed the restaurant since he was a boy."

"Local business owners didn't balk at purchasing goods from the governor's estate?" Ettrian asked.

Lea spooned up another bite. "We charge a fair price, and the money we make goes directly into the city's funds. We don't actually make a profit. Plus, we don't make enough to sustain them year round. This is a seasonal dessert. Only one harvest."

Ettrian made a "hmm" sound, then finished off the last of his sorbet and set his spoon down. "Well, it was certainly worth the trip," he said, then rested his hand on his flatstomach. "Although I think I'll need to walk a bit more before we make our way back."

Lea laughed. "Agreed." She signaled for the server to bring their bill and Iska's, who'd been sitting dutifully throughout the entire dinner eating his own meal while he kept whatever dangers he thought might be lurking about at bay. While they waited, Lea rested her elbow on the table and propped her chin in her hand, then let her eyes drift around the square, happy to see people out and about, enjoying the city.

Once they'd paid the server and said their thank-yous, Lea and Ettrian began their walk back toward her home, Iska trailing a respectful distance behind. She noticed neither she nor Ettrian seemed to be in much of a hurry, so she took them on a circuitous route home, walking along the streets of the shopping district, then through a large, tree-shaded park that was a popular picnicking spot during the day.

When they reached her house, Iska ducked inside ahead of them, mumbling that he would let her mother know they'd returned, and left the pair to make their way inside on their own.

"He's quite good at his job," Ettrian commented. "I almost forgot he was there."

"Iska knows how to walk the line between hovering and privacy," Lea murmured as she watched her guard walk off. "He's one of the fastest wolves I've ever known, so he doesn't necessarily have to be close to keep me safe."

"It's good to have him around, then," Ettrian said. "Your city is a lovely place, Lea, even under siege. Thank you for the tour"

She rolled her eyes. "Thank you for caring enough to keep me company."

He took a step forward and tucked a stray curl behind her ear. "I enjoy spending time with you. And I'm sure there would've been no better guide than the Lady of Errest, herself."

Her heart started to thunder, but before she could reply, he leaned in and pressed his cool lips to her cheek, then her lips. She found herself leaning into his hand when he brushed a thumb across her skin.

Almost as soon as the kiss began, he pulled back and ran a hand down her arm. "Now, I think it's time to get some rest, don't you?"

Lea collected herself, then smiled. "I think you're right. Thank you for a lovely evening."

And before she could do what she truly wanted, which was grab him by the lapels and give him a true kiss, she gave a small nod instead and walked to her room, only glancing back once to see that the prince was, indeed, watching her walk away.

42

LEA

Lea's thoughts kept her up all night. As much as she didn't want to admit the prince's kiss, chaste as it was, had thrown her off kilter, that was precisely what had happened. It had come as a surprise, at least to her, although based on the smile Ettrian gave her when they parted ways, it had been anything but spontaneous.

But then again, why should she be surprised? Hadn't they been spending more time together lately? Breakfast together daily? Developing their own way of speaking with each other? And he flirted nonstop...

And why was she reacting as if this was a bad thing? Ettrian was a handsome prince, after all. How many stories had she read in her life of handsome princes being the pinnacle of perfection in males? He was strong, brilliant, and had a big heart, despite how much he did to hide it. Yes, the cunning creature she'd first encountered in Iladel still lurked beneath the surface, and she had no doubt he would joyfully eviscerate anyone who looked at her sideways, but she was beginning to realize those characteristics she once saw as disconcerting or something to be feared were actually things she'd begun to see in herself.

Perhaps the best thing about Ettrian was that he seemed to want little to do with royal life, which had also been one of the things that drew her toward Jonas initially, despite his closeness with his aunt. The more entangled she became in royal machinations at the palace, the more certain she was that she wanted nothing to do with that life. Clearly, she'd dodged a spear, as far as Jonas was concerned.

Eventually, Lea dozed off, but awoke just before dawn after dreams of golden eyes and gentle caresses kept her from sleeping soundly. Knowing there was no point in trying to sleep anymore, she tossed back her sheets and swung her legs over the edge of the bed, then slid her feet into a pair of slippers.

As she cinched the belt on her robe, she couldn't stop thinking about their dinner, their conversation afterward, the way his hand would brush against hers as they walked home, the touch of his hand against her cheek...

His lips on her skin.

"Air," she muttered, pulling a cloak from a hook by her door. "Fresh air will help me clear my head."

She set her sights on the southeast corner of the wall, where she'd be able to watch the sun come up and ignore every awful thing that was happening to the north and west, for just a little while.

Contentment settled over her as she took a seat between two merlons. It was one of the only places on the wall where her view wasn't marred by signs of her kingdom's war. Instead, all she saw was grassy fields leading to scrubby plants before the beach and sea spread out before her. The sky was just starting to lighten at the horizon, a touch of periwinkle that would shift to pink, then orange soon enough.

As thankful as Lea was for the elves' aid, she longed for the day when she didn't have to pick and choose where to take in the view based on whether or not she might see an encampment or smoke from a pile of burning bodies. Instead, all she'd see would be the rolling expanse of Edhil all around her.

The sky was just beginning to show hints of orange when she heard Ettrian's footsteps coming toward her. She didn't even have to look to recognize his near-silent gait, as she'd never heard anyone walk as quietly as he did. That she heard him at all meant he'd wanted her to.

"I thought I heard you sneaking about." He came to a stop beside her and cocked a hip against the wall. "What are you doing?"

"Can't sleep," she murmured. She hoped he couldn't hear her heart pounding, but knew he likely could. He always could. It was probably what led him up here. At least he hadn't pointed it out yet. She wanted to kick herself for reacting to him this way, but it wasn't exactly like she could control her body's reaction.

"Look at me." Not a command, but commanding enough that she let out a quiet sigh and turned away from the sky, bringing her legs up onto the wall and sitting with her knees bent, her back against the merlon. Once she faced Ettrian, he frowned. "What's wrong?"

Even in the near-darkness, she could clearly see the molten depths of his eyes. "As I said, I can't sleep."

He leaned in closer. "Would you like me to tell you a bedtime story?"

She smirked. "Do you often tell bedtime stories to females?"

"Only ones that are worthy."

Her heart stuttered, but she ignored it and said, "Sure. Let's hear it."

Ettrian slid down so he was sitting on the stone, then patted the space next to him. "Come, I can't have you falling asleep up there. Your mother would murder me if you fell to your death."

Rolling her eyes, she did as he asked and settled next to him. "And you wouldn't feel the least bit of guilt?"

"Because you decided to listen to a bedtime story sitting on a wall one hundred feet above the ground? Gods, no. That would be entirely your own fault."

She elbowed him, but couldn't help but smile.

"So, what would you like to hear?"

She thought for a moment. "You mentioned Gregory and Helena once when we were back at the castle. You said she reminded you of me. Can I hear more about them?"

"A bit of a sad story for bedtime, but I suppose it will do. Although, it does have a happy ending."

"That's all that matters."

"I suppose it starts with King Horace. He was Willem Ristner's great-grandfather, one hundred or so times removed. Possibly more. It was quite a long time ago, in human years that is."

"We typically start our bedtime stories with, 'A long, long time ago, in a kingdom far away.'"

"Whose story is this again?"

Lea mimed zipping her lips, then leaned her head back against the wall and closed her eyes.

"As I was saying...Horace was a dreadful king. Only mildly less so than Willem. Helena's story begins when Horace's former queen died. Once Queen Shyla passed, Horace needed a new queen. He found his betrothal with a woman named Luella. She was Helena's mother and the princess of Teid, back when Dystone's realms were ruled by kings instead of dukes. Luella's husband had passed, and her father presented her to King Horace, who, by all accounts, fell smitten instantly. Many thought it odd, a king marrying a woman in her forties with a daughter who was nearly grown. Most expected him to court her sister, Charmaine, instead, who was much younger and far more beautiful. But planning for the wedding commenced, and the king seemed happy with his choice. Unfortunately, Luella was killed in a raid on the way to the palace the day she was to be fitted for her wedding gown in the capital. If you believe the stories, that is."

Lea smiled at his tone, but kept her eyes closed, letting herself be lulled into a calmer state by his soft, lilting accent.

"Human law dictated that, should a woman pass, the betrothal could also pass to her next of kin. Charmaine, being older, was chosen first, but she managed to work her way out of the engagement. So, Horace opted to apply a literal translation of the law and take Helena as queen instead"

"How old was she?" Lea asked.

"Sixteen."

Lea lifted her head and frowned at him. "She was only sixteen? And set to marry a man who was—"

"Her father's age, yes." Ettrian wrapped an arm around her shoulders and pulled her into his side. "Now, this is supposed to be a story that lulls you to sleep, not sparks conversation."

She considered protesting, but the warmth of his body was far too comfortable to pass up. So she settled in and listened to the rest of the story.

"My own great-grandfather, Gregory, was very much in love with Helena. As you can imagine, he was heartbroken but insisted on coming to Dystone for the wedding as Avorell's representative. Helena's aunt Charmaine was devastated, too, as you could imagine. She felt Helena was far too young and Horace far too cruel. It turned out she'd made a deal with a witch—Kosandra, as it turned out—to free herself from a betrothal to the king in exchange for aiding the witch in her own vendetta. When she realized that meant Helena would take her place, she made it her goal to save her from that fate. She put herself at great risk to help free her niece from Horace's grasp. Because of Charmaine, Gregory and Helena were able to escape Dystone on Helena's wedding night."

"And then your kingdoms went to war," Lea murmured. "Such a happy ending."

The prince chuckled. "We did, yes. But my kingdom didn't go to war simply because our prince wanted a human bride. Gregory and Helena were soul mates in the truest sense–he was able to give over part of his power to give her an elvish lifespan. That doesn't come around often, but when it does, it's a sacred thing. At least in Avorell. Humans didn't share the same opinion."

Lea blinked, then sat up and stared at him incredulously. "Are you telling me Avorell went to war for true love?"

"I wouldn't say that, necessarily," he replied, his expression so flummoxed she nearly laughed. "But true soul mates...that's magic you simply don't disregard."

"Because it means the two individuals are fated to be in love?" Lea tried to keep the smile from her lips. "And tearing them apart could be devastating for them?"

He narrowed his eyes. "If you're attempting to get me to say my people went to war and ultimately shut down our borders because two people were in love—"

"What would you call it, then?" Lea challenged. "If Gregory had simply come home with Helena with no magic tying them together, would your kingdom have gone to war, or sent her packing on the next ship out?"

A muscle flexed on Ettrian's jaw, but his eyes remained cool. "I suppose I see how it might look to an outsider."

"An outsider," Lea scoffed. "Did it ever occur to you that my outsider's perspective might see something in your people that you don't?"

"I thought I was telling you a story?" Ettrian said.

"No, no, this is far more fun," she said, crossing her legs beneath her and leaning against him again. "Now, continue to explain to me how going to war to keep a male's soul mate at his side is different than going to war for true love."

"After the war was done, Helena and Gregory did great things for my kingdom, despite having closed us off from the rest of the world. We were at peace for centuries."

"Until we came along," Lea murmured.

"That's not the point of this story, little witch," Ettrian murmured against her hair.

"What is the point, then?"

"Charmaine, Helena's aunt, seemed to be a bit of a villain at first, having made a deal with a witch to avoid marrying the king and all. But it turned out she was the reason Helena came to my kingdom. Helena was convinced she could not change the course of her life, that she was destined to be Horace's wife, bear a few children, and nothing more. Charmaine showed her otherwise when she helped her flee."

"I feel for her a bit, you know?" Lea said quietly as she sat up and looked at Ettrian. "Helena. When I think about how I was forced into marriage with Jonas, even though it was pretend,...He'd kept so much of himself hidden. What if he'd been just as bad?"

"Why do you think I made sure that marriage was invalid?" Ettrian whispered. "I barely knew you, Lea, but there was no world in which I would allow someone with a heart like yours to risk living in a loveless marriage with a male like Jonas Edrin. I don't believe he's a cruel person, but I also didn't think he had any interest in ruling Jotunheim when I met him. Power changes people, and he was a prime example."

Lea smiled softly. "I don't think I've properly thanked you for that. I know I didn't exactly seem grateful in the forest when we left the palace."

He ran his lips across her temple. "I can think of a few ways you could 'properly' thank me."

She rolled her eyes and nudged him with her leg. "How did Helena fare when she left Dystone?"

"It took her some time to adjust, but once she realized she was really and truly in control of her fate, she flourished. She struggled for months after her mother died, resigned herself to a fate with that monster." He smiled. "I know you say you feel for her, but I don't ever see you resigning yourself to anything."

She smiled. "I also don't see the whole of two kingdoms going to war to keep me in one place."

"You think very little of yourself, Lea," he said after a moment.

"Oh? Why is that?"

His golden eyes held hers. "I'm quite certain there are people in this world who would burn it all down to keep you where you belong."

Once again, her heart started to thunder. Still, she forced her voice to remain steady. "And where do you think that is, Your Highness?"

A small furrow formed on his brow. "I'm sure your mother would top the list of those who would insist you remain here."

She debated only a moment before asking, "And you? Where do you think I belong?"

"Is that a question you truly want an answer to?"

"Yes, I think I do," she murmured, painfully aware of how close his mouth had drifted toward hers.

"I'm a selfish person, Lea." His eyes dipped toward her lips. "What I want isn't always for the greater good. It's often quite the opposite."

Her eyes searched his, the gold in them so mesmerizing she could easily get lost. "I know. Still, I'm curious where you think I belong."

A heavy silence hung between them. Then, he tilted her chin toward him, hesitating for only the briefest of moments before he pressed his lips to hers.

She went still, absorbing the feel of his mouth on hers, warm and soft, and a bit like coming home. Then, just as she felt him pull back, she put her hands on either side of his face and kissed him back. His lips curved against hers as she sank into his warmth.

The world around them faded away, and for a few moments, she wasn't on the wall surrounding her home in the pre-dawn chill. She wasn't in Lindoroth surrounded by war, worried for her friends and family as their enemies bore down on them. Instead, she was free, finally able to do something purely for herself, with no motivation other than simply wanting to. She was on a ship sailing the world, on far away lands meeting new people, experiencing the things she never would if she remained confined in her own kingdom.

It seemed only seconds had passed before Ettrian pulled back and rested his forehead against hers. His glimmering eyes searched hers, and for the first time since Lea had met the prince, she saw uncertainty.

"I think, little witch," he murmured softly, his breath a tender caress over her skin, "I'll let you make that determination yourself."

43

———————

FREYA

The mood inside Byrric's war tent had shifted when Freya and Aer arrived the following morning. The air of suspicion still remained, but the level of hostility Freya had felt between her own kind, the elves, and the Jotnar seemed to have decreased.

When they stepped inside, they found Byrric and the others seated at the table with Vali and Daniel. Neat stacks of paper, tightly rolled scrolls, and leather-bound tomes were now strewn across the table, along with several maps thrown haphazardly on top.

Aer and Freya came to a stop at the head of the table. "What's all this?" Aer asked.

"All of the materials I promised." Daniel's lips tilted into a smirk. "That will hopefully lead to you increasing your trust in me as an ally."

"Prince Fenian and I went with him during the night to retrieve everything from Madrya," Florian explained.

"Against my better judgment," Fenian grumbled.

Freya sent him an amused look. "It's always better to be prepared, Your Highness." She picked up one of the books and turned it over in her hands. It was soft Allanorian leather, sealed shut with a heavy metal clasp. "This is Caelorian steel," she commented to Daniel. Then, running her finger down the spine. "You are fond of our exports, aren't you?"

"I am," Daniel said with a nod. "And I find it far easier to maintain easy access to them by maintaining the status quo, so to speak. With a few added improvements, of course."

"Of course," Aer replied dryly.

"Jotunheim greatly appreciates the opportunity to create our own goods using your materials," Daniel told him. "We will, of course, adhere to the limits of that allowance. Now, shall we get started?"

"You have the floor," Byrric said. He opted to stand, taking up a position between Freya's seat and Aer's.

"My sister and I discussed most of her plans for your kingdom before she left," Daniel began. He gestured toward the pile of documents on the table. "These are her battle plans, detailed maps of each of your realms, and information she gathered regarding specific towns, villages, and all of your capitals."

"I'm guessing that's how she knew about the sewer access to Olthanas," Aer said, scratching his head.

"And why so many draugs slipped into Watoria," Freya added. "One joked that she'd pay a pretty penny if he brought me back to her."

"Not a joke, Queen Freya, I assure you." Daniel's dark eyes, so like Lessia's, held hers. "Lessia knew of your betrothal for years. One aspect of her plan was to remove the prince's intended so as to distract the royal family with the process of finding a replacement. It's quite fortunate that your father sent you off to live with the commoners."

Freya ignored the 'I told you so' look she felt coming from her father. "Are you saying those draugs were after me specifically?"

"No, but that doesn't mean Lessia wouldn't have rewarded one handsomely if he'd brought you to her."

"That's quite brazen," Ana commented. "And stupid."

Daniel gave an appreciative smile. "Indeed. Fortunately for us all, your king threw a wrench in her plans when he announced your betrothal at that ball of yours." He sighed at Aer's surprised look. "My sister was cunning, Your Majesty. She had spies everywhere. How do you think she managed to reign as long as she did?"

"Thumbscrews and a well placed gallows would be my guess," Ruehnar murmured, brows drawn as he picked up a map of Caelora and began looking it over.

"Did she have anyone in Dystone working with Isadora?" Florian asked.

"No. I believe she planned on filling Jonas in if she'd had more time." Daniel nodded toward the documents on the table. "Based on everything she'd recorded and what she'd discussed with me, our cousin Effina was the only other person she intended to plant in Dystone. As far as I can tell, she had set things in motion to ensure Effina would provide Willem an heir. Until that child came of age, Effina would rule as Queen Mother with a set of carefully chosen advisors."

"What about Willem's steward?" Aer asked.

"Benjamin Whitmore was the obvious choice for steward, as he was betrothed to Princess Rosie." He picked up a sheaf of papers and tossed the stack toward Freya and Aer. "Based on everything Dania Edrin told Lessia, Benjamin is well-loved by the Dystonians. His cooperation in my sister's scheme was crucial to Effina gaining the people's favor when she returned as Willem's new wife. As of Lessia's last communication with me, she and Willem had not yet gained control over Benjamin, nor did they expect to. My guess is Effina's plan was to have him killed if he wasn't amenable to their plans."

"Did Lessia's intel provide any insight into who might pose a challenge aside from Whitmore?" Byrric asked.

"No," Daniel replied. "It seems my sister's hubris prevented her from thinking that far ahead."

Vali chuckled. "Thank the gods for small favors, then."

"Agreed," Florian murmured.

"How could she ensure Effina would give him an heir?" Aer asked.

"Magic, of course," Daniel replied. "The same elf witch who gave the true Isadora powers to walk the Between was also quite gifted at helping females conceive."

"That is true," Ruehnar said. "Kosandra was sought after by many females in Avorell for her skills at fertility. Prior to fleeing my lands, her payment for such magic was often quite steep. I would imagine it has only gotten higher since she fled."

"Lord Veldin, what were your thoughts on your sister's plans?" Byrric asked.

Daniel pursed his lips, his shoulders rising, then falling with a heavy breath as he considered Byrric's question.

"Lessia and I had many disagreements," he said after a moment. "From the moment she took over after Crispin died, we disagreed on nearly every decision she made."

"Yet she kept you on as her advisor." Fenian let his statement hang for a moment as he eyed Daniel dubiously.

"She liked to be challenged," Daniel replied. "Only by a select few. She valued my opinion, even though it often differed from her own." He shifted his gaze back to Byrric. "So, to answer your question, Commander, I did not agree with her choice to invade your kingdom. I thought the plan overly ambitious, and her intentions of taking Dystone as well were exponentially more ludicrous." He picked up a thick scroll, sealed tightly with a wax seal. "This is the agreement she made with Dania Edrin nearly fifteen years ago, long before her discussions with Willem Ristner's father regarding an alliance. I've also brought all the intelligence Dania sent, along with my own. My sister's agreements with Willem as co-conspirator and Jonas as emissary are also here. It's worth noting Lord Edrin agreed not to violate the privacy between Lessia and Dania when he acted as courier between Dystone and Jotunheim."

"So he didn't read their correspondence?" Freya asked, not bothering to hide her dubiousness.

"Yes, he seems exactly the type to remain loyal to the female he also helped murder," Fenian muttered, hardly bothering to look up as he put down the map he was scanning and picked up a notebook.

Freya couldn't help but smile at that.

"He has a point," her father said, echoing her thoughts. "Jonas swore to everyone that he had no knowledge of Lessia's plans, but can you truly be sure?"

Daniel shrugged. "At this point, does it matter?"

Freya considered his words carefully. They'd been so focused on whether or not Jonas knew any of Lessia's plans when Lea was in the palace, but ultimately, *did* it truly matter? The best choice would be to move forward, forget he was a factor, and consider any help they got from him as a bonus rather than an expectation.

"All of these agreements are null, of course," Daniel continued. "Although, Jonas can and will be held accountable for violating his terms by conspiring with Dania to help her flee Dystone, as well as conspiring with Willem to murder Lessia."

Freya frowned, unsure if she'd heard him correctly. "I'm sorry, what?"

Daniel shifted cold eyes to hers. "I may not have cared much for my sister, but you cannot truly expect me to let her death go unpunished. It would be a political nightmare, to start, and it will instantly portray me as weak. Jonas will be welcome to challenge me for the Jotnar throne, but if he loses, he will be penalized for his crimes against our late empress."

She hadn't actually considered what might happen to Jonas should Daniel win, but she couldn't help agreeing that leaving Lessia's death unpunished would be poor form for many reasons. Still, it didn't sit right with her that they were all but setting Jonas up for excommunication at best and execution at worst.

"Fair enough," Aer replied with a nod when Freya didn't immediately respond. "Although, you'll understand why that aspect won't be a priority for us."

"Of course," Daniel said.

"We need to craft a plan to draw Willem as far from Iladel as possible," Ruehnar said, moving on. "Which will be difficult, as he knows little of war and doesn't seem ashamed to hide behind his men."

Vali smirked. "He'll be holed up in that palace until one of you drags him out by his balls. I'd be willing to bet he hasn't left since your wedding night," he told Freya and Aer. "There'll be no 'drawing' him anywhere."

Byrric nodded. "I agree. He's no fighter. We should attempt to exhaust his resources as best as possible."

"Then we need to find out where the knights who left Kildin are heading," Ana said. "If they're going to Iladel, we need to pull them elsewhere."

"I would assume they are heading toward Errest," Ruehnar commented. "Aside from it being out of his control, his sister is there."

"Do we truly think he cares about her well-being?" Vali asked.

"He has to pretend to, at the very least," Daniel said.

"Well if that's the case, we'll have a bit more time," Byrric said, "but we still need to handle them before they're able to get too far south."

"I will be able to get the Jotnar knights under control," Daniel said. "Our main focus should be removing the human knights from the playing field." He looked at Ruehnar. "Your other son is in Errest, correct?"

Ruehnar nodded. "He and General Lindesson have secured the city and are in an excellent position to continue defending it, should a larger force come south. We would, of course, prefer to avoid that."

"We should meet with Lindesson and Prince Ettrian to create a contingency plan," Freya said. "Depending on where the forces leaving Kildin are headed, we may very well find ourselves in a position where we have to choose between going to Iladel or chasing them further south."

"Agreed," Daniel said.

"Alright, then," Byrric said. "Let's move on to logistics. We're working with a lot of hypothetical situations and unanswered questions."

"Go ahead and get started without me," Ana said, standing from the table. "I'll go find Zane and work out a squadron of aerial scouts to fly ahead for now."

Byrric nodded. "Don't take too long. We all need to be on the same page for this."

After Ana left, Freya looked around the tent at the motley crew of allies they'd assembled. Elves, Linds, Jotnar, and rebels working together would've seemed a recipe for disaster a few weeks ago. Even now, she wasn't so sure how this would all play out or how much she could trust the newcomers. When she looked at Aer and watched him survey the space just as she was, she couldn't help but be thankful her husband seemed just as wary as she did about the plans they were about to lay out.

"Now that we have our goals sorted," Aer said, "let's move on with getting our agreements in writing. At this rate, we'll be here the rest of the day and into the night sorting out the specifics, and I'd like to get back to saving my kingdom as quickly as possible."

"My son tells me you've all agreed to an elvish bargain, correct?" Ruehnar said.

"We have," Daniel said. "Although I'm still unsure how we plan to do that, considering very little of our agreements involve the elves."

Florian let out a quiet breath, his exhaustion at the idea of helping craft another bargain evident in his dark eyes. He snapped his fingers, and a stack of parchment and pen appeared. "Ruehnar will spell the parchment and ink," he explained. "I will word the agreements to ensure fairness to all parties." He looked around at everyone. "This will take some time, so I suggest we take a break and allow all involved to sort out precisely what they are asking for."

Recalling just how long it had taken to write their own agreement with the elves, Freya couldn't help but agree.

"I'm assuming you'll both want to confer with your own advisors before we sign anything?" Byrric asked Vali and Daniel.

"I've already spoken to our council," Vali said. "We are in agreement that I will make the final decisions and negotiate all terms."

"As will I," Daniel said. "The people who will be my advisors know I will make the best decisions for Jotunheim."

"Out of curiosity," Vali said, his eyes dancing with amusement, "what would happen if one of us attempts to breach our contract?"

"As these are elvish bargains, you would be subject to elvish law," Ruehnar said evenly. "Which means any offending parties would be sent to Avorell for trial and punishment."

"You will be found guilty," Fenian added. "You will also be fodder for Avorell's next Wild Hunt. As my mother is still quite young, that means you will rot in one of our prisons for centuries before being offered the chance at freedom."

Freya bit her lip at the identical looks of unease that filled Vali and Daniel's faces. Something about seeing their composure falter just a bit put her mind at rest.

"Let me be clear," Aer said. "My wife and I don't have the time or inclination to add to our political struggles. Presumably the same can be said for you both. If you aren't prepared to accept the consequences of breaking this agreement or trust that we are not trying to trick you into banishing yourselves from this continent, you can leave now."

"We have just as much to lose in this as you do, Lord Veldin," Freya added. "We have our own agreements with the elves, and we are now willing to add two more to better our chances at saving our kingdom. But you must understand why we would require such strict stipulations, considering the circumstances. We would expect nothing less from either of you."

Daniel sighed. "Fine. Let's get on with it. We'll reconvene at midday." With that, he stood and strode from the tent.

Vali chuckled. "It's a rare day to see his feathers ruffled. It's quite amusing, to be honest." His face turned serious as he looked at Byrric, then Freya. "You're blood, so I am willing to trust you both. I will sign your agreements as requested for that reason only. But I hope that, once this is over, we can move forward with a better relationship built on something other than the threat of imprisonment." The corner of his mouth hitched up in a grin. "Although, it might be fun to see what one of those elf queens is capable of."

"I am happy to invite my wife to Lindoroth to offer a demonstration," Ruehnar said cooly.

Vali shook his head and lifted his eyes to the ceiling. "Perhaps you'll all develop a better sense of humor on the other side of this, too."

44

———

FREYA

The Linds, elves, and Jotnar spent the rest of the afternoon into the evening negotiating the specifics of their agreements. By the time every piece of parchment was approved and signed, the sun had long since slipped below the horizon and Freya and Aer were eager to finally sleep before leaving for Kildin in the morning. It was another night of fitful rest for Freya, and based on Aer's constant turns, for him, too.

Everyone awoke at dawn with plans to leave by mid-morning, giving everyone time to organize their knights and work out who would travel to Kildin with the elves first and how many would follow behind them on foot. When all was said and done, roughly one fourth of the knights would travel to Kildin, while the rest would continue east with the intent of cutting off the knights currently marching south. During the night, Ana and another of her Valkyrie flew ahead to warn Laz they would be arriving within a day, while Ruehnar and a half-dozen of his knights had traveled with Daniel and Vali to retrieve several hundred of their own troops. Half of Daniel's remaining knights in Madrya would begin the march south to Iladel immediately, with a small force directed toward Kildin. A small squadron of elves led by Florian and Fenian traveled to Utgard to retrieve the rebel troops Vali had designated for Lindoroth.

So, just before lunch, the elves transported them all to what would hopefully be their final stop before facing Willem.

Kildin was located further to the north, far closer to the northern border than the area in southern Caelora, where they'd made their last camp. Even still, Freya was startled by how frigid the air was when they arrived in the small village-turned-outpost just outside the city where Lazarus and the others had made their temporary home and command post. The village was small but empty of residents who'd presumably fled the dozens of squat wooden structures when Kildin was attacked. It was close enough to Kildin that getting supplies had probably been easy for the people who lived there, but far enough away that they could live in peace, away from the bustling city. As she stood there taking in the snow-dusted landscape, Freya made a silent promise that those people would return to their homes one day.

Once everyone had their feet on solid ground, Silmar led them toward a small house toward the center of the village.

"Everyone has set up in here," he explained as they neared the house. "It's small, but it will work for our needs."

"Anything will do," Aer said.

"Aerelius!"

Freya grinned when she saw Lazarus standing in the doorway, his face looking far less haggard that it had a few days prior.

Aer rushed forward and embraced his cousin, and Laz's eyes fell shut in relief.

"Lord Cailen," Byrric said with a nod.

"Commander," Laz replied as he stepped away from Aer. Before Freya could speak, he'd lifted her off the ground in a tight hug. "I'm so glad you're both here," he murmured against her hair.

Freya smiled and patted his cheek when he put her down. "I just hope it's not too late."

"I don't think it is." Laz looked at the rest of them and gestured toward the door. "Come, let's get started."

They followed Laz inside, where they found Alyndra Cailen and Collin seated with Tavian Tordove and a sleek-looking lion shifter Freya assumed was her father's general. Ana and Zane sat at their sides.

After receiving hugs from both Alyndra and Collin, Freya and Aer stepped back to allow for introductions.

"Your Majesties, this is General Erlan," Byrric said as the shifter stood from his seat. "He has been holding Kildin since Governor Cailen's death and will brief you both on everything that's happened since."

General Erlan gave a small bow. "A pleasure to meet you both."

"Likewise," Freya said. "Thank you for everything you've done for our people."

"I thank your father for the honor of being trusted with such a task," he replied. He looked at Daniel and Vali, who'd come in behind the rest. "You've brought support, I see."

"We have," Aer confirmed. "This is Daniel Veldin, steward of Jotunheim, and Vali Balthana, leader of the Jotnar rebels."

Laz eyed Daniel but gave him a curt nod. "Lord Veldin. I hope this venture will turn out favorably for us both."

"I hope so as well." Daniel gave Alyndra a smile. "Lady Cailen, a pleasure."

Alyndra didn't do nearly as much as Laz did to conceal her suspicion, but she returned Daniel's smile with one of her own. "We appreciate your aid, Lord Veldin."

"Lord Cailen," Vali said gruffly. "I was sorry to hear of your father's passing." He shifted his eyes to Alyndra. "He was a good leader."

Alyndra's eyes softened slightly. "Thank you. We only hope we can avenge his death properly."

"Fortunately half of that problem has been managed for us," Daniel said. "Now that we're joining forces, we should be able to deal with the other half quickly."

"Quicker, if we spent less time talking," Tavian grumbled from the table, where he was pouring over notes of some sort. "Come, we must get on with this."

Freya let out a quiet sigh but smiled. "Alright, then. Where are we?"

Quickly, General Erlan, Tavian, and Laz went over everything that had happened the past week, reiterating most of what Freya and the others had already heard and adding a bit more about what had been going on since Kildin had begun to empty out of enemy knights.

"Logically, I would assume they are marching toward Iladel," Tavian said. "What we need to decide is how many knights to keep here in case fresh knights are sent in."

"Unlikely," Daniel said. "Willem would've sent them already. I don't believe he realizes the importance of this city in the kingdom he hopes to take over."

"I agree," Byrric said. "And I say that fully acknowledging we've already underestimated him twice."

"Prince Reginald might be able to shed some light on how he thinks," Ruehnar suggested. "Killing Lessia was a power move. That says nothing about his skill as a strategist."

Freya and Aer exchanged a look, and she could see in his eyes that he had the same reservations she did about bringing Reginald into strategy meetings when they were so close to their goal. He'd traveled with them to Kildin, although they hadn't told him many details about why they'd detoured.

"He's not wrong," Collin said from Laz's side.

"Considering you've brought us in, I'd say one more potential traitor in our midst couldn't hurt," Vali said with a grin, ignoring Daniel's venomous look.

"He's not wrong, either," Collin repeated.

"Fair enough," Byrric said, then looked over at the guards standing by the door. "Go find Prince Reginald and bring him here, please."

Rodrick and Perinald each gave a sharp nod and ducked out, leaving Rissen and Cecilia behind.

While they waited, Byrric and General Erlan began going over the more recent updates about Kildin's state. Freya knew she should probably listen, but she couldn't muster the energy to get involved in more discussions. She was so tired of talking, of listening. She itched to spread her wings, fly closer to the city to take in the damage, see what they might be able to salvage. But as she took in Laz, Collin, and Alyndra's haggard faces that held only slightly more hope than they had the last time she'd seen them, she couldn't bring herself to leave just yet. It was also highly probable both her father and her husband would have her guards tackle her to the ground if she attempted to fly off on her own. So, for a multitude of reasons, she opted to stay put.

"What's wrong?" Aer asked, seeming to sense her agitation.

She smiled and leaned against his arm. "Just a bit antsy, is all. I want to go see the city."

"Soon," he promised. He rubbed a comforting hand down her back. "We'll go together soon."

"I know," she murmured. "I won't go running off by myself, don't worry."

He chuckled. "Oh, I know."

A few moments later, Reginald stepped through the door with Rodrick and Perinald close behind.

"You requested to see me, Commander?" He halted when he saw Daniel and Vali. "What is this?" He shifted his legs as if to run. "Who are they?"

"Reginald Ristner, meet Vali Balthana, leader of the Jotnar rebels, and Daniel Veldin, steward of Jotunheim," Aer said.

"We'd like to discuss your brother," Freya added.

Reginald's desire to flee seemed to intensify when he heard their names, but he gritted his teeth and focused on Freya and Aer. "Why are they here?"

"To explore all possible roads toward peace, of course," Vali answered instead. His grin made it clear he was enjoying Reginald's discomfort.

Reginald blinked. "Peace? His sister—"

"And *your* brother," Daniel snapped before the prince could finish. "Let's call us even and discuss this like civilized beings."

"We're formulating plans for Kildin and wanted to get some insight from you regarding your brother's...thought process," Byrric cut in.

Tavian snorted softly.

Byrric ignored him. "We're all aiming toward the same or mutually beneficial goals."

"Your brother's knights and the remaining Jotnar have left Kildin and are marching south," Ruehnar said. "We're hoping you can shed some light on why he might've made such a choice."

Reginald folded his muscular arms and kept his eyes averted from Daniel and Vali. "As I'm sure you've guessed, Willem is no strategist. His choices almost never involve complex decision making. In this instance, my guess would be self-preservation, pure and simple." He frowned. "Why?"

"Because your brother has just recalled thousands of knights from an invaluable city," Daniel said. "It makes no sense, strategically."

"No, it doesn't," Reginald agreed. "And if it were my father at the helm, I assure you, Kildin would still be swarmed with human knights. Again, this is just a guess, but Willem likely sees far more importance in the kingdom's capital than a single realm's. *If* he's sending his men further south, it would be because Rosie is in Errest. Although, he probably knows just as well as I do that she's perfectly safe and unlikely to want to leave."

"If your father had prepared him for leadership in any form—" Tavian began.

"Willem is second only to my father in stubbornness," Reginald said. "Our father was a lot of things, but a poor strategist wasn't one of them. Willem simply always thought he knew better."

"A common Ristner trait, if memory serves," Ruehnar said drily.

Freya raised a brow. "How many Ristner monarchies have you seen, Your Majesty?"

"Enough to know Willem is no anomaly."

"That being the case," Aer jumped in. "I think it's safe to say we can send at least a few of our people into Kildin to assess things more closely. If you agree, Commander?"

"Zane and Ana's reports support what Prince Reginald is saying, so yes, I think that's wise."

"We'll take another pass and meet you outside the western wall," Ana said, gesturing for Zane to join her.

"I'll let Collin run through his thoughts on going into the city," Laz said. "He's been spending most of his days figuring out how to save any people who are still left inside the walls. We've been housing everyone we've found in the village here, since most of the residents fled once they realized the city was under attack."

Freya couldn't help but notice how much stronger Laz seemed now that he was home again. He'd spent so much time worrying for his people, and for good reason. But after his initial reaction to being told he would take his father's seat, she'd been worried he would struggle once given the reins. But watching him now as he and General Erlan laid out everything for Byrric and the others, she was happy to see he seemed to have found a rhythm to being in charge. It looked as though having a solid purpose and no longer having to wait around had strengthened him.

She was also completely unsurprised to hear that Collin already had a plan for entering the city.

"We shouldn't need to worry about cover," he explained when Laz gave him the floor. "You can enter from the west, where the wall has been taken down. There are some areas worth noting where enemy knights might still be hiding," he added, pointing to a few spots on the map, "but our scouts have assessed those areas several times and haven't seen any activity."

"Then what are we waiting for?" Vali asked.

"There's something else." Collin looked at Laz, then Aer. "The city is empty of enemy knights, but it's nearly completely in ruin."

"Worse than we thought when we first arrived," Laz said. "Worse than Watoria," he added with a glance toward Freya.

"Even more reason to get a move on," Vali urged.

"I will take you lot anywhere you want to go if it will get him to shut his mouth," Fenian snapped.

"Fine," Aer said. He held Laz's eyes for another moment, then nodded at the Tordoves. "Take us to the city."

~

MUCH TO FREYA'S DISMAY, Kildin did, in fact, look worse than Watoria. From the field the Tordoves had transported them to on the west side of the city, she could see smoke rising from all over Caelora's capital. Carrion birds drifted in circles here and there, signaling the presence of rotting flesh. The scent of war, of smoke and death and fear, wafted toward them, carried on the light breeze.

That wasn't what drew Freya's eye, though.

A giant hole now cleaved the western wall of Kildin in two. It was more than wide enough to allow hordes of soldiers in without giving the citizens any time to prepare. Wide enough to allow for the complete takeover of the entire city within hours.

"They came through the mountain pass with trebuchets," Collin explained. "It was the middle of the night, so even with sentries on the wall, it was easy enough for the enemy to hide beyond the light line to launch their attack."

"The siege was over before it began," Laz finished.

When Freya looked at Laz, she found him holding firm, his eyes trained on his home with a determination Freya felt in her soul. With a smile, she squeezed his hand.

"We've got this, Lazarus. We'll return this to the home you remember."

He smiled down at her, then put his arm around her shoulder and rested his head on hers. "Thank you, Freya."

"Your scouts are coming," Fenian said, jerking his chin toward the east, where Ana, Zane, and two other Valkyrie were flying in their direction. A moment later, they both touched down on the grass beside them.

"What did you see?" Laz asked.

"Not much, unfortunately," Ana said as she retracted her wings. "But if there are any enemy knights hiding in there, they've done a good job of it."

"We need to focus on the people of Kildin and getting them out safely." Solemnly, Byrric looked back at the city. Then, so quietly Freya almost couldn't hear it, he added, "Whoever's left alive, that is."

"Fortunately this means we won't need to dedicate too much of our own forces to the city," Daniel said. He turned away from Kildin and looked at them all. "We can go in, of course, get the full picture, but we should not linger here too long."

"Then let's get started," Aer said. "I want to know exactly what we're leaving behind when we go to Iladel."

Despite the shattered city that lay before them, for the first time since leaving Iston, Freya felt a bit of hope creep into her heart.

45

FREYA

They walked the streets of Kildin for the rest of the afternoon to assess the damage. By the time they returned to the village several hours later, all were in agreement that the city was salvageable, but it would take significant time and magic to return Kildin to its former glory. Many buildings had been destroyed or severely damaged, but walls and buildings could be rebuilt fairly quickly with the use of the right magics. The rest, the parts that made Kildin such a great city, the morale of the people, would take much longer. Those who hadn't managed to flee the city were either dead or close to it, and Freya knew the best healers in the world wouldn't be able to mend the wounds to the hearts and minds of the people who'd suffered at the hands of the human and Jotnar knights.

After many hours of discussion, the consensus was that the bulk of the knights that remained behind would be Lind earth users and elves, under the combined leadership of Tavian and General Erlan, to speed the process of rebuilding the city walls. Lazarus would continue to offer perspective from a governing standpoint, but military decisions would fall to those with more experience. From there, they would focus on the inner areas to ensure residents had accommodations when they returned. It would be temporary at first, but targeting their earliest effort at physically securing the city would enable it to become a properly guarded stronghold. As most of Kildin's marshals had been slaughtered, Byrric placed General Erlan in charge of selecting new marshals from the Caeloran knights and citizens who remained in Kildin and the nearby areas.

The only remaining issue was to determine which Jotnar officers Daniel would attempt to reach out to in the camps between Kildin and Iladel.

"The Jotnar in Iladel have gone feral without proper leadership," Zane explained as they all sat for dinner in the small house Lazarus had prepared for them. "From what Naedan and I could gather, and Lord Silmar can confirm this," he added with a glance at the elf, "those in the outer camps may be easier to work with than those within the city."

"I agree," Daniel said. "Ideally, we can go into the nearest camp and return with two ranking officers. We will speak with them, and they can then dole out my orders to their own knights."

"Once we have that camp under control, we'll transport our own knights nearer to it," Fenian said. "But not a moment sooner."

"Fair enough," Byrric agreed. "And you're certain you'll be able to pull them under your command, Lord Veldin?"

"Some might take a little convincing," he admitted. "Especially those who prefer the freedom they've found since my sister was killed. I don't doubt I can win their loyalty, but having the elves there to help create a neutral ground for discussion will help immensely."

Freya couldn't help but feel wary about the uncertainty of their new plans. On the one hand, it was completely logical for Daniel to acknowledge he might have difficulties drawing the Jotnar to his command. The fact that he acknowledged it at all put her more at ease with his presence. And, as Zane said, the Jotnar in Iladel needed proper leadership. But on the other hand, if Daniel wasn't able to make his case, and the Jotnar knights became aware of the wavering leadership, the existing war could take on an entirely new dynamic.

"All soldiers seek leadership," Tavian pointed out. "You need to demonstrate you are capable of being the leadership they need. Are you confident in your ability to do that?"

"I am."

"Why?" Ruehnar demanded.

"Because I am the strongest choice they have, Your Majesty. Not to mention, I'm far better than the alternative," Daniel said with a sigh. "The Jotnar follow strength and could care less about ambition. I am stronger than Jonas in every sense of the word, and my goal is to keep Jotunheim safe. As for which army to back, the Linds have a stronger army than Willem's, even without elvish aide. If my knights are given the option to pick a side, they will choose Lindoroth, if for no other reason than it lessens their chances of dying."

"So we get the camp outside of Iladel under Lord Veldin's leadership," Silmar said, using his magic to slide a wooden marker over the camp blocking the pass to Iladel. "If all goes to plan, the Jotnar will turn on any humans within that camp and that will be that." He looked at Byrric and Fenian. "How do you plan to deal with those in the city? They won't be as neatly organized as those in the camps."

"We'll cross that bridge once we have the Jotnar camp in hand." Byrric rubbed a hand over his stubbled chin in thought. "Lord Silmar, you'll transport Lords Veldin and Florian to the camp?"

"I will," Silmar agreed.

"Alright, then. Let's get moving."

FREYA EXPECTED it to take most of the day for Daniel to return with word from the first Jotnar camp, so she was surprised when she and Aer walked into the house and found Daniel, Silmar, and Florian sitting at the table alongside two Jotnar officers just before lunch. Both appeared tall and lean, their long legs splayed out in front of them, with skin so pale it nearly blended into their white blond hair.

"I suppose this is good news?" Aer asked, stopping just inside the door and looked at Byrric.

"That would depend on your definition of 'good news'," Vali said, not taking his eyes off the two officers. It seemed that, despite his relationship with Daniel, Vali hadn't placed full trust in the rest of the Jotnar army.

"Your Majesties, meet General Rayn and his second in command, Lieutenant Forrest," Daniel said. "They have agreed to hear us out."

General Rayn, whose bright blue eyes cast a stark contrast to his alabaster skin, eyed them with barely veiled disdain. "On the condition that we will be returned to our camp unharmed should we refuse." He shifted his pale eyes to Daniel. "I'm only doing this out of respect for my former empress."

"As said empress's brother, I can assure you she would appreciate your loyalty," Daniel said drily, then looked at Aer. "General Rayn is well-respected among his soldiers. Lessia appointed him when she took power, and he has been instrumental in her most recent... ventures." He nodded toward the other male. "She chose Lieutenant Forrest not long after."

"In other words, they had a strong hand in the siege on our wedding night?" Freya asked dryly.

"We follow the orders of our leader," Forrest said simply.

"And if those orders were to change?" Ruehnar asked.

"The Linds don't currently seem able to offer much to entice a change in allegiance," Rayn said with a smirk.

"Most in this room would beg to differ," Daniel said. "Regardless, I am in a position to make your life quite difficult upon your return to Jotunheim."

"If you take power," Forrest countered.

"The only ones who stand to oppose me are Jonas Edrin and a human," Daniel replied. "Suffice to say, I'm confident in my chances."

Rayn leaned back in his chair. "Willem has promised us many things, as has Lord Edrin. More freedom to decide how to train our knights, less restrictive oversight, increased wages."

Daniel angled his head and narrowed his eyes. "And you think I wouldn't be open to doing that?"

Forrest shrugged. "You stood faithfully at Lessia's side for centuries. Why would we think you'd be any different? Maybe Jonas *would* be the better leader."

Daniel snorted. "You know as well as I that you don't truly believe that."

"You do realize Lessia named him heir to avoid anyone assassinating her, don't you?" Florian asked. "No one in their right mind would've chosen him in her place."

"The amount of chaos that would've ensued, the instability, would've been catastrophic," Byrric said. "Fortunately, now you're in a position to choose who will lead you."

"A choice no one else has offered," Daniel added.

There was a heavy silence as the two Jotnar exchanged a long look, holding some type of silent conversation with their eyes. Finally, after a few moments, General Rayn looked at Aer, then Daniel.

"We make no promises," he said as he and Forrest stood from the table. "Regardless of my own feelings regarding this matter, with you, Lord Veldin, our knights have tasted a new type of freedom since the Empress was killed. You are correct as far as Jonas goes. He is no leader and every Jotnar knight will agree with that. Neither is Willem. Unfortunately, many of our kind can be quite...shortsighted."

Freya bit back a snort, but Tavian didn't bother hiding his.

"How much time will you need?" Fenian asked, ignoring his brother.

"Give me one of your kind and we'll be able to move more quickly," Rayn said. "The nearest camp to ours is two days from there on foot. If you want this done expeditiously, faster means of travel are a necessity."

Fenian, Tavian, and Ruehnar exchanged a look.

"You don't have the luxury of time," Forrest pointed out.

"I will go," Silmar said after a moment. "The Jotnar should hear from one of us as well."

"Then one of us should go, too," Aer said. "It's our kingdom, after all."

Byrric nodded. "I'll accompany Lord Silmar."

Fear seized Freya at the thought of her father walking into the hornets' nest that would undoubtedly await in the Jotnar camp. Forcing herself to stay calm, she said "You're needed here."

Byrric lifted his brows. "They need to hear from someone high ranking, Freya. You two are out of the question, so that leaves me. Zane will take my place while I'm gone."

"Of course, Commander," Zane said with a nod.

"He's right, Your Majesties," Florian said as he took in Freya's expression. "The commander's duty is to be your proxy in war."

"This is the position my father appointed him to, Freya," Aer said gently.

Freya exhaled a small breath, doing all she could to keep her expression under control. "I understand that," she said slowly. "But we're talking about sending our commander into the middle of an enemy camp. Taking one elf, no matter how strong," she added with a glance at Silmar, "is not nearly enough to keep him safe."

"Well, you certainly will not be tagging along," Tavian said.

She shot him a glare. "Despite what you may think of my reasoning skills, I'm perfectly capable of acknowledging where I belong."

"I'll go with them," Florian offered. "But we cannot afford to send more, nor would that send the message we want to convey."

Freya ground her teeth together, then looked around the room, taking in the clear opposition on everyone else's faces.

"Put your feelings aside, cousin," Vali said. "And perhaps consider the fact that your father trusted you to keep yourself alive in equally dangerous conditions. He's more than capable of this task."

"The Forest of Ages wasn't an enemy camp with thousands of enemy knights," she countered.

"No, it was worse, because you had no back up and even less of an idea what you would be facing," Fenian said, then turned his gaze to the others. "We are wasting time arguing about this."

"Agreed," Byrric said in a tone that Freya knew better than to push against. "Florian and I will go with Lord Silmar and Lord Veldin, Zane will take my place here, and Lord Silmar will return us once we have a decision."

Lips pursed, Freya looked at her father and nodded. "Alright. Be safe."

He pulled her into a hug. "I'll see you tomorrow."

Then, they were gone.

"Before you get back to...whatever you'll be getting back to," Laz said once the others had vanished, "Lord Silmar left some other news he didn't want to discuss in front of the Jotnar."

Aer frowned. "What is it?"

"He spent some time gathering information while at the Jotnar camp." Laz sighed. "We now have confirmation that the knights that left Kildin are on their way to Errest, not Iladel. They're traveling by boat. Their plan is to travel down the Rimar River toward the Gefhorn Junction and head toward Errest from there."

"Lovely," Tavian muttered.

Freya shook her head. "Willem has to know he's risking massive numbers sending that many knights there. Errest is more well-protected than any other region in the kingdom. It's crawling with Lind and elf soldiers"

"Willem is clearly assuming overwhelming numbers will be enough to handle them," Ruehnar said. "Kildin is destroyed beyond any immediate repair, at least for the humans, so the mines in Errest will be his top priority. I would imagine a large portion of his men will go directly there to ensure they are guarded as well as Iladel."

"Because that's how he'll pay to rebuild once he wins," Aer finished with a sigh. "One of you needs to go warn Ettrian, then."

"I will go," Tavian said. "My brother should be aware of our change in plans as well. We can leave a few hundred additional soldiers here, but I think it would be wise to send reinforcements south. Right now, most of the knights in Edhil are focused on Errest, but Willem is correct in recognizing the value of the mines, they need to be more adequately protected."

"I wouldn't put it past Willem to cave them in if he feels threatened," Vali said. "The bulk of the mines are in the west, correct?"

"They are," Laz confirmed. "Concentrated near the desert's edge below the Gefhorn River."

"We'll send more knights, then," Freya said with a nod. She looked at Aer. "Lea and Perida's focus should be on Errest."

"When I go to my brother, I will confirm what troops, if any, have already been sent to the mines," Tavian said.

"And toward the river junction," Zane added. "It shouldn't take long for the Errestian navy to get their ships on the river, but a show of force on foot will help, as well."

They were all quiet for a moment before Freya said, "I hope we're making the right decision here."

"It is impossible to say, one way or another, whether any choices are the right ones," Tavian said.

"You also don't have many other options at this point," Vali pointed out.

"In other words, we can't unring that bell?" Freya said with a half smile.

"Precisely," Vali said with a nod.

"It's the same choice I would've made," Laz said. "Granted, I don't have nearly the amount of military experience any of you do," he added to the Tordoves and Zane. "But it seems like the most logical choice."

"Common sense isn't exclusive to soldiers," Zane said. "Although, it's a pretty strict requirement."

Aer huffed out a laugh as he stared down at the map, the markers scattered all over its surface. "I guess we'll find out soon enough."

46

LEA

It took barely a day for Lea to realize that, despite her constant irritation with Ettrian, his ability to kiss her silly at every opportunity was making him far more interesting to be around. There was no doubt he'd still drive her insane now and then, but she was more than happy to spend her spare minutes wrapped in his arms, feeling his lips and hands run across her body. They'd ridden into the city the previous day to deliver more jewel fruit to the merchants, and had spent the bulk of their carriage ride to and from with the shades drawn; Lea in Ettrian's lap as he dragged his lips along her neck, her jaw, his hands brushing against her waist and back in ways that were far more chaste than she would've anticipated, or wanted.

Or perhaps that level of propriety was just one more way in which the prince wanted to drive her crazy. She hadn't decided how far she wanted to take their new...whatever it was...physically, but the more stolen kisses they shared, the more it occupied her mind.

And so, when they bumped into each other in the hall the following morning on the way to breakfast, it was those thoughts that had her dragging him into a rarely-used hallway near her bedroom.

"You know, Lady Calliwell, for someone who seemed to have such a strong contempt for me just a few days ago, you can't seem to keep your hands off of me now," the prince quipped as she tugged at his hand.

"Shut up," she murmured as she dragged his face to hers and kissed him. He didn't bother to speak, instead grabbing the sides of her face and pressing her back against the wall. His lips parted hers as he deepened the kiss, and the way her body responded by arching against him had her questioning, again, exactly how far she was ready to take things with him. She gripped his hips and pulled him closer, letting out a breathy sigh as he ran a hand down her side and did the same.

Suddenly, he let out an annoyed groan through gritted teeth and dragged his lips away, resting his forehead against hers.

"What is it?" Lea demanded, her hands frozen on his waist.

"We should go to breakfast," he replied. He straightened his shirt, which had come untucked, and ran a hand through his dark hair, somehow managing to make it look perfectly put together, despite how hard Lea had been dragging her own fingers through it.

Lea smoothed a hand over her tunic and cinched the smooth leather belt that wrapped around her waist, all the while trying to smother the unreasonable sting of rejection. "Dare I ask why?"

"News from the North," he replied, then took her hand and tugged her back into the hall.

"What?" Lea dropped his hand and picked up her pace. "Come on!"

When they reached the dining room, she shoved open the doors, then skidded to a stop the moment she stepped into the sunlit space.

Tavian Tordove sat with her mother, General Lindesson, and Ordona. The sight startled her so much that she jolted when Ettrian stepped in behind her and nudged her forward.

The room carried a heavy silence and an even heavier tension, which Lea knew would likely bring bad news. There was no reason the prince who'd been with Lazarus and Collin would now be in her home unless something terrible had happened.

"Ah, Lea, Prince Ettrian," Perida said. "Good, I'm glad you're here.

Come, sit, so you can hear Prince Tavian's news. He's just arrived from Kildin."

Tavian's eyes briefly met Lea's. His nose twitched in a nearly imperceptible sniff and he sent a mildly disapproving glance at his brother, then shifted his focus to address the rest of the room.

"Your king and queen have joined forces with Daniel Veldin," Tavian began once she and Ettrian had taken seats across from one another. The older prince eyed them both again, his face more neutral this time, although his black eyes had a hint of speculation in them.

"They've done what?" Lea demanded. The way he spoke the words, clipped and precise, as if it was such a simple thing... "Why–"

"It appears his ambitions are much like your dear Jonas, only he has far more support, not to mention skill." Tavian sighed. "He and the Jotnar rebels have agreed to assist Lindoroth in defeating the humans in exchange for your kingdom's support for Daniel taking control of Jotunheim when this is all over."

"And they've agreed to this?" Lea asked, shooting a look at Perida and Ordona. When her mother nodded, she looked back at Tavian. "Again, why?"

"Logic, and a whole host of other reasons you and your monarchs can discuss later. That's not why I'm here."

"Then why *are* you here?" Ettrian asked. "What has happened in Kildin?"

"Kildin is destroyed, but many of its people fled to outlying areas. The enemy knights that were occupying it have left."

"Destroyed?" Lea asked. "What do you mean?"

Tavian gave her a curious look. "Do you not know the meaning of the word?"

"Lazarus and Collin are safe," Perida said, sending the prince an exasperated look. "They're with Freya and Aerelius now."

Lea exhaled in relief. "Oh, thank the gods."

"Assuming things work out with Daniel, they'll continue to remain safe," Ordona added.

"Unfortunately, the knights who left Kildin are heading south on the Rimar river," Tavian continued. "They'll be here in four days time."

Lea looked to her mother, who's shock and dismay were evident despite her attempt to school her features.

"We assumed when Kildin was emptied that they were heading to Iladel," Tavian continued. "It seems a smaller group of humans is heading to the capital to support the forces there, but the bulk of their army is coming here, to Errest."

Perida, sitting at the end of the long table, furrowed her brow. "Why here? What's the significance of Errest?"

"Aside from your realm's mines?" Tavian's eyes flicked toward the door, then back to Perida. "I can only assume it has to do with Princess Rosie being here."

Lea shook her head as she tried to wrap her mind around what was happening. "Rosie doesn't want to leave. She's made that clear."

Tavian shrugged. "Willem does not care. Her presence here is the perfect excuse for him to sack your city. Your best option is to hand her over and hope for the best."

"Even if we hand her over peacefully, the humans are still likely to attempt to burn the city to the ground," Ettrian said. "If the girl wants to stay, let her stay. Giving her back won't erase Willem's desire to take over this realm."

Lindesson nodded in agreement. "Even if we give her back, Willem won't abandon his siege. His larger interest in Edhil is in our resources. Rosie isn't the biggest prize here. She's simply an excuse."

"I'd like more specifics on the deals Freya and Aerelius made with Lord Veldin," Perida said. "In particular, those involving Edhil."

Tavian gave her a nod. "As you would expect, King Aerelius and Queen Freya agreed to certain allowances when it came to Lindoroth's raw materials, with very specific uses and applications the Jotnar cannot deviate from. That includes reverse engineering any spelled objects currently in their possession or using those materials to create weapons against your people. Your king and queen did a wonderful job of tying up any loopholes, however, and each bargain has been sealed with elvish magic."

Perida looked wary, her eyes narrowing as she considered the implications.

Ordona smiled and placed a hand over her sister's. "This is a good thing, Perida. This means if the Jotnar attempt to use our materials for anything outside the terms of their agreement, they'll be subject to elvish law."

"She is correct, Lady Calliwell," Ettrian said. "As long as your people keep up their end of the bargain, the only ones at risk are the Jotnar. Rest assured, elvish punishment far outstrips any you can come up with."

Perida's frustration was palpable. "This feels like we're walking into a trap."

"We don't have many choices," Ordona said quietly. "This is the best possible solution, as I'm sure General Lindesson would agree."

The general held the former queen's gaze as he considered her words, then nodded. "Considering the circumstances, I would say Prince Tavian is correct. I've spent some time familiarizing myself with certain elvish laws, especially those that pertain to bargains. We can dole out our own punishments, of course, but elvish punishments will be a much better motivator."

Ettrian smirked. "The thought of the Jotnar running the Wild Hunt is quite amusing, though. Wouldn't you agree, Brother?"

Tavian actually grinned at that. "Why do you think I helped seal the bargains?"

"Can you two stop speaking as though you want my monarchs to be betrayed?" Lea asked. "Gods above, you're both incorrigible." She narrowed her eyes when Ettrian dealt a gentle kick to her ankles. "Incorrigible," she repeated.

"We need to focus on the bigger picture," Lindesson said with a sigh. "This is about survival. Byrric and Lord Florian are with Freya and Aerelius, as is King Ruehnar. We have to trust that they wouldn't steer them wrong. Our focus now should be addressing the threat headed directly at us."

"Yes, of course." Perida took a sip of her tea, a move Lea knew was to give herself a breath for composure. "Prince Tavian, will you be staying with us for now or do you plan to return to help the king and queen?"

"I will not stay long," Tavian replied. "A potential siege on Errest must be prevented, but you have my brother to assist you with planning. My goal is to ensure you have all the information you need to make those plans."

"Careful," Ettrian said, a smile pursing his lips. "Too many military successes in Errest and I might give you a run for the throne."

Tavian's face went flat, and he let out a short huff, his annoyance so palpable Lea nearly laughed. "Unlikely, but I will take my chances. Not that I have a choice in the matter." He looked at Lindesson expectantly. "We should get everything sorted so I can return to Kildin."

Lindesson dabbed his mouth with a napkin and stood. "We're set up in the drawing room." He looked down at Ettrian, who'd just stabbed his fork into a piece of sausage. "Will you be joining us, Your Highness?"

Ettrian chewed his sausage, then sighed and stood up. "I suppose I can finish breakfast later." He gave a quick nod to Ordona, Perida, and Lea, his gaze lingering a beat longer on Lea than the others, before he followed the other two from the room.

"Wait," Lea said suddenly. "I have one question before you begin your discussions."

The resigned look on Ettrian's face told her he knew exactly where her mind had gone.

"What will happen to Jonas?" she asked. "If we win with Daniel as our ally, what will happen to Jonas?"

Tavian looked at Ettrian, seeming to give him the go-ahead to answer.

"I would be surprised if Daniel didn't have him executed for treason," Ettrian told her.

"He colluded with a foreign enemy to assassinate the empress," Tavian said. "Daniel will be within his rights, both as Lessia's brother and the presumed ruler, to execute Jonas for his hand in Lessia's death. Your king and queen would do the same, and they would be right to."

"Daniel may also allow him to challenge him for the throne," Ettrian added. "It would be for show, of course. Jonas doesn't have the strength or skill for an even match."

"It may not be what you want to hear, Lady Calliwell, but it is the unfortunate business of war," Lindesson explained.

She rubbed a hand over her eyes, then slumped back in her seat. "Yes, I suppose it is." Regardless of her past or current feelings toward Jonas, she had no desire to see him killed. Helping Willem kill Lessia had been the best thing Jonas could've done for his empire, assuming Daniel wasn't worse. Daniel likely knew that, but optics, of course, would never allow him to let Jonas go unpunished.

Lea had been able to keep Jonas safe so far, but she was beginning to fear she was just delaying the inevitable.

47

LEA

Once Lea had finished breakfast with Perida and Ordona, she excused herself to go back to her room, where she found Tyna hovering by the door. She cast a glance down the hall toward Rosie's room, where she thankfully found Iska sitting in a chair across from the door. Satisfied he would keep the princess in one place, she turned back to Tyna.

"I'm glad you're here," Lea said, keeping her voice low. "Come inside." She shoved open her bedroom door, then waited for the pixie to follow her in before shutting it.

Tyna gave her a curious look. "What is it, Lady Calliwell?"

Lea rubbed a hand across her brow. "I need you to keep an eye on Rosie at all times. I know Iska is also guarding her, but you have a different skill set than he does. Mainly your ability to go unseen."

"Of course, but what's the immediate concern?"

"I'm assuming you overheard everything we just spoke about in the dining room?"

Tyna flushed, but nodded. "Yes, of course."

"Good. The moment Rosie gets word that her brother has sent thousands of his knights toward Errest, she'll immediately assume they're coming for her. Any thoughts of not wanting to go back will almost certainly evaporate, and we'll end up needing to lock her away, which is the last thing I want to do."

"Alright, then." Tyna gave a sharp nod. "I'll keep her occupied, watch her day and night."

"I'm going to tell Iska to continue do the same," Lea said. "He's already got a close eye on her, but we can't have her go unsupervised, not for a moment."

Tyna glanced out the window, then looked back at Lea. "We'll take care of Rosie, Lady Calliwell, but I have to ask...what are you going to do about Jonas?"

Lea sat down on her bed, her hands resting in her lap as she considered her predicament. Sadness crept into her heart. "I don't know. How do I tell him that he'll likely be executed by his own people in the very near future? My gut is to help him get away, but even I know that would be a terrible idea." She lifted her hands and let them fall back to her lap. "Despite any kindness he's shown toward me, he's also shown he has a taste for power. That changes who I thought he was entirely."

Tyna fluttered closer. "Be honest, my lady. It might be harder for you to come to grips with that than for him." She placed a small hand on Lea's shoulder. "In some ways, I think he probably already knew this was coming."

Lea pursed her lips in an attempt to force back the lump that had formed in her throat. "I'm sure you're right, Tyna, but that doesn't make it any easier. There's nothing I can do to save him, and even if there were, helping him flee could put my entire kingdom at risk. I can't do that."

"Recent decisions notwithstanding, Jonas seems like a good male," Tyna replied. "I don't think he would ever expect you to put him, a single person, above the well-being of your kingdom. And if he did, well..." She drifted back and let the words hang in the air.

"If he did, that would speak more about the kind of person he is than any action he's shown thus far." Lea flopped back on her bed. "Gods above, Tyna, when did this get so godsdamned hard?"

"I would say the siege on the palace was the likely turning point."

Lea looked up at the pixie, brows raised. "Tyna, was that sarcasm?"

Tyna's eyes widened. "Oh, I apologize—"

Lea grinned. "No, no. It's perfectly fine. Almost refreshing, if I'm being honest. You've been so tense, so it's nice to see a bit of humor come out."

Exhaling a breath, Tyna smiled. "Thank you, my lady. Now...at the risk of being further improper, can I ask a question?"

Lea sat up and eyed her warily. "I suppose."

"What will you do about Prince Ettrian?"

Lea thought for a moment, surprised at her lack of annoyance at the question. "I used to think he was cold and cruel. But I've realized these past few weeks that I respect his methods, his mindset, and his views more than I did initially. His varying levels of deceit made me angry, but does any of that compare to my own deceptions at the palace? Or is that just me making excuses for who he is?"

Tyna smiled. "All fair questions, my lady. I don't think you're making excuses for him." She sat down on the pillow next to Lea. "I've been around a long, long time, met many people and seen many things. What I've seen in you recently are the same things I've seen in other monarchs, other leaders."

"What do you mean?"

"It's a bit like having the wool pulled from over your eyes," Tyna continued. "It's as General Lindesson said. 'The unfortunate business of war.' Only it isn't simply about what type of punishments are dealt out. It's also about what war does to people, how it changes them." She placed a hand over Lea's. "You are seeing how it changed you."

Lea considered how many times she'd pictured shoving green *eitr* down Willem's throat, watching his insides bubble up through his mouth, then watching as his body was devoured by insects, animals, and flames. How she'd reveled in the thought of her world being rid of him in the most gruesome ways imaginable. How she'd imagined poisoning Rosie's raspberry tea, leaving Jonas to rot with the rest of them after he'd left her in the dungeons for a week. How she could barely go a day without eyeing those around her with heavy suspicion.

"Yes, I suppose I am," she finally said. "I'm not quite sure how I feel about that."

"And the prince?" Tyna asked gently. "How do you feel about him?"

Lea kept her eyes averted. "I'm not sure about that, either. It's barely been two days, but he's a welcome distraction. Something to give me a bit of joy between moments of sadness. There are feelings there, I know that. I know I can't ignore them. But I just can't right now, Tyna. It's too much."

Tyna nodded in understanding. "Then don't."

"Thank you." Lea knew she would have to deal with Ettrian at some point. There was no doubt that her feelings for him had grown since returning to Errest. In all honesty, she knew feelings for him began before that, although she couldn't really say when.

But she also knew he would be leaving for Andradath once this war was over. A kingdom halfway across the world.

With that thought, her conversation with Ettrian floated to the front of her mind.

"And you?" she had asked him. *"Where do you think I belong?"*

"Is that a question you truly want an answer to?"

"Yes, I think I do."

"I'm a selfish person, Lea. What I want isn't always for the greater good. It's often quite the opposite."

She'd turned his words over and over in her head the past two days, trying to figure out exactly what he'd meant. His word games had become one of the most infuriating things about him. Elves couldn't lie, but they could find very creative ways to twist the truth.

But would he truly be that duplicitous with her?

With a shake of her head, Lea forced her thoughts back to the present crisis. The plans they were making, the strategies they were considering, all hinged on the actions of others. It was a delicate balance of power and trust. Trust in people who were once strangers, people who were once enemies, and people whose motives varied wildly from hers.

"I'll go speak with Jonas in the morning," she finally said. "I need to talk with my mother and aunt about how we're going to handle the knights coming south, but I can't do that if I'm dealing with his feelings as well as my own."

"Another welcome distraction, then?" Tyna asked with a wry smile.

"These days, they're all welcome," Lea said with a sigh.

48

FREYA

Freya barely slept a wink that night because she couldn't force herself to stop thinking about what might be happening at the Jotnar camp. It wasn't until Aer had silenced her with kisses and the rest of his body that she'd finally managed to fall asleep.

When she awoke, her mind insisted on picking up where it had left off the night before. She rolled toward the window, an east-facing square that framed the Aldridge mountains far in the distance. All she could think of when she viewed the craggy peaks was the palace nestled on the eastern side of the range. Her home.

She pushed away all thoughts of clawing their way out of this war and forced herself to think of the way it had been and the way it would be again. She pictured squires training in the yard, Maghda's stew simmering on the stove, summer dinners in the gardens, and exploring the tunnels with Aer. Eventually, should the gods will it, there would be a prince or princess or two running the halls.

It was a long way off, but she couldn't wait to show her children all the nooks and crannies she and Aer had discovered over the years. The thought of it was enough to bring a smile to her face.

"That's something I haven't seen enough lately," Aer said sleepily, running a hand down her side.

Her smile turned rueful as she took in his sleep-filled expression. "It's hard to smile when things are so dire."

"Then what brought it on now?"

"Thoughts of a happier future." She sighed and placed a hand on his cheek, then rested her forehead against his. "It seems too far away."

"Not as far as you think. I promise."

For some reason his words brought tears to her eyes. Suddenly the mountains she pictured were crawling with enemy knights, the palace halls were filled with leering humans, and the yard where the squires trained was occupied by people who had no business there. It was impossible not to flood her mind with dark thoughts. Her elation that they'd been able to salvage Kildin was slowly being replaced with fear for their next steps, for her father, and for Lea, Perida, and Ordona, who currently had an entire army marching on their city.

"It's alright to cry, Freya," Aer whispered. "It's just me."

And for what she hoped would be the last time during this war, she did.

A FEW AGONIZING HOURS LATER, Byrric, Silmar, and Daniel returned.

"What happened?" Aer demanded as the three males, along with Prince Fenian, walked into the sitting room of the village house where Freya and Aer had been talking with Laz and Collin.

"The Jotnar knights will follow me," Daniel said. He looked relieved, which surprised Freya because he'd seemed so certain the previous day that he'd get their allegiance instantly.

"General Rayn and Lieutenant Forrest are at the Jotnar camp with Florian rallying the troops, so to speak," Byrric told them. "We're getting our own sorted now, then we'll travel to them. I want to be gone by nightfall."

"Some will still need more convincing," Silmar cautioned as Ana and Zane stepped into the room. "But as of now, we should shift our focus to destroying the human camps."

Freya exhaled a breath of relief. She remained wary of Daniel and the other Jotnar, and part of her wished she'd been able to grill the General about his intentions, but she also knew better than to look a gift horse in the mouth.

"Thank you, Lord Veldin," she said. "We appreciate your efforts."

Veldin gave her a nod. "Thank you, Your Majesty. Willem Ristner promised my people a lot of things, but he doesn't know our kind as well as he thinks."

"When do we leave?" Aer asked.

"As soon as possible," Byrric replied. "Zane, Ana, are our troops ready?"

Zane gave a sharp nod. "They are."

"Just awaiting orders," Ana said. "The Valkyrie are getting a bit twitchy, though, so we should probably move out soon."

Freya bit back a smile. It was nice to know that desperate need for movement was a common Valkyrie trait and not something unique to her.

"I would suggest moving quickly, then," Daniel said. "A large portion of my knights are prepared to leave Willem Ristner in pieces. I don't want to keep them waiting."

"Good," Byrric said. "We'll make camp for a night, maybe two, before heading to Iladel."

Aer gave Daniel a curious look. "It wasn't difficult to change their course, then?"

Daniel shook his head. "Few, if any, in that camp wanted to follow Jonas, and those who thought King Ristner was the one to support did so largely because he had little means of actually controlling them. They also haven't heard from Jonas in weeks. Soldiers need a leader and I have spent years presenting myself as a good one."

"Do we need to worry about those who wanted Willem as leader due to his lack of control?" Freya asked. The last thing they needed was a group of soldiers ready to mutiny because their new leader was too strict.

"There weren't many, but those who would oppose me have been dealt with," Daniel replied. "Those who prefer Lord Edrin will be given time to amend their views before we make the choice for them. There is only one other Jotnar camp in the area, which is where I'll be going next."

"What about the camps that have Jotnar and humans?" Freya asked.

"I will need a bit more backup to deal with those," Daniel said. "We can discuss them once we're settled tomorrow."

"Do you still intend to allow Jonas to challenge you if he chooses to?" Aer asked.

"I do," Daniel said. Then, with a quick look at Freya he added, "For what little good it'll do."

"Prince Fenian, you should ready your troops to leave," Byrric said. "Silmar, you'll bring Lord Veldin back to camp?"

Silmar gave a sharp nod. "Of course."

Daniel looked at Freya, then Aer. "We're putting a great deal of trust in one another. Should this all turn out the way we want, with me in power in Jotunheim, Willem Ristner defeated, and you both back on your thrones, I look forward to building a better relationship between our lands."

Aer gave him a smile that Freya was happy to see was genuine, yet reserved. "As do we, Lord Veldin."

With a quick nod goodbye, Silmar transported Daniel away.

"It sounds like it's time to say our goodbyes," Lazarus said.

Freya gave him a sad smile. "I suppose it is."

"I'll give you all a few minutes," Byrric said, gesturing for Fenian, Ana, and Zane to leave with him.

Once Fenian transported them away, Freya turned to Laz.

"Hopefully it won't be long until we're together again," Laz said to her as he leaned in and gave her a hug. "These constant separations are getting old."

"That they are," Aer agreed, pulling his cousin in for a hug after Freya stepped aside.

"If you need us, or have any news, send one of the elves," Collin said.

"We'll do our best to come help you in Iladel," Laz promised. "It'll be a long shot, but we'll try."

"Just keep your focus on Kildin," Freya said as she wrapped her arms around Collin. "Get this city back on its feet. We'll see each other soon enough."

After they finished their farewells, Freya and Aer left the house to find Byrric and Ana. As they walked, Freya couldn't help but worry about leaving Laz and Collin behind. They were most certainly safer in Kildin than they would be if they came with them to the enemy camps and Iladel, but she still wished they were all staying together.

"I wish we didn't have to leave them," Aer murmured.

"Are you a mind reader now?" Freya asked, sending him a small smile. "I was just thinking the same."

Aer chuckled. "Not a mind reader, no. It would just be nice if we could stay put for more than a day or two."

"Agreed," Freya said with a sigh. She slid her gloved hands into the pockets of her jacket and exhaled, her warm breath instantly freezing in the cold air.

As she and Aer walked in silence, the sound of their boots crunching on frozen ground mixing with the quiet din of soldiers in the distance, Freya's thoughts wandered to Lea again. Now that she knew Laz and Collin were safe and Myria was back in Olthanas, the thought of Lea being under threat from half an army gnawed at her mind. The uncertainty of whether help would arrive in time, or whether there were enough knights outside of Errest to combat the enemy, kept her mind whirring with worry. But despite every fiber of her being wanting to take as many knights as she could to Errest and secure one more capital, she knew her place was at her husband's, and her father's, side.

Hand-in-hand, she and Aer made their way down the hill toward the field where Byrric, Ruehnar, and Ana were doling out orders to a group of scouts. As they approached, Byrric sent the scouts off and turned to face them, his gray wings tucked tightly against his back.

"We'll be ready to head out soon. We've sent a few aerial scouts to monitor the road between here and where we'll make camp near the Jotnar. We need to ensure there won't be any surprises after we arrive. King Ruehnar sent several of his knights through the Between with some of ours to secure the immediate area. They're going to take out any smaller human camps between here and the Jotnar camp to avoid any attacks from the north." He gestured toward the mass of knights–Lind, elf, and Jotnar. "Ruehnar and Fenian are making travel arrangements now so we can have the location fully cloaked when we arrive."

"Good," Aer said. "The last thing we need to do is lose any element of surprise we may currently have."

Byrric grunted his agreement. "We're also trying to avoid letting the Jotnar know when we arrive. As of now, they are considered allies, but that's only based on agreements with their leaders. It's best we don't put full trust in those tasked with fighting beside us just yet."

"Good," Freya said. "I thought it was just me being paranoid."

"Not paranoid," her father corrected. "Logical. Despite Daniel's intentions, the Jotnar knights have dealt with too many fluctuations in leadership recently. We can trust that he'll do his job, but even he can't confirm the knights will take to his leadership immediately. Many will likely assume he'll be removed and someone else will come along. Possibly Willem, possibly Jonas. Maybe someone else entirely."

"Gods above, I hope not," Freya muttered. "I've had enough of the surprise entries in this fiasco."

A loud whistle sounded, drawing their attention to where the knights had entered into a formation that would allow the elves to transport them to their new camp as one group.

"I'm going to get things settled," Byrric told them. "Be ready to leave within the hour."

Freya watched as he moved to join Ruehnar, Fenian, Zane, and Ana. She leaned into Aer's side, staring at the mountains in the distance, their peaks shrouded in clouds. They seemed so big from where she stood, stretching for ages to the north and south. When she pictured the palace, it was small, no bigger than a toy, in comparison.

"We'll win this," Aer murmured, his voice low but firm. "Then we'll go home."

"I know," she said with a sigh. "And I know we're in a better position now than we were two days ago. It's just...a lot."

Aer kissed the top of her head and tucked her more tightly into his side.

She relaxed against him, thankful for his proximity and strength. Still, she couldn't shake the heaviness in her heart that reminded her of how much sacrifice their victory would come with. How much had already been sacrificed and how much would continue to be.

She just hoped that when the dust finally settled after all of the battles were fought, they would still have a home to return to.

49

LEA

Once again, Lea barely slept. Only this time, it was thoughts of how she would tell Jonas about the newest developments with the war and his empire that kept her mind from going quiet. When the sun finally rose, she'd resigned herself to her very uncomfortable position as the only person in the house who seemed to care at all about Jonas' feelings and wellbeing. First, his sister was taken from him. Now, she had to break the news that his people and home, and possibly his life, were being taken, too.

She'd spoken to her mother and aunt at length the day before, hoping she could convince them to do something to keep Jonas safe if and when Daniel Veldin took control of Jotunheim. She knew going into the conversation it was probably a fool's errand, but he'd kept her alive at the castle. The least they could do was attempt the same here.

It seemed clear, though, that not killing Jonas on sight when he arrived in Errest was the furthest Perida was willing to go when it came to keeping him safe. And ultimately, it was just as Lindesson and Tavian had said. Daniel Veldin would be within his rights to avenge his sister's death, regardless of how he'd, or many of the

Jotnar, had felt about her in life, and Freya and Aer would be within *their* rights to hand him over.

With an annoyed huff, she rolled onto her back and stared up at the white plaster ceiling. She'd spent hours trying to figure out the best way to broach the topic without making Jonas even more miserable. The more she dwelled on it, though, the more certain she became that there was no delicate way to tell Jonas his empire didn't want him.

A knock sounded at the door. She let out a sigh and her eyes fell shut. She waited until another knock sounded before calling, "Come in!"

When the door swung open, she was expecting her mother, perhaps her aunt, but instead she saw Ettrian leaning against the door frame.

He dragged his eyes over her and her sleep-mussed state and pursed his lips. "Good morning, Lady Calliwell."

Her instinct was to tug the covers around herself and cover her messy hair, but that would give him too much satisfaction. Instead, she sat up. "What are you doing here?"

He took a few steps into the room and shut the door. "I thought I'd come help you hash out this problem that has your mind spinning."

"Oh?" She looked at him expectantly, trying to fight the smirk on her lips. "And what might that be?"

The prince dropped into a chair beside her bed. "You're trying to figure out how to keep that bloody emissary alive."

Lea looked down at her hands. "I can't help it, Ettrian, and it's not fair to expect me to. Yes, he was a bastard in the palace on more than one occasion, but his intentions were always good."

"Those good intentions didn't keep Willem from trying to assault you or his men from eyeing you like a piece of meat." He leaned forward and rested his elbows on his knees. "Nor did they keep you from Lessia's interrogations in the dungeon for a week."

She pursed her lips. "We were both playing a part. I knew what the risks were when I agreed to go back to the palace and so did he."

"Alright. Then what do you plan to do?"

She picked at her thumbnail as she considered his question. "I think—no, I want to talk to Jonas, convince him to try to submit to Daniel, if Daniel would even entertain such a thing. Even I know there'd likely be no competition between the two if the people of Jotunheim are given a choice."

"Do you think Jonas sees it that way?"

Lea's head fell back against the headboard. "I don't know. I used to think he was so smart, that his plans to take the throne from Lessia were sound. But the more I think about our time in the palace, hell, even the time Freya and I spent with him before that...I'm starting to realize he might not be as intelligent as I once thought."

Ettrian's lips twitched. "That's a very long-winded way to say you think he's an imbecile."

Lea shot him a dry look. "That's not what I meant and you know it. I just don't want him to be killed for something he felt he was doing in good faith for his empire. For all of us, even. The world is a better place without Lessia Edrin in it. I think we can agree on that, at least."

"Well, if it eases your mind at all, I do believe Daniel will give Jonas the option of either fealty or death. It's the best course of action if he wants Jotunheim not to be seen as the animalistic place so many view it as."

Lea frowned. "Wouldn't that show weakness, though?"

"Not if he banishes him."

They were silent for a moment as Lea considered what a fall from grace that would be for Jonas. Once a royal emissary traveling the world, now a male in exile. It was sad to think of, but, she imagined, preferable to death. The rebels were unlikely to take him in, especially once their agreements with Daniel were solidified, so he would probably need to leave the continent unless Freya and Aer allowed him to stay.

"What would you do?" she asked quietly, almost afraid to hear the answer.

Ettrian stood, then dropped down onto the bed, next to her, mirroring her position against the headboard. "I would send Jonas a gift for ridding my life of that tiresome wench, then take him on as court jester as punishment." He slid her a look, then smiled at her confusion. "Humiliation can be a far more effective punishment than death, Lea."

She smiled, resisting the urge to move closer to him, to feel more of his warmth. "Yes, I suppose you're right."

He turned onto his side, then ran a finger up her bare arm. "And Willem? What would you see done to him, little witch?"

She tried to ignore the goosebumps that formed on her skin where he touched her, forcing herself to answer his question. "My instinct tells me I'd want to swing the sword toward Willem's neck myself. I think I'd revel in the idea of watching him die." She frowned, then met Ettrian's dark gaze. "I don't want to sink to his level, but what other options are there?"

"Just a quick death, then?" Ettrian raised a brow. "That seems ill-advised."

She sent him a sly look. "Well, at least I wouldn't allow him to live out his life as court jester. At least this way I won't have to stare at his wretched face for the next fifty years."

Ettrian touched a finger to her chin. "It's funny, you know."

"What is?"

"When I first saw you in the throne room in Iladel, I never would've imagined I'd lay in your bed and discuss the most effective way to punish traitors."

Part of her wanted to smile at that, but the other part hated to think of just how much her life had changed in the past two months.

Their conversation was interrupted by another knock on the door. Perida's voice followed. "Lea? Are you awake?"

"Shit!" Lea hissed. In a panic, she shoved Ettrian off the bed on the side out of sight of the door. He hit the floor with a thunk, and she prayed he'd stay there, out of sight. "Come in, Mother," she called out as she hopped out of bed and threw on her robe.

Perida entered, her eyes sweeping the room before settling on her daughter. "How did you sleep?"

Lea shrugged and sat on the edge of the bed furthest from Ettrian. "Well enough, I suppose, considering we have an army aiming to attack us in a few days."

Perida nodded. "We'll handle that, though. We have some of the best knights here to protect our city and people. We both know this city won't fall."

Lea sighed. "I know you're probably right, but even if the city won't fall, how many of our people have to die to ensure that outcome?"

Her mother gave her a gentle smile. "Those knights out there came to terms with those risks years ago, Lea. I understand why you feel the way you do, but what's done is done." She frowned. "What else is bothering you?"

For a moment, Lea thought her mother had realized there was a third person in the room with them.

Before she could come up with an excuse for Ettrian's presence, Perida sat down beside Lea. "This business with Lord Edrin is weighing on you, isn't it?"

"It is," Lea agreed, honestly surprised her mother was so perceptive. "I understand everyone's perspective perfectly, so it's difficult to say 'this is what should be done' with any certainty. I just hate to see him killed or punished when all he really did was make the world a better place."

"Lea, you are going through one of the hardest things a person could experience right now. The things you've had to witness..." Perida shook her head and clicked her tongue. "I've always prided myself on my own fortitude, but the strength I've seen in you lately...I couldn't be more proud."

Lea squeezed her mother's hand. "I know that strength comes from you, though, and Father."

Perida's smile widened, even as her eyes turned sad. "Your stubbornness also comes from your father, although considering the circumstances, that's been quite a blessing.

"Speaking of Father." Lea shifted so she could take Perida's other hand. "There's something I've been wanting to discuss with you," Lea said. "Something Prince Ettrian showed me a few days ago. About Father."

Perida gave her a curious look. "What could that prince possibly know about Orin?"

"Not him, specifically. Just his magic." Quickly, Lea explained what Ettrian had shown her in her Father's study. It was a struggle not to start to cry when Perida's face crumpled and her eyes flooded with tears, but Lea pushed through, doing her best to convey every detail of the night in her father's study.

"I wasn't sure when or how to tell you," she said once she'd finished. "I probably should've right away, but—"

Lea was cut off when her mother pulled her into a tight embrace. For a moment, neither said anything, and Lea could tell by Perida's short breaths that she was trying to hold back tears.

After a moment, Perida pulled back and smiled. Tears tracked down her cheeks, but her eyes were bright. "Lea, you have nothing to apologize for. I know I haven't been as available to you as I should've been since we returned home, so I understand why you were hesitant to bring this to me right away."

"It's not that, Mother." Lea chewed the corner of her lip. "I just... didn't want to give you false hope. At first, I'd almost convinced myself it was some trick the prince played on me, but once that passed, I was worried the magic might be gone and we wouldn't be able to share it with you. But..." she took a breath and smiled. "I know that's not the case. Not just because he can't lie, but because this house is filled with Father's magic. I feel it everywhere I go." She squeezed Perida's hands. "We'll be able to have a proper funeral for him, Mother. Perhaps it won't be perfect, but we can still release some of his magic back into the earth, just as he always wanted."

Perida's smile turned sad as she cupped Lea's cheeks. "I'm so sorry this ordeal has led you to distrust everyone by default. I always question what the prince is up to, but even I can tell he wouldn't be that cruel. Your father would be proud of everything you've accomplished, dear." She kissed Lea's forehead and rose, then smoothed her skirts. "Now, we'll be meeting with General Lindesson shortly. I'd like you down in the drawing room in twenty minutes. If there are things you want to discuss with Lord Edrin, you can go over them with the General then." She stepped toward the door, but when she opened it, she paused and faced Lea. Lea didn't miss that her eyes flicked to the side of the bed where Ettrian had remained hidden, before meeting hers again. "I'm happy you've found something more pleasant to distract yourself with than strolling battle camps, but be careful. Make good choices."

She didn't give Lea a chance to respond before shutting the door behind her.

Ettrian emerged, kneeling and resting his arms on the bed. "Did your mother just give us her blessing?"

Lea raised an eyebrow. "I'm surprised you care about such things."

He shrugged. "I don't particularly. But it'll be nice to know I can take you away after the war without the entire Edhilian navy coming after us."

"Take me away, hmm?" Lea watched as he knelt on the bed, doing her best to ignore the flutters in her stomach. "Where, pray tell, do you plan to take me?"

Ettrian dropped on all fours, eliciting a quiet yelp from Lea that he silenced with his lips. When he pulled back a moment later, Lean smiled at the amusement in Ettrian's eyes.

"Anywhere you'd like," Ettrian murmured, grazing his lips along her neck as he settled himself on top of her. "Someplace far from here."

Lea tilted her chin, giving him easier access to the sensitive skin of her neck. "Perhaps I want to stay in Lindoroth."

"I'm quite certain I could convince you otherwise." He kissed her again, this time long and deep. "At least for a little while."

The flutters returned, this time more difficult to ignore because a part of her knew he was right. "Has anyone told you you're quite full of yourself?"

"You, many times." Before she could reply, he brought his lips to her ear, his warm breath sending a thrill through her body. "But you also can't tell me I'm wrong."

No, Lea thought, *I certainly can't.*

50

LEA

Despite knowing the army heading south should be her main focus, Lea knew she still needed to figure out what she would say to Jonas. Ettrian was of little help, of course, so after breakfast, she met with Perida, Lindesson, and Ordona in the drawing room to work out the best way to address things. Ettrian wanted to be present, but she told him this was something she needed to handle herself.

"I don't think a private conversation is best," Lindesson said, leaning back against a dark wood table and folding his thick arms. "I know it's what you'd prefer, Lady Calliwell, but circumstances like this require more than just a simple conversation."

"Yes, I know," Lea murmured. "Alright, let's bring him in."

Perida looked to Iska, who stood just inside the door. "Iska, if you wouldn't mind?"

Iska gave a short bow. "Of course, Lady Calliwell."

While they waited for Iska to bring Jonas to the drawing room, Lea looked around, taking in all of the details that had, until two weeks ago, been so innocuous to her. The thick shutters, the damper lock beside the fireplace spelled to be unbreakable, and the heavy wood beams that were hidden on either side of the door behind heavy drapes were now a constant reminder of the dangers they faced. All things designed to turn the light, airy space into a fortress.

The door opened, and Lea dropped the hands she'd just been twisting in her lap and stood. Iska walked in, followed by Jonas and Ettrian. She shot the prince an exasperated look, but smiled as she shifted her gaze to Jonas. She was happy to see that it didn't look as though he was uncomfortable or had been lacking anything in his time in Errest. Still, when he entered the room, his shoulders were slightly slumped, and his eyes were heavy.

"Lea," he said with a weary smile.

She could tell by the way it didn't reach his eyes that he knew what was coming, so she didn't waste any time. "We've received word that Daniel Veldin is with the rebels."

Jonas, froze, then sighed. "I suppose that shouldn't come as a shock to either of us." Indeed, there wasn't an ounce of surprise or even sadness in his voice. "Have you heard from Freya and Aerelius?"

"We have," she said with a nod. She sat down on one of the sofas and gestured for him to sit across from her. Ettrian dropped down beside her, propping one elbow on the arm of the velvet sofa with the other stretched out along the back. Lea wasn't sure if the show of arrogance was to remind Jonas just how far he'd fallen or to highlight the relationship Lea and the prince now had. Probably both, if Lea had to make a guess.

"The king and queen have opted to join forces with Daniel Veldin and the rebels," Lindesson said, keeping his eyes trained on Jonas. "What are your thoughts on that?"

Jonas frowned and looked at Lea. "Truly?"

Lea continued to eye him carefully. "Yes, Daniel and the rebels have agreed to support Freya and Aer in defeating Willem."

Jonas leaned back and huffed. He was quiet for a moment, then he looked around the room with a wry smile. "I suppose this saves you all from having to execute me, then."

"Some of us are still open to the idea if you're looking for a quick go of it," Ettrian commented.

Lea ignored him and kept her focus on Jonas. "You know that's not the only option."

"No, but it's the most likely." He leaned forward and rested his arms on his knees as he regarded her with a level gaze. "Even if I swear fealty to Daniel, I helped assassinate his sister, Lea." He flicked a glance at Ettrian. "I'm sure His Highness can attest to standard protocol when it comes to slaughtering a person's siblings."

"Oh, don't look to me, Lord Edrin. My brothers have been trying to kill one another for decades." Ettrian grinned, his pointed teeth on full display. "Makes it tough to take the throne with so much competition."

"Ignore him," Lea said, drawing Jonas' attention back to her. "Will you try to fight Daniel for the throne?"

Jonas shook his head. "No, of course not. I'm no leader, Lea, no matter how much I wish I was. Not in the way my empire needs me to be. We all know that."

"How well do you know Lord Veldin?" Lindesson asked.

Jonas shrugged. "Well enough, I suppose. He was Lessia's advisor, but we were never friends, if that's what you're wondering. He shares blood with Lessia, not me, so I don't think he cared much about me at all."

"Do you think he'll betray our king and queen?" Perida demanded. "Can we trust him?"

Jonas thought for a moment, then nodded. "Yes, I think so. I didn't know him well, but I know he wanted to take control of Jotunheim when my uncle died. I think he realized it was easier and less deadly to be an advisor to the Empress, influence her decisions, but not sit in the crosshairs of any would-be assassin."

"You think he no longer fears it?" Lindesson pressed, seeming unsatisfied with Jonas' answer.

"I'm certain he does," Jonas disagreed. "But now he doesn't have Lessia's vengeance to contend with. The only person who would fight him for the throne is me, and I am willing to step aside." He looked around the room. "He will be the better leader. If for no other reason than he has a stronger desire to fight for it. And I…" Weary eyes landed on Lea. "I'm exhausted, Lea. I knew this was a possibility—"

She frowned, although she wasn't really sure why that surprised her. "You did?"

"Of course. I accepted that death or exile were my only potential futures if I didn't secure the crown. So, I'm willing to help you in any way I can. At this point, I don't have anything to lose. Daniel will get the Jotnar under control, and assuming his agreement with Freya and Aer holds, the war will be over soon. Willem doesn't stand a chance against both of our armies, much less against three," he added with a flick of his eyes toward Ettrian.

"The agreements Veldin made with Freya and Aerelius are bound with elvish magic," Ettrian said. "They will hold, I assure you."

Jonas nodded slowly. "Good. That's good."

"We'll send word to Freya and Aerelius that you'll back Daniel," Lindesson said.

"I will go to them, General," Tyna said, popping into the air beside him. "I would like to see Their Majesties, if I can."

"Of course," Lindesson said. "Thank you."

"So what will your plan be now?" Jonas asked. "I'm willing to help in whatever way I can."

"I wish we knew," Lea said. She'd been wracking her brain for days trying to figure out how to adjust to the change in course that Daniel's involvement brought.

Jonas was quiet for a moment, and he looked as if he was weighing his words carefully before speaking. "While I don't have a specific suggestion," he began, "I would like to just point out one thing."

"What might that be?" Ettrian asked.

Ignoring the prince, Jonas kept his eyes on Lea. "Your magic hasn't failed you yet. Even when you thought it would be useless, it's never failed you."

Lea chewed the corner of her mouth as she considered his point. "You're not wrong," she agreed. "But I don't see how it can help us

now. I'm not mapping out hidden tunnels or warding off Willem Ristner's advances."

He looked at Ordona and Perida, then back to Lea. "As I said, I
don't have any specific suggestions. But considering the three of you
have quite strong earth magic, magic that is connected to this place in
particular, I would consider how you might be able to use that to
your advantage."

Lea frowned as she exchanged looks with Ordona and Perida. She
hadn't really considered what she'd be able to do magically when it
came to protecting her city, at least not on a large scale. Yes, she could
help preserve food, do a bit of rebuilding, but when it came to
helping stop an army, she had nothing.

But maybe...

She gave Jonas a final tight smile. "Thank you, Jonas, for giving
me something to ponder. And I do wish this could all be different."

"I wouldn't worry, Lea," Jonas replied. "I wish circumstances were
different, too, but I think, in the end, we'll all be better off."

THAT AFTERNOON, once Perida and the rest had dismissed her so they
could discuss what they were doing about the army coming south,
Lea decided she wanted to see the city from above, so she slipped out
the front door of her house and began walking toward the main thoroughfare that would take her to the city gates.

As she walked along the sidewalk, people and carriages passed
her in both directions, which she saw as a good sign. Over the last few
weeks things have truly begun looking up. More people were
wandering the market, which was once again a bustling place, and
the restaurants were much more full than they had been just a few
days ago. But she knew Errest had been spared the bulk of destruction because the marshals and the Errestian army had had time to
fortify the city. They had time to call people from the nearest villages
inside and give them shelter. They had time to store non-perishables
that the outside citizens brought in. The same couldn't be said for the

people whose villages were too far away to have traveled to Errest for safety.

She reached the bottom of the city wall, where a nondescript door beside the gate house led to the top. It was guarded, of course, and only a select few were allowed up there. Fortunately, as the governor's daughter, Lea was one of them. She gave the guard standing at the bottom of the stairs a small smile and a brief nod before entering the dimly lit stairwell to the top.

The sun was blinding when she emerged, a stark contrast to the low torchlight that guided her way up the stairs. She took a moment to get her bearings; looked left and right, where marshals and knights stood along the crenellations positioned to watch her from all angles. The presence of marshals on the wall was typical, but the addition of Lindorothian and Edhilian nights was a cold reminder that her city was one could be under siege within just a few days.

Her view of the encampment was much better here from above than it had been from her own house. The only thing between her and the camp was low-lying brush that thrived in hotter climates. The Gefhorn River, which would carry the human ships toward Errest, lay just out of sight beyond the horizon.

After walking for a few minutes, she stopped and leaned against the battlement, resting her forearms on the warm stone. She closed her eyes against the warm desert breeze drifting across the city and allowed herself to imagine this was a typical day and her walk was just like any other she'd taken over the years.

She turned Jonas' words over and over in her mind as she thought about what she could possibly do to help protect her city. *"Your magic hasn't failed you yet. Even when you thought it would be useless."*

A cool hand slid up her back and came to rest on her shoulder, and she leaned back against Ettrian's chest, savoring the strength that radiated from him. Despite that comfort, jealousy flickered in her heart. He was so confident, so powerful, and always, always, *always* so right.

"Is that envy you're aiming at me, little witch?" he murmured.

"A bit," she admitted. "Unfair, I know." She cocked her head. "How can you feel those feelings?"

"The same way I can tell when you're angry." A corner of his mouth hitched up when she turned to face him. "All emotions have a flavor, a scent. I can't always taste them, but yours tend to be so big that they're impossible to miss." He brushed a finger along her cheek. "What's bothering you?"

She huffed out a breath through her nose. "Between my people and yours, we have so much magic. I just don't know what to do with it."

"Alright, then let me ask you this. What is the biggest thing you've ever done with your magic?"

"Perhaps when I began mapping out the tunnels in the palace? Or maybe when I defended myself against Willem?" Lea said, then shook her head. "But that's so simple, so small. I've never had a use for much more."

"The encounter with Willem was anything but small. I wasn't present when it happened, but I assure you, Willem fears you."

"Fine, but it's nothing like Ordona, whose magic has supported the palace walls for centuries, or my mother's. They've both ensured our homes stay standing, are everlasting."

"And you think you'll never be able to do that?"

"Maybe someday. But that doesn't help us now."

"True, but Ordona hasn't been holding up palaces her entire life. Neither has your mother been keeping your home steadfast. They had to go practice in the desert, just like you."

She considered his words for a few moments, studying the intricate embroidery on his tunic. Swoops and whorls of gold, the same color as his eyes, shimmered in the sun.

"Look at me," he commanded. When she lifted her eyes to his, he whispered, "You are the one who gets to decide if your magic is too small."

She nodded slowly, then finally built up the courage to say the words that had been spinning in her mind for days. "Sometimes I wonder...if I should've just kept my mouth shut, stuck with Jonas, continued to pretend to be his wife. If I had..."

"You wouldn't have an army marching on your city?" The shimmer in his eyes sparked with challenge. "And tell me, Lea. What would you have done when you and Jonas were expected to go back to Jotunheim, bear your emperor an heir or two? How would you have been any better off than Dania Edrin, resigned to a fate of doing everything against your will?"

Nausea rose in her stomach as she averted her eyes. She hated him in that moment, knowing she had no argument against him or the vile things he was suggesting she would've been expected to do as empress. He was right, after all. She would've married Jonas, but not willingly. He would need an heir, which she would be expected to bear. The thought of it all, having to force herself to be complicit in such a life, nearly had her vomiting over the city walls.

"I'm sorry," Ettrian whispered, tilting her face toward his and kissing her forehead. "These are things you need to hear, although I'm loath to upset you."

"Then what do you suggest I do?" she whispered hoarsely. "What could I possibly do, Ettrian?"

"Stop feeling sorry for yourself, for one." Before she could snap back, he continued. "Perhaps now is the time to stop waiting for orders and give some of your own."

She held his gaze for a moment before turning away to stare back out at the landscape before her. As the prince slid his arm around her waist and kissed her neck, the seeds of an idea began to take root.

51

FREYA

The next leg of their journey consisted of working to bring all Jotnar under Daniel's control. It took nearly three days to convince the two largest Jotnar camps to join them in their fight against Willem. Some wanted to stay loyal to Jonas, but there weren't enough to warrant any concern. Fortunately, with the help of General Rayn and Lieutenant Forrest, it didn't take nearly as long as it might've if they'd only had Daniel.

Despite the push-back, Freya forced herself to be patient, and wait with her own army cloaked beside the Jotnar, no matter how badly she wanted to storm in and shake the idiots who actually had to be *convinced* Willem Ristner would be a terrible leader. She felt some sympathy for those who leaned toward supporting Jonas, though. According to Daniel, many wanted his leadership because he didn't truly know how to lead, which would give his army more freedom to do what they wished. But others wanted him to come out the victor because he was Crispin Edrin's blood. The former emperor still maintained more respect than the empress he'd left behind, despite being dead for decades.

Once they had the Jotnar camps under Daniel's control, they shifted their focus toward the soldiers that blocked the path from

Saith into Iladel. The largest mountain pass in the Aldridge mountains lay just to the south of the city, and three large human encampments had spread out with the clear intent of preventing anyone from getting through. Based on Ana and the other Valkyrie's reports, only one of those camps had a sizable number of Jotnar, who they would have to deal with before taking on the human soldiers. The mountains in that area were particularly difficult to traverse, so going up and over would've been a waste of time, resources, and knights. Carrying three armies thought the Between would've exhausted the elves and required at least a day of rest before continuing forward. Going the long way avoided that and allowed them to eliminate any human threats along the way, further diminishing Willem's forces.

As they arrived at an area near the pass, a sweeping field strewn with boulders, Freya saw the jagged remains of a burnt-out village nestled at the foot of the mountains. It wasn't the first she'd seen, but seeing the charred wood, now damp and cold, sent waves of anger and hopelessness through her. She rode the anger, letting it fuel her, but forced the hopelessness down. Loss of hope wouldn't rebuild the homes that had been reduced to ash nor bring back the lives of the Linds who were buried beneath the ruins.

"It was one of the first to go, as far as we can tell," Byrric told her. "My guess is Lessia and Willem expected people to flee here, so they were waiting to attack."

"Did you try to save it when you left?" Freya asked.

His eyes were sad. "When I flew past this place, it was fully engulfed in flames. There was nothing left to save."

"Do you think there were any survivors?" The desolation in what was once such a lovely place had that hopelessness pushing at her chest again.

"Unlikely," Byrric replied. "And there's nothing we can do about it now." He gestured toward the long, dark strip in the distance that was the human encampment–three smaller encampments that had joined as one to block the pass. "But we *will* make the ones responsible pay."

Freya glanced back at their own army, cloaked in a magic and shadow as they continued to set up their own camp. Right now, they were on a precipice of sorts. Squadrons had split off to take out the smaller human camps in the area to avoid anyone warning the main camp of the imminent attack, and the Valkyrie and hawk shifters had been monitoring the entire area, so it wasn't as though they were completely inactive. But *she* wasn't doing anything at the moment, which was slowly driving her crazy.

"You should go eat something, get some rest," her father said. "You haven't had to do much the past few days, but the upcoming ones will be difficult."

She grunted her agreement. It had been a frustrating cycle of sending one of the princes into camp, extricating a general and a lieutenant or two, and bringing them back so Daniel could lay out his case. "Somehow I think that might be an understatement," she said wryly. "But you're right."

As she walked away from her father, she scanned the area for Aer. She spotted him near the command tent talking with Fenian and Reginald, but she couldn't bring herself to have yet another conversation about battle tactics. Her father was right—she needed to eat and rest. So, she aimed for the tent where a few soldiers were preparing food.

When she emerged from the tent with a steaming bowl of stew and began walking back to her own, she saw Toskr sitting with a few other elves on logs around a fire. He was a bit off to the side, sharing the space but not quite with the others. She could only imagine what the elves thought of him being out in the open and far from the Forest of Ages.

Part of her wanted to just go back to her tent and sit in the quiet, eat while she waited for Aer to return. Instead, she dropped down on the log next to Toskr.

"Did you eat?" she asked when he smiled in greeting.

He held up an empty bowl. "It was quite delicious."

Freya nodded and took a bite of her stew, suddenly not really knowing what to say. So, they sat in silence for a few moments while the other elves carried on their conversations without them.

"You seem troubled," he observed after a few moments. "Is everything alright?"

A small snort escaped through Freya's nose. "'Troubled' doesn't seem to cover it, Toskr." She took another bite. "We're so close," she said, her eyes drifting toward the mountains. "My palace is just over those peaks. A two-day journey on foot, half a day if I fly. Instead we're stuck here." Gods, how she wanted to fly.

"We'll be through that pass by tomorrow," Toskr reassured. "It will be a simple thing for us to eliminate the human camp, especially now that we have Lord Veldin's knights on our side."

"I know that should be the case," she replied. "The humans don't have magic, there are fewer of them than us, and, in a perfect world, they'll have no idea we're coming." She gave Toskr a rueful smile. "It's a shame it's not a perfect world."

"So you think we will lose people tomorrow?"

"I believe to think otherwise is a fool's dream."

Brows furrowed, he stared into the fire as they lapsed into silence again.

"Your Majesty?"

"Hmm?"

Toskr continued to stare into the fire. "Do you remember the forest?"

She arched a brow. "How could I ever possibly forget the forest? I was nearly slaughtered by every vicious creature in your kingdom."

"Did you ever wonder why I decided to help you?"

"You wanted to escape your punishment," Freya said, meeting his dark eyes. "To get the wights to let you leave."

"Well yes, that was part of it, of course." He flashed her a grin. "But I have seen many people come through the forest. Most become resigned to their fate immediately. The forest is a tricky beast in that way. You were the only one I've seen in centuries who actually fought back and did not give up."

"For as long as you've been in that forest, you've *never* had the inclination to help someone?" Freya shook her head. "I don't buy it."

Toskr chuckled. "You must understand, Your Majesty. Most either get themselves killed or give up and let the forest swallow them whole. You did not."

Freya narrowed her eyes. "There's more."

For a moment, Toskr looked like he might shift into his squirrel form and run off. When Freya gave him an expectant look, he sighed. "Once I knew your story, that you were not yet another traitor to the crown, I will admit that I ...saw an opportunity. You were there for noble purposes. I, as you know, was not."

"So you thought if you helped me on my 'noble' quest, your crimes would be forgiven?"

He shrugged and slurped down the last of his stew. "You cannot blame me for trying. If I could help you prevent further slaughter, perhaps that might help make up for some of my own...transgressions."

"How did you know my story, anyway?" She eyed him curiously. "You said you were told a queen would be in the forest that day. Who told you?"

"I was the knower of all things in that forest, Your Majesty," Toskr said with a sly smile. "Creatures talk, and their words travel over long distances quite quickly."

"Did the wights tell you?" She thought back to the ethereal creatures who glowed blue and menacing in the darkened forest.

"Oh dear, no, they would never do such a thing. I have no doubts they tried to prevent me from finding you." He set his bowl down. "No, it was the creatures who feared you that alerted me to your presence."

"And you didn't fear me?" She raised a brow.

"As I am sure you have noticed, Your Majesty, I am quite skilled with words. My punishment was the only thing in my life I was not able to talk my way out of."

Freya slid to the ground and leaned back against the log, holding her hands out toward the fire for warmth. "Why did you skip out on your duties, Toskr?"

"You might not believe this, but I did not intend to abandon my post. I got very distracted spreading my stories that I did not ensure the village that once existed there was protected."

Freya tilted her head and eyed him. "And what were these stories you had to share? Prince Fenian said you visited a water wight half a day away."

Toskr winced, making it clear he'd hoped she wouldn't ask. "The water wight I was visiting had eyes for a certain pixie. I happened to come across said pixie in a compromising position with a witch and felt it was my duty as his friend to warn him. Pathetic, I know. I got distracted, and those wretches you killed at the end of your Hunt destroyed that village. My village. I was one of its protectors. Not a very good one, of course. They never should have given the likes of me such a job." He averted his eyes and tossed a stone into the fire, then watched as it displaced the embers and sent up a shower of sparks. "I know helping your kind will not bring back those elves, but I am grateful to be part of an army that is helping to prevent such a thing from happening again."

Despite his smile, Freya could see how much that mistake continued to weigh on him. He'd spent centuries atoning in the Forest. Unlike the other prisoners, he'd never been given a chance to run the Hunt for freedom. She could hardly blame him for finding a loophole and exploiting it at the first chance.

"Well, we're happy for the assistance. I know I might not have conveyed this properly, Toskr, but I truly appreciate everything you did for me in the forest. Despite your reasons, you helped get me out of there alive. You made sure my kingdom still had a queen. That's no small thing."

They sat in silence for a few more moments. Freya stared into the fire, losing herself in her own thoughts and allowing Toskr to ruminate on his. Finally, she broke the stillness.

"What will you do when this is all over? When the war is won?"

"When you win your war, you mean?" He smirked. "I would like to return to Avorell, if my monarchs will have me."

She bit her tongue before commenting on how unlikely she

believed that would be. "You're welcome to stay in Lindoroth, too. As long as you don't cause trouble, there will be a place for you here."

"A tempting offer, Your Majesty." He stretched his arms over his head and yawned. "We shall see where we land on the other side of this mess. For now, I think I should sleep."

"Get some for me, as well," she muttered.

He chuckled, then shifted and scurried off.

She sat there for a few moments in silence, watching the night sky, the Valkyrie that slowly circled overhead, guarding them from above just as the knights on foot guarded them on the ground. A part of her wanted to be up there with them, floating on the chilly air, far out of reach of any arrow a human might fire her way. She knew it was wiser to stay on solid ground, though. At least for now.

A few seconds later, Aer sat down beside her. Wordlessly, he took her hand and kissed her knuckles, then lifted his arm so she could tuck herself into his side.

"Almost there," he murmured.

She snuggled against him, letting his warmth chase away the cold night air. "Do you really think so?"

"Of course." He rested his head against hers. "What's wrong?"

"A little bit of everything," she said. "I'm trying not to let pessimism creep in, but I'm struggling." She hadn't wanted to say it outright to Toskr, but even if she wanted to keep her feelings from Aer, it wouldn't take long for him to figure out the issue.

"We've done pretty well these past few days, if I do say so myself," he said. He nudged her playfully. "And since when are you so pessimistic?"

She shrugged. "Since we've become reliant on two groups of people who were considered enemies not five days ago? I guess I'm still having a hard time wrapping my head around the idea of this sudden peace with Lessia Edrin's brother."

"Fair enough," Aer allowed. "But we have ironclad agreements with him. There comes a point where you simply have to have faith."

"I feel like the other shoe is about to drop, and I don't know if that's just an overwhelming sense of dread due to our current circumstances or if there's actually something lingering out there."

"Perhaps both," Aer said after a moment. "It would be unrealistic for you to not feel dread, considering everything that's happening. And we both know anything could happen tomorrow, good or bad. We might approach that human camp and obliterate each one of them, or we might find ourselves in a scenario we didn't anticipate."

"Like with Traust in the valley?" Freya muttered. "Bastard."

"Yes, although it's safe to say we're fully prepared to face him again." Aer twirled a long lock of her hair around his finger. "I think you need to rest, Freya. You don't know what's going to come tomorrow any more than I do. Or the day after, or the next." He stood, then held out a hand to pull her to her feet. With a heavy sigh, she stood. He brushed a thumb across her cheek and kissed her gently. "Come on. Let's go get some sleep."

She smiled, then stood on her toes to kiss him again. It was hard to ignore the feeling that things were likely about to get exponentially worse, but she forced down that fear and wrapped her arms around his waist.

"I love you, Aerelius," she murmured against his warm chest.

"I love you, too."

HOURS LATER, when the camp was nearly silent and the fire in her tent only sent out dim remnants of an orange glow, Freya awoke, shaken from sleep by an idea.

She rolled the idea around in her head, working out what could possibly go wrong, aside from everything, of course. It was crazy, potentially reckless, but if it all came together as planned, it could make the path to Iladel even clearer.

"Aer," she hissed, shaking him awake. "I need to go talk to my father."

"What?" His eyes slowly opened and he kept his arms wrapped

tightly around his pillow. She felt a flicker of jealousy at his ability to wake up so relaxed, considering their circumstances.

"I need to go see my father," she repeated. "And the Princes. And Florian." She swung her legs over the edge of the cot. "And probably several others. Are you coming?"

Aer sat up, rubbing a hand across his eyes. "Are you serious?"

She jerked her chin toward the entrance. "It's nearly sunrise. They're already awake and planning, I'm sure of it."

"And what is this plan of yours?" He gave her an expectant look.

"Hold on. Rini!" Freya called. A moment later, the pixie appeared beside her.

"Oh thank the *gods*, Your Majesty," Rini said, her entire body drooping. "I've been eavesdropping on the Jotnar knights and they are dreadfully boring to listen to."

Freya smiled. "Well, I need a favor. Can you go tell my father to round up the others? I have a plan and I only want to say it once." She glanced at Aer. "After I discuss it with my husband, of course."

Rini eyed Freya skeptically. "Will this plan put you in more danger?"

"I'm already in constant danger, Rini," Freya pointed out gently.

Rini's lips pursed, then she nodded. "Alright, Your Majesty. Right away." She frowned. "I'll be back to help you get ready."

"I really don't—" But before Freya could finish, Rini was gone.

"I'm going to hate this plan, aren't I?" Aer asked.

One corner of her mouth lifted in a cocky smile. "Not necessarily."

52

———————

FREYA

A little while later, after allowing Rini to take care of her hair, Freya and Aer stood in Byrric's command tent. Her father was standing in the middle of the tent, arms crossed with an expression that made it clear he knew she was about to lay out a plan he would hate. Ana stood beside Vali, who leaned casually back in a chair, his eyes amused as he took in the tension around them. Daniel sat, expressionless, beside him, while the elves and Florian watched her with bold curiosity. Rini, ever supportive, appeared and hovered faithfully beside her.

But it was Fenian, wearing a small smile, whose attention drew her the most. She needed elvish magic to carry out her plan, and he was the one most likely to give it. It was a reckless plan, which was why she knew he'd be for it, and at this point, they needed something quick and reckless to speed things along.

"I need you all to hear me out before responding," Freya said, looking at them each in turn.

Vali chuckled. "Oh, this is going to be good."

"Just hear her out," Aer said.

Ignoring them, Freya continued. "I want Fenian to transport me into the human camp." She pressed forward when her father opened his mouth to argue. "We'll wear invisibility glamours and destroy the camp from inside. They'll never see it coming and it'll give us an opening to get through the pass. The elves won't have to expend heaps of energy transporting us all to the other side, and it will quickly eliminate a huge portion of Willem's army."

"A suicide mission," Vali said with an approving nod at Byrric. "You've raised her well."

Ana narrowed her eyes. "It's not the worst plan," she conceded. "But I don't know if I can get behind my Queen, carrying it out."

"Aunt Ana, you and I both know I'm one of the most powerful magic-wielders in this camp, outside of the elves," Freya said. "If not me, then who?"

"Literally anyone else," she replied. "Send in five fire wielders in your place."

"And risk five lives instead of one?"

"If that one life is my Queen's? Yes, precisely."

"Enough," Byrric said. "Of all the reckless plans you've concocted, this might be the worst." He seemed to struggle to keep his voice even. "You expect me to allow my queen, my *daughter*, to drop herself in the middle of an enemy war camp with one elf at her side? Absolutely not!"

A pang of doubt tugged at Freya's belly when she saw the fear and anger in her father's eyes. It was only the second time he'd shown any true type of emotion when it came to her role in this war, and its rarity had her questioning her plan. Very little rattled Byrric Balthana, but when something did, it was worth taking pause.

"It'll work, Father," she said calmly. "I promise."

"I will help, as well, then," Ruehnar said. "My sons and I are the strongest elves here. We will be able to get all of the Jotnar out quickly," he told Daniel.

Florian steepled his index fingers and touched them to his chin in contemplation. "It could work," he said after a moment.

Freya let out a small breath. His approval was exactly what she was looking for. He was their spymaster, and while he might not be keen on sending his Queen directly into an enemy camp, he would never approve of a plan he didn't think they could pull off.

"Perhaps think on it for more than a few moments before making your assessment," Tavian said. "This is, as your commander said, reckless."

"As someone who seems to play an integral part in your plan, it would have been nice if you had consulted me before offering my services," Fenian said drily. "Do not mistake me—it is a good plan. Still, a bit rude of you."

"Can I ask why you are not asking for my assistance?" Tavian asked.

"We'll need you to help your father remove whatever Jotnar might be in the camp," Freya replied. "But Fenian is the one who insisted on seeing my powers at work when we were in your kingdom." She gave Fenian an expectant look. "Isn't that right, Your Highness?"

The eldest elf prince grinned. "I certainly did."

Freya smiled. *Three down.*

"Your King approves of this?" Daniel asked, looking at Aer. "It seems unwise."

"Do I like it?" Aer shrugged. "No. But we're running out of time and options, and I know what Freya is capable of when she has a solid plan. Which this is."

He didn't share the single concern he'd brought up to Freya, which was that this plan relied on her putting her trust fully into an elf prince. Every other situation she'd been in, she'd had at least one of her own with her.

"We're going to have to trust our allies at some point," she'd told him. *"There's no time like the present."*

But when she looked at her father, she saw those same reservations in his eyes.

"You will be going in blind," Ruehnar pointed out. "You have no idea what is going on in there."

"Which is why we'll do some reconnaissance first," Aer replied. "A few will get closer, listen around the camp, get a better idea of where to go in, how many there are, what resources they might have."

Byrric began pacing slowly in front of the table that held an updated map of Lindoroth. It was dotted with even more stone, wood, and metal markers than the last time Freya had looked at it. Finally, he turned toward her. "If Traust is anywhere nearby, he'll know you're listening."

"If Traust were nearby, he'd already know we were here, anyway," Florian pointed out.

"I've been listening, Commander," Rini said. "I've heard nothing of Traust, but I will go back in if you need me to."

"No need," Fenian said. "I want to hear it myself."

They all waited in silence as her father rolled the plan over in his mind. Freya could practically see the wheels turning.

Finally, he dropped his hand. "Alright. Freya, you and I will go with Florian and Fenian closer to the camp. See what we can hear from the ridge. If there's any whisper of Rekyr Traust, this plan is done. Are we clear?"

Freya arched a brow. "Are you saying that as my father or my commander?"

"Both."

"Alright, fine." She gave Fenian an expectant look. "Are you ready?"

Fenian held out his arms and let Florian and Freya each link one of theirs with his, while Freya took her father's hand. "We will return shortly, Your Majesty," he said to Aer.

Aer gave Freya a quick kiss. "Be safe."

"Always."

Moments later, they were crouched on the ridge behind the human camp. It was far enough away that they could observe without being seen, but close enough that they could eavesdrop with minimal effort.

Below them, the human camp sprawled across the pass, forming a horseshoe that blocked its entire width. Small fires dotted the area, but it was still mostly dark. Knights stood guard along the edges, while the bulk of the camp still wore that early morning quiet.

"This might be easier than I thought," Freya murmured. "If most are still in their tents."

"Listen," Fenian said, closing his eyes. Florian and Byrric did the same, so Freya followed suit and trained her ears toward the camp. She called on her air magic, willing the breeze to carry the sounds from the knights up to her on the ridge.

Mutters of home, orders for the upcoming days, disdain toward their king, reinforcements, and mundane conversation were all she heard. No whispers of Traust or damning plans.

When she focused her magic more closely, she could hear a small cluster of Jotnar speaking on the outer edges of the encampment, two hundred to the humans' two thousand. She would've thought it was simply humans putting on Jotnar accents had she not felt the tang of magic when her own encircled their small camp.

They listened for another twenty minutes, long enough to determine Traust either wasn't there or he was very good at concealing his presence. When they returned to the tent, Freya was happy to see that it was her father pacing in anticipation, not her husband. Even though he'd backed her when outlining this plan, she could still feel his worry pulsing through their bond.

"Well?" Aer demanded.

"No sign of Traust," Freya told him. "There are about two hundred Jotnar down there," she added, looking at Daniel and Vali. "Can you get Rayn and Forrest here? Perhaps they can help keep heads cool when we bring the Jotnar out of the camp."

"Consider it done," Daniel said.

She shifted her focus to Ruehnar. "Your Majesty, can you round up a few of your strongest and transport the Jotnar soldiers out of there? The fewer of our own we send it, the better."

Ruehnar nodded. "Of course."

"Pull out as many as you can," Vali told Ruehnar. "Daniel and I will take care of them."

"Ana, take the Valkyrie and provide aerial cover, just in case," Byrric said.

"Done," Ana replied. "We'll just need a few invisibility glamours, if that's alright."

"I'll take care of it," Florian said.

Toskr appeared, shifting to two legs beside Freya. "Do you have a job for me, Your Majesty?"

Freya gave him an amused smile. "Bored?"

"Dreadfully," he admitted.

"As it happens, we could use a distraction," she said. "Are you up for setting a few fires?"

The squirrel shifter grinned. "Consider it done."

"This should go well," Fenian muttered.

Freya looked at Aer. "Are you sure you're alright with this?" She knew he'd never stop her, but the thought of him going through the same emotions and fears he'd dealt with when she'd gone rogue in Watoria was enough to give her pause.

"I trust you," he replied. "You're playing it smart this time." His lips cocked in a crooked smile. "Perhaps you could make a habit of it."

She let out a small breath, relieved she didn't see hesitation in his eyes.

"It's a gamble, to be sure," Daniel said. "But I agree it's a risk worth taking if we want to eliminate those forces."

"Alright, then." Freya looked at the elves. "Fenian, Toskr, and I will create enough chaos for you all to get the Jotnar out of the camp. Once they're gone, we'll burn it all. We'll be in and out."

Fenian held out a hand toward her. "Your Majesty?"

Freya turned to Aer, then gripped his shoulders and gave him a solid kiss. "I'll be back before you know it."

He brushed a thumb along her cheek. "I know."

She looked at Rini. "Take care of him while I'm gone?"

"Of course, Your Majesty."

Freya took Fenian's hand, as Toskr shifted and leapt to her shoulder. "Let's go, Your Highness."

He gave her a mischievous smile. "Time to see what the Huntress of Lindoroth can do."

Then, he swept her off into the bitter, cold Between.

53

LEA

Lea's dreams consisted of soft touches and golden eyes, sweet kisses that belied the male that bestowed them, and a desire that made her all but forget the wretchedness that existed just outside her window. Yet even as that sweetness bloomed, she tossed and turned, chasing that feeling of desire and running from the shadows of pain, fear, and sorrow that tried to snuff it out.

She jolted awake, the last remnants of her dreams vanishing like smoke. She lay there for a few moments, staring up at the ceiling as her heart slowed and her mind adjusted to being awake. As she lay there, something, a feeling, crept toward her. The air felt thick, charged with energy, like the moments before a storm, leaving her skin tingling.

As the sky grew brighter, she contemplated ignoring that odd feeling and staying in bed. Foolish, maybe, but blissful ignorance seemed appealing right then. It tugged at her, persistent in its attempts to drag her from her nest of blankets and pillows. She just wanted to ignore it for a few moments longer...

Finally, she climbed out of bed and wrapped a robe around her body, cinching the soft, silky belt around her clothing. She left her room, then padded barefoot down the silent hallway toward a window that faced north. It was the only direction that mattered these days.

She trained her eyes in the direction of the river junction, where the Rimar met the Gefhorn. The sky was dim with fading night, but nothing appeared out of place. No ships coming down the Gefhorn, no knights on the march. Campfires flickered in the encampment, the only light for miles.

But something was off. She could feel it in her bones. In the way the air tasted in her mouth.

Get dressed and go see, she told herself. It would be the only way to figure out if something was amiss or if her imagination was just running away from her.

Turning from the window to go back to her room, she froze when she saw Ettrian come around the corner. His lips slipped into a crooked smile.

"What's going on?" she demanded.

He reached her and placed his hands on her waist, then directed her back toward her chambers. "Time to get dressed, little witch. The enemy is hardly a day away, and you can't expect to fight them in your nightgown, lovely as it is."

"Already?" She felt panic rise in her chest, but she forced herself to focus on the place where Ettrian's hands seared through her night-dress and into her skin. "It should've taken them at least three more days to get here!"

"It appears they had a bit of help in the form of stolen Lind ships and a bit of Jotnar magic," Ettrian explained. "Your ships are quite fast, in case you were unaware."

Of course they were. The wood used to craft them was almost always laced with some form of earth magic, making them easier to steer and quicker on the water.

Barely a day. She knew it had been just a matter of time before the enemy descended on Errest, but that knowledge did nothing to still her pounding heart. She'd done so much work since coming home. In less than a day, all of that could be completely undone. In less than a day, her city might no longer be hers.

Stop, she told herself as Ettrian pushed open her chamber door. *That kind of negativity will get you nowhere.*

"What will be my role in all of this?" she asked Ettrian.

He shut the door behind them and turned to face her. "I suppose that will be up to you. What do you want your role to be?" He jerked his chin toward her wardrobe. "Get dressed."

Pursing her lips, she began pulling clothes from her wardrobe. No dress today, although her hands lingered on a muslin gown her father had gifted her for her birthday the previous year. Ice blue—the same color as the dress Perida had worn to Aer and Freya's wedding. The dress she'd been forced to wear for weeks in the dungeon, despite it being covered in her husband's blood.

Just like that, any lingering tiredness was swept away by a wave of rage. She thought of how broken her mother had been the first time she saw her after Lea had been released from the dungeons. The image of Perida, her golden skin ashen with grief, cheeks sunken from hunger, with a hollow look in her eyes that still flickered there now and then. The rage Lea felt at seeing her mother so broken began to simmer, a painful reminder of how much had been taken from her family. Her mother was strong, powerful in a way that Lea could only hope to be.

Shoving the memory away, Lea yanked on a pair of lightweight wool leggings from the drawer in her wardrobe and a loose-fitting emerald green shirt from a hanger, then shut the door. When she turned around, Ettrian was sprawled on her bed leaning against the headboard with his fingers laced together, cradling his head.

The corner of his lips drew up. "Don't stop on my account."

The look in his eyes had the rage inside her stuttering out. For a moment, she considered him, debated changing right there in front of him. Something about the way he looked at her, about the way she knew he would look at her body, made the thought even more enticing.

But she wasn't ready. She was barely ready for the idea of taking an elf prince as her lover. "Overwhelming" was too simple a word to describe what it felt like to have him look at her the way he was right then. She wanted to be overwhelmed by him. She knew that much. But not now. Not today. There was too much to do, too many people to keep safe.

So, instead, she let his eyes follow her as she moved to change behind the dressing screen in her corner. His gaze held a hint of disappointment, but the way his smile shifted a bit told her he'd known it'd been a long shot.

Once she was done, she stepped into her en suite bathing room to splash some water on her face. She needed a few moments to clear her head, shift away from her reckless emotions and on to the problem at hand: enemy knights on the river with the goal of seizing her city.

The thought was like a bucket of cold water being poured over her head. How in the world could she focus on elf princes when she could be hours away from death?

But at the same time, what better time was there to be reckless than when her world might be ending?

Later, she thought. *I'll deal with him later.*

She stepped from the bathroom and smiled. "Alright, let's go."

He slid from her bed in a single smooth movement, then held out his hand. When she took it, expecting him to lead her from the room, he pulled her in close and kissed her gently. When he pulled back, she placed a hand on his chest to steady herself and met his golden eyes as he brushed a hand down her cheek.

"Are you ready to save your city?" he murmured.

Her heart thundered in her chest at the weight of his gaze and his words.

"As I'll ever be."

WHEN THEY ARRIVED in the drawing room, Perida, Ordona, and Lindesson were already there, deep in conversation with General Thallan and a few other elf and Lind knights. Jonas had been brought out of his room, but he stood off to the side, a slight frown on his face, his presence clearly still unwelcome. Tyna hovered in the air beside him, discretely keeping a close watch while also hanging on every word.

"Ah, good, you're both here," Lindesson said in greeting. His grizzled face was hard as he looked back down at the map. "Your Highness, your general was just briefing us on what your scouts found when they traveled upriver."

Thallan nodded. "Thank you, General. Once we realized the enemy was on the water, we had hoped to attempt the same trick King Aerelius and Queen Freya managed when humans attacked from the river and board the ships, take them out before they could get too far," he explained as Ettrian walked over to look at the map on the table. "But there are simply too many ships for that to work."

"They will be here by nightfall," Lindesson said. "We've already lost some of the outer villages."

Lea's heart sank. "How many?"

"My scouts found two," Thallan said. "But we did not go very far upriver."

"I took the liberty of doing a bit of reconnaissance," Tyna told Lea. "I only found two other villages between here and Iladel that were raided. All told, there are thirty ships with two hundred men apiece."

"How many Jotnar?" Lea asked. She tried not to think of the people in those four villages who were now without food, shelter, and possibly their lives.

Tyna's eyes darted toward Lindesson and Thallan before responding. "Each ship had approximately twenty Jotnar aboard. Combined with the magic our navy works into their ships..."

Lea's stomach twisted. The fight still wouldn't be even, but any magic that gave the humans an advantage meant more of her people would perish.

"Yes, it seems not all got the message that Daniel has taken over," Jonas said. "Or they simply don't care."

"You took out how many?" Ettrian asked Thallan.

"We were able to sink ten of the ships. Some of the men went down with them, but a few hundred made it to land. We were able to round them up and kill them fairly quickly."

"The Rimar is quite wide as it nears the junction," Jonas pointed out. "I think we can all agree it's strategically unwise to attempt to fight a river battle from land."

"What can we do to stop this?" Perida asked. "We're stronger than them. There must be something we can do to block their path."

Lea gnawed at her lip as she moved closer to the map, listened to the others volley ideas, and turned the whole situation over in her mind. She knew it had been unlikely all of the Jotnar in Lindoroth would've gotten word of the shift in leadership. It was also unlikely every Jotnar knight would be open to that change. Many probably welcomed the idea of a human being in charge, considering how easily he could be overthrown once the war was over. But still, it was stupid for them to think Willem would come out as their new leader when Daniel had turned so many against him.

That being the case, she was more inclined to believe the Jotnar on the ships simply didn't know.

"Could Jonas attempt to give orders to the Jotnar on the ships?" Lea asked, interrupting whatever Lindesson had been saying.

Jonas' eyes widened slightly, but she saw Lindesson, Ettrian, and Ordona exchange a look. After a moment's consideration, Lindesson nodded. "It could work. We need any advantage we can get."

Jonas' jaw ticked. "There are no guarantees they'll listen to me."

"Or that we can trust you," Perida said. She looked at Lindesson and Thallan incredulously. "The reason he's here is because the human king ordered him to come take my daughter! Now you'd ask him to go onto ships belonging to the enemy he was allied with just days ago?"

"I wasn't—"

Ettrian cut Jonas off. "At the risk of sounding supportive of Lord Edrin, there are worse ideas." His eyes glinted. "They will either listen to him or kill him. So, Lady Calliwell, considering your feelings toward Lord Edrin, it could benefit you either way."

Lea pinched the bridge of her nose and huffed out a breath, then let her hand fall to her side as she looked at her mother.

Looking somewhat mollified, Perida glanced at Lindesson. "Alright, then. If it's what you think it's best."

As the discussion shifted toward the best way to get Jonas in contact with the ships, Lea's mind began to drift.

A few months ago, her world had been a completely different place. She'd been at school surrounded by friends, attending dances, and flirting with ease with a male who'd never known war. Her biggest worries had been preparing for their final exams, not getting tricked by Florian in Toxins, and helping Freya settle in as their future queen.

The memories felt so distant now, as if they belonged to someone else. As if she'd lived a dozen lifetimes since then. The weight of it pressed down on her like stones being stacked one by one. Her grief, her anger, sadness, frustration, and the desire to just go back to the easy life she'd had.

"Stop."

The word cut through her mind like a blade. She glanced at Ettrian, who was still discussing battle plans, not bothering to look her way as he sent a word so full of calm toward her. She took a few steadying breaths and forced herself to focus on the conversations happening around her. She wanted to help, needed to help, so she couldn't afford to miss a single detail.

Talk of battle plans continued for the next few hours. By the time Lindesson dismissed everyone, Lea's mind was exhausted. The moment she stepped into the corridor outside the drawing room, she let out a sigh. The air felt clearer already, less heavy with dread. She set her course toward the front door with no real destination in mind once she got there.

"Your misery will be the death of you," Ettrian commented as he fell into step beside her.

"Are you coming on a walk with me?" she asked, ignoring his comment.

"As your guard is currently monitoring the princess, I told your mother I would keep you safe."

Lea gave him an amused smile. "And she believed you?"

He shrugged. "General Lindesson assured her I was trustworthy. Clearly she trusts his judgment more than yours or mine, so here we are."

"That's potentially unwise of her," Lea commented. "But I suppose I won't mind the company."

When they reached a corner that would turn onto the main hall, Ettrian took her hand and drew her toward him, then backed her against the wall. "Look at me." He waited until she'd lifted her eyes to his, then placed his hands on her shoulders. "Don't ever doubt that I have your best interests at heart, Lea. Even if they go against what your mother wants."

Before she could respond, he closed the distance between them, touching his lips to hers in a kiss that was full of softness and heat. It wasn't the same desire she'd felt in her dreams; that was something more deep-rooted that she couldn't touch. Instead, it was something softer. A quiet strength that grounded her a bit. It uncoiled some of the tension that had built in her stomach, replacing her racing thoughts with a bit of calm that she'd been needing all morning.

"Now," he murmured, pulling back a fraction so his lips were only a breath from hers, "how do you plan to save your people? You've been mulling something over since yesterday."

Lea hesitated, feeling the weight of what she was about to say pressing on her. She did have an idea, a potentially crazy one. But it could turn the tide in their favor. She knew from Rini and Tyna's reports that Freya and Aer had launched their own crazy plan, and it had gotten her thinking. It was ambitious—dangerously so.

"Alright. I think I might have an idea," she admitted. It was one she'd been toying with since they spoke on the wall, one so outrageous she expected even him to instantly shut it down. "But I'll need your help convincing...well, almost everyone."

The Prince's eyes sparked with interest. "And here your mother thought *I* was the devious one."

54

FREYA

Campfires flickered around them when they landed in the encampment, cloaked in shadows and magic. Despite her invisibility glamour, Freya found herself crouching slightly as Toskr leapt from her shoulder and scurried into the dim pre-dawn light of the camp, her instinct causing her to anticipate an attack. But as she looked across the camp, at the soft light dancing across the faces of the few men nearing the end of the night watch, her stance eased. Some of the men spoke in quiet tones, others were more raucous, while some quietly stared into the flames. It was an almost tranquil scene, one that gave her a brief, unsettling pause.

Her gaze lingered on a soldier near the edge of the firelight, his shoulders hunched as he stared at the ground. He looked inconsequential, like someone who might have been a farmer or a merchant had he not been here. For a moment, pity flickered in her chest. These men seemed so ordinary, not the vicious monsters so like Willem Ristner that she'd pictured in her mind. They were only men, not unlike the knights who fought for her.

Her hand twitched, hovering near the hilt of her dagger as her stomach knotted.

"I know what you're thinking." Fenian's voice broke through her thoughts.

"Somehow I doubt that," she muttered.

"Do not mistake their stillness for harmlessness," he replied, his eyes scanning the camp as he shifted impatiently. "The moment they sense us, they'll act. They are soldiers, Your Majesty. It is what they are trained to do."

Freya swallowed hard, her resolve fully settling back into place. They were just men, yes. But if given the opportunity to do what she and Fenian were doing now, they would take it and do the exact same thing. They were still the enemy, no matter how normal they seemed in this moment.

They waited silently for a few minutes, neither inclined to speak as Toskr did his work.

"He's taking too long," Freya muttered, sliding her dagger from its sheath. "Do you think they saw him?"

"Quite possible," Fenian replied. "It should not take this long to set a few fires." He huffed out a breath and nodded. "Alright. You stay here, distract them until the squirrel does his job. I will go set the outer fires."

Freya's eyes widened. "Distra—" Before she could finish her protest, Fenian was gone. A moment later, she realized he'd lifted her glamour as well.

She had half a breath to decide what to do, barely enough time to curse the prince for leaving her exposed. The knights around her, about a dozen, froze, then immediately jumped into action drawing swords and raising bows.

Instinct told her to glamour herself, but Fenian's words rang in her mind. *"Distract them."*

Gritting her teeth in annoyance, she drew her sword, then gathered her magic in her other hand and formed a handful of magic daggers beside her. She could take a dozen men. Not easily, but she could do it.

"Their queen! Seize her!"

The men charged, and she let her daggers fly. Three men went down instantly, but the others made it past. She parried the sword of one, then planted her boot in the chest of another, shoving them both stumbling backward. A sword swung at her head, and she ducked, slipping a feather from the vambrace at her wrist as sliding it cleanly under the human's sternum. An arrow whizzed past her ear, then another, as two men attempted to tackle her. Her wings flared out on either side, the force sending the two men tumbling to the ground just as the fires Toskr had been sent to set rose up in the center of camp, crisscrossing throughout the tents. More arrows flew and she dodged them both while she continued to hurl magic daggers at the cluster of men. She heard shouts from further away, and she prayed they were in response to the fires and not reinforcements coming to help the men she was fighting. She ducked another sword, then drove her blade into the gut of a man beside her and sent him sprawling into two men behind him. Another sword, another parry.

Then, out of the corner of her eye she saw a blur of motion dive into the group of knights attacking her just as flames rose up behind them. Toskr skidded to a stop next to her, deftly catching an arrow in his hand that was mere inches from her face.

She barely had time to register his presence when another soldier charged her, sword raised. She reacted on instinct, tossing a ball of raw magic at him and a dagger at the one beside him. Toskr darted forward and attacked a third, shifting effortlessly from elf to squirrel and landing on the man's back. Freya blocked another blow as Toskr shifted again and snapped the man's neck. He shifted again, launched himself at another knight, and did the same. Panic seemed to set in around camp as men fled from the fires that were quickly overtaking everything.

A sharp pain sliced through her arm as another sword missed her neck by inches. She ignored the pain and forced more magic into her hand, continuing to fight as tents went up in flames around her.

She blasted her own fire out, forcing the men back and giving herself precious seconds to figure out what the hell to do. Murdering Fenian was currently at the top of her list, but that would have to wait.

"All of the fires are set!" Toskr snatched another arrow out of the air and sent a blast of magic toward the man who'd fired it. "We only need the prince to do his part!"

As if on cue, a wall of flame went up at the perimeter. It started at four points and quickly spread out, forming a ring around the entire encampment. Suddenly, Fenian appeared beside her.

"Apologies, Your Majesty," he said as he punched the knight he'd appeared in front of.

Freya shot him a cold glare but didn't bother wasting time with anger. "Now?"

"Yes, that would be wise."

Freya dropped a protection spell around them, then as one, they both dropped to the ground and slammed their palms into the dirt. Twin blasts of power combined with torrents of flames shot out, sending all the knights around them flying backward before the flames overtook them. The soldiers who'd been so hellbent on killing her moments ago screamed in agony, the sound a gut-wrenching thing that had bile rising in her throat.

Cries echoed from all around them as they continued to send out their power, fully engulfing the camp. Freya's heart thundered, but she refused to let pity cause her to waver. More fire, more magic. Fenian lifted his hand, raising the fires higher, higher, higher. The flames roared, trapping their enemies in a blazing inferno. Freya threw down one last ball of fire, and with that, the camp was consumed.

"Enough," Fenian commanded. "It is done."

Toskr leapt to Freya's shoulder and latched onto her leathers. Wordlessly, Fenian took her hand, and the cold, bitter air of the Between cocooned them as they left the camp, leaving behind only the raging fire and the final screams of the dying men.

THE SUDDEN SILENCE of their own camp was jarring when Freya, Fenian, and Toskr arrived. The sun was just beginning to break over the horizon, a pale gold that would've been peaceful if Freya hadn't been so damn furious.

She yanked her hand from Fenian's grasp and shoved him away. He staggered back, an enraged look filling his features before his lips broke into a grin.

"'Distract them?'" She swiped at the healing slice on her neck, wincing. "What the hell were you thinking, you godsdamned menace! I nearly lost my head!"

The prince straightened, dusting off his tunic as though her shove meant nothing. "The squirrel was taking too long to do his job." His eyes flicked to Aer, Byrric, Ruehnar, and Florian, who were rushing toward them. "It all worked out precisely as it needed to."

She took a step toward the prince, her fury urging her to do things that would most certainly go against any agreements of peace their people made. "You nearly got me killed!"

"And me," Toskr added. "I nearly died, as well."

"You were taking too long, rodent!" Fenian snapped.

"You left her?" Aer demanded. Magic flickered at his fingertips, snaking up his forearms. "You left my wife in the middle of an enemy camp?"

"Alright, enough!" Byrric barked, stepping between them all.

"Explain yourself," Ruehnar said to Fenian, his tone brooking no argument. "Now."

"As I said, Ratatoskr was taking too long to do his job," Fenian explained. His voice was so calm and unbothered that Freya nearly shoved him again. "In order to get in and out in a more timely manner, I chose an alternate path."

"Without telling her first," Florian said flatly. "Do you not see how that could've gone terribly wrong?"

Fenian shrugged. "I had faith in your queen to make the right choices, which she did. She survived the Hunt, after all. If you have doubts about her abilities, that is your problem."

Aer's face turned absolutely murderous, but before he could step toward the prince, Freya put a hand on his arm to stop him.

"I saw no need to go back and forth about a minor adjustment to our plan that I knew you would agree with," Fenian continued. "It would have been a waste of time. Much like this conversation."

Freya's magic flared inside her, but she reined it in. Fenian was right. They would continue arguing like this and getting nothing accomplished, or they could focus on the task at hand.

"Did you get all of the Jotnar out?" she asked Byrric and Ruehnar.

"We did," Byrric confirmed. "Daniel and Vali and the others are... handling them now."

"Well, the camp is destroyed," Freya said. "So, it should be clear from here to Iladel."

"Then it's done," Florian said. "We need to drop the matter and move on."

"Very well." Ruehnar ran a hand over his chin. "Commander, we should send a few of our knights out to confirm there are no survivors."

"Agreed." Byrric looked at Freya and Toskr, then, grudgingly, Fenian. "Good work, you three."

Before they could go back to the command tent, Rini appeared beside Freya.

"Oh, good, you're both back," she said breathlessly. "I've found Reykr Traust."

"Where?" Byrric and Freya demanded.

"He's patrolling the streets in Iladel," she explained, her breath sending tiny puffs of steam into the cold morning air. "He's watching the city."

"And likely knows we're coming," Florian said. "Did you go to the palace?"

"No, Lord Florian. I only wanted to find Traust." She looked at Freya and Aer. "Should I return?"

Byrric nodded. "Go to the passages. Keep an eye and ear on everything. If Willem gets a whiff that we're close, you come to us."

"Of course, Commander. Your Majesty, do you need anything from me before I go?" she asked Freya.

Freya didn't miss the way Rini's eyes drifted toward her hair, the tight braids a mess from fighting. "No, Rini, I'll be fine. Just be safe. Stay out of sight."

Rini gave her a sharp nod, then disappeared.

They all began walking toward the command tent, but Freya forced calm into her steps, walking slower than the rest. Her pulse was still racing from the confrontation in the human camp, but she knew there was no time to dwell on that now. It was done and over. No amount of scolding or bickering would change the prince's methods, nor would they convince him he'd been reckless.

The plan had worked, though. As the rising sun continued to break over her own camp, still shrouded in magic, she comforted herself with that thought.

55

LEA

Lea took a deep breath before knocking on the door to her mother's chambers. Even though she knew Perida and Ordona would likely think her plan was reckless, they were running out of options. They knew that. All Lea had to do was convince them her plan would work. She hadn't decided what to do if they said no, but she shoved that thought from her mind as soon as Perida called her inside.

Perida and Ordona were sitting at the small table near the bedroom
window, postures tense. Steaming cups of tea sat untouched beside a small map
of Edhil that was spread across the table. For the first time since they had
returned home, Lea saw a bit of fear in her mother's eyes, something she always
tried to shield her from.

"Lea," Perida said, standing from her seat. "Has something happened?"

Lea's eyes flicked to her aunt before she took a deep breath. "I have an idea. You're both going to think it's crazy, but I think I know how we

can help block the humans from reaching Errest." She looked down at the map on

the table, then at her mother. This plan of hers was crazy, too crazy, too over

the top. But it could save their entire realm within mere moments if it worked.

All they had to do was see that. They *had*

to.

"We already have Jonas and the elves working to get the Jotnar off

the ships." He'd left almost immediately after their meeting with General

Thallan to begin. "What if the three of us combine our earth magic to dam the

river, block the ships from coming any closer?"

There were a few beats of tense silence, during which Lea saw no

less than half a dozen emotions cross her mother's face. Ordona moved first,

though, a flick of her lips that shaped into a small, skeptical smile. She

folded her arms and looked to her sister, allowing her to be the one to speak.

Lea already saw the refusal in Perida's eyes, but she held her breath, hoping

she'd be wrong.

"So?" Lea asked. "What do you think?"

ETTRIAN WAS LEANING against the wall across from Perida's chambers

when Lea stormed out of the room a short while later into the sunny hall.

"How did it go?" he asked, although the glint of amusement in his eyes told her he knew precisely how well it went.

"Terribly," she snapped. She began walking a brisk pace down the hall, not bothering to wait for him to catch up. "Aunt Ordona seemed open to it, but Mother won't even consider it! It's too dangerous, the risk of something going wrong is too high, and, of course, she doesn't want me anywhere but here in this house, in that damned drawing room, sequestered with everyone else who's too helpless to contribute!"

Ettrian ignored her snark as he kept pace with her down the hall, his arm brushing against hers with each step. "I suppose that's not so surprising. That room is built like a fortress, after all. Although I have a feeling Ordona might be able to sway your mother. Give her a bit of time. She has a way with words, that one."

Lea scoffed. "I won't hold my breath." She stopped at the hallway intersection that split toward the guest rooms, then took a deep, calming breath in an attempt to exhale out her anger. "In the meantime, I need to check on Rosie, tell her what's going on. I feel like she's been more amenable to talking the past few days. I don't want to backslide now that her people are coming to attack us."

"As I've said before, you are too kind for your own good, Lea." He stepped closer, then trailed a finger down her arm and linked his fingers with hers. "Come find me when you're done."

She tilted her chin up and took the kiss he offered. "I will."

The corner of his mouth kicked up into a smirk. "And if you decide you'd rather I just take her to the middle of the desert and leave her there,

let me know."

She rolled her eyes and shoved him back, then wiggled her fingers

in a wave. "Goodbye, Ettrian."

As she walked toward Rosie's room, she tried to smother her

irritation at her mother and aunt. Yes, it was infuriating that she constantly

felt like she wasn't doing enough to help her people, but it also wasn't

terribly surprising that Perida was so against the idea. She'd just lost her

husband, nearly lost her daughter, and was faced with losing everything else,

too. It was a bit surprising that Ordona hadn't spoken in support of Lea, but

she *was* Perida's sister, after all. If Ordona thought it

was a good idea, she knew her sister well enough to know she needed some time

to mull things over on her own.

When she reached Rosie's door, she knocked softly, listening

closely for a reply from within. When she heard Rosie's quiet "come in," she

pushed open the door. Rosie was sitting in the chair beside the window. Her

half-eaten lunch was sitting on a tray on the table next to her. When she saw

Lea, she gave her a slight smile that didn't quite reach her eyes.

"Hello, Rosie," Lea said, shutting the door behind her. "How are you doing?"

Rosie's bottom lip quivered slightly as her eyes filled with

tears. "I was just thinking about how much I want this all to be over."

Lea sat down on the edge of the bed. "It will be soon. One way or another."

"Not soon enough." Rosie dropped her gaze to her lap, where she was twisting her fingers. "I heard the servants talking. I know my kind are on their way to attack the city."

Lea felt a pang of sympathy, a feeling that had slowly been supplanting her annoyance with the girl. For a moment, she watched Rosie, taking in the exhaustion that seemed to have finally caught up with her.

On impulse, she stood and held out a hand. "Come for a walk with me, Rosie."

Rosie looked up in surprise, hesitation clear in her expression. "But...I thought Errest was going to be attacked? Isn't it too dangerous?"

Lea gave her a small smile. "We have some time, yet. There's nothing we can do here, so we might as well make the most of this lull."

After a moment, Rosie took Lea's hand and got to her feet, and they walked out into the hall together. The princess's gaze flicked around the halls, her posture shrinking a bit each time a knight or guard walked past. Lea tightened her grip and quickened her steps, navigating them through the halls and outside to the estate's wall. When Lea shoved open the door that led to the bridge, the afternoon sun blasted them both with blinding light and heat.

Rosie's eyes widened slightly when they stepped onto the stone wall. "I wondered how you got out here. I saw the wall from my window."

"It's my favorite place to come when I want some peace and quiet,"

Lea explained, shutting the door behind them. "Aside from my garden, of course.

Come. Let's walk."

She hadn't been entirely sure why she brought Rosie up to the wall, but now that they were there, she knew exactly where they needed to be.

Slowly, she began leading Rosie toward the northern wall.

As they walked, Rosie looked out over the landscape, past the dwindling trees and toward the desert.

"We don't have any deserts in Dystone," she commented. "I always thought this part of Lindoroth would be a dry, dusty place." She flushed, glancing away. "I'm sorry, that sounded—"

Lea waved a hand. "It's fine. I understand." She gestured toward the landscape. "And now? What do you think?"

"It's far lovelier than I expected," Rosie admitted. She went quiet for a few moments, and Lea forced herself to wait patiently. Finally, Rosie looked up at her. "I've been wondering..."

"Wondering?"

"If you think I'll ever go home." Twisting her hands, she heaved a breath. "If my brother loses this war, I mean."

Lea considered her words carefully before responding. The wrong answer could set the princess off, and what Lea needed right now was for her to be calm and on her side, not panicking and trying to flee at the first sign of human ships.

Lea frowned down at her. "Is that what you want?"

"Why didn't you leave me in Iladel?"

"I already told you, I didn't want Willem to take any of his anger toward me or Ettrian out on you."

"You're so certain he's that cruel? Cruel enough he would hurt his own sister?"

"Perhaps. If Isadora—the real Isadora—is to be believed, Willem was horribly unkind. Punitive, harsh. That's why she was so content to hide away in Madrya, in an empire known for its vicious rulers, rather than return to Dystone and marry him."

"But Dania had already taken her place," Rosie replied. "Isadora wouldn't have been able to marry Willem."

"I'm fairly certain she would've found a way," Lea said drily.

"Likely murder Dania in her sleep, if I'm being blunt." She paused at the corner where the wall turned toward the front of the house. "Rosie, Willem threatened to throw you in the dungeon when you tried to stop him from trying to take me for himself. You showed an inkling of fear, of concern, for someone who wasn't him, and he threatened you. How long do you think it would've been until his twisted mind began thinking you were completely against him?"

Rosie pursed her lips and turned her head away, the denial in her eyes so clear Lea wanted to shake her. "Where are you taking me?"

"Not to toss you over the edge, if that's what you're worried about." Lea cocked her head to the side. "You need to see the outside world, see what war looks like instead of hiding behind the walls of a palace or the governor's home."

Rosie hesitated for a moment, then nodded. "Alright."

Lea turned and continued around the corner of the house, revealing the encampment that stretched out before the city. She heard Rosie's breath

catch when she caught sight of the tendrils of smoke rising to the west, but

Lea didn't comment. Instead, she kept walking, letting Rosie take in everything

around them. Part of her felt a bit guilty forcing Rosie to take in the breadth

of the camp, the rising smoke. But at the same time, she couldn't find it in

herself to care enough to soften her approach.

When they reached the front wall, Lea rested her hands on the warm

stone, leaning against it as she stared out over her city, where the sun cast a

cheerful gleam, taunting everyone below with its cheeriness. Far in the

distance, beyond the dark strip of forest, the Gefhorn River stretched across

her lands. The enemy was close, closing in at that very moment. She could feel

it as she watched movement ripple through the camp, soldiers gathering together

to make their formations and march against the humans seeking to trash her city.

The idea of using her earth magic to stop the humans came back to

her. Frustration at her mother and aunt resurfaced, but she forced it down.

She'd need another plan, another solution, but that would have to wait.

She turned to the girl beside her, physically only a few years

younger than her, but so, so childlike in every other way. "Can I ask you something?"

"Of course."

"Where were you when your brother and Lessia launched their attack

on Lindoroth?"

"I'd gone to bed hours before. Why?"

"Did Willem ever come to check on you afterward to make sure you

were safe?"

"No." Rosie frowned. "Again, why?"

"So with the exception of me and my mother, you haven't seen any

of what this war has done to my people?"

Rosie's expression turned wary, and for a moment, Lea thought she

might try to run back inside.

"No, I haven't," she finally said.

Lea nodded slowly, then pointed toward the smoke. "Do you see those bodies burning, Rosie?"

Rosie sniffed. "Yes," she whispered.

"Those knights got to leave this world in ash. Their deaths may

not have been peaceful. I can guarantee they weren't, actually. But at least

their bodies get to leave this place peacefully, respectfully." She clenched

her jaw, then let out a quiet breath. "Do you know what happened to my father's

body? My uncle's? The rest of the people that were murdered at Freya and

Aerelius' wedding?"

Rosie sniffed again and shook her head sharply. "No, I don't."

"They were left to rot in a pit behind the palace, picked apart by

insects and birds." She waited a moment. Then, when Rosie looked at her, eyes

filled with a mix of shock and revulsion, she asked, "Where is the respect in
that?"

Rosie was silent for a moment, her expression so indecipherable that Lea wasn't sure if Rosie believed her or not. "I just want to go home,"
she finally murmured, breaking Lea's gaze. "I don't care what awaits me there."

"Will Benjamin be there for you?"

Rosie nodded. "I know what you must think of him, but he's always
been so kind to me. I want to go home to him. If I'm being honest
—" She looked
down at her hands. "If I'm being honest, I feel safer with him than my own
family."

Lea considered that for a moment. "Do you think he supports Willem
with all of this?"

"I don't know," Rosie confessed. "I don't think so. I haven't
heard from him in weeks. I assume it's because of the lack of ships coming from
Dystone, but he has his own fleet. I thought he would've at least attempted to
reach me."

Lea had considered that as well but chose not to read too much into it for the moment.

"I just want to go home," Rosie said again.

"I promise, Rosie. When this is all over, I'll make sure you get
there." Lea took her hand and shot one last look toward the river. "For now,
let's go prepare for your people to launch their attack on mine."

Rosie's hand trembled in Lea's. "I think...I believe you now."

"About?"

Rosie took a deep breath. "My brother didn't send any of them here
for me. Not Lord Edrin, not these ships."
"No, he didn't," Lea murmured. "And I'm very sorry about that."

56

LEA

Although Lea hated the thought of being confined, she only put up
a minor protest when Lindesson insisted they barricade themselves in the
drawing room again.

"It's the safest place in your home, not to mention the city,"
Iska had told her as they walked down to meet the rest of the
household.

"Oh, I know," she said with a sigh. "I just feel so useless
sitting there, stuffed in that room."

"It's for your own good," Tyna said with a sharp nod. "No one can
get in there."

"No one will get into the city, Tyna. Those humans will be dead
before midnight."

"You put a lot of faith in our knights," Iska commented. "But
anything can happen."

Lea sent him a sidelong look. "It sounds like you should have a
bit more, sir." She glanced at Tyna. "You'll make sure Rosie is
comfortable?

Not too worked up?" It hadn't slipped past her notice that Rosie seemed fond of

Tyna, no matter how much she tried to feign disinterest.

"Of course, My Lady."

An hour later, not long before sunset, the drawing room had once

again been turned into a fortress. The windows were shuttered tight against the

setting sun, the flue sealed. Blankets and cots had been brought up, as well as

a cart of food and water in case they had to stay the night. Everyone in the

house, from the maids to the Queen Mother, were sealed in the room, hopefully

safe if the humans got far enough to try to break in. The fear of what was

looming outside the city weighed over the room, keeping voices low and

expressions tight.

Perida, Ordona, and Lea sat around a table, their voices hushed as

they talked about what would come in the next few days. As her mother and

Ordona continued to speak, Lea's eyes drifted around the room and landed on

Tyna, who, true to her word, was hovering near Rosie like a shadow, doing all

she could to keep her calm.

"Well, I don't think you should discount the idea simply because

of what you think might happen," Ordona was saying. Lea pulled her attention

back to their conversation, which had been slipping toward Edhil's rule.

Lea frowned. "What idea?"

"Oh, your aunt believes I should push to govern Edhil on my own,"

Perida said with a sigh. "With the General as advisor, of course. The thought

has crossed my mind, Ordona, but I'm simply not convinced our people would have

me." Her voice trailed off as she looked around the room at the people gathered

there. "The laws are what they are. In the absence of a male successor, the

other governors, our monarchs, and the Errestian council will vote."

Lea eyed her mother with speculation. "I don't think you believe

that. I think you want to govern Edhil, and I think you'd be wonderful at it."

Perida gave her the briefest flash of a smile. "Perhaps. If

nothing else, I'll push to stay on as an advisor, at least during the transition."

"Good," Ordona said. "There's still so much you can offer this

realm. Although, I don't think you should let the idea of ruling it yourself

slip away so easily." She gave her sister a wry smile. "Considering who the

governors, king, and queen are, I'd say you have a fair chance at being

appointed."

"Yes, a fair dose of nepotism always garners support from

the people." Perida took a sip of her tea. "For now, Lindesson will continue to

lead until things are smoother."

"I think you underestimate your people's ability to adapt," Ordona

said, adjusting her skirts beneath her.

Perida shrugged. "I'm also not opposed to letting life get a bit

quieter. After everything that's happened, it might be for the best."

Lea could tell in the way her mother refused to meet her gaze that she'd been contemplating this for a while. Yes, the Edhilian people might be

willing to adapt, but the idea of a quieter life in a quieter place would be

understandably enticing, considering how things had been going the past two

months. To hear Perida, usually sharp-tongued and quick to act, now speaking as

if she were giving in to outside pressures so easily, was a bit startling.

She could see it in her mother's eyes, though. Losing Orin had

been sinking in more for both of them since they'd returned. They hadn't talked

about it much with each other, but now that they were here, they needed to

process that loss, grieve, move on.

When she looked at Perida, she saw her mother looking back at her,

understanding filling her eyes. She leaned forward and took Lea's hand, then

Ordona's. "When this is done...maybe we could take a trip somewhere."

"I think that sounds perfect," Ordona said. "A celebration."

Lea forced a grin. "I love it."

Perida patted her hand, then leaned back in her chair and looked

around the room. Finally, after a moment, she looked back at Lea. "Do you truly

believe that plan of yours could work?"

Hope flickered in Lea's chest, but she shoved down that spark and

kept her voice steady. "I know it will, Mother." *And if it doesn't, at least we died trying.*

"Did the Lady of Errest change her mind?" Ordona asked with a smirk.

"Oh, you thought it was a good idea all along," Perida shot back.

Ordona shrugged, the movement so very queenly. "The only way you would agree to this insanity is if you came to the decision on your own. If I pushed, you would've never considered it."

Perida pursed her lips, but amusement glinted in her eyes.

As if on cue, Ettrian appeared beside her. His quick eyes assessed them in half a breath, then settled on Lea. "I take it opinions have evolved?"

"It would seem so," she replied with a relieved grin.

"Not to rush you all, but if you want to carry out this plan, we need to hurry," Ettrian said. "I'll need to update the generals."

"Shouldn't we discuss–" Perida started.

"We'll discuss the details when we get to the river," Lea cut her off. "I already told you everything."

"She's right," Ettrian said. He looked at Perida and Ordona. "I would suggest getting changed, first."

Lea looked at her mother and aunt's attire. Her own leggings and tunic were fine for what they were about to do, but the fluffy skirts and tight bodices her mother and aunt wore could end up being a hindrance.

"No need, Your Highness," Perida said, smoothing her skirts. "Let's just be on our way."

Rosie rushed over when she saw them standing. "Where are you going?" she demanded.

Lea did her best to hide her wince, forcing a placating smile onto her face instead. "We have to take care of something, but if all goes as planned, I won't be gone long at all."

"And I will be here with you, Princess," Tyna said. She touched a small hand to Rosie's arm. "I wish I could go with Lady Calliwell, too, but it's safer for us to stay here."

Lea didn't miss the hurt in Tyna's words, but she knew better than to comment."

"You'll be fine, Rosie," Lea soothed. "Tyna will be with you." She glanced toward Iska, who was standing beside Tyna. When he saw her look, he nodded. "And Iska will be with you, too. He's kept me safe all my life. I promise, he will do the same for you." She pursed her lips. "And Rosie?"

The princess's tear-filled gaze met hers. "Yes?"

"Try not to do anything stupid while I'm gone." She squeezed Rosie's hands. "Alright?"

Rosie sniffed, then nodded. "And then I can go home?"

"As soon as possible, Rosie. I promise."

Rosie's lower lip trembled, then she stepped back to stand beside Iska.

"She'll be fine with me, my lady," Tyna murmured to Lea once Rosie was out of earshot. "No need to worry."

Lea smiled. "I appreciate you, Tyna. Truly."

Tyna smiled and gave a small curtsy before drifting back toward Rosie.

Ettrian held out a hand. "Are you ready?"

"As I'll ever be." Lea took his hand, then her mother's. Perida gripped Ordona's, then she nodded.

"Hold on, then," Ettrian said.

Then the gray, swirling cold air of the Between enveloped them, and they were gone.

57

LEA

It was twilight when they arrived on the banks of the river junction. The air held a damp stillness, silent save for the lapping of water against the shore where the Rimar and Gefhorn converged. The junction spanned the width of both, funneling the rushing Rimar into the narrower Gefhorn and giving Lindorothian ships ample space to spread out and block the enemy's passage toward Errest.

Across the waterway, the masts of the stolen Lind ships, now maneuvered by humans, coming toward them cast an eerie shadow against the darkening sky, and Lea could just make out shadows moving about the decks. It was an ominous sight, one that probably should've terrified her. Instead, it only fueled the flames of her anger.

"We should've come sooner," Perida muttered as she took in the scene before them. "Damn it!"

"Our timing is fine," Ettrian murmured absently, his eyes a bit distant. "I told Thallan and Lindesson this was a possibility, so they already have a plan in place."

"How do you know?" Perida snapped.

His eyes shifted back into focus briefly and he looked down at her and tapped his temple. "Because I'm speaking with the generals of your army and mine right now."

Perida sent a shocked look at Lea, who realized she hadn't ever told her mother about Ettrian's mind-speak.

"It's okay, Mother." Lea placed a hand on her mother's arm. "We need to wait until they get to the junction, anyway." She squinted toward the ships and looked up at Ettrian. "How many humans came south on land?"

"Several hundred. Our squadrons took out most of them last night, mainly raiders and shore patrols, but now they know we're here." He smirked down at her. "They don't know *you're* here, though, which is quite good for us."

She exhaled slowly, continuing to watch as the ships drew closer. "We can do this, right?"

"No time to doubt yourself now," Ordona said. She gave Lea a quick smile. "You're running this show, after all."

Lea tried to return her smile, but it came out as more of a blanche. Despite Perida's frustration at their timing, she and Ordona exuded a quiet confidence that Lea couldn't seem to grasp ahold of. They had centuries of experience honing their magic to fine points. She'd not even a decade.

Her idea suddenly seemed monumentally stupid.

"My ladies," Lindesson said when he appeared at their side with General Thallan. "Our knights are in formation on the eastern and western banks. They await your signal." He looked at Perida. "Thank you, Lady Calliwell. Your people will not forget this."

Perida gave him a faint smile, and Lea wondered if her mother was having regrets about what was in no way a foolproof plan.

"I have my squadrons doing their best to distract them," Thallan said. "We have removed all Jotnar from the ships and Lord Edrin has been speaking with them. As their de facto leader, few have put up a fight. The human knights are beginning to focus more on what is happening on board and less on the banks. They know we march alongside them, but they have done nothing to stop us."

"That's a bit unnerving," Lea said.

She looked out over the area, at how the Rimar narrowed slightly just before it widened into the Gefhorn. *There's so much water,* she thought. *This was a terrible idea.*

A hand came to rest on her shoulder, and she relaxed a bit at Ettrian's presence. "Don't worry about the water," he said. "Pretend it doesn't exist."

She continued to watch the ships, trying to find comfort in Ettrian's presence, but struggling. One turn and those boats would be on their way to Errest, the width of the Gefhorn making it nearly impossible to stop their forward progress.

"They're nearly there," General Lindesson said. "Ladies, best of luck. Our hearts are with you all."

"Likewise, General," Perida said.

When Lindesson and Thallan were gone, all that remained were Lea, Perida, Ordona, and Ettrian, with a handful of his own knights at his back. Lea looked at his soldiers, then at Perida and Ordona, all so confident, so suddenly sure about what they were about to do. So much more experience, so much more strength.

"You have that strength," Ettrian whispered. "They're your blood. This is your land, Lea. It's your magic. It's their magic," he added, gesturing toward the Linds making formations on the banks, now shielded by a massive protection spell that shimmered over them. "What belongs to them belongs to you. Use it." Then, he turned to the elves behind him and snapped a few orders in elvish. Moments later, they disappeared, followed by the bulk of the elvish knights on either side of the river. The ships were almost there. Moments away.

"It's time, Ladies of Lindoroth," he said. "Do your worst."

He stepped back, then Ordona and Perida each took one of Lea's hands.

"Ignore the water," Ettrian said in her mind. *"Take back what's yours."*

"Lea, darling, thank you for this," Perida said. "I couldn't be more proud."

"Alright," Ordona whispered. "Let's go."

Lea tightened her fingers around her mother's hand and aunt's, and took a deep breath. Her power responded to her instantly, despite the panic and fear that nearly had her faltering.

The ships were seconds from the river's mouth when Lea saw the water begin to ripple and tremble. Her power surged within her, then flowed out of her in a current with Perida and Ordona's. The three streams of power joined together, and as they did, the ripples on the river's surface turned to small whitecaps. Mud from the river floor quickly began to churn the water, turning the whitecaps russet.

The first ship had just reached the junction when rock and mud pressed up from beneath the water, causing it to run aground in the widest part of the river. The two ships along side it made it a bit further before their progress was also halted.

"Keep going!" Ettrian ordered.

She felt Perida and Ordona's hands quivering in hers as they continued to funnel their magic into the earth that cradled the river. More magic joined theirs, water and earth users along the river banks adding support to Lea, Perida, and Ordona's magic, working to divert the flow and prevent humans from abandoning their ships.

But it was Lea that dragged boulders up from beneath the mud, Perida that piled them atop one another, further damming the river, and Ordona that dug deep trenches on either side to keep water from flooding the shores. As one, they turned the wide, rushing Rimar river into two streams, fully stranding the fleet of human ships in the middle. Shouts rang out from the boats as, one by one, the ships struck the rocky dirt that now formed an island in the center.

Shouts sounded from the river as flaming arrows flew from the boats to the knights that were hemming the humans in. Magic crackled as air and spirit magic blocked the arrows' paths, causing them to burst into harmless sparks that drifted toward the water. The humans' only options were to attempt to flee the ships or stay where they were.

Lea, Perida, and Ordona kept pushing their magic into the river bed, reinforcing it with boulders from underground. When the churning waters slowed to a gentle flow on either side of the stranded ships, humans scurried about the decks like rats, bringing a grim satisfaction to Lea's smile.

"Do we wait them out?" Perida asked, still clinging to Lea's hand as more arrows flew toward the shore.

"They'll surrender soon enough, I'm sure," Ordona replied.

"It might take awhile," Ettrian said. He nodded toward one of the ships that still bobbed in the water, unable to pass due to the narrow straits and beached vessels. "That one there has a persistent captain."

Lea's lip curled in frustration. "Let him tire himself out, then."

"Wisdom would dictate they surrender," Ettrian said. "But they're soldiers, so they're going to try to find any way possible to get out of this mess." Suddenly, an arrow flew in their direction, but Ettrian threw up a shield before it could strike any of them. "Clearly, wisdom isn't their strong suit," he said with a sigh.

One of his knights appeared beside him. "What are your orders, Your Highness?"

Ettrian jerked his chin toward Lea, Perida, and Ordona. "Take them back to Errest." Before Lea could protest, he touched a finger to her lips. "Berate me later. Those creatures are about to flood these shores. You don't need to be here for the ensuing slaughter."

Perida touched her elbow. "He's right, darling. We've done all we can. The rest is for our armies to handle."

Lea turned and looked at the ships. They were stuck in the mud, all the knights continuing to scramble around the deck, sending arrows sailing toward the shore. Each one bounced against the magic that arced over the water.

"Now is not the time to argue, Lea." Ettrian's tone was far more serious than she'd ever heard. He pulled his sword, holding it as if it weighed nothing and was merely an accessory to his fine clothing. No armor to weigh him down, just his magic and a single blade.

As she took him in, she felt something flicker there. Not envy of his confidence, although that would certainly be understandable. It was something more, something that was a mix of reassurance, gratitude, and fondness.

She stepped toward him and laid her hands on his chest. "Just... come back to me. I—I don't want to lose you. Not so soon."

His lips curved into a smile as the weight of her words settled over them. "Is that an order?"

"Don't be an idiot," she replied as she curled her fingers against the rough fabric of his tunic. She could feel the magic woven into it, protecting him. "Just come back to me."

He touched his lips to hers. "Don't you worry, little witch. I'll see you soon."

She closed her eyes as he rested his forehead against hers. "You'd better." She stepped back and joined hands with her family and waited as the knights took their arms.

Moments later, they were home.

The drawing room was startlingly silent compared to the sounds of shouting soldiers and rushing water. The knights Ettrian had sent them home with vanished almost immediately, leaving them in a room full of scared people.

"I'll update them," Perida said. "You two sit and rest."

Not needing to be told twice, Lea and Ordona collapsed onto the nearby sofa while Perida moved to talk with Iska. Although she held her chin high, Lea could tell her mother was as exhausted as she and Ordona were. The effects of expending all that magic had left them drained, mentally weighed down.

It had been worth it, though.

"You did well today, Lea," Ordona said, patting her hand. "Your father would be so proud."

Lea smiled. "You did, too, Aunt Ordona. Thank you for believing in me."

"It was a good plan, dear." She pursed her lips, then exhaled sharply. "You and the prince..."

"Aunt Ordona..."

Ordona held up her hands. "Your mother worries and so do I. Are you sure about him?"

Lea thought for a moment, her mind going back to all of the moments she and Ettrian had shared since he arrived in the palace.

Good moments and bad, they all flashed through her mind as she considered her aunt's question. It was so loaded, so filled with heavy implications that she didn't know how to answer honestly.

"No," she finally said. "But that's alright. For now, I'm sure I want him in my life. That could change, although I don't see that happening."

"Well, you're both young enough that you don't need to be sure about anything," Ordona said. "Just be careful, please? I know your Mother has spoken to you already, but I'm fairly sure she didn't convey her concerns fully. He didn't give her the best first impression, as I'm sure you can understand."

Lea smiled. "He didn't give me the best first impression, either. But I'd like to think my judgement is fairly sound, at least when it comes to my happiness."

Ordona put her arm around Lea's shoulder and pulled her into her side, then rested her head on hers. "You sound just like your mother when you say that. Hold onto that knowledge, alright?"

"Of course," Lea murmured. Her eyes suddenly felt so heavy as the weight of all they'd just done settled on her. At the same time, she was filled with a satisfaction of knowing that, for now, they had managed to keep their people safe.

"Rest now," Ordona whispered, stroking Lea's hair. "Your mother will be back soon."

Lea barely heard her finish her sentence before she drifted off to sleep.

58

FREYA

Freya and the others remained settled around the ruined human camp until the following morning. Despite the carnage, Daniel, Vali, Ruehnar, and Byrric all wanted to take a look through the remains of the camp for any usable supplies or weapons, so they waited until daylight came to begin packing up. As the night passed, Freya remained on high alert, unable to get more than a few minutes of restless sleep here and there. She spent most of the night training her ears for sounds of human survivors slinking from their camp who might still pose a threat. Even with the Valkyrie patrolling above and her knights and their allies patrolling on foot, the excitement of the night wouldn't allow her any rest.

The weight of the coming days lay heavily on her, and the dread gnawing at her mind made rest impossible. Iladel was the final stop, their last stand. If they didn't succeed, that would be the end. Their kingdom would be lost to the human king, her people would be in even more danger than they were presently, and she would die a failure. Success in Iladel was the only option, the only path forward for her kingdom.

When Aer rolled to his side and tugged her a bit closer, a bit of calm eased itself into her tired muscles.

"Sleep, Freya," he murmured. His eyes remained closed, his lips barely moved, but his grip on her was strong.

"Much easier said than done." She slid a hand across his arm. "I'm trying."

He slid closer and rested his head against her arm. "Close your eyes and count to one hundred," he said. "Slowly. It'll help slow your mind down."

She smiled. "When did you become a sleep expert?"

"Since my wife tosses and turns so much it's impossible to fall asleep naturally," he replied.

She smacked his arm playfully, but did as he suggested and closed her eyes. Slowly, she began to count, picturing each number as it passed through her mind.

Eventually, she managed to drift off, but she was asleep barely an hour when Rini burst into the tent in a fit of excitement and pixie dust.

"Lady Calliwell has done it!" she exclaimed, jolting them both from their sleep.

Aer propped himself up on his elbows. "What do you mean? What has she done?"

"She and the other Lady Calliwell and your mother grounded the human ships last night. Tyna has assured me that the humans will not reach Errest."

"Oh Rini, that's excellent news!" Freya exclaimed. As Rini continued to rush though the explanation of the success in Errest, Freya's uneasy mind finally began to settle as her concern for Lea eased a bit.

"Thank the gods," Aer muttered as he tugged a tunic over his head. "Hopefully that'll draw Willem and Traust's attention away from Iladel for a bit."

"Come," Rini said. "The commander wants to get started early, before we can risk any news traveling north about our defeat of the humans."

Freya and Aer rushed to get dressed as Rini flitted around nervously.

"Relax, Rini," Aer said when she flew toward Freya with her comb in her hand. "The commander won't start without us."

Freya snorted, but forced herself to be patient long enough for Rini to whip her hair up into a tight braid. "Have you met my father?"

The corner of Aer's mouth kicked up in a smile. "On second thought, I suppose we'd better hurry."

The cold air outside the tent felt sharper than the days leading up to this one. The sky was clear, the sun bright and deceptively cheerful, as though the weather itself celebrated Lea's success in Errest.

They rushed across camp toward the command tent, where they found everyone awaiting their arrival.

"Finally," Fenian said with a huff as he stood from his seat. "I take it your pixie has told you of your friend's victory?"

"She has," Aer replied. "What other news is there?"

"Your river will need to be dredged of bodies and ruined ships," Tavian quipped.

"We'll head toward Iladel," Byrric said, ignoring the prince. "Ettrian and the Generals have everything in hand in Errest, so we need to keep our focus here."

"Will you be returning to Kildin?" Freya asked Tavian. Part of her hoped he'd stay, as two elf princes were certainly better than one.

"No," he replied. "Kildin is secure enough for now. I will be of more use here."

"Good," Aer replied. "We'll need as much magic as possible once we get to Iladel."

"Rini, have you been into Iladel yet?"

Rini nodded and drifted closer to the map. "Yes, he is still quite active in the city." She pointed toward the central part of Iladel. "He's been patrolling the skies, zigzagging across the city all night. Human and Jotnar knights are crawling the streets."

"He had to have seen the fires, then," Freya said with a nod. "There's no way he doesn't know we're here." She turned to Daniel. "Any thoughts on how you'll reach the Jotnar knights in the city?"

Daniel folded his arms and held her stare, then his eyes flicked to

Fenian. "If you care to give me a ride and a boost to my magic, I can go speak to their General at any time."

"I'll keep an eye on the ones here." Vali gave them a crooked smile. "They seem to have taken a liking to me."

Daniel sent him a level stare. "I have lieutenants to do that."

"I don't think going into the city is the best option," Byrric said. "It's too risky."

"Your commander is right," Ruehnar agreed. "Of all the soldiers in this kingdom, the ones in that city are the most unpredictable. Even if they'd beg for Lord Veldin to be their ruler, we would not be able to trust them so soon."

"You don't think it's even worth trying?" Freya asked. "I would imagine the opportunity to offer up a human bloodbath would be quite enticing."

Byrric nodded. "I agree. But it would also remove any element of surprise we may still have. Our best option is to get into the city and turn as many as we can once we're there. It's a risk, I know."

Daniel drummed the fingers of his left hand against his right forearm and stared through the open tent door toward Iladel, still hidden beyond the mountain. Finally, he sighed and raked a hand through his thick black hair. "Alright, I see your point."

"Then what's our plan?" Aer asked. "I was hoping Traust would turn toward Errest, but clearly that's not going to happen."

"We'll leave at dusk," Byrric said. "We'll remain cloaked, travel through the pass, take one last night to rest, then travel the Between once we get closer."

As Aer and the other leaders began to discuss the finer details of their plans, Freya's mind drifted toward the possibilities that awaited them only a day away. Tomorrow she'd be back in her city. She'd see her palace again. They would face down the monsters who tried to take everything and absolutely obliterate them.

She couldn't help but smile to herself at that.

Vali came to a stop beside her. "I've had that look on my face a time or two. Dare I ask?"

"I'm just thinking about how much I'm looking forward to pulling those wretched creatures out of my home," she replied. She saw no reason not to be forthright. "And I'm thinking about how we'll pull it off."

"We'll do it," Vali said with a nod. "You'll have your home back."

She raised a brow. "Confident, are you?"

"And you aren't?" Vali chuckled. "You're nearly as cocky as I am, Freya. Don't forget that tomorrow, because what we'll face in the city and at the palace will be the worst you'll have seen so far."

"I know," she murmured. Her thoughts went toward the people who were still trapped in the market, all of the others who were in hiding. She could only pray that they'd all been able to stay hidden as well as the people in Watoria. Considering most of the knights in Iladel were human, the people were more likely to be successful at concealing themselves with magic.

"I'd hoped Traust would go to Errest," she said.

"You and your father are not in Errest," Vali replied. "And this Traust fellow is clever. I'd be willing to bet it was his idea to send that army to Errest, not Willem's."

Freya nodded. "True. It *is* a good distraction, assuming you know nothing about him and think he's just looking for the biggest reward."

"Yes, but for him, the biggest reward is your head on a platter." He smirked when she rolled her eyes. "Errest is a grand prize, but Iladel will provide maximum destruction." He looked around the room, at the mix of elves, Jotnar, and Linds, plotting their next move. "Fortunately, we have more than enough magic to defeat him and those creatures Willem Ristner calls soldiers."

"Let's hope so." Freya sighed as she glanced around the tent, taking in her husband, father, and their allies, all planning their final push against Willem Ristner. Their last stand. It was something she never would've imagined facing if someone had asked her six months ago. She wondered where they would be if she and Aer had known on her first day at Aldridge what was coming. Maybe they could've done things differently, somehow prevented all of this from happening.

But for now, all they had was the path fate had laid before them.

Their kingdom was under siege, and they were the last line of defense. For better or worse, they could know tomorrow what the fate of Lindoroth would be.

59

LEA

Lea awoke the following morning feeling more hope than she had in weeks. True, this had been only one battle, but their success here would hurt Willem Ristner far more than any so far. The loss of life had been on par with the battle at Watoria, but the financial loss, the access to Errest's mines that would now be that much harder to achieve, was even greater. Freya and Aer still had quite the fight in front of them as they headed into Iladel, the final leg of their journey home, but at least Lea felt confident that they now had one less thing to worry about.

When she arrived in the dining room for breakfast, she was greeted
by her mother and aunt, Generals Lindesson and Thallan, Ettrian, Jonas, and
Tyna. Rini floated in the air beside her sister, her wings fluttering gently as
she spoke.

"Lea," Perida said, holding out her hand for her to sit and join
them. "Rini was just updating us on how things are going up north."

"I've reported your success to the King and Queen," Rini said as

Lea took her seat. "They are planning to move on to Iladel tonight, but they're still working out how to get Daniel in to speak with the Jotnar inside the city."

Lea frowned and spooned some eggs onto her plate. "Can't they just do what General Thallan did and remove them all to the outskirts?"

"That would require sending too many of my kind into your city at once," Thallan explained. "They will pull some and hopefully they can convey the message, but there is no guarantee." He looked at Jonas. "However, Lord Edrin has been quite successful with the Jotnar we pulled from the ships. Most seem amenable to Daniel Veldin's terms."

Jonas nodded. "It's no secret my kind hate the humans. For most, they follow Willem because he was allied with Lessia. Now that they see a third, better option, one who isn't an outsider, they're open to hearing Daniel out."

Lea's brows rose. "It was that easy to get them to flip?"

Jonas chuckled. "No, not really. A few were amenable without convincing, but it took some time with many of them. And some simply couldn't be convinced, but fortunately, that number was fairly small."

"They've opted to join the soldiers resting in your desert, instead," Ettrian said with an unsettling grin.

"About two thirds sided with us," Jonas continued. "But that's not a huge number. Not many of my kind came down here."

"Because they're all in Iladel fawning over Traust," Rini said.

"Willem is on the throne, but Traust is running the city. I'm not entirely sure when that shift occurred, but it's clear Willem has lost standing with his men and the Jotnar."

Fear gripped Lea as she thought about Freya being in that city with Traust and thousands of knights who were ready to do his bidding. She could only pray that Daniel was better at convincing the Jotnar to come around than Jonas had been. He had to be. And, she reminded herself, Freya and Aer had many experienced, intelligent people with them who would be able to help navigate dealing with someone like Reykr Traust. If they couldn't...

"I'd like to see the river," she said, forcing herself to change the subject. She had to focus on what was in front of her, not what was far away and out of her control. "I want to see the damage."

Lindesson frowned. "I don't think that's wise, Lady Calliwell."

"Nor is it necessary," Thallan agreed.

She looked around at the males before her. "You don't think I can handle seeing what *I* helped cause?"

"There's nothing there you should want to see," Ettrian said.

She shot him a glare. Of everyone here, she would've expected him to back her. "I just need to see that it's done."

"Once the water users let go of their magic and the earth users began filling the trenches, the floodwaters washed away the bodies of those who'd abandoned their ships," Ettrian said. "The ships drifted downriver, and with no one to steer them, they crashed into the banks. All that's left to see is a giant mess that could take days to fully clear away."

She narrowed her eyes, seeing straight through his attempt to

downplay what she was certain was much more than just a 'mess.'

"Water and earth users have been hard at work redirecting the flow

of the river to prevent it from becoming blocked," Lindesson continued.

"There's nothing more you can do there."

"I can help the other earth users," she protested.

Perida stepped forward and gripped her hand. "There's a lot that needs to be done here in the city that I need your help with. We need to

organize getting help to the villages who've been overrun. Now that we can

safely leave the city, we have to move quickly." She glanced toward Rosie, who

was pacing in front of a window, twisting her hands nervously. "And I need you

to get that girl out of here before she wears a hole in my carpet."

"I think it would be best to spend more time with Rosie," Tyna whispered. "You've come so far with her."

"And she'll be put on a ship back to Dystone in three days time," Lea shot back. Perhaps it was unfair, but she simply didn't have it in her to

care an ounce about Rosie at the moment. The girl didn't want to go back to her

brother, that much was clear, so there was no need to babysit her and make sure

she didn't get herself killed by trying to escape. If anything, her will to

live had gotten stronger after her conversation with Lea about Benjamin.

"Kindness costs nothing, my lady," Tyna said. "And what good will

seeing a thousand dead bodies truly do for you?"

This time, Lea's glare was directed at her attendant. "Shouldn't you be on my side?"

Tyna straightened her back and lifted her chin in defiance. "I always am, Lady Calliwell, even if you don't believe so."

Instantly, Lea's frustration was replaced with chagrin. "Of course I believe that, Tyna. It's just very frustrating. I'm part of the reason we were so successful, yet I can't go see the results?"

"Our people would do well to see you," Perida said. "Word has reached them about stopping the humans, and now they need guidance."

"And as your mother pointed out, the princess has some energy to burn," Tyna said. "Perhaps you could bring her with you."

Lea sighed and looked over at Rosie, still nervously tugging at her fingers as she stared out the window. Her mother and Tyna were right, but it didn't change how she felt. "Fine." She looked at Ettrian. "But I want to hear *everything* when you get back."

Lips pursed, she turned on her heel and crossed the room toward where Rosie stood. When the Princess saw Lea approach, she dropped her hands.

"What is it? Is—"

"Everything is fine, Rosie," Lea said. "Would you like to go into the city with me?"

Rosie's eyes widened. "Into—why?"

"Because you need to get out of this house for once, and I have a job to do." Lea smoothed her hands over her dress. "And it's a lovely day."

"What job do you have to do?"

"Well, I'm still the governor's daughter, even if he isn't with us," Lea said. "So, now I need to go into the city and meet with my people, see who needs help with what now that they can begin preparing to leave the city, make sure everyone from the outside has safe harbor."

"Is that really something I should be present for?" Rosie asked. "Your people hate me."

"They don't know you," Lea replied. "And if you're that worried, just don't speak. Help with what I ask you to help with, but other than that, just be my shadow. You'll be fine." She frowned at the look of nausea on Rosie's face. It was very hard not to be annoyed with the girl's reactions to seemingly simple things, but Tyna was right. It wouldn't hurt her in any way to show some extra kindness. "What's wrong?"

Rosie exhaled heavily. "There's just...something I've been meaning to say." She gnawed on her lip so hard Lea thought she might draw blood.

Finally, after a few painfully long moments, she continued. "I wanted to be your friend. Back at the palace. I wanted us to be friends."

Lea's jaw tightened, but she forced herself to relax. "I don't think—"

"No, please let me finish." Another deep breath. "I wanted to be your friend, so when Willem told me to get close to you, I thought it would be the perfect opportunity to do that." Each word sounded deliberate, rehearsed.

"But I see now that I let my loneliness cloud my judgment. I know he wasn't trying to help me. I see that now. I was just so, so lonely and..." Her words cut off as she swallowed back her tears.

Lea felt a pang of pity, so she made her voice as gentle as possible. "I know you wanted to be my friend. I also knew Willem was using that

to his advantage." She put a hand on Rosie's shoulder. "I don't blame you for
it, Rosie. Truly."

Rosie nodded and let her gaze drift back toward the window. "When
I saw you leave yesterday—you went out there and quite literally faced your
enemy...yet you didn't look scared." She looked at Lea and frowned. "How?"

Lea shrugged. "Unyielding rage will do that to a person."

Rosie's smile turned a bit happier. "Fair enough." She looked at
Tyna, who'd just drifted toward them. "Alright, then. What are we doing?"

60

LEA

A lighthearted feel had settled over Errest in the wake of the river battle. Lea, Rosie, and Tyna spent the entire day in the city checking in with citizens, most of whom seemed lighter on their feet, eager to plow ahead and put this war behind them. The whole city seemed to have picked up speed in the past few days now that the immediate threat had been neutralized. The war wasn't over yet, of course, but there was enough of a lull now that the people were finally loosening their grip on their fear.

For Lea, speaking to the citizens and businesspeople was a distraction just as much as it was a necessary task. Despite Rosie's fear, most people barely spared her a glance. Yes, some cast wary or even hostile glances toward her now and then, but Lea's presence seemed to quell any concerns about the human princess' presence in Errest.

One by one, they approached the grocers, innkeepers, apothecaries, smiths, and anyone else who might have a skill that could assist the villagers who'd lost their homes during Willem and Lessia's siege. Most were happy to help however they could, although there were a few who resisted on the grounds that they didn't want to use up their wares so soon after one victory when the kingdom was still teeming with enemy knights.

Lea supposed she could have her mother, backed by Lindesson, come down to the city and order people to comply, but that would never be the right approach with her people. Certainly not if she wanted them to have confidence in her mother's ability to lead Edhil. So, she thanked them politely for their time and moved on.

By the end of the day, the square was bustling with business owners and craftspeople finalizing plans to get assistance and supplies out of the city. Carpenters and smiths would travel to the nearest villages to meet with the locals and work on a plan to start rebuilding. A few volunteers would work with citizens to gather food, clothing, bedding, medicine, and other supplies to bring to the villagers. Lea couldn't help but smile at the fact that food and shelter, things that had been absent from the lives of many of her people for weeks now, would soon be on their way.

But as she, Tyna, and Rosie wrapped up in the square just before dusk, she couldn't shake the feeling that something was still unresolved. As she watched dusk fall over her city, a strong, resilient city that was *finally* safe after weeks of stalemate, she couldn't shake the feeling that something still wasn't done.

"What is it?" Rosie whispered as Iska held open the door to their carriage. "What's wrong?"

Lea waited until the three of them were settled in the carriage before answering. "I just feel like...like it's not enough."

"What's not enough?" Rosie asked.

Lea chewed on her lip and watched as the streets began to slip past out the window. "Me. What I'm doing. I want to do more."

"But you've already done so much, my lady," Tyna said, placing a hand on Lea's shoulder. "What more do you expect yourself to do?"

Lea frowned. She knew exactly what she wanted—no, needed—to do, but she didn't dare say it aloud. Not yet, anyway. "I don't know."

Rosie smiled, but Tyna gave Lea a wary look, so perceptive that Lea had to avert her eyes. Knowing the pixie, she already knew precisely where Lea's mind was, but that wasn't a conversation she needed to have with Rosie in the carriage. So, she smiled at them both. "Let's go have some dinner. I'm sure I'll feel better after some food and rest."

As they rode the remainder of the way home, Lea turned over in her mind how she would talk to her mother about what she wanted to do. She wouldn't like it, but it had to be done. But for her mother to agree would require patience, a gentle approach.

Hopefully, she wouldn't come to regret it.

"I WANT TO GO TO ILADEL."

Perida and Ordona, who'd been seated at the dining room table eating dinner with Ettrian, froze. Lea had opted to discuss traveling north in the morning the flesh out her plans more. She'd intended to address it with her mother calmly, but by the time she'd gotten up, bathed, and worked up the courage to talk to her mother, anticipation and urgency had caused any sense of diplomacy to vanish.

Ordona recovered first. "And why would you want to do that?"

"Because that's where I'll be most useful." Lea pulled out a chair and sat across from her mother and, very intentionally, beside Ettrian. "You saw what we did on the river. I want to go to Iladel and put my magic to use with Freya and Aer and the others."

Perida glanced around the room at the servants who were still present. "Could you all give me a moment with my daughter?" She waited while the servants filed out of the room, then looked at Lea, fear flickering in her eyes. "Absolutely not."

"I'm not asking permission, mother." Lea squared her shoulders. "Only for you to support my decision, even if you disagree."

"Might I ask what brought this on?" Ettrian asked as he continued to cut into his eggs.

Lea took an even breath and looked at him. His golden eyes were unreadable, so she couldn't tell what he thought of her plan. "I can't just stay here coordinating the distribution of food and clothing when my family and friends are out there fighting."

"We just lost your father." Perida's voice cracked and her knuckles were white as she gripped her fork. She swallowed hard before continuing. "I can't bear the thought of risking your life, too."

"Freya and Aerelius are out there right now fighting for us," Lea argued. "I need to be there with them!"

"They're the King and Queen," Perida shot back. "Being who they are, people will expect them to fight. Your place is *here*. Where you're safe and protected and not a target!"

"Which is precisely what you will be if you go there," Ettrian said. "Willem despises you. If he knows you're there, he'll either want to take you or kill you."

"He's right," Perida agreed.

She sent a disbelieving look at Ettrian. Of course the first time he and her mother see eye-to-eye would be on something she wanted, but wasn't getting, both of their support for. "I can handle Willem."

Ettrian shrugged and sipped his wine. "Perhaps."

His nonchalance made her want to scream but she refused to react. The last thing Lea wanted to do was leave her home on bad terms with her mother, but that same sense of urgency that'd had her hurrying through the halls was continuing to build inside her. She turned back to Perida. "This is something I have to do."

Ordona put a gentle hand on her sister's arm. "Per..."

Perida's shocked gaze jerked to her sister. "You're siding with her? Ordona, she's nearly died too many times already!"

"And each time, she's found her way out," Ordona said patiently. "Yesterday's victory should show you that."

Perida looked between her daughter and sister, her eyes filled with so much panic it nearly undid Lea's resolve. Lea hated seeing her mother in pain, and the last thing she wanted was to risk putting her in a position where she might lose her daughter so soon after losing her husband. She couldn't step back now, though. This was too big, too important. So, she took a deep breath, willing herself to hold her ground.

"I need to go, Mother."

"And if I tell the prince not to take you?"

Lea met her gaze, unflinching. "Then I'll find another way. Another elf."

Ettrian took a sip of his tea and set his cup down and addressed Perida. "To be fair, Lady Calliwell, I'm not under your command. That would be my father's role."

If looks could kill, Ettrian would be dead under Perida's glare, but Lea could see her resolve faltering.

After a long silence, Perida's glare shifted into resignation. "You'll keep her safe? By your side at all times?"

"You have my word," Ettrian said with a nod. Lea noticed a faint flicker of amusement in his eyes, no doubt sparked by Perida's newfound trust in his ability to keep Lea safe.

"Then I'll support you," Perida said. "But if it gets bad, if things go too far south..."

Lea leapt from her seat and rushed around the table, then threw her arms around Perida as she stood from her chair. "Thank you, Mother," she murmured into Perida's dark curls, so similar to hers. "I promise I'll have Ettrian, or whatever elf is nearest, carry me out of there. I promise."

She pulled back, keeping her hands on Perida's shoulders. It was then that she realized her mother no longer wore that gaunt, starved look she'd had when they'd first came home. She looked stronger, less like a prisoner and more like the female who would run Edhil.

"Don't thank me." Perida slid her hand over Lea's. "Just be careful."

Lea squeezed Perida's hands and kissed her forehead. "I will." She stepped back and looked at Ordona. "Take care of her?"

Ordona nodded somberly. "Always." She glanced out the window. "Now, you'd better hurry. They'll have started by now."

Lea let out a huff. " Alight." She kissed her mother again, then her aunt. "I'll be home soon."

With that, she rushed from the room.

～

THE DOOR to Lea's room fell shut softly as the weight of Lea's promises to her mother weighed on her.

"I'll be home soon."

Only an idiot would say such a thing with so much certainty right before going into battle.

"No going back now," she murmured, shaking off the thought. Now was no time to doubt herself. Quickly, she began pulling clothes from her wardrobe, refusing to give herself time to reconsider. After some digging, she pulled out a pair of leather pants, a fitted tunic, and the boots Freya had given her their first day of class at Aldridge. As she stepped behind her dressing screen to change, her mind raced over the details she was still working out about her trip to Iladel.

She'd just tugged on her pants when she heard her door open and, a moment later, the sound of a body flopping onto her bed.

"You threw me to the wolves a bit in there," Ettrian said. "Next time, I'd appreciate a conversation first before you volunteer my transportation services."

Thankful the screen kept her face hidden, Lea pulled her tunic over her head. "Would you have said no if I'd asked in private?" She tucked her shirt into her pants, schooled her features, and stepped out from behind the screen. "I didn't think it would even be a question."

He sat up and swung his legs over the side of the bed, his face more serious than she'd ever seen. "You expected me to jump at the chance to carry you into what will undoubtedly be the single most deadly battle this war will see? You thought I would be eager to do that?"

She frowned. "Yes, actually. Well, not eager, but willing."

He stood up and stepped closer to her. "Your mother is grieving, Lea. She's given you her blessing, but you must know what this is doing to her."

"Prince Ettrian Tordove, are you *worried*?"

"Of course I'm worried," he said, taking another step closer and resting his hands on her waist. "I've grown quite fond of you, in case you hadn't noticed." He touched his lips to hers in a soft kiss, then smirked. "It would be rotten luck if you went and got yourself killed so soon after you've realized how madly in love with me you are."

She smiled, her lips curving against his as her fluttered at his feigned nonchalance. "Then I suppose you'd better keep me safe." She leaned back and put her hands on his cheeks. "If things get bad, you'll get me out of there. We can discuss...other things when we return."

He chuckled. "You and I both know it's a fool's dream to think it will be that simple."

He kissed her again, and for a brief moment, she considered abandoning the idea and simply waiting out the war with Ettrian in Errest. It would be so easy, and all they'd have to do is wait for word from Iladel that the battle was over. Then they could go off to wherever it was he planned to take her first, get to know each other properly, the way they might've if they'd met under normal circumstances.

"I noticed you didn't deny your love for me," he taunted as he pulled back.

She met his eyes, struggling for a moment with her response. "Having that conversation now...it feels too final, Ettrian." She placed a hand on his chest. "Whatever we have to say to each other...I don't want it to be the last thing we say before going into battle."

He grinned. "Then I suppose *you'd* better keep *me* safe."

Lea smiled and swallowed the knot of apprehension that was forming in her stomach. "I'll do my best." Then, she stepped back. "Tyna?"

Instantly, Tyna appeared. "Yes, my lady?"

"Would you mind checking in with Rini and finding out where we should land? I don't want to get myself killed before I've even had a chance to fight."

Tyna gave her a quick nod. "Of course. But first..." She snapped her tiny fingers, and a strap of leather appeared in her hands.

No, not a strap of leather. A weapon's belt. Lea's heart twisted.

"I thought you might need something to hold your blades," Tyna said quietly. She hooked her hands together behind her back. I managed to smuggle it out of the palace. I hope I wasn't too presumptuous."

With a soft smile, Lea took the belt and ran her thumb over the soft leather, trying to ignore her aching heart. "This was my father's." He'd worn it nearly every day. It was part of his uniform, something she'd watched him put on and take off frequently over the years. It was a small part of him, right there with her.

"Indeed," Tyna said. "I think Lord Calliwell would be honored for you to bring a part of him into battle."

Lea looked at Ettrian as she struggled to contain her tears. "Help me put it on?"

He touched a finger to her chin and kissed her, then took the belt. "Of course."

"I'll be back soon," Tyna said. "Be ready when I return."

Lea took a deep breath, then rested her hand on Ettrian's arm. "We will be."

61

FREYA

The next morning, the sun broke over camp, casting long shadows across the tents and soldiers hurrying to prepare for the day. A light snow had fallen the night before, coating the grassy field in a thin, crunchy sheet of icy white. It would melt within a few hours, but Freya couldn't help but stare at the glittering crystals as the rising sun shone across them. They added a hint of beauty to what was otherwise a dire scene. There was a tension lingering over the camp, one that Freya could feel straight through her flesh to her bones. As Rini helped her dress for the day in her fighting leathers, her hair twisted up into a braided coronet, she tried her hardest to remember the strength and skill she'd wielded in Watoria. A different city, different stakes, but she and her people managed to win. They would do that here, too.

She looked to the skies as she and Aer walked toward the command tent. Valkyrie circled the area, watching from above for any sign of attack or ambush. The night had been quiet, so Freya could only surmise that Traust either hadn't picked up on their presence, or he was biding his time. She wasn't sure which was worse.

Aer must've sensed her unease, because he slid his hand in hers.

"Remember, we're in this together," he murmured as they neared the tent. "We'll get through this."

She gave him a rueful smile. "I wish I had your confidence."

He kissed the top of her head, then pushed open the tent flaps and walked inside.

The command tent buzzed with tension and activity. Maps and scrolls sprawled across the central table, illuminated by the soft flicker of lantern light. Thankfully, a smoldering brazier still put out heat in the center of the space, making it a bit more welcoming. Freya stood beside Aer as they approached the table, her hands clenched at her sides, eyes scanning the drawn lines that detailed their plan to retake Iladel. The faint murmur of voices surrounded her—Byrric, Vali, and Ruehnar outlining strategies, Daniel and Fenian exchanging clipped words about troop placements, Ana and her Valkyrie discussing how they would spread out their kind.

"Ah, good, you're here." Byrric glanced up from where he was studying the map of Iladel and the surrounding area with the others.

"We're here," Freya said with a nod.

"Where are we with our plans?" Aer asked.

Fenian gave them a short nod as they approached. He tapped a spot on the map that showed the outside of the palace. "A quarter of our forces will land here, at the rear of the palace. We'll take the mountain tunnels in." He dragged his finger across the map toward the city. "The rest of us will arrive in various points across the city."

"I'll be in the city, correct?" Freya asked, examining the small wooden markers on the map.

"Yes," Byrric replied. "King Ruehnar, Prince Fenian, and I will lead the elves and Linds into Iladel. Lord Veldin and General Rayn will lead the Jotnar in and ensure cooperation of those within the city."

Daniel inclined his head toward Rini, who was hovering beside Freya. "Your attendant reports there are almost none of my people remaining in your palace, so the bulk of my knights will be with me in the city. His Majesty was kind enough to bring two of the remaining Jotnar in the palace to me last night, and they are prepared to support whoever we send in to fight against Willem."

Aer exhaled a breath. "That's something, then."

"It's going to be much more difficult to have that level of success in the city," Byrric cautioned. "There are only about thirty Jotnar remaining in the palace, but there are hundreds in the streets, not to mention at least a thousand humans."

"I'll bring my fighters along with some of your people to the palace," Vali said. He gestured toward the elves. "Some of their kind, too, for a bit of extra magic."

Ruehnar cocked a brow at Tavian. "Tavian will bring some of our knights to the palace. A small squadron, but enough to give you added strength against the humans."

Tavian looked as though he would rather do anything else, but he gave his father a curt nod and didn't argue.

"His Majesty will go to the palace, as well," Byrric said. "Freya, you and I will work with Prince Fenian, Florian, and Lord Veldin to coordinate the Jotnar once we breach the city." His eyes flicked to Daniel for the briefest of moments. "I have no doubt Lord Veldin can get the Jotnar in hand, but it will be messy at first."

She nodded, looking at Aer. They'd known they would be separated during the fight—a necessary tactic, but neither liked it. It would be foolish to have both monarchs in the same place, though, and Aer knew the palace and its grounds better than Freya did.

"The knights in the city are more complicated," Daniel admitted. "But I'll handle them. They'll follow me, Commander. Don't worry."

"My knights are prepared to leave," Fenian said. "I would prefer to return to my own kingdom some time this century, so if we could get on with it, please."

True fear began to flicker in Freya's chest; fear mixed with anticipation. She was eager to leave the camp and be in the city. She wanted to fight for it just as she'd done for Watoria. But at the same time... this was their last chance. If they wanted to prevent this war from dragging out even more and stop further bloodshed, this was their last, their only, chance to eliminate their enemies. She was thankful they only had Willem to deal with, but until they could get Lessia's knights under Daniel's control, they would be at huge risk.

"Alright," Byrric said. "Let's go over this one final time. I want to be out of here within the hour."

The plan was sound, but the thought of separating from Aer left her uneasy. They'd fought apart before, but not like this—not with the stakes so impossibly high. She couldn't help but notice the potential weak spots in their carefully thought-out strategy, points where there were too few knights or possibly too many, the city streets most of them weren't familiar with, and the palace that was riddled with secret passages Willem–and likely Traust, at this point–knew about. Too many places to hide, too many places to lay in wait and launch a surprise attack.

They had been forced to split up in Avorell, she reminded herself. That had turned out fine. It was difficult, but they'd come out on top. She refused to believe they wouldn't do the same this time.

She looked around the room and couldn't help but smile at the level of support in the room. They *would* do the same this time. There were too many people there that had too much to lose. Between her and Aer, Daniel, and Vali, who all vied for their land, and Ruehnar and the princes, who simply wanted to get *back* to their lands, there was certainly no lack of motivation among them.

If only that were enough.

Satisfied they could all work out the rest of the details themselves, Freya turned to Aer. "Come outside with me?"

His eyes softened as they shifted away from everyone else in the tent and focused on her. "Of course."

When they stepped into the snow-flecked air, Freya leaned forward and let her head come to rest on Aer's chest. As he circled his arms around her, she wrapped her own around him. "You'll be careful," she said. Not a question, not a command, but a need for reassurance.

"Always. And you," he replied as his arms tightened. "Promise me, Freya. Don't do anything stupid."

She smiled into his chest and breathed in his scent one last time.

For once, she didn't feel tears threaten as they said their goodbyes. Instead, his presence gave her a strength she knew she wouldn't be able to get through this battle without. "I promise."

When they parted, her heart ached much like it had in Avorell when they said their goodbyes before the Hunt. They would get through it, though. If they could survive this long, if she could survive the insanity that was the Wild Hunt, if they could make it through the wilds of Lindoroth and the battle at Watoria, they could survive this. They had fewer enemies to tackle, a human king who was hemorrhaging support, and more allies than they could've anticipated.

As she stood, prepared to leave with Fenian and the others in the center of their snow-dusted camp, she had to force herself to think about their chances of winning. They might not come out of this alive —but that wasn't a possibility she was willing to accept.

Not yet. Not ever.

62

FREYA

Those who traveled to the city split into six groups, all consisting of a mix of elves, Linds, and Jotnar. The smallest went to the outer edges of the city to look for citizens who might be sequestered like those Freya had found in Watoria. Their goal was to get as many remaining citizens out as possible. General Forrest and Lieutenant Rayn led groups to help get the Jotnar within the city under control in the hopes of avoiding too much bloodshed. Freya's group traveled to an area a few blocks off the main square, where the streets were eerily quiet. The remaining knights surrounded the city, forming a tight circle that would keep any enemy knights who tried to attack contained.

Freya knew the city was crawling with enemy knights. Yet here, to the untrained eye, the city seemed at peace. Of course, it was a lie. The moment Freya got her bearings, she saw shadows lurking between buildings, men patrolling on rooftops, and a very distinct lack of magic lingering in the air. She had never realized how tangible her people's magic was until its absence made itself known. The thought of it no longer saturating every brick in her city made her fury rear its head.

"Easy, there," Fenian murmured from her side. Then he frowned. "Where is the rodent?"

"I'm not sure," she said, frowning. "I haven't seen him since last night." But now that she thought about it, it *was* strange Toskr hadn't caught a ride with her like he normally did.

"Finally gave into cowardice, most likely," Fenian muttered.

She sent him an exasperated look, but then let her magic flare outward, shimmering as it crept down the streets that stretched away from the square. A cluster of Jotnar lingered on the street to their left, while a small group of humans patrolled the streets to the right and behind them.

"See if you can find the Jotnar general," Byrric told Fenian, gesturing toward where the Jotnar patrolled. "Bring him back to us."

"Do you think this will work?" Freya asked Daniel as Fenian vanished.

He shrugged. "We've done well so far, so I'll remain optimistic."

"Let's hope their logic is as sound as yours, then," she replied. "I'm going to get a look from above. I'll keep the glamour on."

"Alright, but be quick," Byrric said. "If Traust is here, he'll most likely see right through it."

She nodded, then flared out her wings and leapt into the air, the rush of wind momentarily silencing her thoughts. The moment she rose above the buildings, she inhaled, thankful to finally be flying above her city. The sharp tang of ash pricked at her nose, causing her fury to ignite just a little bit more. She hated that it had taken this long to get back to Iladel. Yes, everything she'd been doing in her absence had been to salvage Lindoroth. Yet as she looked out over Iladel, she couldn't help but wonder how many people she could've saved had they made it there just a day sooner.

As she cast her eyes toward the hills and the palace hidden there, she took solace in knowing that Willem's weak, pitiful human eyes would never be able to see through her glamour. She'd concluded recently that Willem's hatred toward her kind wasn't just because they weren't human. No, she was certain part of that hatred stemmed from jealousy of the power that he would never have. Even if he took her lands today, he would never have the level of power required to keep them.

The grim satisfaction that she was so close to him, flying so near the palace but unseen by him, was subdued when she remembered that Traust could likely see her right then, just as he could probably see the Valkyrie soaring over the woods outside the palace, led by her aunt. She wouldn't be surprised if he was standing on the battlements watching her hover above the city, readying himself to take aim. Perhaps he was already on his way.

It didn't matter, though. Her arrival in Iladel wouldn't be a surprise to him. He expected her, her father, and whatever army they'd managed to muster up to appear sooner or later.

She took a few moments to circle over the city one last time, taking in the streets that were empty, save for the Jotnar and humans lurking there, and the market that was covered in scorch marks, but still concealed by a thick bubble of elvish magic. She knew they would need to get there and help the people who'd been in trapped for weeks, but for now, she had to trust that Ettrian's magic would continue to hold.

After a final check to make sure their other fighters were in place, all hidden under glamours she could barely detect, she swung around and headed back to her post.

The streets were still quiet when Freya touched down beside her father just as Fenian returned, a furious Jotnar knight in tow.

"What is the meaning of this?" the knight demanded. His eyes widened when he took in Daniel, then narrowed to slits. "I heard you'd been sniffing around, poking for bits of the Empress' power." He spat on the dusty cobblestone. "Best of luck with that. We have our leader."

Daniel eyed him cooly. "Is that so?"

"It is. So you can take your ilk and leave, unless you all want to die." He sneered at Freya. "Starting with that pretty queen."

She arched a brow. "Flattery will get you nowhere, General."

His sneer deepened, this time mixing with disgust.

"Shall I find another?" Fenian asked, gripping the Jotnar by the back of the neck.

Daniel held the knight's gaze for a moment. "Are there any other ranking officers in the city?"

"I'm the general in charge of this city," the knight replied. "So if you think—"

His words were cut off when Fenian snapped his neck. As his body slumped to the ground, Fenian looked at Daniel. "We don't have time for this."

Freya turned to her father. "He's right. If Traust doesn't already know we're here, he will soon enough. We have to move."

"If he was telling the truth, there is no one in charge of the Jotnar right now," Daniel said. "Don't bother searching for another. Go round up—"

As he spoke, heavy footsteps echoed from both ends of the street. Freya turned, her pulse quickening as two groups of Jotnar rounded the corners. The thrum of Jotnar magic reached toward them, and in a matter of moments, they would sense the glamour that surrounded Freya and the rest of her party.

Just as the thought formed, she saw one, then another stiffen as they sensed their magic. Confusion flickered on their faces as mutters rippled through the group. Then, the one at the front, a short male with chin-length blond hair and a cruel face, smiled. He lifted one leg, then stomped his foot down on the cobblestone, sending a wave of magic through the ground, rattling the stones beneath their feet.

"I know you're there," he taunted as the shaking ebbed. "You might as well reveal yourself."

"Do we think he knows how many of us there are?" Freya murmured to Byrric.

Byrric's wings flared out behind him as he gripped the hilt of his sword. "Unlikely."

"Let me speak with them." Daniel looked at Byrric. "I will try to convince them to stand down."

Fenian grinned, a feral look that made Freya glad she was on the same side as him. "Have at it, then."

Daniel unsheathed his sword and stepped forward. The moment he moved outside their glamour, the Jotnar before them took up a defensive stance. The one at the helm held up a hand, telling his followers to hold.

"Lord Veldin," he greeted. "I was not expecting to see you here."

Daniel nodded. "I've come to help get Jotunheim back to how it should be. My sister is dead, but—"

"Lord Edrin is our leader now," the male said. "Not you."

Freya tensed, then slipped a feather into one hand.

"Lord Edrin is currently captive in Errest," Daniel said calmly. "He has agreed to support my rule."

The male sneered. "I'd like to hear that from him if you don't mind."

"That will be a bit difficult, considering the aforementioned captivity." Daniel let his eyes roam over the crowd. "I think we can all agree that I will be a stronger leader than Jonas Edrin."

The knight drew his sword, and the two dozen males behind him followed suit. "I think we'll take the weaker option, if it's all the same to you."

And with that, he lunged forward, and it was only by sheer luck, or perhaps thanks to centuries of experience, that Daniel was able to bring up his sword quickly enough to block the blow.

Instantly, Freya and Florian dropped their glamour, revealing the breadth of their squadron. The slightest of hesitations rippled through the Jotnar. For a moment, Freya hoped they would pause, but when their leader shouted a command, they surged forward, despite their inferior numbers.

The street erupted in chaos. Within seconds, the two groups merged, the sounds of metal hitting metal ringing out in the empty street. Freya knew it was a matter of minutes before reinforcements arrived, so they had to work quickly.

Freya's heart was in her throat as she caught a Jotnar's blade on her own, the impact shuddering up her arm. Before she could take a breath to recover, he threw out a whip of magic. She ducked, then lashed out with her blade and sliced the knight's leg and stumbled back a step. Her magic surged in her veins, hot and unyielding. She summoned her daggers and let them fly into the cluster of knights surrounding them. She desperately wanted to grab one of the Jotnar by the neck and shove him at Daniel, for him to see reason, but she barely had time to duck the swinging of swords, so her attention remained wholly on the fight before her. Numbers alone told her that her side should come out on top, but the longer they fought, the more knights they would lose, and in a city filled with enemy knights, that could prove deadly very quick. That thought alone had her funneling extra magic into each movement and letting her instinct guide her strikes.

Then, above the din, she heard, "Stand down!"

The command registered just as two Jotnar lunged toward her. Instead of greeting them with her blade, she shoved one away with her boot and hit the other with the pommel of her sword, sending both stumbling back.

"Stand down!" The voice called again. This time, Freya registered a distinct Jotnar accent.

So there is *another ranking officer in town.*

One of the Jotnar before her lunged forward, bloodlust clouding his eyes, but she blasted him with her power, sending him stumbling backward. The second knight spun and scanned the area for the source of the command.

"Listen to your leader," she snapped as she summoned three daggers and poised them to strike. "He said stand down."

Freya looked around, her eyes landing on Daniel where he stood beside a male with shaggy red hair. His face was haggard, making him look like his exhaustion had become an enemy he couldn't shake. As Freya scanned the crowd, she saw that most of the Jotnar were either dead or held at sword point by one of her own, but those who weren't had held up their hands.

Despite the male's weary expression, his face remained hard. "As the new general," he began, glancing toward where the previous general lay dead on the cobblestone, "I'm ordering you all to stand down while I speak with Lord Veldin." When he looked at Freya and Byrric, his lips twisted slightly. "I will hear them out."

Sliding her blade back into its sheath, Freya stepped over the knight sprawled on the ground and walked toward her father. Muttered curses sounded from around her, but to their credit, the knights obeyed their new leader.

"Do you think they'll go for it?" she asked Byrric.

Byrric sheathed his own sword. "Let's go find out."

She glanced up at him, took in two large gashes on his forehead. "You should let Florian heal those."

Absently, he swiped at his forehead with a bloodied hand, doing nothing more than smearing blood across it. "I'll have plenty of time for healing once you're back on your throne. Come on."

She shook her head, but didn't bother arguing as she followed him toward Daniel and the Jotnar General.

Daniel was already speaking earnestly when they approached, so she kept her lips sealed and allowed him to lay out his argument. She noticed his sword was still in his hand, his fingers wrapped loosely around the pommel, almost as if he forgot it was there. Something about that casual stance eased her mind a bit. "You may not care about Lindoroth," he was saying when they came to a stop beside them, "but we both know Willem's war will spill into Jotunheim if it isn't stopped. We need to protect what is ours, Sandson."

"And why do you think you're the best one for the job?" Sandson replied. "Why not Lord Edrin? Lessia named him heir, after all. Clearly she had faith in him."

Daniel snorted. "You and I both know why she named him heir, and it certainly wasn't due to his military prowess. Get your soldiers to follow me so we can ensure that human filth never touches our lands."

Sandson jerked his chin toward Freya. "And what of the Lindorothian monarchs? Our leader stole their crowns. How are we to believe they won't retaliate?"

"The second Willem succeeds in securing the Lind crown, he'll turn on you," Freya said. "If you don't see that, you're—" She cut herself off before calling him a fool. "Misguided. Jonas is currently being held in Errest, and all of the forces Willem has sent to take the city have been destroyed. We *will* defeat him, with or without your help. But as Queen, I would much prefer we end this war on good terms with one another." She looked around at the carnage around them. "As good as can be expected, considering."

Sandson's jaw clenched as he considered her words. "It's mostly humans in the city. You won't find much Jotnar support."

"Where are they all?" Daniel asked.

"Traust ordered most of our kind out of the city." Sandson scanned the sky. "He'll be here soon, I'm sure."

Freya didn't miss the way his tone changed when he mentioned Traust. If she didn't know any better, she'd think he hated Traust just as much as she did.

Then, she heard it. The rattle of armor. Pounding feet on cobblestone. Easily a hundred, if her ears weren't betraying her, and they were about to come around the corner.

"Time to make your choice," Freya said.

Sandson held her gaze for a moment before looking at Daniel. His lips thinned as he scanned the battered remnants of his knights scattered on the street. He gripped his sword tightly, and for a moment Freya thought he might refuse. Finally, he returned his gaze to Daniel. "Fine." Then, raising his voice slightly, he addressed the rest of his knights. "We'll follow Lord Veldin."

Freya turned to see the reactions of the Jotnar knights and was unsurprised to find sour looks on some of their faces. Even so, they were soldiers, and good soldiers followed orders. Thankfully, these seemed to be good soldiers.

"I suppose it's time to test that newfound loyalty," Byrric said, drawing his sword. "Prince Fenian, take our new friend and help him spread the word. The King and Queen have returned to Iladel, and if the Jotnar want to survive to see the end of this war, they'll stand with us."

Fenian gave a sharp nod before gripping Sandson's arm. Before they vanished, Sandson raised his voice and spoke to his knights.

"Stand with Lord Veldin, and we will return home soon." He flicked a gaze toward the end of the street where the sound of approaching human knights had grown louder. If possible, the disgust he wore was greater than he'd shown Freya. "I will return shortly."

Let's hope so, Freya thought.

Freya let her magic pool in her hands. Facing the end of the street, she flared out her wings.

A moment later, hordes of human knights came pouring into the street from both ends.

Reykr Traust was leading the surge.

63

FREYA

Blind rage mixed with determination coated Traust's features as he led his men into the square. He didn't spot Freya or her father right away, but she knew it was only a matter of time. Before she could decide whether to announce her presence or stay silent, chaos erupted around her. It was hard to tell how many human knights Traust had brought with him, but it was immediately apparent it was too many for her side to take out quickly.

Three humans charged her, and she leapt into the air, knocking two back with her wings and two more with her boots. She summoned her daggers and sent them soaring toward all three, then flew like a shot above the battling knights. She wanted to get to Traust. She *needed* to get to him. The sounds of clashing steel, shouted commands, and groans of the injured rose around her as she flew.

Then she saw him. He was cutting through a crowd of Linds as if they were dolls made of straw, ducking elvish magic as he headed directly toward her father, who was deftly fighting off a handful of humans, Florian at his side. Between Florian's magic and Byrric's strength, they were making quick work of them. They didn't need her help.

But Traust was getting closer, and she was *not* going to let some centuries-old vendetta destroy her family.

So, to avoid being an easy target for the rest of her enemies, she touched back down, surprising two humans who were just about to take on an elf. The sharp, metallic end of one of her feathers made quick work of them; then, perhaps stupidly, she aimed for the hulking beast that was now no more than ten feet away. Before she could reach him, though, Byrric shot into the air and took off down one of the side streets.

"He is going to the market!" Fenian shouted from beside her. "I have sent some of my own to assist with removing your kind before the wards around it fail."

She nodded, then pushed forward, using her magic, her blades, her sheer anger and hatred, to take down any knight that came at her. She felt the slice of metal against her arm, but ignored it in favor of taking the head off a human knight. A hit to her ribs with the pommel of a sword barely fazed her as she drove her dagger through the gut of another and sent five of her magic daggers soaring toward two more.

Then, Traust leapt above the battle and took off toward where Byrric had just flown.

Her father had given Traust a choice: take out Byrric or Freya, but he wouldn't get both.

No. Absolutely not.

She spread her wings and leapt into the air, ignoring Fenian's shouts as she sped off toward where her father had gone. An arrow flew past her ear, then another, and she quickly changed course. She flew through the streets of Lindoroth, desperately trying to catch up, but Byrric and Traust were far faster than she was.

She soared above the streets, trying to ignore the scent of smoke that got stronger the closer she got to the market, where the battle had spilled past the square into the streets, but as the sound of the fighting in the square ebbed, she heard the sounds of clashing metal in other parts of the city. The battle was fully underway.

She flew past the blurs of flashing steel, the sparking flicker of magic, the bloodied faces and screams and shouts of the injured and dying. And she ignored them all.

When she reached the market, she scanned the chaotic scene before her for her father. Lind and elf knights fought against humans, battling past them to get to the market, which was fully engulfed in flames, although they seemed to be licking at an invisible barrier, not the wood and stone structure itself.

Her relief at the wards still being in place was short-lived, though, as she focused her attention on locating her father and Traust.

Finally, she found them. They stood among the wrecked street, swords locked. Byrric was holding his ground, but something was wrong. His movements were off and he almost seemed sluggish.

His head wound. It's weakening him. With that thought, she burst forward, forcing her body to fly faster than it ever had.

She was almost there when she saw Byrric falter, his knees dipping ever so slightly under Traust's assault. She gave a hard flap of her wings, trying to fly faster, faster, faster. She was almost—

Traust yanked a dagger from his hip and buried it into Byrric's shoulder. He staggered, falling to one knee. Freya dove, the world blurring around her.

"No!" She swooped low, yanking a sword from the chest of a dead knight, then landed with a force that felt like it could've cracked the cobblestones, placing herself between them.

"Freya, get out of the way!" Byrric roared from behind her.

"Not a chance," she shot back, her wings flaring.

Traust laughed, the sound low and venomous. "Perfect," he sneered. "Now I can kill both of you at once."

Freya widened her stance and forced a smirk onto her face, doing her best to wipe away any visible signs of fear. There was so much fear. "You can try."

"Cocky bastard, just like your father." Two knights ran toward him, clearly hoping to be his backup. His face twisted in fury. "No!" he roared. "These two are mine!"

Before they could respond, Traust threw out his hand, knocking both men back with what little magic he possessed. Then he lunged toward her. Freya sidestepped, her wing striking out like a blade and crashing against his breastplate. Traust growled, turning to attack again, his strikes almost too fast to see. She let her other senses guide her: the sound of armor shifting as he swung a sword, the change in air pressure as his wing crested through the air to hit her.

Freya spun, her stolen sword meeting his, then drove her knee into his gut. Another wing strike sent him stumbling. Again and again, she pressed her advantage—spin, kick, wing—relentless in her assault. He wasn't taking her off guard this time, and she certainly wasn't going to fly off in fear. Every step back she forced him was a victory, and she reveled in each one.

She let her own fury fuel each movement, each bolt of magic she fired his way. Feathers hadn't fazed him before, so she didn't bother trying this time. But her daggers, the ones that never failed her, made of dense air magic, did exactly as she demanded. One in the side under his armpit, another in the neck of his armor, another behind the knee. Despite how terrified she was for her father, her instincts chose not to fail her in that moment.

Not dead, not dead, not dead.

Traust continued to swing his massive sword down at her, but the magic that had ripped open the flesh beneath his arm hindered his movements. He tried to lift a foot to kick her back, but her blade had sliced the tendon behind his knee, so all he succeeded in doing was stumbling forward. Freya dodged out of the way, then kicked her foot out and tripped him, sending him sprawling to the ground, his sword falling from his hand and clattering away.

Another sword lay a few inches from where he fell, though, and he gripped the hilt, then leapt to his feet and swung. She saw the handle just before she ducked the blow—her father's sword. Seeing it defiled in the hands of someone with so much hatred for her only served to fuel her determination.

With a growl, she plowed her foot into his stomach, sending two more daggers into the soft flesh behind his knees as she kicked. Byrric's sword fell to the ground as Traust lost his footing, his legs no longer willing to hold up his massive weight. Her magic was starting to wane, but she couldn't let him see that.

Another kick, but he stumbled forward, now wielding his own dagger.

Movement drew her attention to where her father lay on the ground, distracting her just enough that she nearly took Traust's blade to her gut.

His sword. Byrric's hand was inching toward his sword. As she duck and spun, she caught his eye, and in that moment, his intentions became clear.

Traust lunged at her again, and she side-stepped out of the way, positioning herself in front of her father's form.

"You think you can protect him?" Traust roared, drawing a second dagger. "He's as good as dead, little girl!"

He lunged, and this time, Freya didn't bother fighting back. She stepped out of the way once more, sending Traust off-balance enough that he didn't catch himself before falling forward...directly onto the sword Byrric had positioned to point up.

The sword had been sharp enough, or perhaps magical enough, to pierce the front of his armor, and the *thunk* of metal on metal told her it had cut clean through to his back. But he continued to thrash as he tipped to the side.

Before he could get his hand high enough to pull the sword out, Freya grabbed a spear from the ground beside her and drove it under his helm, plunging it straight through his neck and obliterating his spine.

She let the sword fall to the ground. Normally she would've basked in her victory, but it hardly registered that they'd just killed Reykr Traust. Her immediate thought was of her father, who lay on the street, bloody. She dropped her dagger and ran toward him, skidding to a stop on her knees beside him.

"I was supposed to do that," he admonished when he saw her. His face was pale, far more so than a normal blade would've done. "Ore powder," he murmured.

"No!" Panic surged in her chest. *This can't be happening.*

She'd come so far with no more major losses

He'll heal. He'll heal. He'll heal.

Ore powder is what killed Mother. It killed Salazar. It killed—

"Freya." Her father's calm voice jolted her out of her panic, despite how weak he looked. "Calm down. Go get help."

"Florian!" she screamed. "Get over here!" She looked around frantically, trying to see where her potions master was, only to remember she'd left him fighting back in the square.

"Go get help, Freya," her father repeated. "Florian will have an antidote, but you need to go now."

She nodded, then wiped away her tears and spread her wings, preparing to take flight.

Suddenly, there was a flash of light to her left. She looked up, and the sight before her nearly caused her to weep.

A squadron of knights, human knights, bearing purple and gold crests on their armor, launched themselves into the fray. Not the blue and green of the Ristner house, but something else.

They immediately took up arms against Willem's knights alongside the elves that had appeared with them.

She didn't know whether to be relieved or terrified, but then she saw a flash of whipping white hair as Queen Nalaea fought her way through the battle toward Freya and Byrric.

For a moment, Freya thought she was dreaming. Hallucinating as she took in the hordes of human soldiers now fighting *beside* her people and her allies, not against them. Between that and her father dying at her feet, Freya was struggling to make sense of everything around her. Nothing felt real and yet...her father was *still* lying at her feet, humans were *still* fighting against their own.

Freya was jerked from her reverie by a cool hand shaking her shoulder and the *thud* of magic hitting the ground around them. A shield encircling them, protecting them from the battle. She looked up and found Nalaea gripping her shoulder, trying to pull Freya to her feet.

"I will take him," she shouted. "You are needed at the palace!"

"I'm not leaving!"

Aer is at the palace. Your throne is at the palace.

She shoved the thoughts away

"She's right, Freya," Byrric said with a cough. "You need to go help Aerelius take back your thrones. He needs you."

"Shut up." Freya pressed harder on his stab wound and tried not to let her panic send her spiraling. She looked back at Nalaea. "Who are they?"

Nalaea's smile was wry, and Toskr appeared beside her looking proud, Rini fluttering in the air beside him, a smug look on her face.

"What did you do?" she demanded.

"There are some who value family over power," Nalaea said. She shoved Toskr toward Freya. "Now, go!"

Before she could protest, Toskr grabbed her hand. "It's time, Your Majesty."

She took one last look at Byrric's bloodied face and saw the terror that was barely concealed in his eyes.

"Go, Freya," he said with a cough. "Go defend your crown. Take back your palace."

She couldn't believe he was sending her away. Every ounce of her wanted to fight him on it, tell him she most certainly would not leave him. But when she looked up at Nalaea, she felt suddenly reassured. Whether it was the queen's magic or Freya's faith in her father's judgement was anyone's guess. Whatever it was, it made her decision a simple one. She needed to take back her throne. If her father died right now, it would all be in vain if she didn't have her crown in the end.

So she kissed her father's hand, one of the only places not covered with blood. "I'll be back. You'd better be here."

"I will," he promised. "Go."

She leapt to her feet and took Toskr's hand. They'd barely made contact before he whisked her away.

64

FREYA

Toskr took them to the tiny door under the drawbridge. It was the only place Freya and Aer never went as children, aside from the time Aer dared her to fly under the bridge to confirm its existence. It was also the only place in the palace unlikely to be guarded by humans. Now there was no reason to fly beneath the bridge. For the first time since Salazar Harridan ascended to the throne, the drawbridge was closed. The moss-covered stone beneath was finally exposed to the sunlight that trickled through the clouds.

A mix of awe and unease swirled in her chest and she let her gaze travel upward, toward the towering walls and corner spires silhouetted against the sky. It was no longer the palace she had left behind —it felt colder, more imposing, as if the very walls had absorbed the weight of Willem's tyranny. But it wouldn't stay that way.

Toskr shifted beside her, his sharp eyes scanning the surroundings with sharp intent. "It's too quiet," he murmured, his voice more grave than she'd ever heard.

She checked the bond she shared with Aer and felt his heart racing with exertion, but there was no indication he was injured.

Unlike Father.

Her father, who she'd left lying in the street beside the body of the male who'd wanted to kill him, Freya, and probably anyone else who still possessed Balthana blood.

Traust was dead. It was still hard to comprehend that they'd done it. She and her father had killed him. *She* dealt the killing blow. Part of her felt that honor should've been Byrric's, but it was no matter. Traust would never come after her or her father again.

And now he was gone. Her father might be gone as well. The vision of his blood seeping through her fingers was like a brand in her mind. All she could hear was his raspy voice telling her to go defend her crown. She didn't know where he was or if Nalaea had even managed to get him off the street in time to find help before he was gone.

Gone, gone, gone.

A small hand touched her shoulder, and she jumped, swiping away tears that had begun to leak from her eyes. She smiled when she saw Rini's face hovering beside her.

"I see that face, Your Majesty," Rini said. "Your father needs you to focus on this."

Freya exhaled another slow breath. "I know." She turned and faced the door again, which looked as if it led to a fairy tale world. Solid wood, curved at the top, with a thumb latch handle. Freya could feel magic oozing off of it, so she knew it wouldn't be as simple as pressing the latch.

"Harridan blood?" She looked at Rini.

She nodded.

"I would pull out that pretty dagger of yours if I were you," Toskr said.

She did as instructed, pricking the tip of her finger and releasing a small drop of blood onto the latch. Instantly, it released and the door opened into the yawning darkness.

"Are you ready?" Toskr asked.

She took a deep breath, then nodded. "I am, but you need to go back and help the others. There are enough reinforcements here."

"Nonsense, Queen Freya." Toskr put his hands on his hips and looked up at the palace. "This is precisely where I should be."

She shook out her arms in an attempt to flush out the stress of worrying about her father's injuries. "Alright. Let's go."

As Rini led them into the darkened chamber, Toskr leaned toward Freya. "I'll bet you never expected you would go into your final battle alongside a pixie and a squirrel."

A smile twitched Freya's lips. "Yet here we are."

"I think we're quite competent, thank you," Rini said haughtily. "Now focus."

Freya summoned a ball of light in her hand and set it floating in the air beside them. It was a small, gentle light that fought back some of the damp gloom around them. A narrow twisting staircase rose upward, the torches hung in the sconces, cold.

"Aer and I never explored this one," she whispered as they began their ascent. "I wonder when the last time someone came this way was."

"Many, many years, Queen Freya," Rini replied. "Which is why we're using this entrance and not another."

They continued on slowly for a few minutes, with no one speaking until they reached the top of the stairs and arrived at another door.

"Is it true this is where they used to toss prisoners for executions?" Toskr whispered.

"That's always been a rumor, but—"

"Yes," Rini said. "Wait here." Without giving any more explanation, and without waiting for permission from Freya, she vanished, returning a few heartbeats later. "Alright, the coast is clear, but we must move quickly. Vali and King Aerelius have pushed the humans back to the gardens, but Willem is hiding in the throne room with several Jotnar guarding the doors. He believes they are still loyal to him."

"Well, then, I suppose we should go." Freya stepped toward the door, her heart galloping at the thought of her throne being within arm's reach.

Rini took a deep breath and followed her. "Yes, we should."

With that, Freya pushed open the door.

When she stepped into the torch-lit space, she was surprised to find they were in the hall that led directly to the throne room. Surprisingly, no one stood guard up ahead, although Freya could feel the intense pull of magic coating the door. Willem had either sealed himself in somehow, or he'd been locked in by someone else.

"Elvish magic, Queen Freya," Toskr murmured. "Quite effective at keeping evil human kings locked away, but tricky to get through without the help of an elf."

"Good thing I have you, then."

"Yes, about that–"

Freya felt the press of the air shifting beside her as Fenian arrived, cutting off Toskr's words.. "What is it?" she asked.

"I thought you could use some assistance," the elf replied.

"So your mother sent you?" She gave him a small smile.

He actually had the decency to look abashed. "Well, yes, but I thought it was a solid plan." He looked toward the door. "And the squirrel won't be able to get you through the spell Tavian put on that door."

"Ah. And I suppose you can?"

"Indeed." He held out an arm. "Shall we? I promise to let you draw first blood."

Rini let out a small huff but didn't argue.

A moment later, they were in the throne room where Willem Ristner sat on her throne, surrounded by human knights.

No, not her throne. A crude, dark monstrosity that held none of the richness of the Harridan thrones sat in its place. Its twin sat beside it. *Her* throne was gone, along with Aer's. Pieces of Harridan history Willem and Lessia had the audacity to toss aside, likely burned or rotting in the mass grave behind the palace. They thought removing the thrones would erase the Harridan reign, its legacy, but clearly they knew nothing about Lindorothian determination.

And with that, her fury ignited.

She didn't bother drawing her weapons. He knew what she and the elf prince at her side were capable of.

"*This* is your grand show?" Willem's eyes flicked between her and her companions. "Two elves and a flying rat?" He scoffed. "You're even more pathetic than I thought."

Freya opened her mouth to retort, but Fenian raised his hand and sent a wave of fire toward the dais. The knights surrounding Willem instantly went up in flames, their screams echoing in the high-ceilinged room. The fire consumed them within seconds, leaving only ash and lumps of melted steel behind.

Willem's face turned deathly pale.

Freya gave Fenian a nod of thanks, then smirked at Willem. "I suppose now you understand the true cost of stealing from me."

His throat bobbed as he swallowed. "And what might that be?"

"The world is now against you, Willem." She gestured toward the window. "Elves, Jotnar, and now, more humans are obliterating your men out there."

His jaw clenched as he absorbed her words. "It's no matter. I can go home, regroup. There are others in this world who will support me."

Fenian snorted. "Did you miss the bit where your *own people* are against you?"

Willem attempted to grip the hilt of his sword, but changed his mind halfway there and instead turned to flee toward a door behind the thrones.

"Coward," Freya muttered, walking toward him.

Just as his fingers would've found purchase on the door, Fenian materialized before him, leaning casually against the frame. He was having far too much fun with this, but Freya couldn't say she blamed him.

He chuckled as Willem stumbled back in shock, his arms wheeling as he tried to regain his balance. "Going somewhere?"

Willem spun and ran toward the main entrance, but Toskr leapt forward, shifting in mid-air and landing on his shoulder. He latched onto Willem's neck with his claws and dug his needle-sharp teeth into his ear. The ear-splitting scream Willem let out would've been comical under other circumstances.

Rini darted forward, tossing a handful of pixie dust into Willem's face just as Toskr shifted, one arm wrapped around Willem's neck, the other around his head. "That's for my sisters, you rotten, rotten creature!"

"What shall we do with him, Queen Freya?" Toskr asked, tightening his grip on Willem's neck. "Shall I snap his neck for you?" The human king's face went red, then purple as his air supply diminished. His eyes had taken on a gray sheen thanks to the pixie dust, with tears streaming down his face as he struggled in vain to wipe it away.

"Let him go," Freya said, finally drawing her own blade. She considered using magic, but she wanted to do this with her hands.

Toskr released Willem and shoved him forward. Now free, Willem attempted to swing his sword toward Toskr, but Toskr sidestepped with ease.

Fenian dropped onto the arm of one of the thrones. "Have at it, Your Majesty. Let me know if you need assistance." He flicked a finger, summoning a sword from where one of the knights had dropped it before being incinerated. "This might do a bit better than your dagger, though."

Freya couldn't tear her gaze from the pathetic human in front of her, continuing to swing his sword blindly at each sound.

She reached out and took the offered blade. "Rini, clear his vision."

"Of course, Your Majesty." Rini waved her hand, and Willem's eyes refocused.

With a growl, he charged toward Freya, sword raised. She deflected the blow effortlessly. The crash of steel on steel echoed through the room. Her magic continued to simmer just below her skin, itching to be put to use. Not this time, though. If Willem Ristner thought the only difference between them was a bit of magic, she would show him exactly how powerful she was without it. She countered every swing, driving him back step by step. Each move was precise, calculated, and she put all of her physical strength into each blow.

Willem's attacks grew more frantic as his wild swings began to exhaust him. Freya could see the fear consuming him as his movements became more uncoordinated. Finally, as his movements slowed and breathing became labored, Freya succeeded in driving him back against the wall. As she pressed forward and their swords crossed, she leaned in, letting her blade slide slowly down his until his neck was perfectly positioned between both blades. She pressed a bit harder, and the edges of each blade dug into his skin, drawing twin drops of blood.

His chest heaved with exertion as his wild eyes searched hers. "How do you plan to kill me, then?" he spat.

Freya opened her mouth to respond, but there was a shift in the air behind her. She froze as a growl rumbled through the room. She turned her head slightly, and realization hit.

She looked at Willem, unable to conceal her small smile. "Oh, I'm not going to kill you," she said softly as she stepped aside. "They are."

Any of Willem's remaining bravado shattered as Collin and Laz flanked her in full wolf form. A loud hiss sounded from behind them, and Myria stalked forward. And behind them stood Aer and Lea, their magic coming off them in waves. Ettrian had joined his brother near the throne dais, watching with unabashed amusement.

"You took a lot from me, Willem Ristner." She took another step back and tossed the sword Fenian had given her aside. "But I've already gotten my retribution. Traust is dead. My family is avenged. Now it's their turn."

Willem's sword clattered to the ground. He looked from Freya to the others, his mouth opening and closing, searching for words that would do him no good. Even this close to death, he seemed to fight against defeat, his body poised as if to flee one last time.

But when Myria swiped out a paw, tearing through the leather of his pants and into his thigh and drawing a high-pitched shriek of pain, Freya saw it finally register. Willem Ristner knew this was the end. His reign over the humans was over. His line was ending. With no sons to pass his crown to, his brother would be the one to see the Ristner line carried on.

Willem Ristner was, really and truly, a dead man.

"He's all yours," she murmured.

The last thing she saw before Fenian took her back to her father were Willem Ristner's terror-filled eyes.

65

LEA

Lea could've stood there all day beside her cousin, savoring the sight of Willem Ristner cowering against the throne room wall. She would never feel more gratitude toward her queen than she did in that moment, watching Laz, Collin, and Myria stalk closer to the human king. She stared at Willem's terrified face and smirked, happy to let this moment stretch just a little bit longer.

She felt the flicker of spirit magic as Aer let it pool in his hands beside her. Whatever fury she felt, she knew his ran deeper. Willem hadn't just taken Aer's father—he'd stolen his home and defiled it with greed. The halls Aer had played in as a child were now smeared with blood, and the courtyard where he'd trained as a boy had become a holding ground for human prisoners.

In that moment, her cousin was no longer the lighthearted prince she'd grown up with. Now, he was a king on the cusp of vengeance. The anger she felt over her own losses intensified as she thought about how painful the memories of his coronation would be.

Willem's eyes darted around the room, his panic rising as he found no escape. When his gaze landed on the two elf princes leaning against the thrones, his fear twisted into a sneer.

"You aren't even going to help them? With all of your great elvish magic?" His tone was mocking, but the fear in his eyes didn't lessen. Blood continued to gush from his thigh, but Lea couldn't tell if it was the blood loss or fear that had his face taking on a gray pallor.

Fenian chuckled. "You think any of them need our help getting rid of you?"

Ettrian dropped into the throne Willem had just occupied and slung one leg over the arm. "We're here for the entertainment and nothing more. I haven't seen a well-deserved execution in quite some time. Feel free to take your time, Your Majesty. Just be sure to let Lady Calliwell take a bite or two." He clicked his teeth menacingly, his fangs on full display.

Lea smiled at that.

Aer's cold glare didn't leave Willem, but his lips twitched in amusement. "Gladly." His voice was deathly cold. "I see that look on your face, Willem. You still think someone will come to your aid."

Lea snorted. She extended her hand to summon her vines, the same thorny tendrils she'd used to defend herself against Willem in the gardens. Slowly, they crept over the window sills and floor, inching toward Willem. "Did you ever even lift a blade? Or did you sit in your stolen palace like the coward you are?"

Aer sent out twin ropes of magic, letting his power spread across the floor toward Willem at a glacial pace between Laz, Collin, and Myria.

Myria, trembling with rage, let out a low, guttural hiss. Willem's gaze flicked to her as she flexed her claws slowly against the stone floor.

Willem's face darkened with anger, though his trembling hands gave him away. "You're weak," he spat at Aer, then turned his glare on Lea. "The both of you. You'll just have your pets—"

The rest of his words choked off as Aer's magic lashed out, wrapping around his throat in a glowing noose. "And that's where we're different, Willem." He stepped closer as Willem writhed against the tightening magic. "I don't mind sharing this moment."

Lea's vines surged forward, binding Willem's wrists and ankles to the wall. The thorns bit deeper, drawing blood as they pierced his skin. Beside her, Aer's magic squeezed, cutting off Willem's breath as his face turned purple.

Pathetic, Lea thought as she watched him struggle.

Myria let out a low, guttural growl. Her claws scraped against the stone, leaving deep grooves. Willem's gaze flicked to her, panic flashing in his eyes.

Myria hissed, then lunged. Her claws raked through Willem's torso, severing flesh and bone. He screamed, but the sound was cut short as Aer's magic tightened, and blood bubbled past his lips.

Distantly, Lea heard Ettrian's approving laugh, but it was too far away, too detached from this moment. This cruel, glorious moment. She let her vines tighten their grip, curving so the ends pierced through Willem's shoulders.

Willem screamed, his bloodshot eyes darting to Lea and Aer as Laz and Collin leaned back on their haunches. Myria's tail flicked once, then twice as she crouched low to spring. Aer let his spirit surge, his power holding Willem by the throat, arms, and legs. The human king thrashed and tried to scream, but the only sound that came out was a sickening gurgle as he choked on his own blood.

Lea stood there for a moment and watched as Willem finally realized he'd been defeated. Gory as it was, it was a sight she would commit to memory and carry with her every day for the rest of her life. Grim satisfaction spread through her as she touched her cousin's arm.

"Have at it, cousin," she said to Aer, tightening her vines' grip on Willem.

"Take him down," Aer growled.

Laz, Collin, and Myria lunged.

The room filled with the wet, visceral sounds of tearing flesh and cracking bone, punctuated by Willem's strangled cries. His struggles slowed, then stopped entirely as the life drained from him.

And then, as suddenly as it had started, it was over.

The silence that followed felt heavy, almost sacred. Blood pooled beneath Willem's mangled body, soaking into the stone. Lea stared at what remained of the man who had taken so much from them, committing the moment to memory.

Finally, she let out a slow breath and turned to Aer. "It's done."

Aer's magic faded from his hands, and for a moment, he simply stood there, his shoulders rising and falling with each measured breath. Lea touched his arm, and his eyes slowly slid toward hers. His hardened expression softened as he pulled her into a bone-crushing hug.

Laz, Collin, and Myria all shifted back into their Lind forms. Myria's eyes were red with tears, and the fury that pulsed off of Laz and Collin was palpable. Lea held out a hand toward Myria, who still looked as if she hadn't quite left the lioness behind. Gingerly, she took Lea's hand and closed her eyes, exhaling a slow, measured breath.

"I need to go home," Myria said, looking at the princes. "To tell my mother, my brother..." She pursed her lips and swallowed. "I need to tell them."

For once, Fenian didn't look annoyed about acting as transport. "I will take you. I need to report to our forces throughout Lindoroth, let them know the fighting can end."

Ettrian came to a stop beside Lea. Instinctively, she leaned against him, allowing herself to relax just a little.

"We need to go back to the city, let them all know the king is dead," Aer said.

Ettrian slid a hand up to Lea's shoulder. "Then let's go."

66

FREYA

The market that had been in chaos just an hour earlier was quiet when Freya returned after leaving Willem to his death. The reinforcements Nalaea brought had made quick work of their enemies, and now the streets were littered with the bodies of human knights, all bearing the blue and green emblem of Willem Ristner's house. Her own kind and many elves and Jotnar lay there, too, but in much smaller numbers.

She and Toskr stood there for a silent moment, Rini hovering beside them. It had all ended so quickly, and seemingly in their favor. Willem's knights who'd opted to surrender were lined up in rows in the market square, with Ruehnar and Daniel pacing in front of them.

Freya could still hear pockets of fighting in other areas of the city, but her singular focus was on finding her father and confirming Nalaea had done what she'd promised. There was no sign of the elf queen or Byrric in the market, nor did she see the man who'd been fighting alongside Nalaea when she'd arrived.

"Where are they?" she muttered to no one in particular.

Rini cleared her throat. "I will find them, Your Majesty."

Once she'd vanished, Freya and Toskr strode toward the cluster of humans on their knees and came to a stop beside Daniel. "Is this all that's left?" she asked.

"Here, yes," he confirmed. "Our knights will make quick work of the rest. Lindoroth is yours once again."

"And your father is safe," Ruehnar said. "He and I have sent officers throughout your kingdom to inform the other camps that the war is done."

Freya's eyes fell shut as relief settled over her. "Thank the gods."

"And the human king?" Daniel asked her. "What of him?"

"I'm sure Aerelius and the others will be along shortly to recount his death."

Daniel gave her a slow, appreciative nod.

Freya turned to her friend. "Who were they, Toskr? The humans who came with Nalaea?"

His eyes drifted over her shoulder. "I'll let them tell you."

Freya followed the direction of his stare, then nearly crumpled when she saw her father standing beside Florian and Nalaea. He was bloody and looked weak, but he was on his feet. With a sob, she launched herself at him, burying her face in his shoulder as she cried with relief. He was safe. He was whole. He was alive. Her father was *alive*.

It was then that she noticed the two humans standing behind him. One was short with gray hair and piercing blue eyes, while the other was much younger and more regal-looking despite his dented and blood-spattered armor.

Slowly, Freya extricated herself from Byrric's embrace and looked the men over. "Who are you?" she asked.

The younger man stepped forward and bowed his head. "Benjamin Whitmore, Your Majesty. It's a pleasure to make your acquaintance."

Freya dragged her eyes from Benjamin to the older man at his side. "And you?"

"Silas Brisbane, Your Majesty. I'm told my daughter is currently... under your care."

"Daughter?" She blinked, then turned shocked eyes on Nalaea. "What—"

"Lord Brisbane is Isadora's father, Freya," Nalaea said. "As I said, some people value family over power."

"Surprise," Toskr whispered.

FREYA REFUSED to have any further conversations without Aerelius present, partly because he was her husband and king, but mainly because she knew the discussion they would need to have with Silas Brisbane and Benjamin Whitmore would take far more time than they had to dedicate while standing in the midst of a ruined city. So, after Aer and the others returned to announce the human king was really and truly dead, and after Byrric, Fenian, and Daniel doled out orders for their knights to get to work clearing the streets, Freya and Aer escorted all necessary parties to the throne room.

Freya tried to ignore the way the throne room looked now that it had been stripped bare of all Harridan influence. The beautiful thrones, golden touches, and Harridan colors that would unfurl along the wall would come later, when replacements could be made for the one Willem and Lessia had burned. Dina and Oliver, ever the steadfast servants, had made sure everything that hinted at Willem or Lessia's presence was gone, along with Willem's remains. Although, Freya wasn't sure she'd ever be able to look at the wall beside the throne room door without seeing Willem's ruined body again.

What was harder to ignore was the look on Lea's face as she took in the room. Fury first, then sadness. Freya nearly told Ettrian to take her home, but Lea had just as much a right as the rest of them to hear from their new allies.

As she and Aer sat on two chairs Dina and Oscar had placed on the dais to act as temporary thrones, she tried to find a smidge of happiness, the thrill of success, satisfaction, anything. When no logical emotions came, she assumed she was probably still in shock.

So, as was her habit, she ignored it and took Aer's hand. "We made it, my love," she whispered as he sat beside her.

He gave her a smile. "I knew we would." He looked at the rest of the room's occupants, his eyes looking over Silas Brisbane, Isadora's father and owner of a massive fleet of human ships, before landing on Benjamin Whitmore. "Now, let's hear how this all came to be. Lord Whitmore, as you are currently steward in Dystone, I'll start with you."

"Of course, Your Majesty." Benjamin stepped forward and cleared his throat. He seemed a bit nervous, Freya noted, but not the least bit wary. "The Ristners and my family have been close allies for many generations now, which is how my betrothal with Rosie came about. About a year ago, my father approached me and asked what my thoughts were on helping the crown acquire some new territory for Dystone. I agreed, as I knew that had been something Willem's father, the late king, had wanted to do for a large portion of his reign. A few months ago, my father told me the elves were leaving their shores and your kind were joining with them to march on Dystone. He said we'd acquired a new ally with Lessia Edrin, but we had to act quickly to ensure our kingdom's safety. Willem said we needed to seize Lindoroth before you could launch an attack on our lands."

"And you were amenable to that?" Aer asked.

Benjamin ducked his head. "I was, Your Majesty. Willem seemed desperate, panicked, as if he truly feared for the safety of our kingdom. I never knew the Linds to be a vicious people, but I took him at his word because he was my king."

"What changed your mind?" Freya asked. "Clearly something changed, considering our current circumstances," she said, gesturing toward Nalaea and Silas.

"Lord Brisbane approached me about one month ago, just before your wedding." Benjamin looked at Silas. "If it's alright, I'd like to allow him to tell this part."

"Your Majesties," he said with a nod. "Not long after the king and queen left for your shores, I received a letter from Dania Edrin. In it, she explained everything—how she had replaced my daughter when

Isadora was a child, posed as her for the past ten years. She said all the things you would expect someone in her shoes to say—it was never something she wanted, she'd been forced by her empress, and she wanted us to know the truth. She also told us where we might find Isadora, if we were so inclined."

"She wasn't planning on returning," Freya murmured. "She never intended to go back to Dystone." She looked at Reginald, who stood to the side, his face a mask of shock. When he felt her stare, he met her eyes and shook his head, clearly unaware Dania had decided to leave Dystone permanently.

"I had no idea, Your Majesties," he rasped. "We planned to leave, but only if we couldn't get Willem out of the way."

"It sounds as though she had other plans," Fenian murmured.

"Continue," Aer said, flicking a hand toward Silas.

"I am a curious man by nature," Silas went on. "Christopher Ristner, Willem's father, had been quite insistent on my Isadora marrying Willem, but it had never been lost on me that she and Prince Reginald had developed a friendship of sorts." He looked at Reginald. "My wife and I assumed when the betrothal was formalized, that friendship would wither." He cleared his throat. "I immediately thought the letter a fake, so I began digging. I'd heard of an elf witch who'd come to stay in Dystone, so I sought her out. She was, by all accounts, a gifted seer, and I thought she might be able to cut away some of the cobwebs and show me the truth. She did, and more. When I learned what had become of my Isadora, my wife and I— there was no question that we would do anything to get her back, even if that meant going against our king."

"A wild guess—was her name Kosandra?" Freya asked.

Silas nodded. "It was, Your Majesty."

"Lord Brisbane contacted me immediately," Benjamin replied. "I spoke with the witch, as well. She informed me that Willem was keeping Rosie locked in the palace. I've heard tales that elves can't lie, so I took her at her word just as I had Willem. I love Rosie, so when I heard she'd become a prisoner, I simply couldn't stand by any longer."

"She wasn't a prisoner, though," Lea said. "Rosie had free run of the place, as far as I could tell."

"Willem was always very clear that she was not to leave the palace grounds," Ettrian said with a shrug. "Presumably, the palace gates were locked. Technically, Kosandra did not lie."

"What was her goal, though?" Freya asked. "How did telling you both these things benefit her in any way?" She'd believed Fenian when he said Kosandra would've had ulterior motives to helping Isadora and Willem, but she still couldn't see the logic in putting so much effort into sowing discord among the humans.

Vali chuckled. "Brilliant."

Freya frowned. "What?"

Vali's smile turned into one of appreciation. "The Ristner's chose the Brisbanes and Whitmores to marry into their line due to the size and skill of their armies. Turn those armies against the crown, and the kingdom will be turned on its head."

"Why, though?" Aer looked at Ruehnar. "How does a war in the human kingdom help an exiled elf?"

Ruehnar shrugged. "Boredom would be my guess. She was the catalyst for the last war between the humans and elves, too. She had no reason to do that other than greed. My assumption is this time is no different."

Freya sighed and dragged her gaze back to Nalaea. "And where is Kosandra now?"

Nalaea's answering grin was feral. "Awaiting the future queen of Avorell in the Forest of Ages."

"Then I suppose we both managed to tie up some loose ends," Aer said.

"How did this... alliance come about?" Freya gestured toward Nalaea and the two human men. "The last I heard, communication between Avorell and...anywhere was all but nonexistent."

Nalaea's gaze flicked to Rini, Tyna, and Toskr, who hovered off to the side, all three looking abashed. The two pixies fluttered forward.

Tyna took a deep breath. "I spent a good deal of time with Princess Rosie in Errest. She wanted nothing more than to be home with her betrothed, and she was quickly becoming convinced Willem was precisely what we all knew him to be." She looked at Benjamin. "So...Toskr, Rini, and I took turns..." Her face went beet red, then the rest of her words came out in a rush. "We visited Lords Whitmore and Brisbane and told them everything."

"Then we went to Queen Nalaea and–" Rini exhaled and looked at Freya beseechingly. "Oh, Your Majesty, I *know* you had agreements in place with the elves, but we just thought–"

"Your pixies suggested I encourage Lords Whitmore and Brisbane to join your cause," Nalaea said. "As Kosandra has been a thorn in my side for centuries, I thought we might kill two birds with one stone, so to speak. Return the witch to Avorell while also liberating Lindoroth."

A silence hung over the throne room as everyone absorbed Nalaea's words.

Finally, Freya smiled at Toskr and the two pixies. "So, this is where you three were when you weren't around?"

Rini and Tyna slumped with relief, and Toskr stood a bit taller.

"It was, Queen Freya," Toskr said. "I hope we didn't overstep."

Aer cleared his throat when Freya couldn't think of a response. "We'll table this discussion for now, but we'll need to cover this in more detail later." He looked at Silas. "Lord Brisbane, you said you wanted to get your daughter back. As you know, she's currently a prisoner of war. She conspired with Willem Ristner to destroy not only our kingdom, but the empire of Jotunheim. Why should we hand her over?"

Freya's heart ached at the sadness in Silas' eyes.

"You have every right to try her for her crimes," Silas said. "But I failed my daughter, Your Majesties. I would like the opportunity to right that wrong."

Freya and Aer exchanged a look. It was an impossible choice—try Isadora for her crimes against Lindoroth, just as they would any other prisoner of war, or allow Isadora to try to start over, free of the influences of Willem and Lessia. By her account, she'd begged her parents not to marry her off to Willem, told them of his cruelty, but those pleas had fallen on deaf ears. They had followed through with their plans, despite her wishes, and she let her resentment and hatred toward them grow. Obviously the Brisbanes had no way of knowing how their daughter would end up, and Isadora was responsible for her own actions, of course. But still—allowing Isadora to live out her life went counter to everything they'd been fighting for the past month.

"That will need to be a longer discussion, as well," Aer said after a moment, turning back to Silas. "We'll have her brought to Iladel. You can visit with her, at the very least, until we come to a decision."

"Thank you, Your Majesties," Silas said with a bow.

Freya looked around the room, letting her gaze fall on each person present.

Aer squeezed her hand, grounding her. She looked at him, seeing the fatigue etched into his features that mirrored what she felt inside. He gave her a weary smile that spoke of relief and the weight they now bore together—the weight of their crowns, of rebuilding their kingdom, and of ensuring the people they'd crafted allegiances with continued to stay true.

"That's enough for today," Aer murmured to her.

She nodded, letting his words settle in her heart as she looked around the room once more. The throne room was a blank slate, a reminder of what they'd lost, but a symbol of their victory. They would rebuild, make their land a thriving place that spat on the memory of Willem Ristner and Lessia Edrin.

Aer stood from his seat. "We'll reconvene tomorrow after we've all had a chance to rest. We have a lot to discuss," he said, his eyes going to the humans. "I have a feeling those discussions will demand far more attention than we have to offer at the moment. The servants will arrange accommodations for you all."

One by one, each of the room's occupants left. When the room was empty, Aer took Freya's hand and kissed her knuckles. "We should rest, too."

Freya nodded. "Yes, I suppose we should."

Rini fluttered to her side. "Your chambers have been prepared for you both, Your Majesties."

"Thank you, Rini," Freya said with a smile. "We'll be right there."

Rini curtsied. "Of course, Your Majesty."

Once she left, Aer stood, then walked slowly toward a window that faced east. Wordlessly, he held out a hand for Freya to join him.

When she stepped to his side, she wrapped an arm around his waist and followed his gaze. Together, they looked out over their kingdom, at the city of Iladel far below, the glittering ocean beyond. It was theirs, once again. The war was over and the future, uncertain as it was, belonged to them.

Tomorrow, they would begin to rebuild it.

67

LEA

The first thing Lea did when she returned home after she gave her mother and aunt the news of their victory was visit Rosie Ristner's room. Now that news was spreading that Lindoroth had emerged victorious, word would get back to her about her brother's death. Servants wouldn't bother holding in their excitement, nor would the city hold back on ringing out the bells of celebration. Rosie, despite everything, deserved to hear it from Lea.

She found the princess in her bedroom, sitting on her bed reading a book, the door open for once. Or at least, she was pretending to read a book. Lea wasn't convinced the look of concentration Rosie wore was entirely genuine. She hesitated in the doorway for a moment before knocking lightly on the frame.

"He's dead, isn't he?" Rosie said without looking up, her voice barely a whisper.

Lea stepped inside the room, her boots scraping softly against the wood. "He is. Lindoroth is back in my people's hands."

"Did you do it?" Rosie's voice was tight, her eyes still trained on the page before her.

Lea hesitated before responding. "I...yes, I had a hand in it." She took a few more steps closer, then stopped when Rosie's sharp eyes shot to her. "I thought you deserved to hear it from me."

Rosie stared at her, waiting. Then after a few silent beats, she scoffed. "What? No 'I'm sorry, Rosie'?"

Lea let out a measured breath. "I am sorry for your loss, Rosie, but I will not insult you by pretending I'm sorry he's gone. He tried to destroy my kingdom. He killed my father, my uncle. We both know this is the ending I wanted."

Rosie held her gaze for a moment, then let the book fall in her lap. Her eyes continued to simmer with anger, but then that shifted toward sadness and finally, something Lea thought looked strangely like relief, before the tears started. Great, hiccuping sobs that had the princess sitting up, holding a hand to her chest.

Lea rushed toward her and sat down on the bed beside Rosie, then wrapped an arm around her and pulled her close. The princess fought her for a moment, but her attempts to push Lea away were so half-hearted even she knew it was pointless to pretend. Instead, she let Lea hold her while she cried.

They sat like that for a few minutes, Lea letting her get it all out and Rosie allowing Lea to give her that small bit of comfort.

Once Rosie had settled a bit, her sobs smaller, sighs hitched, Lea leaned back and put her hands on her arms. "There is some good news."

Rosie eyed her dubiously. "Somehow I doubt that."

"Benjamin is here. He arrived in Iladel not long after I did."

Rosie sat up, her eyes wide, tears forgotten. "Benjamin is here? Truly?"

Lea nodded. "He came to help us. He came for you."

Rosie's lips parted, her breath catching. "He came for me?"

"He did. And if you'd like, I can take you to him when Ettrian and I return to Iladel in the morning." It was the one thing she'd been adamant about with Freya and Aer before she left.

For a moment, Rosie looked as though she might cry again, but then a tentative smile broke through the storm of emotions on her face. "Yes, I would very much like that!" Then she deflated. "Wait. If he was here to help defeat Willem..."

"He was here to defeat Willem, but he came because he hadn't heard from you," Lea said gently. "He didn't say it outright, but I don't think he's been getting any of your letters."

Rosie's eyes fell shut, then she smiled and wiped away her tears. "It's no matter. He's here now. He will take me home and..." She frowned. "Who will rule Dystone?" Panic filled her eyes. "My kingdom—there's no ruler!"

Lea took her hand. "I don't know. Legally, Reginald is next in line." She pressed forward when Rosie's face went stormy. "It's how these things work, Rosie, and he may not even want it."

"Oh, he will," Rosie muttered. "This is what he wanted all along, wasn't it?"

"Not like this," Lea assured her. "But save that for tomorrow, alright?" She smoothed back the princess's red hair. "For now, just sleep peacefully, knowing Benjamin is waiting for you."

Rosie nodded. "Yes, you're right. And I suppose Reginald wouldn't make the worst king." She smiled. "He is a Ristner, after all."

Lea smiled tightly, still utterly flummoxed at how quickly Rosie could slip into a deferential role. She hoped that wouldn't cause her problems in her marriage, but somehow, she didn't think it would.

She squeezed Rosie's arm. "You'll be alright, Rosie. You have people who care about you, but I want you to make sure you care for yourself, too."

Rosie gave her a small smile and nodded. "I know. Oh!"

Lea frowned. "What is it?"

"Lord Edrin—what will happen to him?" Rosie's cheeks reddened. "I—he was always quite kind to me at the palace, even though his aunt was just dreadful."

Jonas. She'd barely thought about Jonas since she'd left Errest. "Daniel Veldin will take control of Lindoroth," she said. "I'm not entirely sure what will happen to Jonas once they return."

"Yes, I suppose I can understand that." She sighed, then, to Lea's surprise, leaned forward and wrapped Lea in a tight embrace. For a single heartbeat, Lea froze, not sure how to respond. But when Rosie's arms tightened, she returned the embrace, patting a tentative hand on the princess's back.

"Thank you," Rosie said, her words muffled in Lea's hair.

"For what?" Lea asked. She frowned when Rosie pulled back and looked at her.

"You didn't have to show me any kindness once you took me from Iladel, but you did." She gestured between them. "And this...you could've just left me to find out about my brother from gossiping servants, but you didn't. I don't know whether I would've done the same in your shoes."

"Hopefully, we never have to find out." Lea patted Rosie's hand and stood. "Plan to leave first thing tomorrow. And Rosie?" She waited for the princess to meet her eyes. "I *am* sorry for all you've lost."

LATER THAT NIGHT, Lea found herself up on her home's battlements again. The silence in her bedroom was thunderous, but the quiet that hung over the city wasn't quite so weighty. It was a peaceful feeling, filled with the knowledge that their enemies had been vanquished and soon they'd be able to open the city gates once more.

She wanted to sleep, knew she needed to. Ora had brought her a pot of tea to her room, but no matter how many cups she drank, she couldn't get her mind to stop racing over all that had happened over the past few days. She also couldn't quite wrap her head around the fact that they were safe. Willem Ristner was dead and she had a hand in killing him. It was a heady feeling, knowing she'd been able to accomplish the one thing she'd wanted more than anything this whole time.

And yet here she was, pacing the walls, unable to sleep because she couldn't get the image of his terrified face—the face he wore just before she and her cousins tore him apart—out of her mind.

Quiet footsteps sounded at her back, and she smiled.

"You look like you could use another distraction," Ettrian said, coming to a stop beside her. Together, they leaned against the wall and stared at the flickering lights of the encampment.

"I'd say that's putting it mildly. I helped dismember, disembowel, and behead a man today, and now I can't get the image out of my mind." She looked down at the wall, then at him. "Will it stop? Ever?"

Ettrian brushed a finger along her face. "Eventually, yes. If you were anyone else, I would say you will get used to it, but I don't see you finding yourself in a similar situation anytime soon." He smiled when she leaned into his touch. "I hope not, anyway."

She looked up into his golden eyes and watched as he studied her. "What is it?"

He touched a thumb to her lower lip. "I was trying to decide whether this would be a good moment to kiss you. You know, to distract you."

A smile forced its way onto her lips. "You should always kiss me, Ettrian," she whispered.

"Always?" He turned her so she was leaning with her back to the wall and lowered his lips to hers in a gentle kiss. "As in, forever?" Then a second, this one setting her insides on fire.

She considered his words. Forever for him meant something much different than it did for her. For her kind, forever might be a thousand years. For an elf...it could easily be double that. But that was a problem for another day.

"Forever...is a distinct possibility." Her heart picked up a bit as all thoughts of war and murder slipped away.

"Is that so?" He drew a hand down her side. "Does that mean you've considered where you'd like to find yourself, now that we're on the other side of war?"

Now that we're on the other side of war.

In that moment, the weight of their victory settled in her chest, just as something lifted from her shoulders. Grief, anger, hatred... it all felt a bit lighter now that she knew the cause of it all was gone from this world. She would carry them with her for a long time, perhaps always, but they didn't weigh her down now the same way they had yesterday.

She turned her head, looked out over her city, then beyond it, to Edhil and the whole of Lindoroth. She thought back to their conversation about returning to school, finishing her education. It all just seemed so... small.

She wanted something more, and when she looked at the prince, whose golden eyes were searing into hers, she knew she wanted it with him.

She placed her hand on his chest, then ran her fingers through his dark hair. "I want you to show me the world, Ettrian."

He cupped her cheek in his hand, then let his hand drift down her neck, then her side, before curling his fingers around her hips. "The world, hmm?" He kissed her deeply, his touch filled with a gentleness that surprised her, then rested his forehead against hers. "That's quite an ask for someone who considered me a 'stupid elvish bastard' not two weeks ago."

For once, she didn't have a quip to throw back at him. She was too consumed with the way his hands moved, the way his body felt pressed against hers. "Let's just say my feelings have evolved."

He ran his lips along her neck, then stopped at her ear. She shivered at his nearness, then curled her fingers into his tunic as she pulled him closer. "Evolved to what, little witch?"

Her hand found the back of his neck, her fingers tangling in his hair as she dragged his mouth to hers in a kiss so searing and full of passion, she didn't need any words to convey the emotions.

Even so, she pulled back, separating their bodies just far enough to whisper, "I think I might be falling in love with you, Your Highness."

His eyes held hers, flickering with happiness. "And I, you."

And in that moment, Lea knew all would soon be right with the world.

EPILOGUE

It was nearly three months before Freya and Aerelius could have their official coronation ceremony. By the time they were able to plan the celebration they all so desperately wanted, and needed, spring was well underway. The air was clear, the trees were lush with foliage, and the palace gardens were ripe with blooms, all helped along with a solid mix of earth magic from Lea, Perida, and Ordona. There were no signs anywhere of the horrors that had swept through the palace or the kingdom.

Instead, the throne room, now returned to its former glory, brimmed with life and light. Sconces flickered along the walls, their glow making the golden curtains shimmer like flames. The tapestries that once adorned the walls had been returned to their rightful place, and flowers from the gardens spilled from vases scattered throughout the room. A long, red carpet ran from the door directly to the dais where two beautiful thrones, carved from Caeloran oak by the elves as a gift from the Tordoves, now stood. The arms were wrapped in leather from Allanor, the edges dotted with Errestian emeralds, and the finest Saithian silks covered the cushions. Much like the royal wedding, the thrones now encompassed every aspect of Lindoroth.

The gown Rini had chosen for Freya was ice blue and scattered with opals, its gold embroidery catching the light each time she moved. The back was open nearly to her waist, leaving her wings on display. And, just as she'd done on Freya's wedding day, Rini dusted Freya's wings with a smattering of pixie dust, giving them an ethereal glow befitting a Valkyrie queen. Aerelius, of course, had insisted on matching, so he wore a doublet in the same shade of blue, stitched with the same gold thread that ran through Freya's gown.

But it was the crown on her head that Freya noticed the most. It had been a phantom these past few months–there but not. Its weight grounded her, reminded her of who she was, what she'd lost, and, most importantly, what she'd won. People had come from all across the kingdom to watch as Ordona set their crowns on their heads, while Florian spoke the official coronation words. Now, as Freya sat beside her husband and watched their subjects talking, laughing, drinking, *living*, she smiled. Aer took her hand, lacing their fingers together as he laid a kiss to her knuckles.

"You're quiet," he murmured.

"I'm just taking it in," she replied. "All of it. All of them."

Her gaze swept across the hall, lingering on the familiar faces scattered around the room. Ana, now happily employed as the palace physician, sat at a table with Vara and a few other Valkyrie. Vara had been on one of her journeys, having returned only for the ceremony before she would continue on her way. Lazarus and Collin stood with Myria near a table laden with food, deep in discussion. Lazarus and his mother had brought Kildin back from the brink, with rebuilding well under way in the city, and Lazarus settling nicely into his position as Governor. Myria had fallen right back into her role as a proper lady of Saith, with her brother running the realm, while Collin's cousin had easily taken over for Collin's uncle as governor. Ordona stood nearby speaking with Perida, who'd been elected governor of Edhil in a landslide. Ever the leader, Ordona had been spending most of her time in Errest acting as one of Perida's advisors.

Toward the back of the room, near the door, Reginald sat with a group of Linds, seeming to be regaling them with some story—no doubt about his travels. He'd refused to take the crown in Dystone, instead handing it to Benjamin Whitmore, who was reshaping the kingdom into something newer and better. Although the people of Dystone had considered Willem a good ruler, the machinations behind closed doors indicated otherwise. Benjamin and Rosie had married in a royal wedding that, by all accounts, rivaled Freya and Aer's in grandiosity.

As Freya thought about how Reginald had willingly handed the crown to Benjamin, she couldn't help but think about Jonas. Daniel had tried him for conspiring to kill Lessia, but, after conferring with his advisors, had agreed to excommunication instead of execution. Jonas now lived in western Jotunheim not far from Utgard, slowly rebuilding his life. Toskr, who'd opted not to return to Avorell, had also taken up residence in western Jotunheim, although he still spent a fair bit of time visiting Iladel.

It was Lea who brought Freya the most happiness, though. She and Ettrian, who'd been traveling to one place or another for the past two months, stood near a window in the corner of the hall. Lea had her back to the wall and Ettrian stood in front of her, an arm braced on the wall beside her as he whispered in her ear. The smile on her face as he spoke, the laugh that sounded briefly over the din, the love that poured from them both, had Freya's heart nearly bursting.

"You still worry about her," Aer said, leaning toward her.

"I do," Freya agreed. "He's an elf prince with a claim to their throne."

"I don't think you need to worry." Aer gestured toward the other Tordove princes who stood speaking with Byrric and Florian. "Ettrian isn't the one with interest in the crown."

Freya smiled at him, amused. "So I don't have to worry about Nalaea and Ruehnar forcing her to run the Wild Hunt?"

Aer shook his head. "I don't think Ettrian would allow it, anyway." He chuckled. "Although, Lea might insist on it if there's any hint they find her unworthy."

Freya's eyes found Nalaea, standing with Ruehnar, watching the room just as Freya was, and followed her gaze. The queen's expression was calm, almost...happy as she looked at Ettrian and Lea. "Somehow I don't see that being the case."

A cheer erupted from the far side of the room, drawing Freya's attention to where Lazarus and Collin were toasting with a group of Iladel's most prominent business owners. The city, like the rest of Lindoroth, was on the path to recovery. Soon, its streets would be full to bursting with patrons, tradesmen, and travelers.

"Freya," Aer said softly, pulling her from her thoughts.

She turned to him. "Hmm?"

He smiled and held out a hand. "Dance with me?"

At some unseen signal, the music began to play a bit louder. They stood, and she let him lead her to the center of the hall, the crowd parting for them as they began their first dance as the King and Queen of Lindoroth.

"So, what comes next, my love?" Aer asked, touching a kiss to her temple.

"We travel around the kingdom, like we planned," Freya replied, leaning into him. "See our people, help where we can. Be the king and queen this kingdom needs." She hesitated, then, "Or is there something more?"

He cleared his throat, then looked down at her. "I want... I don't want you to think I'm not content with what we have, and I know we talked about waiting, but I want..."

She smiled at how flustered he seemed. "A family?" She laughed as he spun her, then pulled her tight, their lips a breath apart.

"We nearly lost everything," he whispered and tightened his hand on her waist. "I want the world with you and I can't fathom leaving it without seeing our children."

She bit her lip, then closed her eyes as he leaned down to kiss her softly, giving no care that the entire room was watching them. When he pulled back, she held his gaze, so deep and piercing she could feel it in her soul. She twined her arms around his neck as they spun in a slow circle. "As it happens, I've been thinking the same."

Hope sparked in his eyes. "Is that so?"

She cupped his cheek in her hand. "I want to build the perfect future with you, Aer. I've always wanted that."

For a moment, they held each other's eyes. Then, quicker than she could react, he dipped her low and kissed her with far more passion than was appropriate for their circumstances. But she didn't care. As he righted her, leaving them both breathless, she grinned, unable to contain her happiness as it all sunk in. Their kingdom was safe. They were back in their home making plans for the future. Her heart filled with a certainty that they were ready for whatever came next.

For the first time in ages, Freya allowed herself to believe in the promise of tomorrow.

THANK YOU!

Thank you so much for taking the time to read *The Valkyrie's Triumph!* If you enjoyed it, I'd love it if you could take a minute to leave a quick review on any of the following sites:

Goodreads

Amazon

ABOUT THE AUTHOR

Lucy grew up "down the shore" in New Jersey, where her love of the mythological was born when her middle school English teacher introduced her to the Odyssey. After high school, she received Bachelor's degrees in Psychology and English Literature before continuing on to her Master's degree in Library and Information Science. In her spare time, Lucy loves to read, cook, and go hiking with her husband and two daughters. Chaos is her debut novel.

Stay up to date! Hop over to www.lucyroyauthor.com to sign up for Lucy's newsletter, follow her on social media, and read up on news and other bookish things!

X x.com/LucyRoyAuthor

instagram.com/lucyroyauthor

pinterest.com/authorlucyroy

bookbub.com/profile/lucy-roy

amazon.com/Lucy-Roy/e/B07P5PYG5M